THE OTHER
SIDE OF NIGHT

DOROTHY JUDD

Cover photo credit: August Judd aged 2
Photographed by Dorothy Judd

I AM SELF-
PUBLISHING

🐦 @iamselfpub
www.iamselfpublishing.com

Reviews

'They'll get over it' is a well-worn phrase, used to gloss over painful happenings, but do we ever 'get over' the events of early childhood, and our reactions to them? This is Dorothy Judd's second novel, and here she digs deep into what makes us all tick, as she unfolds the story of Emmy the little girl who becomes Emily the artist.

Emmy lives in South Africa, brought up largely by a black African nanny called Lizzie. Emmy gets under your skin, as you follow her journey of losses, of longing. Judd, a deeply respected child psychotherapist, is uniquely qualified to write in this way, burrowing back into childhood, our inner world of dreams and desires, awakening all our childhoods, and giving us new perspectives. She has a light touch in approaching perennial philosophical questions about identity. Both Emmy and Emily ponder on these.

As Judd's small son called tomorrow 'the other side of night,' so readers can, through the pages of this book, both joyful and painful, reach understandings that the adult Emily eventually achieves. ...'most everyday things are beyond the ordinary, they seem to contain the whole world'. Our memories may go slip-sliding away, but Judd helps us return and reassess. 'Resilience' is multi-faceted, and loss can be converted into creativity, as both Emily and Dorothy Judd show us. *The Other side of Night* is a book that's hard to forget, as is Emily's quest for understanding and wholeness.

Judith Edwards Author of *Love the Wild Swan*.
Former consultant child and adolescent
psychoanalytic psychotherapist.

In this fine and haunting novel, we follow the life of artist Emily Samuels from traumatic earliest childhood to successful late adult life. Rarely has a novel conveyed all the stages of life so richly and authentically. As Emily's paintings slowly change in fine detail, we see why an artist would keep a visual inventory of life at that same time as understanding how chance happenings affect choices for generations. Judd wears her personal skills as psychoanalytic psychotherapist and artist lightly in this riveting sweep of history.

Valerie Sinason, poet, writer, and psychoanalyst

Written with intensity, confidence and flow, it's an engrossing and rewarding novel. Dorothy Judd has a superb eye for the minutiae of texture, colour and form whether in nature, material or food. She explores with great insight the subtle resonances of her different characters' encounters. Her heroine Emily has a journey to make from her difficult and abusive childhood in South Africa to serene rural life in Suffolk and then London. Seeking love, connection and creative expression above all, as an artist Emily finds ways of repairing her losses.

Sylvia Paskin, poet, writer, and editor

'The other side of night'
My son Luke, aged 3, when meaning 'tomorrow'.

To produce a perfect pearl the oyster needs some piece of matter, a sandcorn or a small splinter round which the pearl can form. Without such a hard core it may grow into a shapeless mass. If the artist's feelings for forms and colours are to crystallise in a perfect work, he, too, needs a hard core – a definite task on which he can bring his gifts to bear.

E. H. Gombrich *The Story of Art*, Phaidon, 1951

Death is that side of life, which is tuned away from us, unilluminated by us: we must try to achieve the greatest possible consciousness of our existence, which is at home in both of these unlimited provinces, inexhaustively nourished out of both . . . .

Rilke, *Briefe aus Muzot*, 332-3

The most demanding part of living a lifetime as an artist is the strict discipline of forcing oneself to work steadfastly along the nerve of one's own most intimate sensitivity.

Anne Truitt (sculptor)

There is no despair so absolute as that which comes with the first moments of our first great sorrow, when we have not yet known what it is to have suffered and healed, to have despaired and have recovered hope.

George Eliot, *Adam Bede*

PART ONE:
CHILDHOOD

'Our experience of life is made up of split seconds of the present, which we attempt to order and string together like beads in a necklace. But that is a false construction, a conceit. In my paintings I attempt to capture a paradox: the impossibility of coherence, to capture a moment in time which is lost and unrepeatable.

If anyone was to write a book about me, the only way that it could come close to my experience of life would be if it was pieced together of fragments, details, chaos and order, unintegration and integration, paucity and richness, missing bits, like an incomplete papier-mâché construction that aims to convey the spirit of someone.

Maybe, then, in the shadows would emerge some shapes.'

Emily Samuels, painter, 1944 –
Portrait of an Artist BBC Radio 4, 18 August 1981

1948

Her fingers spider-walk along the arm, over the bumps of the raspberry-pink cardigan, into the little creases, down over the hill to nestle in the dark space between her mother's hand and body. The child lies still now, her head resting on mother's tummy. She can hear rumblings like waterfalls, or like water going down the plughole, which make her laugh. The laugh is forced.

Now she can't hear anything.

'Mommy, Mommy, wake up. Mommy, nough playing, wake up. Please. Please stop!'

'Mom-*meee*.'

The child pulls away, and looks at her mother's head on the kitchen floor. The neck is crooked, like a broken bird she saw once in the gutter. She begins to feel strange in her tummy. Shaking her mother's heavy arm, she squeezes the hand. It's cold. It has lost its bones. But the space between the arm and body is warm. The child begins to shiver, and puts both hands in the small space that is warm.

The clock ticks in a soft, furry way.

She holds the cold hand between both hands, (like when they play 'one-potato-two-potato-three-potato-four,') and tries to warm her. The hand feels funny, sort of like Walkie-Talkie-Doll Susan's hand.

'Mommy, want drink. Juice. Juice for Emmy, for Em'ly. Warm juice, *please* Mommy.'

Big choking tears block her throat. Now her mother's chest is wet with mucous. The child's lank fringe hides her broad forehead, her cheeks and chin are wet.

Emmy doesn't know how long she cries for. Shivering, she thinks of getting her special blanket and putting it round herself, and over her mother.

Sometimes she plays a game where she puts her mother to bed, and tucks her up, 'Here, Mommy, you have *tickly-nankin*, goodnight-sleep-tight-don't-let-the-fleas-bite', and then she gives her a kiss (and switches the light off if they are playing in her own room where she can reach the light, but if it is in her parents' room she has to stand on the dressing table stool,) and goes out and almost shuts the door. And then she comes back straight away, announcing, 'Morning time!' Even if her mother wants to stay there tucked up she says 'No, get up, Mommy!'

Now Emmy fetches *tickly-nankin* from her room, but it doesn't feel like fun. The world is closing in, walls are tipping, the floor isn't flat, everything is sort of dark grey, she wants her mother to stop this game, *Wake up and be Mommy, or, or . . . .* She doesn't know what else, but she must, must wake *. . . . Daddy!* She knows her father doesn't come home until late, after bath time, and she doesn't know when that is. Sometimes she doesn't see him until the other side of night.

Missis-van-rensber-nextdoor pops into her mind, *but Mommy says she's very old.* And Emily knows she can't open the front door all by herself.

A half smile crosses her face as she runs to find Lizzie in the kitchen, where everything is quiet and still, *so same.* She climbs up on the step-stool to look out the back window into the yard. Lenin starts to bark, rousing himself from his sleep in the shade. She watches him stand, stretch, yawn with his big pink tongue hanging out, walk until his chain restrains him, and curl up again.

Lizzie's door across the yard is shut. *But . . .* , she puzzles, *Lizzie went away . . . . Something about a holiday. And John? He's gone this week, Mommy said, gone to see his mommy, on the farm.* 'LI-ZZIE! LI-ZZIE!' The silence bounces back, swallowing her up in its vastness.

She runs back to her mother and covers her with the small blanket. The feet stick out. Emmy averts her gaze from her mother's face. *It's not the same, not right, she's the wrong Mommy. Her face doesn't . . . doesn't . . . taste right.* The child wants to shout and bash her and scream, but she can't, she just whispers in a sort of high squeak, as helpless as a moth trying to penetrate glass to get to the light, 'Mommy, please, *Mommeeeee.* Stop it Mommy! Stop being sil-*lee!*'

She walks her fingers up the arm again, and tickles her to try and make her wake up, but when the skin feels like cold Plasticine, she only makes them walk along the cardigan. The big arm won't move.

She doesn't want to go under the blanket any more, and there's no-where else to go. Now Emmy's pants are wet and she's scared because she hasn't wet her pants for ages and ages.

The phone rings, one, two, three times, and then stops. Emmy thinks she should phone Daddy. She reaches up and lifts the receiver and hears a loud buzzy noise, like her father's voice, so she grabs it with both hands, and listens, holding her breath. Then there is silence. With one finger she turns the roundy thing over the numbers and moves it – it's quite stiff – and then she takes her finger out of the hole and it whizzes back to where it was. The buzzy noise has stopped and she doesn't like the quiet. Emmy won't choose four, which is her own number because she's four; she likes the fat number: *two roundy shapes,* joined in the middle. She makes the dial move all the way round, then lets it go and it zooms back again. She puts back the heavy receiver. But then lifts it up again to hear that nice growly sound, and leaves it lying on its side so she can still hear it when she walks away.

She doesn't look like Mommy any more, stealing a look at her mother. *Maybe Mommy went out and this . . . this funny lady's 'tending to be her, wearing my Mommy's pink cardigan and my Mommy's blue fluffy-fluff slippers.*

Emmy is shivering so much that her teeth are clattering against each other. Her tummy hurts, and she wants to cry and cry for ever. She's too cold to change her pants, but she pulls them off and kicks them away. Then peels off her wet socks. She won't fetch clean clothes from the drawer, because it's her mother's job and she should be here.

She goes to the Kelvinator and takes out a bottle of milk with a loose silver top which falls on the floor. Drinking from the heavy bottle, milk dribbles down her chin, and then she puts it back, leaving the big door open. She feels a bit better now.

Everything will be alright soon, maybe Mommy will wake up . . . or come home . . . or something.

The child's breath snags on a thought: *Maybe she's very sick.* But then her mother is never very sick. *Missis-vanrensber-nextdoor, yes, get her to help, maybe she can call a . . . a namulace.*

Pushing a chair up to the front door, she pulls herself up onto it. The knob turns, but the door won't open. She moves the chair a little so she can pull hard, but still it won't open. She remembers Mommy and Daddy putting a key in the keyhole, so she looks for one, but can't find it.

She notices a letter on the door mat. She pushes it out through the letter flap, and then a piece of paper with writing on it. She waits, and listens. It feels right to push things through the letter box. Maybe someone will see them.

She turns around on the chair and stares at the silver milk bottle top on the kitchen floor and now it's a shining light and she stays there, shivering, with this light. Everything else goes blurry except this light. She can't take her eyes off it.

The house becomes even gloomier, like when a thunderstorm is about to break out. Emmy sits on the lounge couch, her hands white from being squeezed between her knees, her legs dangling over the edge. The big mirror is covered with a sheet. The clock sounds muffled and slow, now it's only *tock . . . tock . . . tock,* without the *tick.*

Each room has been full of visitors for days – her granny and cousins and aunties and others. She can tell that their hello-smiles are not real smiles. They have hushed conversations that Emmy can't hear. Her father is in his bedroom most of the time, or sits very still in the lounge with a rug over his legs. She looks at him from across the room. He seems so far away. She wants to sit on his lap, but is frightened because he looks broken, *only not so broke as Mommy*.

No-one except Lizzie spends time with her – at bath-time and bedtime and breakfast – in-between dashing all over the house making tea and washing up and tidying. Lizzie is the only one Emmy has been able to cuddle – besides Lenin, who sighs as if he's a real person, and wags his tail even if he's sleeping.

Emmy whispers into his ear, 'Lenin Lenin, my little Leniny!' She spends hours on the floor with the Labrador, stroking his velvet ears.

On one of these strange days Uncle Mickey sits by the child, 'Lucky Lenin! *He's* okay isn't he, Emily!' Emmy feels shy and wishes he'd go away.

She hears the word 'funeral' and Aunty Sarah puts Emmy in her best dress, the dark-green fine corduroy one with a lace collar. Her mother let the hem down months ago but it's still too short. Emmy tugs at the skirt to try to lengthen it.

Granny Gella's mauve veil that hangs from her hat makes her face look misty. It matches her mauve hair. She lifts it to leave a red lipstick mark on Emmy's cheek, and a syrupy smell furls from the old woman.

Even more people arrive. Aunty Sarah puts an arm around Emmy's shoulders and squeezes her before walking across the room in a rustle of black taffeta, mopping her eyes with a lace handkerchief. The child watches the skirt disappear into the hallway.

The house rapidly empties of people and she is left at home with Lizzie, John, and Lenin. And a new colouring-in book.

She wants to ask Lizzie 'What's a furenal?' But she doesn't.

She squeezes past John who is polishing the lounge floor, and wanders into her parents' bedroom. It's exactly how it always is: the dressing table mirror – *it's not covered up, not blind* – with two side mirrors, where she can see herself not looking at herself. *There's Emmy*, with her hair in bunches and green ribbons, *and another girl, just standing there all alone*. She quickly looks away, at the round box that she knows houses the powder-puff that she likes to play with. And there is the glass tray with pointed patterns like daggers cut into the glass, containing long snappy grips with teeth like sharks that her mother puts in her hair.

The big bed shrouded in its dark red candlewick bedspread is there too, as always. Emmy stretches out a finger, touches the tufts of the quilt, and strokes it gently. It feels cold against her palm.

She's sure that her mother has just gone somewhere, and that she'll come home. *Soon*.

Or someone will find her, simple as that, and bring her home.

She remembers one of her silkworm moths, lying really still, and never ever waking up again.

That night she dreams that she's digging in a pile of builders' sand, even though in the dream she knows she shouldn't. She can hear her mother saying, 'You'll get ringworms, and worse!' Then she uncovers a shoe box, like the box her talcum-powder-smell tissue-paper-wrapped wetting doll came in. Opening it, she finds Grandpa Maurice, very dead, a yellowy colour, shrivelled up, his brow wrinkled like a barnacle, the veins round his neck standing out. And he's as small as a doll.

She won't tell anyone her dream. It's too horrible. Especially because Grandpa Maurice isn't dead. But the dream doesn't go away. When she's alone in the lav or in the dark she thinks of it, for months and months.

1969

Emily puts on the kettle for the third time. Each time it boils, she is distracted by small tasks, or by reading a phrase or two in the latest review. She takes the milk from the fridge, butters some burnt toast that is cold and hard. She doesn't want to read the article, and yet if she doesn't it will irritate her all the more. She glances at the first part:

> *It is shocking that Emily Samuels can reduce interiors to pattern and colour, yet they still 'read': she selects a small corner of a room and it is at one and the same time an abstract of lines, colours, textures and patterns, as well as a table, a rug, a woman in a long patterned dress, shadows, wallpaper, curtains. If not for the fleshy skin of the face, the woman would be indistinguishable from the room. The mind cannot see both concepts at the same moment, and so the viewer's vision jumps from one to the other. That is the shock, for it brings to mind how much we choose to read the world around us in its everyday appearance and how much we are missing, how a painter like Samuels draws us to the invisible and to the unconscious.*

'And how he misses the bloody point!' she exclaims. She knows she's not painting the 'unconscious' or the 'invisible'. *That Edward Durrant!* She paints what she sees; she cannot paint what he calls the 'everyday appearance' of the world – what she sees is *her* everyday, her way of making sense of the everyday. She doesn't know why she reads reviews.

She makes her tea at last, just as she likes it: dark as wet York stone. Marcus could never make it right for her. She cuts the toast into triangles, like Lizzie used to, spreads Marmite, and enjoys the hard crunchiness as she chews. Sitting at the kitchen table to get this over with, she reads:

Samuels gathers fragments and juxtaposes them so that they are retrieved, things that would otherwise be lost, now in a formal relationship with other elements occupying the same spatial plane, giving the whole gravitas and beauty.

She reads on, how Durrant compares her with Nolde, Bacon, and with Vuillard. Emily considers looking at some Nolde, and revisiting Bacon. But no, why should she? Vuillard, yes, she knows about that affinity, and loves some of his interiors.

She thinks about her show, about the woman in that painting being her, of course, even if she was painting a model. Now, sitting at the table resting her chin on her hand, stroking the smooth grain of the pine, she feels how she is part of everything around her, how we are all made of cells and molecules and light and shade and colours and textures, and how we and all the things around us are part of the whole, subtly changing all the time. This connectedness sends a frisson down her spine.

Glancing again at the review, her cheeks colour with a rush of anger at how insensitive egocentric people can be, how they define her for reasons of their own. Why is it '*shocking*' if she does not privilege people and make them stand out against a background? Somehow Durrant reminds her of Marcus.

But then she knows how easily she sees a face in a flower, or a fat dancing lady in a tree that sways in the breeze – she too personifies everything. The ochre hills in the Welsh Black Mountains became the muscular thigh of a lion, its pelt worn and thin, battle-scarred in places. The velvet creases of her blouse right now in the hollow of her elbow are the curvaceous lips of a woman. In the rent in a chair's fabric, she sees a deep wound in flesh, a wound which does not bleed because the person has died a long time ago. It cannot heal.

She doesn't want to analyse everything, but she knows why she sees everything this way: she is groping to find the truth of a world that is both visible and hidden, where there is presence and absence at one and the same moment, and where she is part of the universe and not alone and separate from it all.

She paints because she has to, because through painting she can be sure she exists. If she doesn't, the little silver light inside is in danger of being extinguished. And then she would cease to exist.

A few months later she has a successful sell-out show at the Arnold and Sons gallery in Dover Street. She refuses to be interviewed.

Instead she writes down some of her thoughts, for that is the only way no-one can interrupt her or force her into corners. Perhaps she will let Angela Bellamy see her writing, for she is a critic she quite likes, who shows a fresh openness and does not try to categorise her.

So, with a bottle of French country red wine at her side to fuel her courage, Emily begins.

> *I look at this wall and see sparkling stars. Lower down, brown marks are the little seats on a big wheel, the kind you have at a fair – only one is missing, so it's not a perfect circle. The line of the desk lamp intercepts the frame of the picture behind, and I can cut it exactly in half by moving my head a fraction.*

Her eyes dart up and then down at the words, up and then down, over and over again, like a watchful bird.

If I raise my head, the reflection in the glass of the picture moves up and down, it's no longer a reflection – of the windowsill – but the view from a porthole, of waves half covering the window, up and down.

How laborious and slow it feels, to write all this down.

This isn't really satisfying because the reflection or 'wave' is a straight line, and waves can't be straight.

She frowns, straining to see through preconceptions.

So I look at the shadow and the bright light from the sun through the window on this same patch of wall, and before I can think about it, it's gone, the wall is plain magnolia. Then I move my eyes a fraction, onto the pear, well, it's not a real pear, it's a metal container made to look like a pear, quite squat and not as beautiful as a real pear would be, with a stalk at the top and a join where the top part meets the bottom. The stalk cuts across the prickly pear postcard behind it. I could go on seeing the way the prickly pear now has a mouth (the stalk) but my eye is drawn to that metal pear again. I have to make it into something: it is a bell on top of a fat shape, no, it's a fat person hiding beneath a blackish costume, like a woman in a burka. But why is there a stalk sticking out of her head? Maybe that's a periscope so she can see, for there is no eye slit. The space or shape between the woman and the small gourd next to it is a vase, a vase of pearly cream like a shell . . . .

Emily stops, her head floating on the wine, her hand aching from writing fast, and re-reads what she's written. She knows it could seem crazy to anyone else. But then, she thinks, if that is her vision . . . . Perhaps she shouldn't bother. Perhaps the paintings should speak for themselves. She can always tear this up. Gulping more wine, she goes on:

Everything can become something else, and the something else becomes the dominant thing, and I lose the fact – in the moment, not altogether – that this is really a handle to a window-catch, because it's much more alive if it's a duck's head swooping down towards the water; or if that's a baby, a real gigantic baby lying on its back and looking up, and not a cloud.

And if I don't make everything into other entities, things would be boring or . . .

She pauses, and remains still for a few seconds before she continues,

. . . dead, and I wouldn't paint the way I do. It's easy to see people as animals or birds or big babies or sometimes monsters or grotesques, to see parts of things as something else, to see the bumps on a tree as breasts, or a hole in the bark as an anus, to go dreamy and let my eyes lose focus and be surprised by what can happen. If I try too hard, it doesn't work – I have to look through and past and beyond and into things. I can always – nearly always – make them jump back to the ordinary world, with all the horrible feelings that brings. Oh dear. Words dance and slide and pop out unexpectedly. So much easier with paint, to paint over things. Or to transform them . . . .

I think what I'm saying is that I have to look at something long enough, and then I discover an aspect that has never been seen by anyone before: I discover the unexplored in and behind and under everything, and that has to include the air all around, the light, the changes from moment to moment.

Why click back to what people call 'normality', when my vision is endlessly magical? Or maybe not 'magical', but a world, a universe, saturated with beauty . . .

She pauses again, then writes,

... and with such fear. I have to admit there's a kind of raw terror in seeing that untamed overwhelming beauty. I don't know why it's terrifying, why it makes my heart race. Maybe it's because as we grow up, we try to name and explain everything, and if we glimpse a universe that we cannot rationalise we are no more than primitive organisms at the mercy of infinite space, and laws we don't understand, and probably chaos. So, I'm writing all this to explain what cannot be explained, that I know I can't ever pin down this miracle, but I can spend my life attempting to capture fleeting intimations ....

When people talk, I don't have to listen. I can see whatever I want to see in and around them, in objects in the room, and then later I can remember exactly what I was looking at because my mind has 'photographed' everything. Months and years later it is still there for me to find, like looking through an old catalogue. The images are never moving, they are frozen moments. Even if it is a memory of running I see slice after slice of time, like stills from a film, the colours with the intensity of the real moment.

1970

The branches bend in the wind, some dance and sway, some remain still. Even the sharp blades of the aloe move with the troupe, playing their part too. The warmth of France makes it easier to imagine living alone. For two weeks, Emily is staying in a small cottage in the Gers. She needs to be alone to paint. It is a small step towards that big step, a preliminary to her 'emigration' to Suffolk.

She prepares her canvas, covering the whole surface in cream emulsion, the colour of wild primroses. When it is dry, she places it within the 'v' of a low clothes horse, for she has not brought her easel. It props at a good angle, although the lower area is awkward to reach. She has not failed to notice on the mosaic concrete table the small fish-shaped spatters of chalky bird droppings, and the smoky smudges – pink and white, like ectoplasm – where some splodges have lain but been removed.

She lays out her tubes of oil paints in an orderly row. The poetry of the names is part of the process, like a litany, beginning with the three whites: *flake, titanium*, and *zinc*, each different in its translucency when mixed with other colours; then on to *lemon yellow*, and the two *cadmiums* – yellow and red, followed by *vermilion*. Then, abruptly, *Prussian blue,* which looks almost black. *Ultramarine, cobalt* and *viridian* follow, then onto earthy *yellow ochre*. She ends the rainbow with *raw sienna, umber, burnt umber*, and finally *ivory black*. Oh yes, she has forgotten *rose madder*. She smiles as she places her old friend, *Rose Madder*, for whom she has a particular fondness, after *vermilion*.

Her actions have the precision of a surgeon preparing his tools. The swollen new characterless tubes lie next to their old dented crooked-shouldered neighbours, whose torn and worn labels are smudged with fingerprints, whose screw-tops sometimes sit at an angle like cocked hats, whose contents may last one more session – until, reluctantly, she throws them away.

She remembers how she used to keep all her used tubes, a huge cardboard box full, until a journalist interviewing her noticed them, and referred to 'Samuels' *detritus*, like cigarette stubs, signifying death'. She was so appalled that she threw them into a black plastic bag and wrote to him that they were now indeed despatched in a body bag. But somewhere she knew he was right, that the subject of death was never far away, and that for most of her life she has battled with its presence. The presence that is all about absence.

The setting-up has a sense of ceremony, of ritual, of expectation and anticipation, as well as fear. She never knows if she will meet blankness, or worse: hopelessness. Blankness is at least a type of limbo – painless – and could carry a whisper of a hope of *something* to alter it, but when hope is muffled by a miasma of despair, or all her efforts destroy her aspiration, she is faced with the mess of her paintings as a small child. When she was four. And a half.

That time, twenty-one years ago, that time of a perpetual scream in her throat. Something like that scream, which nothing could alleviate, is still there in a corner of her mind, or when things go really wrong she feels she is back in an empty tin with un-scalable shiny reflecting sides. If she had cried as a child her cries would have echoed back. Perhaps she did cry, but she cannot remember. She can only remember the voiceless emptiness, the void.

Yes, she lived in that silent scream, and the self-loathing that came after it, for years and years after her mother died, when Phyllis and Georgia – and Grandpa Harry – came into her life.

Her father was there. But not really there.

She pulls herself back to the scene where it is the turn of the paint brushes to be laid out. She knows that this ritual can take her away from all that. Not right away, but to a place where she has a voice.

Here, each brush has a character of its own. The squat chisel-one of hog hair, the tear-shaped sables, the longhaired Chinese ones, those whose handles have long lost their varnish and whose wood is stained with colour – or by now a brownness. There are the oblique-angle brushes of synthetic hair, the cheap little decorators' brush, the pastry brush she bought for one shilling, the hardened ones – like someone whose joints have seized up – that she tries to coax back into mobility, and the ones which have lost most of their hair, but still have a use, even if it is to scrub out part of a painting or to gouge through thick wet paint, or to stab with small harsh dots. The sables are the most sensuous; she sometimes strokes her lips or her neck with one of them, to conjure up being in her mother's arms. She won't part with any of her brushes – even when, like a puppeteer who is curious about the effect of bringing new characters into her repertoire, she handles and admires and occasionally buys new ones.

She feels that each brush is a person, and when she paints she is merely an agent for it to do what it wants. Not until she is involved in a painting has she a sense of which character will emerge from which brush, for there could be feminine brushes and masculine, crossover ones that struggle with their gender, child ones and wise old ones, foolish ones and serious ones, crazy brushes and intelligent ones, exhausted ones and energetic ones, those who are blind and those with visual acuity. Above all, there are the firm vigorous brushes – the four-square chisel ones, although it can vary – who are on the side of life and those – the balding ones, the old thin ones, sometimes the glossy sables, even the pointed sable with a cherry red lacquered handle – who are convinced that death is everywhere and that it is winning the battle with life. Sometimes those saboteurs mock the lively ones, call them 'stupid', 'naïve'. But she has to give each a chance to express its particular vision. If she tries to persuade or control the outcome, she is faced with something different, that might be impressive as a painting with intellectual quality, or sometimes a prettiness – but it lacks the passion of the dialectic, the perpetual search for integration that is as elusive as the play of light and shade on leaves moving in the breeze.

1945

In one of the long hours when Emmy's parents are out and Lizzie is watching over her, she turns her attention to a little helicopter. With practised expertise, she swivels the propeller around with her finger, the finger that reminds her of her father's rhyme about Peter Pointer. She smiles without knowing that she is smiling, repeating the action. And drops the helicopter.

She crawls into the bathroom, to the edge of the bath, rumpling the hard canvas curtain in her fat fists, making crackling sounds, then shakes it to make loud swooshy sounds, again and again, tidal watery sounds. She pulls herself up and peers down into the empty bath, her plump lips making 'bubba, bubba', evoking bubble-bath times. Reaching down into the bath, she feels its sleek sides with her palm, then stretches to almost touch the shiny silver taps, and asks Lizzie to help, 'Mor mor'. Lizzie smiles and shakes her head. Emmy withdraws her hand and stands there, looking at the taps and then into the bath. Her foot knocks over a shampoo bottle on the floor. She plumps down to the floor to pick it up, then pulls herself up by holding onto the bath stool, gently bangs the tap with the bottle, trying to make the water flow. She puts the top in her mouth, for she knows that mouths are where things can open and flow, but to no avail. Shaking it, she watches the soapy contents slosh back and forwards, then lets the bottle slide into the empty bath, where it rocks forwards and back until it come to a standstill. She looks at it for an instant, then plops down on the floor again, and crawls away from the bath. She's had enough of things that don't work or go away and leave her.

She goes over to Lizzie who is sitting on the bath-stool, and climbs up to hold her broad thighs. The nanny lifts her onto her lap. She looks at Lizzie's bright green beret, and reaches for it, but withdraws her hand, not sure if the wish is forbidden. She never sees Lizzie without something on her head, a *doek* or a starched white hat or a beret; perhaps it's part of her. Tentatively Emmy proffers a pointed finger into the other's smiling mouth, frightened of and yet attracted to those most white teeth. 'Izzie Izzie,' she says, very seriously. Lizzie withdraws the small hand and kisses it.

Plump feet indented by the soft straps of slippers, whose tiny starry-centred buttons echo the glints of light in two blue-grey eyes. The slippers wear through at the toe and her knees become as tough and dirt-ingrained as the garden-boy's hands. Months later the flat soles take their share of wear and tear, as dimpled knees soften and straighten, and the vast world becomes a more accessible place, a place to be stretched up to and explored.

But many things are still beyond reach and are high-as-the-sky – door handles, cups on tables, sometimes her mother's lap.

The wooden cage with bars is now rarely used for keeping her from excitement. Grass and stones and soil can briefly be savoured in her mouth until someone's finger pokes them out. Her mother is especially clever at probing in and hooking out whatever it is. Emmy scrabbles to fetch a smooth grey pebble; she has to taste it and feel it and quickly pop it in her mouth. With her back to everyone, she sits on the grass with the fat stone in her mouth, rolling it around with her tongue. Poking her finger in her mouth, she feels the smooth wetness, her chin glistening with dribble.

'What's that child doing! Quickly, Rae, something in her m. . .' her father shouts from across the lawn.

Her mother's shadow is upon her immediately, 'Oh my God! Come on Emmy! Open up, no no *no!*'

Turning her head away, the child wants to hold onto the pebble all the more.

'Come on darling, please Emmy, *pagh,*' loudly making the sound of revulsion. '*Pagh pagh!* Show Mommy, come on, be a good girl!'

Emmy turns towards her, confused, no longer able to enjoy her prize. Her mouth has been invaded by a finger. She sees the pebble briefly plop onto the grass.

'Good girl! Well done, Emmy!'

There it is, shiny and beautiful for a second, before her mother grabs it and hurls it over the fence and into the field beyond.

'All gone!' Mommy exclaims.

Emmy takes a deep breath and lets out a wail, her finger in her mouth, her tongue quivering in an empty space. Her mother is flustered.

She picks the child up and hugs her, 'Oh Emmy darling, come on, Mommy had to do that, you know you *mustn't . . . . You could swallow* it!

'Jake, you know, I think she'd swallow something in order not to surrender!' she calls to Emmy's father.

The child doesn't understand why they all worry, for they let her put big things in her mouth, like the foot of her rag doll, or her stuffed giraffe. And food, all kinds of food.

Now, sitting on her mother's lap, she is shown her cardboard book of cats. Her sobs quieten into a few sniffs and then stop; she scratches at the picture of a kitten, wanting to pick it up and feel it.

'*Miaow, miaow,*' the child says.

Oh, the thrill of upright dashing – even though big nappies chafe between her legs – with the big cousins, same as them at last – well, almost the same – quick, quick, before a sudden crash landing. The intense adventure is tempered by fear of what might be around the corner and finding herself alone. She holds onto a stool for support, but then it moves, the ground tips, and she crashes down. Her mother appears, helps her up, and smoothes her dress. She has to totter on her own, for mother has walked away.

Another day kittens are chased, picked up, squeezed, their furriness incorporated in her eager mouth for a brief moment of satiety before they wriggle and scratch free, or are dropped. She picks one up again, and, incomprehensibly, one of the big cousins shouts at her, smacks her, and grabs the kitten.

Sudden despair again, joy extinguished as abruptly as a snuffed candle. She cries for her mother or father or Lizzie, but they are not there. The fly-screen blocks the doorway. Howling and screaming from the depths of her being, full of clawing rage she lies on her tummy on the scratchy ochre grass. Cheeks redden as they graze the ground and small fingernails scratch at unrelenting umber earth. *No no-one nothing,* only a sick bleakness, falling dizzy death.

She is lifted skywards, up to the blinding hurting light as suddenly as a mouse caught by a hawk, but not to meet her death. It is her father. She kicks and flails, but there is sunlight after all. Wrapped in a tobacco smell, big arms and a solid chest, she breathes in gasps while he pats her back, makes resonating brown-velvet sounds while the hard bump on his neck vibrates. Her tears are kissed away by his bristly mouth – 'starsh!' she complains – and her damp forehead is stroked and restored to its wide clear countenance.

The world is full of wondrous things: bright petals that fall and flit, which her father calls *flutterbies*, and droning fast purposeful buzzy creatures. Little things with legs like hairs that make sandcastles and disappear down inside them, and if she treads on them they go very still and broken. White bitter-milk oozes from the insides of the leaves that grow by the veranda when she plucks them. If snapped, fat sticks crackle like flames, and, inside, they have a dry sponge that looks like marshmallow but tastes of nothing. Dots in the sky swoop and dart. And white soft flower-stars can be pulled apart, with yellow hairy middles. Little brown snails move along slowly, carrying a stone on their back; their soft heads disappear if she touches them.

There are round orange balls, each with a little knobbly bump, that people unzip and give her the squashy insides to eat, called *naartjies.* And a tree full of cloudy purple little balls that shine like Lizzie's face if she rubs them, and which she can eat as well. Happy leaves as high as the sun, that dance and shiver; others as big as elephants' ears and as bitter as poison. Cotton wool clouds that are anything conceivable or inconceivable, and that sometimes rush so fast that the world moves and she feels wobbly and has to plonk down. Light green purses, which open up to reveal rows of tiny sticky pale eggs. And a breeze that sounds like lots of loud whispering and the comforting shooshing of her mother's voice.

Years later, she thinks back to the diaphanous cellophane of a grasshopper's wings, that caught a rainbow of colours and had a pattern as fine as the blue circles of her mother's eyes. Rich brown soil that was part of her father's large hands. He dug it, played with it, absorbed it under his fingernails; shared it, and sometimes magically produced a *songololo* from its midst, which she held on her palm until its attempts to burrow frightened her and she dropped it. She watched it with desire and abhorrence as it wriggled away and she wiped both palms on her dress with a shudder. Her father smiled. The *ticktick* of crickets, indistinguishable from the sound of the rotating sprinkler, was still there.

1946

She protests when she is alone at night, alone except for the black shadows of lions, and curtains that move by themselves, while her mother and father are together, together in their big most comfortable bed, feeding each other sweets, Emmy is sure, looking after each other, without her. Partree, her best bear, named after A Partridge in a Pear Tree, is tucked up in her bed, comforting for only a little while. *Tickly-nankin* is there too, of course, while her tongue pulsates around her thumb. Her other hand is between her legs. But nothing assuages an indefinable longing. She awakes from dreams of being chased, or dropped, or lost.

One night, Emmy dreams that Partree's eyes stare at her like an evil witch's eyes, bright orange, and poke into her. So she braves the dark passageway to their bedroom – the passage can't be scarier than her dream and her bed – dragging her pillow behind because that's a Rule. (The other Rule is that it has to be a bad dream – she can't just get into their bed because she wants to.) Her words, 'Bad dream', are the only clear thing in a tumble of shapes and shadows, and she is allowed in next to her mother's warmth and softness.

Her mother's breathing gets slower and heavier. Emmy imagines she's the koala bear she's seen in a picture, wrapped round a tree trunk. Her father is snoring. She's not sure if she's safe, or still alone. She begins to feel frightened, because now it's clear they're both deaf and blind and their minds are far away. She tries to breathe in harmony with her mother but becomes breathless with effort, because Mommy breathes much too slowly. If only it were morning-time, to be deluged with lemon-bright sunshine as the curtains are swished back, when Lizzie brings orange juice with the layer of sugar among the pips at the bottom of the glass.

The next night she holds her mother around the neck for longer at kiss-goodnight-time, knowing she can't make her stay and stay. Empty blackness inside, desperately wanting something to fill it up. Their big bed, warmer than a bear's, beckons when her mother leaves the bedroom, even though it didn't soothe her the previous night. *Go now, lights on in the passage. Before I get more scared.*

Finding her asleep in their bed later, like Goldilocks, her father carries her back to her own cold bed. Her parents are amused; she feels misunderstood. There is no place of absolute safety. She has to continue to fight her solitary battle with the dark shapes and noises of the night.

The other side of night, her mother tells her she got a fright when she pulled back the eiderdown to find her there. She feels bad that her mother can get a fright from her.

1947

Her mother holds her in her gaze; even when Mommy is reading or knitting while Emmy plays, she knows she is there.

But when her mother and father hold each other in their arms she feels shut out, wants to break them apart. Sometimes she squeezes between them. She doesn't know why that makes them laugh.

But Lizzie is always light, even though she is dark as night, as reassuring as Maltabella porridge, she of the starched white apron, the *doek* on some days, the bottle-green beret or the white cap on other days, the steady smile, the plump bosom and capacious lap, encircling arms, pink palms and fingernails, skin like a ripe plum, yet her knees are hard and rough. If her eyes and nose and mouth have particular features, they are not registered by the child. A presence, as comforting as the African sky, leans over her.

Lizzie takes her for early morning walks in a large pushchair with an iron rail all around, the seat facing forwards. She voyages forth into the open, where sunlight casts long shadows – a tranquil world after the tumult of the kitchen smelling of fried bacon and shoe-polish, flies circling around the twirl of fly paper, and dark corners.

Each setting-out has a sense of exploration, a wrench from home, an ambivalent journeyer on an inevitable wave of discovery. Strange new others sometimes appear on these expeditions, to be viewed obliquely or denied existence altogether with glance askance. A turn of her head right round always re-establishes Lizzie, her white starched cap in dazzling contrast to her blue-black shiny face, all framed by the floppy scalloped edge of Emmy's blue-and-white polka dot bonnet.

Pale purple beds of fallen jacaranda flowers beneath the pushchair wheels make comforting plump *pop-pop* sounds.

She finds herself standing one day in a big hall, a place with grey light, strange people, a few big people and lots of little ones like her. She holds tight onto her mother's hand, sensing a bleakness and desolation about to descend on her.

This is Hopscotch Nursery where the big cousins used to go, so now she's catching up with them. Only they are not here any more. Just these new others. Hiding behind her mother has a sense of futility, for she cannot alter what is another inevitable part of an overwhelming plan, like when they decided that she had to sleep in her own bed at night. Her mother stays, though, while Emmy keeps an eye on the silver bracelet glinting on her mother's arm, and slant-wise explores sand trays, water troughs, little jingly bells and wooden carts. Ann is there too: big fat Ann, over-the-road-Ann, Ann with deep dimples instead of knuckles on the backs of her hands, Ann of six toes on each foot caused by eating orange peel – or so the cousins say.

Emmy finds herself being bundled into Hilda's red car, her mother in the front, and Ann and lots of other children all squashed in the wooden floor space in the back, and driven home by Hilda. So disaster has not befallen after all.

But then the inevitable does happen, and the whole procedure is repeated on the other side of night in order for her to be left there, abandoned, for a time that never ends, with Ann who doesn't count because she isn't Mommy. She isn't even Ann's sister Shirley, of Annashirley. It's no comfort to know that Shirley isn't here because she's too young, and she'll be here next year, they say, whenever that is. Ann's presence makes Emmy miss Shirley all the more.

Distorted golden windows with black dividing bars angle out across the radiant lake of floor, a polished floor smelling of sawdust in butchers' shops, mingling in Emmy's mind with visions of blood soaked into it, dead animals hanging up, and no-one protesting. Empty space and no Mommy, only the big lady with the brown eyes.

Emmy stays inside herself: that way perhaps the world is not coming to an end. She peeps out warily at this unpredictable place. That tall dark big lady, Miss Jeffries, with a brown-velvet voice like her father's, is worth holding onto with her eyes, even though she is busy with so many others. She knows Emmy's name and takes her to the toilet – there are rows of them and they are little so she doesn't have to pull herself up and she doesn't feel shy with this big lady. And then there are rows of washbasins, all the same. How strange. Like the little dwarves' beds in the book about Snow White at home. She holds onto this thought, like her mother's hand the day before.

They all sit on little red chairs – again, all the same – forming a circle, to have a piece of apple and half a cup of milk before the story. She realises that they all have to do the same thing at the same time. She would like more milk, but doesn't know how to ask for it, and watches the child next to her spilling his as he gazes dreamily before him. He has a string joined to a funny thing in his ear, and he talks in a misty way. His one eye turns inwards all the time, and the other goes all over the place, so she never knows what he's really looking at or what he's saying. Emmy stares at him, just like she stares at everything.

She cannot know when the big boys will hurtle into her as if she were not there, or when someone will try and take her spade from her hands, but she begins to know with some certainty that the big lady with the brown eyes and pale-brown voice will usually be somewhere when most needed. With more certainty she learns that there will be Circle Time every day, with apple and milk, and sometimes 'tanas. Her mother comes to the rescue every day with Hilda and they take her and others home in the red car. That is certain too. But some days this happens after a short and busy time when she could have played and played, but on the days of scuffed knees, the long, long days, her mother does not come until late.

On one of those long days, the large wooden cart chases Emmy down the path, and no matter how fast she runs, it runs faster and catches her up and bangs into the backs of her legs and mashes up the skin so much that it bleeds. In that whooshing turning moment that carries the sun away, of scattering children and tumbling trees, and then such silence and stillness as she lies on her back staring at a sky framed by branches, not even the big lady appears until later. By then the bright stuff that is more red than blood itself, that glints in the sun with the purplish iridescence of a beetle's wings, has been applied to her wounds. Eventually the big lady wipes her cheeks where tears have made inroads through the grime, and some semblance of order and safety is restored.

Emmy's first sense of public failure, of humiliation, is being expected to strike the triangle in time to music played on the piano. She hears the beat and taps the metal bar with a baby wand. Now she has a chance to make proper music, like the big cousins on the piano at home. A silver sound sparkles out, a sound as bright as water splashing in the sun, but not at the right time. The harder she tries, the more the grownups shake their heads. Other children play the tambourines, drums, cymbals, xylophones, bells, castanets, triangles, all at the right time, filling the hall with dancing sounds, but all she can do is stand in a bubble of her own gloom.

Another day the piano rings out sounds which make a familiar moving shape: 'The Farmer's in the Den.' Her big lady, Miss Jeffries, is making the piano work. Emmy is caught in a knot of confusion: her special lady far away playing for everyone, *but perhaps she's really playing for me.*

Emmy is chosen to be Jan's wife, Jan with the pink bulging tight skin and the shaved white bristles all over his head that she wants to stroke. His damp spongy hand holds her's and she feels a current of happiness flowing from behind her ears and down her back. She wants to stay like this, securely by Jan's side, but now she has to choose a baby. She looks round the circle. There are no babies anywhere. Miss Jeffries tilts her head expectantly, piano-hands poised in mid-air. A hotness rises into Emmy's head blurring her vision. She grasps the nearest hand: of the big girl with long pale *mealie*-colour plaits like Gretel in her book at home. Emmy is surprised at her boldness in claiming this big beauty who she has admired from afar. No-one seems to think it wrong. The Gretel-girl smiles and joins her in the inner circle, soon to choose her nurse. By the time Emmy has wondered why the baby has to choose a nurse when she isn't hurt or ill, and how a small boy with frightened mouse-eyes who isn't wearing a white hat with a red cross on it can be a nurse, the nurse chooses a dog. Her sense of that this far-from-home new place is capable of many strange developments is further stretched by the excitement when the dog is patted by everyone. The dog is a boy with spots all over his face and limbs. She speculates whether his covered parts and the skin under his orange hair suffer the same fate. From a little way away he looks light brown instead of pink.

Miss Jeffries tinkles on unquestioningly while the other large grownup who never knows who Emmy is continues to bustle the children into the parts assigned to them.

Ah well, Emmy thinks, at least they seem to have forgotten her earlier performance on the triangle.

'Kinnaqueen,' Emmy imagines, is two royal personages joined Siamese-like, wearing identical crowns. She is held up on her father's shoulders to see the passing of the Royal Train – King George VI and the Queen and the two princesses – but only sees crowds, lots of little flags strung high up like dolls' washing on a line, a whoosh of the reflecting windows of a white train, and clean chunks of white gravel around the track. This must be the King who was a merry old soul counting out his money . . . and who wanted some marmalade for his bread while the Queen was eating bread and honey.

1948

Emmy wanders out into the back yard, then back through the scullery and the kitchen. *Inky pinky ponky* . . . . The litany goes through her head . . . *Daddy bought a donkey.* Words, more words, the same words, a rhythm, Daddy's rhyme. She finds herself in the passage, and the hall . . . *Donkey died, Daddy cried* . . . . But it begins to irritate her, like being stroked in the same place over and over again. *Inky pinky ponky* . . . . *Daddy bought a donkey* . . . . She can't stop.

Jacob Samuels emerges shoulder-stooped from his bedroom, his face as if crushed, a drop of clear mucous hanging between his nostrils. Lenin comes up to his master and wags his tail, trying to lick his hand. Jacob blows his nose in a big handkerchief before gently brushing Emmy's shoulders, and taking her by the hand to the scullery. The dog follows.

The fluorescent light shines helplessly on this bright day. Lizzie is wiping soap-bubbles off the floor with a rag in wide sweeps.

'Lizzie, the um . . . child . . . . You know, you can . . . can you look after her now, a bit?' He adds, not looking at Emmy, 'Em, you stay with Lizzie? *Ja?*'

Lizzie nods knowingly to her master, '*Ja, baas,*' rising from her knees, and dries her wet hands on her apron. Jacob backs out of the room.

Lizzie sits on the step-stool and lifts Emmy onto her large, soft lap, wrapping her in her big brown arms. The nanny smells of cooked potatoes and clean washing. She sings to the child in her own language, rocking forwards and backwards all the while, on and on. The gentle up-and-down lullaby is punctuated by click-sounds from time to time, like the odd thorn tree growing on rolling hills. Emmy's crying simmers silently, and then erupts in big sobs from her depths. The outburst subsides, as she nestles into Lizzie's large, soft breasts. She almost goes to sleep. Lizzie still rocks, humming her sombre song.

Through her unmuffled ear, Emmy hears the buzz of her father's deep voice in the distance, talking on the telephone.

Further sobs rise up inside her, more for the love of Lizzie than the big dark place of her mother's absence, day after day, night after night. The child makes herself wake up, because the world keeps slipping away into a murky place. So she lifts her head, and looks deep into Lizzie's brown-black eyes with their yellowy whites, and asks,

'Mom . . . Mommy?'

'*Ay yai yai*, is not easy, not easy my little Em'ly, sometimes maybe the ancestors is wanting to have the *Missus* with them up in Heaven, or sometimes out of the blues the Lord wants a good Mommy up in Heaven . . . . Oh no no no, sometimes they jus' sick, not your white doctors, not the *songoma*, is going to get the person better, nothing,' shaking her head. Emmy has never heard Lizzie speak so much to her.

'But *why*, Lizzie?' her bottom lip quivering. 'Why?'

'I don' know, my sweet-haat. Jesus took my Ruthie just the same.'

She searches Lizzie's face for more clues, looks into those brown eyes, darker than her father's, notices the fine red wriggly lines on the pale creamy-yellow around the brown ball, looks deep into the black middle bit, and it fills her with a warm feeling in her tummy.

Who is Ruthie? she wonders. 'I haven't sorn Ruthie. Me's your child,' she says.

Lizzie smiles and says 'You are my chil', but there's four, four other childs. There's my Harrison, he's nineteen – good boy; and Metcalf, seventeen, always in trouble. . . ,' shaking her head, '*Tsk tsk* . . . . Then there's Pretty, age fourteen, leaving school; and then Baby – Queenie – age twelve. Ruthie, now she would be fifteen now this Chris'mass.'

'But Lizzie, who looks after them? Why don't they come and play here?' The woman smiles, shakes her head, and wipes her brow with the back of her hand, exposing palms as pink as Chappies chewing gum, and shakes her head again.

'I have to werk. Course I miss them. What can I do, I have to werk. Your Mommy and Daddy, your *Daddy*, is good, good to me. I have to find money to pay for the school. Nearly all the African children not with their Mommies. My mother – their gran'mother – look after them, my childs, in Natal, on the *plaas, ja*, on the farm. She's old, ver' ver' old, but she look after them ver' well. One day, when I'm old also, I look after *their* children in Natal and keep chickens and grow *pampoens*.'

Emmy burrows her head into Lizzie's neck and stays still, thinking of all those children without Mommies. And then she remembers her mother and gets that wobbly feeling inside.

She wants to stay with Lizzie's lovely dream of pumpkins surrounded by chickens and plump piccaninnies with big tummies.

1949

She slumps on the sofa, as floppy as her rag doll Rosie. She opens a book, then drops it, pulls at a loose button on the sofa.

Her father is at work, Auntie Sarah at the hairdresser's, and Lizzie is doing the washing in the back yard, shouting loudly in her jumpy language that sounds like dice being shaken in a bakelite cup, to John, as if he's a long way away, and laughing.

Emmy wanders out, briefly swishing her hand in the sudsy water in a vast tin bath. Lizzie's solid arms are in and out of the water, her sleeves rolled up. The child wonders why the water runs off Lizzie's brown arms so quickly – *Look, they look dry* – while hers stay wet. She notices small cubes of Reckitt's Blue, and wet sheets puffing out in the wind like sailboats. The smell is so tangible and fresh that her lungs feel peppermint-cool from breathing in the flapping air around them. But still her tummy feels empty.

She returns inside. It is all dark now. Climbing back on the sofa, she drags up Sailor, her favourite doll: a lanky boy wearing a faded blue and white striped suit. Rusty marks dot the fabric in broken lines where the skeleton of his wire armature has rotted through. One side of his smiley face is squashed in; try as she might, she cannot pull it out. His smile is crooked. He looks sad. She scratches at his always-open surprised blue eyes. He doesn't blink. The child turns Sailor over. She pokes her finger into a small hole in the seam, widening it. She turns him face upwards again. Golden sawdust comes out of the rent in a slow trickle, forming a pile like an ants' nest. *He's bleeding, pooing. I'm hurting him.*

I squashed his face, only she can't remember when or how. She doesn't know if she wants to cuddle him. Swooshing the sawdust off the sofa, she drops the doll on the floor. *All gone.*

Momentarily, she rests her cheek on the plump seat. Her eye catches the big beads and wooden cotton-reels threaded on a thick string, among her dolls and bricks. The beads don't fall apart even when she tries to separate them. Touching them one by one she intones her mother's voice, '*Mmmmn, nice.*' A fat feeling in her chest rises up, like a warm bubble. Up and up to her throat.

She glances over the edge of the sofa at the splayed doll. *Broken. Still broken. Can't fix.* Like the beetle she squashed with her finger.

The beam of light, bright sunlight, focusing warmly on her, holding her in the arms of her mother's mind, has gone out, leaving a cold darkness. Emmy's face, like her mother's face, is like a house without windows.

She continues at Hopscotch Nursery, although it is like another country now, across a divide that she cannot comprehend.

She seeks out Miss Jeffries sometimes, to tell her how many days until her birthday when she will turn five, because Miss Jeffries is really interested. Or, sometimes, she finds her just to be near her. When she plays near her, she can imagine whatever she wants and feels safe. Miss Jeffries never disturbs her games with *her* ideas, like the other teachers do, or like some children do.

One day Emmy asks Miss Jeffries where her wife is. The tall woman gives a little laugh and says she hasn't a wife, nor a husband.

'What's your Mommy called?'

'My mother died years ago, but she was called "Margaret".' The teacher gets a faraway look in her eyes, as if she's looking at something deep inside herself. Emmy feels shivery. And then Miss Jeffries smiles softly and takes the child's hand. Emmy looks up at that beautiful face and they both go to find the others.

A plump woman with long, dark curly hair and circles of rouge on her cheeks wafts up the garden path, past the line of poplars and the rockery, followed by a girl of about seven or eight, also with long, dark curly hair, only hers are in ringlets. The girl wears a yellow tiered dress printed with small Scottie dogs. The woman and child are followed by Jacob who has brought them in the Buick.

Emmy watches from the lounge picture window, sure that these strangers cannot be anything to do with her father. He must have found them somewhere, helped them from some danger, maybe they need to use the phone. Or perhaps the woman is trying to sell something.

Emmy plucks leaves off the purple plant in the pot by the window. But no, now they are sitting on the lawn, and her father is calling to Lizzie for tea. Emmy hides the broken leaves behind the curtain.

'Emmy, Emmy love, where are you? Em, come out here, will you?'

She wants to hide.

He enters the house. She can hear him along the passage, 'Emmy, come on then! Some important people for you to meet!'

Turning from the window, 'Who are they?'

'A friend of mine, called Phyllis. And her daughter, Georgia.'

'But, where's their *Daddy* then?' She feels pleased that she got straight to the point, a way of catching hold of something through the muddle of thoughts piling up.

'You mean, Georgia's Daddy? Phyllis's husband? Oh, he's . . . he's in Cape Town, actually. They . . .' He hesitates and when he speaks again his voice sounds cross. 'Anyway, that's none of your business. Come out now.' He pauses to check her appearance, briefly holding her shoulders before brushing her long fringe out of her eyes. He wets a corner of his handkerchief with spit and wipes her chin.

She has no choice. She follows him out into the bright sun, narrowing her eyes against the glare.

The large woman is sitting in the bamboo chair; her flesh oozes through the gaps. The big girl perches on her mother's lap like a bird too big for its nest. The woman wears fancy rings on every finger except her wedding finger.

'This is Emmy, Emily, my little girl.' *Little, not little,* she thinks, pulling herself up to her full height. 'And Emmy, meet Phyllis, and Georgia.'

Phyllis peruses Emmy from head to toe as if considering some wares in a shop. Georgia looks uninterested, has a glum look on her face as she twists round to fiddle with her mother's macramé belt, plaiting and unplaiting the cords. Emmy watches open-mouthed, intrigued by this new big girl who behaves as if she owns her mother. It is Georgia who breaks the silence.

'Mom, when are we going to OK Bazaar? You *prom*ised. And I told you I feel sick, car sick,' in a voice that Emmy thinks of as watery yellow. 'You know that kind of car always makes me sick.'

'Alright Georgie. Have a drink of orange juice, that'll help. And say hello to Emily – Emmy, is it?'

'Hello, Emmy,' says the older girl without shifting her gaze from her mother's belt.

Emmy is more perplexed. Georgia is not like the cousins, or her friends, or girls at school.

Emmy notices her father sitting in a chair that is very close to this other woman, so close that their knees almost touch.

Jacob starts to dispense the tea that Lizzie has brought, from the best pewter tea pot.

'No, Jake, let me. A woman's job.' Phyllis gets up awkwardly from her low position, after firmly removing Georgia. The girl looks as if she will topple over.

Emmy is longing to go back inside when Lenin comes up and licks her hand. She hugs him with her whole upper body, laying her face on his hot back.

'Oh, so you like dogs. Jake, what did you say his name was? Stalin?'

Her father smiles, 'No, Lenin.'

'Same difference,' says Phyllis. 'But careful, Emily, dogs have germs, can give you diseases. I'm sure she knows that,' glancing at Jacob.

Phyllis peeps under the fly net, as if gaining a preview of a bride, 'Ooh, *farfel* cake, one of my favourites. Who made it, Jake?' Her tone is suspicious.

'My mother makes it, brings it round when she visits.'

'Apricot jam. I approve. Some people have started using plum jam. Not the same. Good, some cream.'

She cuts herself a stout wedge, puts it to one side, and then asks the others if they want some.

'I'm bored, Mom,' the big girl whines.

'Well, Emily, after tea show Georgia your toys,' sighs Phyllis.

'Yes, Emmy, after tea. That's a good idea,' says Jacob.

How can her father bring these two people here in this way, she thinks – not asking her, not warning her, trying to make her play with this girl who looks *so . . . so full, so full of this mother, this Phyllis. Georgia doesn't need me.*

Not looking at them, Emmy continues to stroke Lenin, sitting on the grass.

She glances up at her father's face and sees an expression she remembers from long ago, from that time before, before the world tipped: as if a light has been lit in his eyes, as he smokes his pipe and twinkles at this fat stranger.

After another tea on the lawn a week later and an outing to the Zoo Lake another day, she knows that everything is funny, not right. But she can't do anything about it.

Then there follows a trip to the zoo with all four of them, when Emmy clutches her father's hand so tightly that he has trouble extracting his wallet to pay for elephant rides. Georgia eats the monkey nuts that are supposed to be for the monkeys, and when her ice-cream falls in the dust Jacob quickly buys her another. Emmy thinks that if that happened to her, he would have washed the ice-cream and given it back to her. Phyllis and Georgia laugh unkindly at the chimpanzees. Emmy doesn't think the chimps are funny; in fact she worries about the animals' feelings being hurt.

Silver-sun leaves on the poplars dance in the wind, butterflies dive and twirl, long fronds of a banana tree wave, 'Help me, help me!' Detail upon detail. Raindrops race each other down the windowpane; red mud erupts between her toes when she plays in it. She doesn't feel hungry these days – except sometimes, when Lizzie sits with her while she eats. Things slip and slide and tip.

She covers a page in her colouring book with thick crayoning, ignoring Dumbo's outline – even though he looks cute – pressing as hard as she can, breaking crayons in the process, her hands becoming hot and speckled with wax, her fingernails dirty, on and on, until not a fragment of white remains on the page.

One Saturday her father calls, 'Emmy, come here, love. Want to talk to you.' A feeling of dread spreads from Emmy's head downwards. He never wants to speak to her in that voice, a voice that tries to be ordinary but underneath is as cold as the wind in winter.

She walks slowly into the lounge. She has begun to walk silently without realising it, her heels hardly touching the ground.

'Emmy! Don't creep around like that! You gave me a fright! Like a ghost,' he remonstrates.

But you called me in, so how can you get a fright? she thinks. He has that stinky dark wee-wee-colour drink now, and it's only afternoon. She had a sip of it once and it burnt her throat like fire.

Jacob is sitting at one end of the sofa. 'Come and sit here, Emmy,' patting the seat next to him. She sits near him on the broad arm of the Chesterfield, and he puts an arm around her waist. 'You know Phyllis, and Georgia? Well, Phyllis and I are going to get married. Next month. And she and Georgia are going to come and live here, after that.'

Emmy closes her eyes. Her stuttering thoughts of *No, Why, But, Stop, Can't,* clatter like pieces of broken china in her head. Half opening her eyes, she knows he is waiting for her to say something, for he is looking at her while he gulps his smelly drink. She thinks she might cry. She tries not to. A cold wind is blowing down her back. Drumming a heel against the sofa, she manages 'Why?'

He seems at a loss, 'Well, *why*? That's a funny question! Don't bang on the couch like that. Because "Y"'s a crooked letter and you can't make it straight.'

Now she feels like crying all the more. She turns her head away.

He says, 'Well, darling . . . ,' taking another gulp of the drink, 'it's because I . . . ,' and his talking speeds up, 'I love Phyllis, and she loves me, and so we are going to get married and live together. Simple as that. And Georgia goes wherever her Mommy goes!'

She remains still and stiff. Alright then, if children go where their Mommy goes, I want to go to my Mommy, she thinks.

'Emmy, come on, this is for you too y'know. For you to have a . . . mo. . . a woman in the house, to look after you.'

'But there's Lizzie, Daddy, you *know* there's Lizzie.' She feels some relief in coming out with this, but she doesn't know why she's really crying now, why her throat feels blocked.

'Yes, of course there's Lizzie. Phyllis really wanted to bring her nanny – Virginia, Veronica, whatever – but I said *no*, we have to keep Lizzie. You see, Emmy, I am trying to do what's best.'

Neither mention her mother. She has not been mentioned for months by either of them. Emmy senses that she is over the hills and far away, or up in the clouds, and that no-one is trying hard enough to get her back, and she can't do it all by herself. All this proves that her father has forgotten all about Mommy.

He gets his handkerchief out of his pocket. She thinks it is for her. He wipes his eyes. The lump in her throat gets bigger.

Just when Hopscotch Nursery becomes more of a familiar place – though a place with something missing all the time, like cheese with holes in it – and the days have a definite shape which pass quickly, and she knows she will always be fetched by Hilda in the red car, and Shirley is there too, Emmy is moved to a brand new place, called Kindergarten, where there is no Miss Jeffries and no Shirley.

Here the teacher's nostrils flare out as if she's smelling a bad smell all the time. Emmy is no longer one of the bigger ones, but has to start all over again being one of the little ones.

All the children lie on little canvas beds and have to be quiet for a long time every day; some even fall asleep. She can never do that; she doesn't want to be seen with her eyes closed, for they may think she's asleep when she's not, and she might miss something. The curtains picture rows of flowerpots with different flowers in them, of which she knows every detail. They muffle the glare of sunlight but not the sounds of cars, birds, voices, ticking clocks, sometimes hammering, and droning flies.

They have a lesson called 'Hygiene'. Miss McKenzie, her dyed orange hair in neat curls, asks, 'Now, children, when you have a bath, do you know what you must wash first?'

Emmy watches Gary Rosen, who always puts his hand up.

'Yes, Gary?'

'Miss, um, your, my legs?'

'Good try. Well, you must all remember to wash your *faces* first. Then your bodies, and *last* of all, between your legs. Because, because you want to wash your face while the water is clean, don't you?' Emmy feels herself going red. She imagines the teacher's private places: she discerns soft saggy titties hanging like *lappies* beneath that maroon fancy jersey. Below the tight-as-a-drum corseted tummy she conjures up an area of shadowy hair like Phyllis's, masking mysterious creases, craggy caves and flaps, folds and holes.

Emmy's ten year-old cousin Carl shows his *pookalie* to the servants one night while her father and Phyllis are out. He pulls down his striped pyjamas and prances around, laughing. Georgia is looking cross, but he clowns around all the more. Emmy notices Lizzie smiling, shaking her head, and wiping her brown face with her pink palm that looks as if the dark skin is worn away, in the dim-light kitchen smelling of Flit.

Lizzie, having to sit up until the parents return, perches on a stool in the scullery, her beret askew against the wall as she dozes, her knobbly bare feet crossed.

Emmy doesn't know what to make of Carl's performance as she watches from the passageway. She feels excited, and then sick and dizzy. Rooted to the spot, unable to move, to get back to her bed.

1950

Black and white photographs in the album show a plump open-featured happy baby, well cared for in a pram with a ruffled fly-net, as if gift-wrapped. In some pictures a smiling mother looks on or holds her lovingly. Sometimes a beaming black woman in white uniform stands proudly behind the baby. A father, tall, dignified, a humorous twist to his mouth, in wire-rimmed spectacles, comfortably holding hands or small bodies, or watering a parched garden. Moments frozen and sometimes blurred by the Box Brownie, later the concertina Kodamatic with its bumpers and chrome protuberances.

Emmy pages through photos of clean Viyella Start-Rite children in hand-knitted tight bumpy cardigans, squinting into the winter sunshine. Girls' floppy hair bows; boys' long khaki (even though they're in black-and-white) shorts; tiny party dresses with frills, white socks and white sandals; long party tables on the veranda laden with little bottles of lemonade, jellies, cakes. Rows of friends, rows of cousins, aunties, children graded according to size, small to big, standing like soldiers. The first day in the new school uniform; the *braaivleis* on the beach; the Game Reserve meal; the roadside picnic; the aunties and uncles in London.

Mommy.

And then she isn't there any more.

The arrival of Phyllis and Georgia, and Grandpa Harry and Grandma Milly, just like that, as if that is supposed to happen; cousins' ballet performances, Georgia's *pas-de-chat* on the lawn – all frozen moments of an unreal reality, ways of going beyond memory into tributaries of time.

There are few photographs of children crying, none of adults fighting, of black men and women toiling, of sick people, of ordinary conversations, of real intimacy, of toilet or bath times.

Another day Emmy pages through the heavy albums, returning to the pictures of her mother: that small one where Mommy is crouching down and smiling; her body, arms and legs a safe house surrounding Emmy's little body. The child is crying in the photograph while her mother smiles at something or someone out of the frame. Now she feels a blocked lump in her throat that spreads up to her ears.

Decades later, Emily studies snaps of even earlier days, of wide-hipped, large-thighed, dark-lipped women in swimsuits, smiling at the camera, posing like starlets. Of a smiling Mommy-and-Daddy leaning into each other's bodies with Botticelli grace, cigarettes erect, as glamorous as any *de Reske* or *Stuyvesant* advertisement. There is a troubled long-dead grandmother – her mother's mother – with an anxious watchful look. The other grandparents smiling roundly beyond Emmy's memory; ancient photos of Lourenço Marques; Valentino-haired father holding a baboon; or, as a boy in a black full-length swimming costume belonging to his big sister, (which, he said, 'hung so low that it revealed everything.') Sometimes white waterfalls ('where the light got in,' her father said) give the photos a religious grandeur.

At Kindergarten, she is given her own square of garden to dig with a big fork. Then she is given a packet adorned with a picture of blue cornflowers. Inside are tiny bits of dust, to sprinkle over the soil. The teacher calls the dust 'seeds'. Emmy is puzzled: *seeds make babies, don't they?*

For weeks, the only colour on her plot is the seed packet on its stick, and some green plants. She is told they are weeds. She doesn't want to pull them up.

Eventually straight-stemmed grey-green plants produce tight buds and then crinkly blue flowers as perfect as the packet picture. They are a miracle, which she is sure could not have sprung from her own efforts of digging, scattering seeds, watering with a fine shower from the little tin watering can with ducks on it. Perhaps a fairy put them there. She imagines real little babies also growing out of the soil, and wonders if they would be high up on stalks, or low down on the ground like the pumpkins her father grows.

Cornflower blue. Sky-blue. Baby-brush blue. She feels a vague shiver of connection with her mother.

'You can pick them now,' Miss McKenzie tells her, 'and take a bunch home for your Mommy.' Emmy can't say, 'She's not my Mommy,' let alone, 'My Mommy's *dead* !' She looks at the big lady and nods.

Phyllis smells the flowers and smiles, 'Ta. Lovely, Emmy. Isn't the school clever to grow them.'

At meal times, Emmy stares at the bunch of blue flower babies while the talk from the grown-ups and Georgia flows around and above her.

Kindergarten continues to be a strange place where she doesn't feel she really belongs. At least Hopscotch Nursery – at the beginning, anyway – had her mother at both ends of the day.

But she joins in all the activities and knows that the teachers think she's clever. She can tie bows because her father taught her with a shoelace and a story about a tree, a pond, and a snake.

Emmy sits on the grass with the other children, cross-legged, her skirt making a tight tent over her thin legs; or climbs up the slope of the slide instead of bothering with the steps; or makes an arch, arms upstretched with another child, in a game where children go under the archway, until it's her turn.

Others twist the iron chains of the swing while she sits on it, round and round, tighter, making the seat rise higher, and then they let go, and she laughs at the streaky world unfurling with dizzy speed. Sometimes she stands on the swing and goes really high, legs pushing and arms pulling, the clanking and whining noises filling her head, until she thinks *What if the chains break,* or *What if it goes over the top*, and her knees go wobbly and she slows down.

She runs barefoot, or walks with her arms out as if balancing on a tightrope when she has to walk over stones to fetch her sandals. She likes Ingrid because she has a straight thick fringe and her black bobbed hair looks like a drawing in a comic. She and Ingrid balance along a tree trunk that lies at the edge of the playground, their arms like wings.

In long grass, Emmy finds a big black *tok-tokkie* beetle with a back like a tiny corrugated roof. Cupping it in her hands, she feels very important as children crowd round to see it. She is not scared of its hairy feelers.

During 'wet play' when all the children have to stay indoors, she invents a game of going from table to table, sliding her hands on the surfaces, walking and then running around one table, faster and faster. Ingrid joins her and they run round and round, their hands chasing each other, laughing. Then the two of them chant 'One potato, two potatoes, three potatoes four, five potatoes, six potatoes, seven potatoes more', piling their hands up and up over each other, always ending in giggling chaos.

A teacher watches Emmy dance in her vest and pants in 'Musical Movement' and says '*Ag,* shame'. This confirms Emmy's sense of there being something wrong with her, as uncomfortable as having thorns in her socks. Years later she realises that 'shame' means 'cute'.

It is here, in this Kindergarten that, without any thought, she takes a little peach-coloured knitted woollen purse with a few big brown pennies in it from the desk of a child who, with perfect blonde curls, looks like a big doll. The purse has a small flap secured by a tiny pearl button. Emmy has hardly enjoyed the sense of possession before the teacher enquires loudly after the missing item. She clutches it in her fist, looking straight ahead. The teacher insists they all look for it, and that no-one can go out to play until it's found. Emmy wants to disappear into a hole in the floor like the genie in the pantomime. She crawls around under the desks on all fours, pretending to hunt, while the other children search too. Through the forest of desk and chair legs, scraps of paper on the dark floor, black cracks between the floorboards, brown and purple shadows, heavy black lace-ups, grey fluff, other children somewhere there too, moving, she hears the teacher's command,

'It has to be somewhere. Things don't just *disappear*. Unless it has legs! Come on then! Or you'll all have no playtime!'

After a terrible frozen dark space of time, Emmy places the purse next to a table leg, straightaway snatches it, 'Found it!' she says, holding it up.

'Oh, still warm,' the teacher mutters as she takes it. 'Alright then, all out to play now.'

Emmy is haunted by shame. She didn't want the pennies, only the hand-knitted purse, a soft-warm safe holding thing.

Emmy is running along little paths at the Wilds pretending there's shark-infested water all around so she mustn't fall in, when Phyllis calls her to sit by her and her father. Georgia is already on the rug – lying face-down and having a tantrum.

'If we wait for Georgia there'll never be the right moment,' Phyllis says. 'Ciggy please, Jake.'

Emmy pulls her rose-pink dress under her bottom so the dry grass isn't scratchy, and she gets comfy, because it's clear something is going to happen. She rummages in Phyllis's face for clues.

Phyllis is smiling but worried at the same time. Her father's eyes are smiling in a way Phyllis's never do. The lit cigarette goes from his lips to Phyllis's. He's holding her arm.

Lenin isn't taking the opportunity to sleep – he's trying to read Phyllis too, with his long dripping tongue – which has begun to disgust Emmy – hanging out. But she tries to concentrate on Phyllis, who says,

'Guess what?'

Oh God, Emmy thinks, how can anyone possibly guess. 'What? Tell us! You're going to buy a new car? We're going on holiday? I can have a kitten? I can tell it's something good.'

'*Shuddup*, Emmy! Let her get on with it!' Georgia muffles Emmy's words as effectively as Cousin Carl's fountain of wee on the Game Reserve camp-fire.

'You know you mustn't say "shut up," Georgie. Listen, we're going to have a baby.' Phyllis looks plump and important.

Emmy's first thought snags on the 'we' – why *we*, who's *we*? Oh no. She can't believe it. *A baby*! Her world has tipped, again, like Chicken-Licken when the sky fell down. Like being left at Nursery School, or banging her head so hard on the sticking-out window frame as she ran with a windmill. Like leaving Pretoria for ever. Or the big, big thing that rocked her world irrevocably, that she cannot place in its proper place amongst all the others so it ceases to be on her mental map. And least of all can she place the bad Harry-things that are a lumpy blur.

She utters the only thought she can: 'What's wrong with us, then?'

Phyllis laughs.

By now Georgia is excited, wants to know '*When*?' and says, 'I'll help!' Emmy sits there looking, looking at details, as usual. The ash on Phyllis's cigarette has got so long that it's about to drop off by itself, the sole of her white wedge-heel sandal is more worn away in the middle, her red toenail polish that the hairdresser paints on is flaking off her big toes, but it still looks like wet cherry-flavour jujubes after the sugar is sucked off. Her lipstick is half worn off too. Daddy is still holding Phyllis's arm, and now he's putting his arm around her shoulder. There is thick dust sitting on the ledge of stitching that runs all around his shoes. Georgia is lying on her tummy talking to Phyllis, looking up, smiling.

The Wilds look different now. It will never be the same again.

An untidy, loose V of geese fly over, making a cranky, heavy machinery noise.

Emmy swallows the hard lump in her throat and it goes down into her chest where it stays and won't melt, like swallowing a sweet the wrong way.

'What're you thinking, Emmy?' asks her father.

She shrugs, wiping her sweaty upper lip on the puffed sleeve of one shoulder as she gets up, before hoisting up her *broekies* because the elastic is loose. And stands behind him, her arms around his neck. She rests her cheek on his hot-from-the-sun Lenin-smell Brylcreemed smooth head. He frees a hand to hold her forearm.

Some things haven't changed.

She tightens her hold, feels like squeezing him harder, wanting to strangulate him.

'Jake, you know, that child looks as if she's in a *dwaal*, a dream, half the time.' Grandma Gella solidly fills her wicker chair, watching Emmy.

'What d'you mean, Mom?' Jacob Samuels scratches the bristles on his strong chin with its Sunday growth. 'Don't think so,' frowning.

'Just look at her now, as if she's . . . .' The old woman puts her knitting down on her lap. 'Oh I don't know . . . sort of behind a veil. Can't have been easy for her, you know, Rae dying like that.'

Gella Samuels darts a look at her son, before she lifts the gold-rimmed bone china cup, and sips her tea.

Jacob shrugs, slightly shaking his head from side to side. 'Well she has a good life now, that's what I say. Phyllis is very devoted to her, as well as to Georgia of course. Treats Emmy as if she were her own flesh and blood. You know that. Very lucky. What more can we do?'

Gella knows this is not meant to be a question, but a defence of his position.

He adds, 'Y'know, Ma, Emmy's stopped that silly business of sleeping across her bed – I think I told you how ever since, since she, since Rae passed . . . since we . . . lost Rae, Emmy slept across the top of her bed – y'know, where the pillow is. I'd find her like that every night, would straighten her, make her lie properly, and an hour later she'd be back again, across the top, pressed against the headboard. Anyway, she doesn't do that any more.' He breathes out forcefully.

Gella notices his tension, his way of fiddling with his chin. She feels a familiar pain in her chest, and worries if she remembered to take her tablets after lunch. She hears her own mother's voice, 'You can only do what you can do,' and briefly calms herself.

They sit in silence, watching the two girls in identical dresses with white sailor collars, made by Phyllis. Georgia's is yellow and Emmy's sky blue, with embroidered daisies on the collars in corresponding colours. Emmy's collar has the added colour of mulberry stains. Georgia is pushing a doll's pram and Emmy is trailing after her, saying something. Turning round to face Emmy, Georgia blocks her ears, shouting, 'Not listening, not listening!' From where the adults sit in the shade of a syringa tree they cannot hear the rest of the children's exchanges.

Gella knows that her son is broken somewhere inside, that he has not recovered from the death of Rae, from his guilt at not insisting that his wife seek more treatment for her heart. She knows how hard it is for him to accept Georgia, brittle angry Georgia, who sees her own father regularly and rejects Jake. Jake once said flatly to his mother, 'Georgia comes with the territory.'

His shortcomings so reflect her own that she cannot really help him with his loss, nor help him to help Emmy. Whenever she senses his difficulties, she feels a familiar constriction in her chest. She doesn't know any more if she's upset about her son, or herself, or Emmy, shaking her head imperceptibly.

'Anyway, what's the point of talking about Rae, now?' Jacob continues, assuming his mother is still focussed on the same subject. 'Surely it would only open old wounds. When she's older, maybe. But then . . . . ' He cuts a slice of granadilla cake, and offers his mother another.

'Better not,' the old woman replies. 'Got to watch my weight. It's good, though. Phyllis makes a good sponge.' Gella wonders what he had been going to say, but doesn't ask. She picks up her knitting and continues with a purl row, hardly needing to look at her nimble fingers and the white wool dancing around the clicking needles as if by magic.

After a few minutes, Gella says, more to herself, 'White's always safest. Or lemon yellow. Don't like pale green, or apricot. There's a new colour they call "aqua". Pale aqua. Don't think I like that either.'

Jacob gives her a little smile. 'Yes, Mom. Phyllis is getting mostly white things, though she thinks it's a boy. She's quite a collection of bootees and matinee jackets already, and I think those things with *broekies* sort of built in. Romper suits? Yes, a few romper suits, made by Ma Green.'

Gella feels a prickle of competition with the other grandmother, Phyllis's mother, but tries to ignore it. She never liked Milly Green, even before there was a family connection, and least of all does she like her husband, Harry Green. She can't put her finger on it. Something about him. Those close-set eyes, ruddy complexion. She gives a slight shudder now, recalling his clammy skin. Is it because of Harry that she doesn't like Milly, or Milly in her own right? Her . . . snaky side? Gella thinks of the way Milly's tongue darts over her lips and retreats so rapidly that she can't be sure she showed it at all. No, she concludes, it's Milly's way of being there all the time, there for Phyllis and Georgia, because she's got the time, and although unstated, she makes out that Gella is not doing enough.

Gella has lived alone for over thirty years. She is used to having conversations in her head.

The two girls have moved closer to Emmy's father and grandmother. Emmy seems to be giving up their game and is lying on her back on the grass, her stick-thin arms above her head attempting a shady canopy. She lies very still. Her dress billows up in the breeze, revealing her skinny long legs.

'Hate you like poison! Going to tell on you!' Georgia calls. The older girl zooms away with the pram at top speed. A wheel bangs into the rockery and a doll hurtles out as the baby carriage topples on its side.

Emmy rolls onto her tummy to see what is happening. Georgia runs inside screeching 'Tell on you! Mom-mee, *Mom-mee!*'

Gella notices that even now Emmy does not come to her father, nor to her. The child rests her head on her forearms. The old woman sighs at all these things she can't fix. Especially big things, like . . . . She doesn't like to spell it out. She is surprised at her own mother's voice, Taube's voice again, and she can see Taube with her hair swept back from her high forehead, her large bosom and tiny waist, repeating, 'You can only do what you can do'. This has become something positive, and not the weak state of doubting if it will make much difference.

She knows that she can show affection to this lost grand-daughter.

Gella gave up feeling that she could shape her own life, play a part in her destiny, with the death of her second husband, Raphael. That was in 1916, when he was killed in action in South-West Africa.

She had found Raphael's return from the front overwhelming in its intensity, the way he pulled her to him, his great hunger; the thinness, almost hollowness, of his spare body, and yet that strength in the way he made love to her. She discovered how something can be so strong that it almost hurts, but that when she went with it she felt the greatest joy of her life. She had never experienced anything like that before, or since. No wonder she conceived her son that week.

Gella glances now at Jake, her colour flushed, thinking, of the secrets we carry to the grave.

She pauses in her knitting, purporting to study the pattern, and fiddles with the counter at the end of her knitting needle.

She remembers that afternoon, barely an hour after his return, when they drew the curtains on the glare, the sun glowing through the flowery fabric, and Raphael not waiting to undress her. The sheets wet with perspiration. Only later he had the time to savour her, to peel off her silk stockings, and her slip, and her brassiere. To marvel at her with the tenderness of a mother with her baby. But it was his initial passion that she returns to over the years.

To be killed so soon after that was inconceivable.

He had left his seed inside her, alive and growing.

Jacob Raphael, she called the baby. His birth was powerfully reminiscent of his conception: passionate and strong, tipping over into excruciating pain, but joy too. Gella's mother helped her to raise him, and so did her sisters, and sisters-in-law.

Her thoughts turn to Lionel, her first husband. She needs to recall him now, or it would feel disrespectful. She sees him in his grey flannel suit and his greased-back black hair. His small stature. But even if she tries she cannot recall the feel of him; he died from a rare cancer when they had been married for only a year.

It was the second death – when she was twenty-nine, in love, and pregnant with Jacob – that destroyed her faith in shaping her destiny.

And then, thirty-two years later, when her daughter-in-law Rae died, Gella was staying with a niece in a suburb of London that had not been wrecked in the Blitz. Of course she flew back to South Africa and was there for Rae's funeral, going through the motions, but feeling quite numb. Her fatalism protected her: after all, this is what happens in life.

Even the stories that emerged of what the Germans had done in the war did not really sink in, in all their horror and immensity. If you pile on more losses, you become more numb – or crazy. How wrong she was, she realised, to have thought they could escape persecution when her parents brought her and her five brothers and sisters from Poland to South Africa in 1901, when she was twelve.

As a child, living in the Orange Free State, Gella's Afrikaans was almost as good as her Polish and her English. She spent her days looking after the chickens and the ducks, making clothes, cooking and baking. Her father was away for weeks roaming the countryside with his cart pulled by a mule, selling everything from needles to nails, ribbons to embroidery thread, buckles and buttons to collar studs, hair restorer to blood tonic, floor wax to calico and buckram, from gripe water for babies to elixirs for lovers. Her mother struggled to feed them, as well as – through the goodness of her heart – Hymie the lodger, who was 'Not the full shilling,' as her father used to say. There was not enough money for Gella to go to school after the age of fifteen.

She crocheted through all events; the only thing that changed was the type of white – sometimes cream – cotton or wool she used, its tone or thickness, leaving a trail of antimacassars, doilies, collars, ponchos, baby blankets, purses, table centre-pieces, and one shoulder bag.

Now Grandma Gella calls to Emmy, for she has an uncomfortable feeling in her heart. 'Em! Emmy! Come here love! Come and see Grandma!'

The child raises her upper body on her elbows and peers towards her as if she is a long way away.

'Nothing wrong with her eyesight, is there, Jake?' Then, loudly, 'Come on then, little chicken! How about some cake?'

The child gets up slowly and walks towards them, bits of dried grass sticking to her knees and elbows.

Holding the bamboo arm of her grandmother's chair, her eyes briefly scan the old woman's face, and then she looks away. Gella strokes the fair hair back from the child's high forehead, saying, 'Come and have a cuddle then. Come on, sit on my lap.' Emmy watches and waits while Grandma places her knitting back in its cloth bag with wooden handles. Emmy is glad that the white knitting is put out of sight. She likes that bag, though, with handles like the rockers on her dolls' cradle, and flowery fabric that reminds her of something long ago.

Gella turns the child round so that her back is towards her and half lifts Emmy onto her lap, 'Climb up! Come on then, your old Granny isn't as strong as she used to be!'

Emmy sits stiffly on Gella's solid legs, legs covered in thick stockings like bandages beneath a heavy silk petticoat and crepe navy dress, her feet stuffed into court shoes, flesh swelling out of them like bread rising in a tin.

The old woman gently pulls the girl back towards her and the little body bends into her grandmother's bosom, her neck softens, and her head lowers. She becomes as slack as a puppet whose strings have been released.

'Lizzie's half day off today, Ma. I'll get some more tea,' Jake says.

Gella puts her arms around Emmy and whispers in her ear, 'So how's my little girlie then? What've you been up to? How's school?'

Emmy does not know how to reply to so many questions.

'You haven't fallen asleep have you! Cake?' her grandmother whispers.

'Ye-es, please,' she replies softly.

'You'll have to jump off my lap then!' Emmy remains there, not having realised that it was cake or a cuddle. She wishes she had said 'no' to cake. She climbs down and sits on the grass with her legs crossed, pulling the fabric of her blue dress tautly over her knees.

Grandma passes her a white gold-rimmed plate with a fat wedge of granadilla cake on it, and a silver cake fork. The child cuts a triangle of cake with the side of the fork and stuffs it in her mouth with the palm of her hand. She savours the lemony icing and crunches on the granadilla pips, even though Georgia calls it squashed-fly cake.

'My word, you're enjoying that, aren't you! You're lucky Phyllis bakes such good cakes!'

Emmy eats another mouthful, watching an ant carrying away a crumb. She drops a few more crumbs to see what happens. Imagining that she is a giant and the ant is in the normal world, the blades of grass a jungle of tall trees, her eyes stop focussing on the grass and the ant and the other ants rushing to the scene, for she wants to curl up with the sweet cake in her mouth, her arms wrapped around her knees, and . . . . And she doesn't know what, because she can't think what she wants or where she is, except that she's all alone somewhere and there's no-one, no Grandma, no Daddy no . . . *no Mommy. Only Grandpa Harry. He* . . .. She begins to shiver, and cups her hand over her closed lips.

'What's the matter now? Aren't you feeling well, Em'ly? I thought you were enjoying the cake.' Gella sounds irritated; her efforts have not been rewarded. She looks at her watch – the old Timex with its aged yellow face, that just keeps going. 'I'd better get back to Hillbrow.' She pulls her cardigan round her shoulders.

Emmy blinks, and remains motionless.

A strong wind rattles the syringa leaves, seed pods drop like hail, and branches creak.

Gella covers the cake with a fly net and carries her knitting bag towards the cool house. 'You can't be lolling there all day, now can you, Emmy?' she calls over her shoulder. 'Strange child. Could have done with that second cup of tea that never appeared,' she mutters.

Emmy curls up into a tighter ball, her knees bunched under her chin. She begins to feel that she is part of the wind and the falling seed pods. Something rises in her chest. She wants this to go on and on. She sees pictures in her mind of Snow White in Georgia's big book, Snow White making friends with the deer and the birds and the wolves in the forest.

She pores over that book whenever Georgia is not around – before the older girl can snatch it back and say 'It's *mine*! *My* mother gave it to me! *Who* said you could have it?' In a particularly cruel moment one day Georgia added, 'Now I'll have to uninfect it.'

Emmy doesn't know why she is drawn to that story, why she thinks she is Snow White, even though Snow White's hair is black as ebony and hers is yellow as sand. When the hunter takes Snow White into the forest to kill her, she turns the page rapidly even though she knows he spares her. That picture makes her choke: her throat closes up and she feels like vomiting.

She likes to pore over the page of Snow White in her glass coffin.

'Come on Miss, whatchyou doing, lying there in a tempest!' Lizzie, back from her afternoon off, wakes Emmy from her reverie. The nanny looks different now, not in her white uniform, and wears a dark green beret instead of a *doek*. The child remains still.

'Whatchyou want? Piggy back? Okay then, come on, piccannini!'

She crouches down and lifts one of the child's arms and wraps it around her neck. Emmy climbs onto Lizzie's broad back.

'Your Daddy gone to take *Ouma* back in the car. Where you go now? The *Missus* give you bath? Inside, you go inside. Too much wind not good, too much spirits in the air.'

Emmy is not listening to the words but to the sound of Lizzie's voice, a voice as soft as Clydella pyjamas. She wishes it could go on for ever; then she'd sleep well, and not have those frightening pictures in her head of spiders and snakes. And sometimes of Grandpa Harry. She squeezes Lizzie tight round the neck. The nanny gently eases the grasp.

'I take you round the garden now, for a ride, then you go inside. Orright? You jus' like my little Queenie, my baby, in a blanket like this while I werk.' Lizzie's hand reaches behind her back and holds the small bottom comfortingly while she walks the gravel path round the big garden, past the proud cannas, past the sprinkler with its reassuring heartbeat, each footstep making a loud scrunch.

She lowers the child gently by the back door, opening the fly screen for her to enter the fluorescent-lit kitchen.

Emmy does so, silently, unsteadily.

Emmy kneels up in the Buick to keep Annashirley in sight, until they round the corner. Then she looks down at the glassy sparkling buttons of her cardigan.

They are moving house, from Pretoria to Johannesburg. Emmy does not comprehend that she will never see the old house again, with bobbly glass on the lav window, long dark corridors, a shady veranda for all the laden party tables, and never again play in that garden with Vasco the cat sleeping beneath the poinsettia trees, the presence of Ann and Shirley over-the-road beyond the chicken-wire fence.

She cannot think about the place of Mommy, with her dressing table. And the hard tile kitchen floor.

The new house has builders' sand in heaps all over the garden.

Vasco treads daintily across the gleaming parquet floor in the illuminated lounge. How did he get here, already? He looks as if he belongs.

1951

Watching the cake mixture swirl and whirl and fall back upon itself, glisteningly smooth, in the bowl of the Kenwood merry-go-round mixer, Emmy senses a familiar wall building up between her and Phyllis. The child is locked into this position, with no way out.

'You're always arguing, Em-*meel*-ee! Blerrie stupid child!' 'Blerrie' is Phyllis's word for 'bloody', which no-one is allowed to say.

Emmy refuses to call her Mom or Mommy.

She sees her step-mother as enormous furious waves, waves which can drown her as easily as when her Minnie Mouse tin bucket was carried away for ever off Durban beach, and even her father couldn't get it back. What else can she do now but stick to her ground when faced with this power?

The outcome is predictable, but she stays on the step-stool, leaning against the Kelvinator, eyes fixed on the eruptions of dough, ears full of the whine of the machine and her own voice, all imbued with a greyish-red hue. 'No, I didn't. No, I don't. No, I won't. No. No. No. No I can't. *Don't care!*' – words like more sand to build up the battlements to keep out the encroaching tide, but at the same time whipping the waves up into greater determination.

A slap stings her thigh, not felt as physical pain, only outrage. The child hangs onto *When-I-grow-up-I-won't-hit-my-children* in her head, refusing to cry, to give this monster-wave any satisfaction. Her rigid resolve enrages Phyllis further, 'I'll teach you!' and a further slap resounds.

Emmy dashes to her bedroom; corridor, doors, and walls falling about her. She has to get there before she can allow the volcano inside to erupt. Banging her bedroom door shut, she throws herself face down on the bed, immersed in the sickeningly familiar knowledge that life is not worth living, that she would rather die, if only she could press a button and end her life, it's much more difficult to live than to die, that she hates Phyllis, no-one loves her, Daddy can't really care because he sides with Phyllis. She remembers with a worse pain the longing for her mother, and being teased by Georgia for crying out for her, and for Miss Jeffries at Nursery School . . . . Her cries are now choking gasps, *only Grandpa Harry . . . no-one.*

Her sobbing is interrupted by the sudden entry of Phyllis shutting all the windows, 'So the neighbours can't hear', and rushing out, slamming the door behind her. The rage within Emmy builds up to a crescendo, as she sees in her mind the familiar image of a shiny biscuit tin, herself a small creature within, unable to scale the steep sides. She screams more loudly. Phyllis returns, racing towards the child, and slaps her again and again, saying '*Now* I'll give you something to cry about!'

Silence of breath held while Phyllis re-slams the bedroom door behind her. The end.

Emmy is full of a snarled madness; a seething, bubbling wound of excrescences. Sobs rise up again like a coil even though she tries to hold her breath for ever and ever . . . to die . . . to show Phyllis . . . to bring absolute peace. Looking down at the slap wealds she scratches her thighs, adding her own stigmata to those inflicted. This causes further unstoppable crying.

Beyond the throbbing in her ears and chest and throat, she hears the scrunch of the Buick's tyres in the drive, then a car door slams. She waits, facedown, head hidden in her arms, for the moment that may pull her back from the edge of the world. There is a long wait, broken by lumpy inhaled sobs rising through her body. Then, holding her breath to strain to hear, voices beyond. What is she telling him?

Her father comes in quietly, sits by her on the bed, strokes her back, her shoulders, talks softly. A space is made for a fresh upsurge of sadness, of such bleakness, as new sobs rise to the surface, yet now the anguish is tinged with a clarity and a warmth instead of the earlier amorphous mess. He calls her 'darling', mutters something about being sorry.

She knows she cannot argue her case, cannot untangle the knot of shame over her absolute despair, her madness, cannot understand where Grandpa Harry is in all this, cannot attempt to appropriate her father as an ally against Phyllis; cannot break up their indivisible alliance and love for each other. Implacable Phyllis reminds her of the bas-relief of the monolithic Voortrekker Monument on the sugar bowl, beneath the fly net fringed with beads.

Phyllis is so fat now, because the baby will soon be here. 'I'm sick of being preggers,' she says. She looks like a whale, especially when she's in the bath. Emmy can feel the baby kicking sometimes: it moves under the surface like the whorls of ringworm she once had. She's not so fed up about the baby now. In some ways it will be sweet, she thinks, and her friends will be jealous, (or 'jell' as Phyllis calls it, always reminding her of jelly,) because she'll have a real baby to play with, not just a doll.

She is puzzled, though, how they made it, because she can't possibly imagine them doing things like Georgia told her, with their *pookalies* and all that. Georgia says that Emmy's Dad has little squirms, (which remind Emmy of worms,) and that they must have got into Phyllis to make a baby. She feels proud of her Daddy's squirms.

Then one day Phyllis gets pains, and her waters break. Emmy remembers the picture in her Children's Bible of the waters dividing. Her father drives Phyllis to hospital.

The next day, he takes Georgia and Emmy to see the new baby.

Lizzie has specially whitened the girls' shoes with Meltonian, so now they have that fresh damp smell. Auntie Sarah has washed their hair.

Her father gives each girl a bunch of flowers. Emmy doesn't know if they are for the baby or for Phyllis. She walks almost on tiptoe into the long room as full of flowers as a flower shop, lined with rows of high iron beds like cots with bars, with a Mommy in each one, and an identical little metal sort-of roasting tin on a trolley by each bed. Georgia goes straight to her mother and pulls herself up onto the bed. Phyllis hugs Georgia.

Emmy says softly, 'We've brought flowers for your baby.'

'It's not my baby, it's your baby, yours and Georgia's!'

Emmy doesn't want a share in the baby.

Everyone is talking all at once, and Phyllis looks pretty and a bit different, her face sort of shines as if there's a light inside her and her tummy isn't quite like a whale any more, only like a big balloon. Emmy strokes her own inner arm, which feels nice and silky. Everyone is looking at It in its box next to Phyllis.

She peeps at It. Just like a wetting doll. Very still, and tiny, and perfect. She can't believe it's got a big-boy name – Alexander – and that it's her brother, though Georgia pointed out that it's Emmy's '*half*-brother.' Emmy does not realise that it is Georgia's half-brother too, but assumes yet again that Georgia is fully rightful.

Alexander gives a creaking-gate whine, wrinkles up his face so that he looks as shrivelled as an old balloon that's had all the air let out. The moan becomes a cry. Emmy feels a little frightened. Her father lifts him up – oh God, she hadn't thought how awful it would be to see Daddy with It – and gives the baby to Phyllis. She watches wide-eyed as Phyllis opens up her nightie and puts it there, on her titty. Emmy sort of knew, but at the same time didn't really know, that this would happen. Alexander snuffles around like a blind red rat until he finds the bump, and sucks on it like he's had years of practice. Phyllis tenderly feels the baby's face and head with an outstretched forefinger as if she's blind and wants to get to know every little inch. Then Phyllis asks her father something in their special language about the *kleintjie* and Emmy is sure she's being talked about. Her father turns to look at her, and answers in their language. The child forces a sweet smile, still standing by the bed.

A busy nurse with a big wart on the side of her nose like a witch comes to tell her father that Visiting Time is over. He says, 'Sure, I'm taking the kids home in a minute.' Only a 'visitor', Emmy thinks. At least Georgia is one too.

Georgia makes a big show of having to leave her mother, her tentacle arms tightening around Phyllis's neck.

'Oh Jakey, can't she stay a little longer? Alright Georgie, you'll come again tomorrow; and I'll be home soon.'

As is the way with Georgia, the more she is indulged the more demanding she becomes. 'Put that baby *d-ow-own!*'

Phyllis passes the tiny bundle to his father, who gently places the infant in the cot. Alexander begins to cry in a repetitive *wha-wha* way.

Her father gently but firmly unwinds Georgia's arms from his wife's neck, and carries her out crying. Emmy follows behind, casting a look at Phyllis's tortured face.

Now that Phyllis is busy with the baby, or sleeping, there are even more stretches of the day when Emmy is alone than with someone, and the hours lying in bed waiting to fall asleep at night feel longer than ever: watching the green 'N'-for-Northcliffe neon light in the distance for the count of twenty-five, changing to a red star for five seconds, and then the 'N' again, never totally predictable by counting. She imagines she falls asleep with her eyes open – always watchful, always needing to appear awake, even when alone in the dark.

In the album there is a page of black photo-corners on black paper, framing nothing: a non-reflecting mirror on which she gazes and speculates about the lost-and-gone-forever moments.

She turns the thick pages, to find the small black and white photographs.

This person is now dead . . . *buried* . . . *perhaps just a skelington* . . . . She cannot make sense of that. They don't know they're dead, do they? And they don't even know about her. Then she wonders what would happen if Phyllis died, or Georgia, or baby Alex. Or her father. Or her.

She does not think, now, that her mother *has* died.

She imagines a world of being only her with her father all to herself, and no Phyllis. But eating away at the corner of that world, like woodlice eroding a log, is a frightening sense of not being able to live without Phyllis, or is it her father?

The scrutinised faces give no real clues to the transformed present-day adults. She cannot believe that her parents could ever have been children, let alone babies. And how could her father be *older* than Phyllis, and yet be the youngest in his family, whilst Phyllis is the oldest in hers? The more she ponders the more baffled she becomes.

She has heard tales of their childhood adventures, of one penny being able to buy so many sweets, of their parents who sailed to South Africa on ships from places which really were the other side of the world, of people who couldn't speak English. Of the scarcity of good food; of a bull charging down the street; of Jewish shop windows being smashed, Jewish names being changed. And of unbelievable daredevil exploits; of feet splayed from barefoot dashing all summer, unable to squeeze into second-hand shoes, or shoes cut open to accommodate growing toes. She pictures these action stories, like Uncle Alec's films, shown again and again, though in her imagination they are in colour, not black and white.

And yet her mother is rarely mentioned. Her father seemed to have stopped talking about her from the day she died.

Stories delay Phyllis's or her father's departure before the long night alone. Phyllis always tells the poems or stories *she* likes, like *Winnie the Pooh*, giving an atmosphere of a faraway country where, in the illustrations, Christopher Robin looks like a girl and is cared for by a nanny who isn't black, and where he kneels to say prayers. There is a place called a 'Common' full of rabbits, and doctors with old-fashioned fat bags, and rhymes that she only half understands; and adventures with the same old dilemmas for she's heard them all before and Phyllis thinks they're very funny. Phyllis reads *The Water Buffalo*, and *Millions of Cats*, and *Aesop's Fables*, and *Peter Rabbit*, and the sad tale of *Jemimapuddleduck*, or *Jemery Fisher* who's always paddling about in the wet, and the Greek myths that Emmy can't understand but she is left with frightening brightly coloured pictures in her mind of people with eyes as big as saucers, or snakes growing out of their heads.

Her father makes up fantastical stories, some becoming her classics and retold or embellished. He seems to enjoy them as much as she does. One favourite is about frogs that keep being eaten by ducks. So the frogs call a meeting, and one clever frog suggests that they each tie a string onto a back leg, with a stick attached. Then when the ducks swallow them, the sticks get stuck across their beaks. That stops the practice: but was it that the ducks learnt by experience, or did the frogs rescue their trapped friends and relations by pulling on the sticks?

Bathed in the half-light glow from the passage Phyllis sometimes tries to sing Emmy to sleep. Propped on an elbow, Phyllis's lighted cigarette is a moving beacon of threatening hot ash or flying sparks. Her voice is as soothing as her comfortable fleshy arms and yet its quavering out-of-tuneness and smoker's cough carries a discomfort like the hot ash. *Joshua, Joshua, sweeter than lemon squash you are, yes, by gosh you are, Josh-u-osh-u-aaa . . . .* The songs and their rocking rhythm become as familiar as Emmy's own body, *Go to sleep my baby, close your pretty eyes, angels are above you, peeping at you darling from the sky . . .* , like Lizzie's presence, like something as deep as the smell of a rose with its layer upon layer of perfume, or the crowing of a cock that is home and peace and the very centre of being alive, in all time, time that is present and past and future.

In the Big School, smelling of polish and disinfectant, where Georgia has been for two years, Emmy and the other new children are shown rows of iron coat hooks, and she's told by the big lady with yellow curly hair that hers is the one with the picture of a red aeroplane above it. She sees her name on a small card. Emmy is pleased that she has her very own hook, that they are expecting her.

Phyllis is there, beyond the dividing glass window, with Alexander in his pushchair, but Emmy knows that she and all the other mothers are going soon.

She sits in the classroom with her back as straight as a ruler, in her proud new green ribbons, and can cope with Phyllis's departure, which she discerns by darting a sideways look. Cynthia and Sandra are in her class, and Lesley and Arlene, so she doesn't feel too strange.

She wishes her father could take her to school, but he always has to go to the office, or to important meetings with someone called 'Pappert', or 'Lane' whose wife, she hears, is 'twice his age'. Or he has to visit 'Fuchs Ware' or 'Cheeny Chains'. Her father always calls people by their surname or company name – he keeps first names for his best friends and family.

Emmy learns new rituals at this school, like the whole class being told to fold their arms and place an index finger on their lips when they have to be quiet, or to put an arm up when they know the answer to a question. They all learn to stand up when another teacher enters the room, chanting in unison, '*Geoie mŏra, Meneer Venter*' or whatever the name is, in Afrikaans if it's an Afrikaans lesson, or otherwise in English. Sometimes they all have to rest their heads on their folded arms. If a child is very naughty, they have to stand at the back of the classroom, but this particular fate doesn't befall Emmy. She is good at being good because she can't take her place for granted: she can hardly believe that she too is given new exercise books, and a stick-pen, and a pencil. They are all told to take their new exercise books home and cover them.

Teachers spend ages writing on blackboards, and then rubbing it out, sometimes wetting the felt blackboard cleaner first. Their hands and clothes are often chalky. Emmy thinks blackboards are really grownup and a sign of real school – like inkwells, dipping pens, and exercise books marked with red ticks.

She learns writing and spelling and sums and Afrikaans every day. And how to do the right thing in order to please the teacher, to follow the many rules. She has trouble remembering which way small 'bs' and 'ds' face, so she solves the problem by remembering that 'd' always faces the door. When they move classrooms the problem returns. Afrikaans is quite easy, except for the strange spelling – she knows some rude poems in Afrikaans anyway – and again she feels grownup: that she is catching up with Georgia, and is so much bigger than Alex.

Sums are nearly always about oranges, sometimes about apples, or cakes, or swimming pools. They all have to work out their cost, weight, volume, distribution, sometimes imagining cutting them up. She is sure she'll never need to know all that; all that effort in learning how to manage oranges. Sometimes the problems are about sweets, which is much more fun. She sees a face in some sums (-1-) and spectacles (-0-0-) and fat ladies (8 8) and swans (2 2 2). Laboriously she has to learn her tables, reciting them in unison with the class, the voices beaming light amidst dark shapes in her mind. Mostly, she doesn't remember them very well; she becomes dreamy and mouths the incantation whilst the others can be relied upon to come out with the right pattern.

Emmy and her friend Denise write 'Class 2a, Greenside Primary School, Rustenberg Road, Greenside, Johannesburg, Transvaal, South Africa, Southern Hemisphere, Africa, The World, The Universe' on the covers of their rough books.

Phyllis doesn't take her to school any more, for she can go on her bike with Georgia. The burrs of blackjacks stick to her grey woollen socks in the winter, and in the summer her bike's handlebars are so hot that she has to hold them with tissues.

They have to cross the field on the corner with long grass like straw, or go round it. They are told never to walk there because of snakes, but Emmy rides fast, ignoring the group of black men sitting on orange boxes gambling loudly with cards and dice in a corner of the field, as she traverses along the narrow path. Once she bumps over a fat snake. For the rest of her life she cannot ride a bike along a narrow path without wobbling and falling off.

Playground games and crazes are the best part of being at school. She watches Georgia and her big friends skipping over a long rope held between two girls, 'Rosie, Rosie, apple tart, tell me the name of your sweetheart. A . . . B . . . C . . . D . . . ,' each syllable punctuated by jumping over the whiplash rotation of the rope. 'Salt . . . Mustard . . . Vinegar . . . Pepper . . . .' Fasterandfaster, their chunky bodies looking too big for the same uniform that Emmy wears.

But soon Emmy and her friends have their own skipping games, and marbles and charms. She buys charms in 'lucky packets', containing a few pastel coloured little sweets and a picture card, or she swaps charms, or wins them. She feels bountiful – like when her father brings home some free samples from his business – when she scoops a win of a big round of charms. The more she wins, the better she becomes at the game.

She hoards her charm collection in an old Black Magic box, grasping fistfuls and allowing them to trickle through her fingers. Scrabbling in the box makes that scratchy sound like waves on the shore dragging pebbles. She finds old favourites, or rare ones, or the delicate coloured glassy ones of ballerinas or wash boards or Dumbo. Somehow these always remind her of cool water splashing in a clear aquamarine swimming pool.

Hopscotch is a game she plays all the year round, but without the possible gain of charms. The playground and the driveway at home nearly always carry the hieroglyphics of chalked games, unless the rain has sluiced them away. When it rains it really rains, or, out of the sky hailstones drop, as big as eggs, which can break windows. Once she had to shelter under the kitchen table.

She walks with her friends along shady avenues of dappled-trunk plane trees, to the public swimming baths. Their towels are specially folded like Chinese spring rolls, with a neat tuck at one end, to enclose their *cossies*. Emmy looks forward to the pink and green popcorn which squeaks softly on her teeth when she chews it, while she lies on her tummy sunning herself. She cools off in the chlorinated splashy-loud pool when she needs to wee.

There is a large picture on the classroom wall of a red post-box, houses, a street, gardens full of neat flowers, people, and a policeman wearing a rounded high hat looking like Mr Plod in *Noddy*, all glowing in a faraway clean country called England.

'Describe the picture in your rough books,' instructs Miss Tickle in her tight emerald-green jersey-suit, gold buttons straining over bosom and corset, permed curls framing her powder-pink red-lipped face and big beaky nose.

Emmy dips her stick-pen into the inkwell. The nib emerges with darker-than-blue blobs like snot from which a purposeful metallic smell unfurls, and has to be wiped with blotting paper. She re-dips it more delicately, wiping it along the edge of the china inkwell, and copies the date on the blackboard – *Tuesday, 16th July, 1951* – noticing the light-and-dark-blue ink's speckled variations in her grown-up curvy joined-up loops.

She turns to Mavis next to her, 'Do we have to do a heading?' Miss Tickle swoops upon this misdemeanour. The warm picture, the motes of chalk-dust in the sunlight, the optimistic date, all shatter as Emmy is called to the front and told to hold out her hands. She closes both eyes tightly as the wooden ruler slaps one palm and then the other with a twang as hard as Miss Tickle's corseted bum. The pain tears at a hurt deep inside, more than at her stinging palms.

The feeling of not being understood is further borne out when she writes a story with the phrase 'Granny even said . . . .' Her early attempt at an emphatic style is squashed as Miss Tickle corrects it, 'Granny Evans said . . . .' Emmy cannot explain.

Mavis – Mavis McGrath – has skin as white as her milky-white silky hair, hair always braided, tied and tartan-beribboned in long thin loops behind each ear; Mavis, with strands of stray silk as fine as silkworms' thread around her face, skin so white and transparent that pale mauve veins glow through her temples. Mavis, who blushes as red as a ripe pomegranate, especially once when standing by Miss Tickle's desk, and the teacher bellows,

'Now if you're going to make a smell like that don't stand by my desk! *Ag sies jong!*'

Emmy is shocked that Mavis, of all people, with her Persil-white socks, is capable of farting! Who'd have thought she had a bum? And fancy a *teacher* talking about such things.

Now if it was Hannah, Hannah Olifant, that would be different.

Hannah smells faintly of the rhinoceros enclosure at the zoo. Her jersey has holes in it, she wears boys' big grey socks which roll down her legs, her hands are never clean, and there seem to be permanent marks under her dribbling nose. Her new exercise books look old and battered before she's filled the first page. When she writes her tongue lolls out the side of her mouth like a pink slug.

Emmy feels sorry for Hannah, and so she agrees to go and play with her after school one day.

Hannah Olifant lives in a house on the outskirts of a suburb at the end of an un-tarred road, with piles of old washing machines and rusty bits of cars, mattresses and junk where a garden should be.

Hannah's grandfather's eyes are pale and cloudy; his face looks as if it has been drawn in thick oil pastels, his brown felt hat is tied on with bits of twine. He leans on Hannah as if she's a walking stick.

A litter of puppies with pink plump tummies and porridge-spattered soft fur play around the yard, smelling richly of something vaguely familiar, yet lost. Emmy longs to keep one puppy forever. The rubber tyres on ropes on which Hannah's brothers swing attract her attention, but soon the puppies compel her to return.

They chew Emmy's fingers with new needle-teeth and climb over her legs. There is a boy puppy – with a penis like a little white paintbrush – who she is sure wants to live with her. Hannah's mother nods in agreement, but adds, 'Ask your mom'. Emmy thinks that these poor people are abundantly rich, despite their house smelling funny, and not having a nice garden with a green lawn, a sprinkler, and a garden-boy.

'No. No puppy. Puppies grow into dogs you know,' Phyllis says.

As if I didn't know. Grownups can be so stupid.

'But we have Lenin. Why can't we have another dog? It would be nice for Lenin to have a friend. And . . . and I know one of the puppies wants me, wants to come and live with me . . . .' She feels like crying.

Phyllis laughs, and then ignores Emmy.

''snot fair . . . . But Phyllis, please, listen, Hannah's mommy lets her have puppies, even though Hannah's mommy hasn't got a daddy, I mean a husband, only an old man, I think Hannah's grandfather.' Emmy's face is clouded by her fringe and her frown. 'And Hannah's mom's legs are covered in sores and the skin, the flesh, rolls down over her shoes like . . . . like thick trousers.' Phyllis gives her one of her strange looks, as if she thinks there's something wrong with the child. Emmy tries to ignore her, to continue, '*She* manages, Hannah's mom, so why can't we?'

Phyllis carries on reading the newspaper, chewing her baby finger, as she often does.

Emmy calls her a cruel step-mother in her mind. She vows to have lots and lots of pets when she grows up, *no, as soon as I leave home, as soon as possible, I'll have twenty dogs . . . . That will show her.*

She cries into her pillow, locked again in the metal box of hopelessness. Surely her mother would have let her have a puppy; she's sure her father wants a puppy. Why doesn't he make Phyllis change her mind? She's glad she laughed when Phyllis broke her finger trying to hit Vasco the cat but hit the iron bed-frame instead; clever Vasco running under the bed. Vowing to run away the next time Phyllis smacks her, she wonders why she doesn't run away now. When she told Phyllis that before, Phyllis laughed and said, 'I'll pack you sandwiches.' So she decides not to tell her, to just go. Now.

She can't climb out of her bedroom window because there are burglar bars. Tears of rage stop as she creeps out of the back door as it drowses in late afternoon sun, like the palace in the *Sleeping Beauty* where everyone is asleep for a hundred years. Excitement is dampened by further tears of self-pity as she strides down the road, the way ahead blurry like swimming underwater, the longed-for puppy subsumed by familiar clouds of despair. She doesn't care if she gets lost. *They'll be sorry. Hah! That will show them.*

She plucks a leaf from a hedge as she marches on, and another and another, leaving a trail of shredded leaves, until a sting pierces her hand and the world explodes in a crimson whorl of despair. The hurt is so sharp that there is no alternative but to run back to Phyllis.

Phyllis laughs at Emmy's predicament and does not miss the opportunity to point out that the child still needs her. For once Phyllis's laughter is a relief after the solitary escape and the pain. At least this time Phyllis doesn't say it was 'God's punishment' for running away, but instead says 'Pride comes before a fall'. Emmy is confused, because she didn't fall over. Phyllis finds the tiny splinter-sting and triumphantly extracts it with tweezers, 'The bee will have died from stinging you. That will serve it right!'

The fumy ammonia from the applied antidote makes her eyes water again. Some order is restored and she walks away sadly, pondering if it was her punishment for hating Phyllis . . . . She tries to work out that it was the bee's fault that she was stung, surely . . . ? So it died . . . but what if it's Phyllis's fault that she hates her, why isn't Phyllis ever punished? *Perhaps she knows I hate her and that serves her right. But she has Daddy always, and that's not fair.*

A sense of further doom lurks around the corner of her mind at all these thoughts of hating, because hating is not allowed. Phyllis says, 'Hating makes you ugly.'

And yet one day her father comes home with a puppy – not it seems in response to her requests but just because Phyllis and he decided it would be a good idea to have a watch dog, and Lenin isn't much of a watch dog, but more of a house dog.

This so longed-for little puppy lands in her life, like when Phyllis had a baby. Only that wasn't longed for. How grownups make these big things happen, and there's no warning. Emmy has a strange feeling of wanting to cry, deep within the joy of this new arrival.

Her father decides on the name of Jock (of the Bushveld). It's hard to see how this little soft puppy could be a watch dog, or indeed have the fighting spirit of his namesake.

Jock sleeps on one of Alex's old baby blankets in a big basket in the neon-lit American kitchen. Her father says that when Jock's older he'll have to sleep in a kennel outside. Emmy often sits by the puppy and sometimes curls up in his basket with him although her legs stick out. Lizzie laughs at her; Phyllis tells her to stop being so silly. Georgia is out with her friends for much of the time and does not seem to care much for dogs.

By now Vasco the cat has died. When he died Emmy couldn't believe it. The vet had to 'put him to sleep' as he was very ill and couldn't eat. For weeks she would expect him to be curled up in the shade in his favourite place on the rockery, or pouncing on beetles on the veranda at night, but when she met a world that went on and on without Vasco, when Lizzie still brought her freshly squeezed orange juice every morning with its sediment of sugar and pips and she would sweep up the sugar with her finger and lick it, she felt that horrible heavy feeling in her throat, and at times a choking sensation. She returned to worrying about going to sleep, in case she died.

Sometimes Georgia seems happy to play with Emmy. These games stretch out into dramas: a stage on which teddy bears, stuffed dogs and wetting dolls have high temperatures and sometimes die.

Emmy puts wetting-doll Jenny up her dress – she won't fit properly because the bodice is tight – and they pretend that Georgia is the doctor examining her to make sure the baby is alright. Emmy pretends to be very sick, vomiting and coughing. Then she pretends the baby dies, there and then. She didn't think Georgia would allow her to have this pretend, but she does. She squeezes real tears out of her eyes as she solemnises the death – she's good at forced crying if she looks in a mirror – but giggles break through uncontrollably, spoiling it all.

Real large spiders get run over on the drive and are buried in matchbox coffins adorned with flowers and registered in scratched letters on small slate headstones.

Dolls are given gateaux which she and Georgia make by layering Marie biscuits with rainbow coloured icing sugar, topped with hundreds-and-thousands, and then sliced into perfect triangular wedges, which have to be eaten by the girls because the wetting dolls' rosebud mouths can only take the teat of tiny bottles.

She and Georgia share a room while Granny Gella has Georgia's room for a few months. The girls both catch not only the same range of childhood illnesses but also a ball that they toss from one bed to the other in the long days they both have to spend in bed. Phyllis always comes in when one of them is out of bed, and scolds them, 'I *told* you . . . .' Emmy wonders how Phyllis always knows when to come in. It's never so bad being shouted at if they are both in trouble.

Phyllis shouts at Emmy in the bath one evening and Georgia starts to cry too. Phyllis stops in her tracks,

'What are *you* crying for!' she says to her daughter.

The misted-over shiny taps become Emmy's whole focus: one with 'H' for Hate, and the other 'C' for Cind, fat drops of water forming beneath each one like snot until they can't hold on any more and they let go, *pling*. She stops crying.

1952

Now there's new baby, Paul, in the family. Again a huge change that no-one asked Emmy about. But he is sweet, and Emmy often gains the treat of licking out his bowl of Nutrene. He sleeps for much of the day. Phyllis is busy with him at bath time and feed time. Georgia doesn't seem to notice him.

Walking home from school one summer day a man is blocking the narrow path across the corner field. Emmy is reminded of the Scarecrow in *The Wizard of Oz* with straw hair, hair the same colour as the dry long grass, grass almost as tall as she is. He smiles at her in her green checked summer school uniform, then stares hard as he puts his finger through the flies in his trousers. It's the sort of joke that Cousin Carl would make. She doesn't know what to do, or if she's supposed to laugh. But she feels as if an icy knife is going through her heart. She considers running back along the path towards school.

Last time she ran away from something, from the wooden cart at Hopscotch Nursery, it still caught up with her and bashed into her. Her parents said she should have turned off the path that time. She wants to go home, to the after-school butter-syrup biscuits, so she stays still thinking how to get past him.

Ohmygod! It can't be his finger. One of his hands is holding it. *It's got big and amazing.* She tries not to look but her eyes are pulled towards it like a magnet. She feels spiked to the ground. Opening her mouth to cry, no sound emerges; her head is full of clear pictures like a photograph yet it feels like a dream. *Perhaps it is a dream.* Like a dream she's had before. *Or, like . . . .* Time stops.

He's walking towards her, still staring at her, but with that peculiar big thing like her father's or Cousin Carl's only much too big, and rubbing it up and down up and down as if he's in a sort of trance, '*Asseblief,* hold it, hold it, *maisie,* I'll give you lot of *lekkers,* sweeties, *baie lekkers,* as most as you wants.'

She's so scared, not sure if she'll ever get past him, too bad about the snakes in this field, this is the worst snake in the world. His eyes look at her in a troubled way, cross-eyed like Cousin Morrie, or is it Grandpa Harry – but he's dead isn't he? She begins to feel sorry for this scarecrow, he's so desperate. He makes her feel special, as if he's come to find her; but she feels sick at the same time, sick in her stomach, and her throat begins to retch. Perhaps if she does what he asks, he'll let her go home. She should have listened to Phyllis and Daddy, and not walked across this field on her own. Serves you right, Georgia would say.

So she holds that hot big thing, which can't be called a *pookalie* any more, and he holds his hand on top of hers in his desperate way and moves it fasterandfaster, so fast that it becomes a blur, and she sees his face contort, and the veins in his neck stand out purplish under his pale skin. She thinks he's having a nepileptic fit like Jonathan at school. Suddenly he gasps as if he's dying, and whitish stuff like snot, no like half-cooked egg-white, comes out of it and goes all over her hand and over his big freckled hand with orange hairs on the backs of his fingers like an orang-utan, and he says, 'Thank you thank you, *danke, baie danke.*'

She squeezes past him and runs – too bad about the promise of sweets, even though they're her best thing – wiping her hand on her checked dress while runningrunningrunning for home past Mrs Berman's house-on-the-corner with the round windows like eyes, past the granadilla fence, past Leslie's house, quickly glancing over her shoulder, no, he isn't following, up the drive and the side of the house to the backyard, remembering the picture of Peter Rabbit coming home in tatters.

Emmy won't tell Phyllis. She would be furious. She is sure she shouldn't have touched the strange scarecrow man. *Sorry sorry sorry* . It has to be a secret. She can't tell her father, because he'd be shocked that she knows about big things, even though she thinks she knew anyway, before.

She hears Lizzie and John talking, no, shouting loudly to each other in their language in the back yard. Perhaps they know; perhaps they saw it. Lizzie laughs in a cackly way. Emmy feels ashamed.

She sweeps through the dangling fly screen beads over the back door and into the kitchen.

Everything is the same. So still and quiet. Except for her heart pounding like a bat in a cage, trying to get out. Perhaps Phyllis is having a rest. Dropping her school case, Emmy notices that the pram is in the shade in the yard, the fly net pulled over it. Baby Paul must be sleeping. She feels like tipping the pram up, for him to come crashing screaming out. Lenin comes up to her wagging his tail. Stroking his head, she's pleased that someone treats her normally. But he gets all excited sniffing her dress and her hand, and licks it. Feeling more sick, she washes her hands under the kitchen tap, using lots of Lifebuoy. And sniffs them. Now they only smell of soap.

She stands by the lounge door.

'Emmy, that you? What's the matter?'

'Nothing. . . .' Silence. *How does she know?* 'What d'you mean, Phyllis?'

'Mean what?'

Again Emmy is silent, though she thinks anyone would hear her heart clattering like hail on a roof.

'Come here', Phyllis calls, sounding cross, not turning her head away from her magazine, as Emmy enters the room. The child goes over to her step-mother and stands by the big Chesterfield chair covered with the lords and ladies material.

'What happened?'

'Nothing.' Emmy starts to cry, not meaning to cry, not wanting to explain, sure she'll get into trouble. But she can't help it. The more she tries not to, the more she sobs. Phyllis puts *House Beautiful* down, gets up, puts her arms around Emmy, and tells her to sit on her lap. Lenin is there, licking her knees, trying to make her better. She sobs and sobs in big gasps like rocks in her throat.

Phyllis gets impatient, 'It can't be *that* bad, whatever it is! Come on, cough it up! I haven't got all day!'

In a flurry of confusion, the child's mind is full of the stranger and his big thing and the stuff and the strange excitement of it all and the feeling she's dreamed it all before. How can she possibly tell the story. And now Phyllis is getting impatient. But the next minute she seems to soften, for she says,

'Come on, try. You'll feel better if you do.'

So Emmy does. She talks about a man on the path across the corner field – noticing her step-mother's body stiffen beneath her – and rushes on with the story, hoping Phyllis won't notice that she should never have been walking across the corner field in the first place, '. . . and his finger was in his trousers, I mean his flies, only it wasn't his finger, I thought it was, I thought it was a joke, and then, and then . . . .'

Phyllis becomes very quiet and tense; Emmy can feel her holding her breath; she doesn't know whether to go on or not. She pauses.

'Go on!'

So she does. Looking at the floor, her eyes fixed on the herringbone pattern of the parquet, Emmy describes '. . . his *umn* . . . *pookalie* changing into . . . something else, and he wanted me to sort of move it, with him, and then, and then . . .' She can't say any more. She doesn't have the words. She's scared. With sickening familiarity she feels that life will never be the same again. She cries again. And then Phyllis stops comforting her; she seems to be angry, and the child remembers all the times Phyllis has been angry with her. She can't express the hopelessness of being on someone's lap when she needs comfort but they don't give it, so she becomes angry too, and she shouts, not looking at her step-mother,

'And then he *made* me hold it on and on up and down 'til he had a fit like Jonathan at school and then he said "*Danke,* thank you very much," and he sort of changed, to being . . . very kind. But I ran home 'cos . . . .' Another wave of crying makes it impossible to talk, and then the child refinds her anger, 'I was *baie bang,* and now I don't know what . . . . But please don't tell Daddy. Or Georgia.' Only now does she turn around to glare at Phyllis.

Phyllis sits there, her eyes looking cloudy in their own way as if there's a thunderstorm about to break out in her head, and she says she's 'very sorry', and 'this should never have happened', and 'he's a sick man.'

Emmy doesn't understand, because he didn't look sick, and she's the one who feels sick.

Then Phyllis says, 'We must call the police, but first you must have a drink of water.' It's what she always suggests if a child gets a fright or gets stung or falls over. So Emmy fetches one.

'And don't be silly about not telling your Dad. Of course he has to know.' She knew Phyllis would tell him everything.

She takes a mouthful of water, holding it in her mouth for a long time, unable to swallow, until she forces herself with a loud gulp. She feels a bit better. The spotlight is certainly on her, even more than when she dropped a brick on her toe, or the time she was *deliver-us* (like in the Lord's Prayer they say at school, 'deliver-us from evil') and had an extremely high temperature – which must have been the evil. That time Phyllis said she was so hot that she could have scorched the sheets.

She feels even better when Phyllis says, 'Fetch my keys and unlock the sweet cupboard and help yourself.' Emmy can't believe it. 'But first wash your hands. Properly.' A fresh wave of worry rushes over her: something really very extremely bad and extremely serious must have happened to her to warrant this unimpeded access to the sweet cupboard. She takes one chocolate and one Liquorice Allsort – her favourite kind with hundreds-and-thousands on it. Phyllis wants to know what she's chosen. She shows her.

'Only two? Emmy, you *must* be shaken. Have more. Gowon. Jelly babies? The sugar'll do you good.'

'No thanks, Phyllis. I feel a bit sick.' Phyllis feels her forehead.

'No temperature' – the ultimate gauge of whether anyone is really ill or not. The chocolate is melting in her hand.

Phyllis goes to dial the Police. She knows the number off by heart, 'in case'.

'Emmarentia Police Station? Greenside, did you say? Same difference. Can I speak to a woman – a lady? Why? Because I have something delicate to report.' Emmy thought only babies, or lace, some flowers, or fairies, were 'delicate'. Once Granny Gella said her stomach was 'delicate'; the child thought it meant that the food was caught up in all those saggy wrinkles.

Phyllis tells the child to go out of the room. Of course she listens outside the door. She lets Lenin lick the chocolate on her palm, and hears Phyllis telling the policewoman about her daughter aged eight. She hears the word 'penis', and another long word like 'mastrating'. Then Phyllis calls her in, her hand over the receiver.

'Did you say his hair was . . . yellow?'

Emmy pulls herself up to her full height. 'It was the same colour as the veld, and he had orange hairs on the backs of his fingers, and his check shirt was dark blue and light blue and his trousers khaki-colour, with dark brown stitching and he wore *tackies*, dirty worn-out white ones, and he smelt funny like John only different, and he had red cheeks, and under his shirt I saw a torn white tee-shirt, and one of his teeth in the front was crooked when he smiled . . . .'

'My God, that's enough! What's the matter with you! I can't tell her all that. How d'you remember it all?' Emmy could have gone on and on, for her head is bursting with how his big thing was almost red, but the lump on the end was purple, and there was a scary gaping hole at the end like a fish's mouth, and the stuff that poured out like lava in her

book about volcanoes smelt of . . . . She couldn't think what
. . . . Perhaps a sort of fishy scrambled egg smell, she wasn't
sure. And there was more orange curly hair peeping out of
his flies. She knows they need the details, to track him down,
so she can't understand why they don't want to know all this.
Like afterwards, when the thing went kind of mushy and he
was so grateful, and he stuffed it back into his trousers, she
noticed that one of his fly buttons was missing. It's too scary.
Scare Crow. That must be where the word comes from.

Now she thinks she's a lucky fish that Phyllis doesn't want
to know any more. Perhaps Phyllis thinks it's all made up, for
attention. No, even Phyllis would know she couldn't possibly
have made this up.

She hears her on the telephone saying 'No, I don't think
that's necessary. No, I don't want to put her through that.
No thank you Officer. I'm sure I've told you everything.'
And then, after a few seconds, 'Of course I'm sure she's not
making it up!'

Emmy thinks she'll be scared for ever. She so wishes
it hadn't happened. Perhaps it's her own fault. Perhaps
she should have run backwards, even if it was the wrong
direction. Or run into the *veld* with big snakes. She thinks
Phyllis would have been more sorry if she'd been bitten by a
snake and was dying.

'The police now have a Report on him and will keep a
Lookout. They may catch him and put him in Jail,' Phyllis
proclaims.

In Emmy's mind she sees the Monopoly board, *Go to
Jail. Do not pass Go, do not collect $200.* Poor Scarecrow, she
thinks. Or does it serve him right? Now he'll have to live on
bread and water for ever – if they catch him.

Phyllis calls, 'Lizzie! Go to Paul. . . he's crying.' Sitting
down, she says 'I'll read you a story, Emmy, until Georgia
comes home, because you've had a big shock. And from now
on Georgia will *have* to take you to and from school, and you
must *never* go in that field again.' While straightening her
skirt and lighting a cigarette, she adds for good measure, 'If I

got hold of that man I'd give him the hiding of his life.' Emmy believes her.

Yet, in a way, Emmy knew about his big thing – she doesn't know how – so it wasn't a complete surprise. She saw it in full colour like a Cinemascope Technicolor bioscope, and not shrouded in shadows in her mind where it was before – perhaps from Georgia telling her how babies are made. Only she doesn't exactly remember what Georgia said and her class at school hasn't had the film about all that yet.

She remembers how she felt sorry for the man. He needed her so much, and that made her feel powerful and important.

That night Emmy tells herself to dream of something nice, like a holiday by the sea, because she doesn't want to dream about the Scarecrow. But it never works, telling herself what to dream. She dreams about *The Wizard of Oz* film, and one of the Munchkins is sort of crazy, and wants her to eat something that she doesn't want to eat, and he's pushing it into her mouth and she tries to keep her mouth closed but he tells her, 'It's nice, oh please *please* for my sake', and so she opens her mouth just a little and then he's Grandpa Harry and pushes the whole lot in and she feels full of bad stuff and she's choking and wants to vomit and she's so scared that she can't cry. She wakes up and this time she's in no doubt about going to Phyllis and Daddy's bed, she doesn't care what they say.

She quickly feels her way along the dark corridor to their bedroom, forgetting the rule of bringing her own pillow. When she gets there she's not sure whose side to go in. She stands at the foot of the bed looking at the big shadows like bears on the walls. She usually goes next to her father, but now she feels muddled.

Phyllis half wakes up, 'Wha'sa matter? Who's it?'

The bad dream qualifies her for entrance. She climbs in next to her step-mother.

Her shadow is squashed and small now; it follows her much closer than when it's gigantic and spread out. She can't lose it like Peter Pan. It bends up tree trunks and walls and over stones, thinner than a locust's wings. She moves suddenly, to trick it out of its persistence. *Copycat, stole a rat, put it in your Sunday hat.*

Echoes of peeping in the mirror and trying to catch unawares the girl who lives behind the glass, or trying to see the orchestra of tiny people who inhabit the inside of the gramophone by peering through the circle of dark little holes from which the sound emanates. When she searches she thinks of her mother somewhere high up in rays of slant sunlight.

The white fire sun lends sharpness to stains on the front wall: pale patches spread out as they dry, gobbling up the wet-from-the-sprinkler drab areas.

Impatient for the figure of Phyllis at the top of the road, Emmy tugs at a bulging canna pod – rough-skinned, like her father's Adam's apple – and tears it open to find the palest green sticky seeds. She squelches them between her fingers and tosses them away.

And waits.

Ants march up the wall in a grey quivering line.

A lizard with brown and black tapestry-skin and fine twig-feet, his whole body vibrating with each heartbeat, darts his tongue out before disappearing so quickly that she wonders if she imagined him. Like the scary scarecrow man and what popped out of him.

The inside of dried half-moon seed pods reveal black dots, like spent caps from a cap gun.

Warm green smell of damp soil.

Tufts of coarse grass under her bare feet.

She picks at a scab on her knee from when she fell off her bike, to make it smooth. The slight pain makes her more determined to pull it off. *Eina!* She doesn't care that she's made it bleed again. She bites into the scab with her front teeth until they meet, then spits the two bits out. An ant finds a fragment and soon a crowd of ants are investigating and beginning to drag it off, like illustrations in her *Book of Knowledge* of men labouring to build the pyramids.

A black man digs a hole by the side of the road, piling up ochre earth with each blunt sound of the shovel.

More waiting.

Walking towards the corner creates the expected, for there appears the familiar rounded shape not much taller than Emmy. Phyllis has come back on the bus from town, after being at Daddy's office.

'*Phy – llis*!' she calls, shading her eyes from the sun. Lassoing her with her voice. 'Hi Phyllis!'

With a knowing smile her step-mother says as she approaches, '*I* know why you've come to meet me!'

A flash of a memory of the promised present from her father's office – that Aladdin's cave of music boxes, painted pencil boxes with roll-top lids, delicate paint brushes, plastic ballerinas – bursts in her head, pushed in all around by the complexity of having half forgotten that there was to be a present, wanting to be believed that she simply wished to meet Phyllis from the bus-stop.

Phyllis smiles her twinkly smile. 'Ooh! You only came because you knew . . . ! I know you!' She seems to know Emmy better than she knows herself; her step-mother's version is always the definitive one.

When Emmy plays with the present – of a pink plastic bench with a blue plastic man seated on it – she feels sad.

She wanders into the bright kitchen to find Lizzie, who is always there beneath the curly flypaper dotted with prey like musical notes, or out in her thunder-dark room in the backyard.

Conversation is scattered over the Saturday breakfast as messily as the table strewn with plates of French-toast crumbs, jam, cinnamon sugar, little pools of yellow butter, and half a bowl of cold *Taysty Wheat*. Flies home in on the scene, drumming away, not settling for long on anything, like Emmy's mind. Above, the mobile twirl of flypaper claims a few victims amid the generalised noise of voices.

Georgia, in playful mood, asks 'How old are you, Emmy?'

The patchwork of sounds become momentarily sharper.

'Eight,' clear as a bell, Emmy's well-brushed hair in long beribboned bunches propping up her sense of dignity.

'*Agh*, I told all my friends you were *seven!*' Emmy struggles between a sense of this familiar tease meant to demean her by making her younger, and a real fear that Georgia has got it wrong again, that Georgia really doesn't know. For no sooner than her age is only one year behind Georgia and she thinks she might catch up, the older girl has a birthday and pulls away by two years.

Incomprehensible words take over again, amid laughter and crumbs and the newspaper, and the silver dinner bell ringing to summon Lizzie.

She is rescued again by Georgia, 'Hey Emmy, what d'you want to be when you grow up?'

'What?' stalling for time.

'What, pot, stick your head in a coffee pot, when it's ready, pull it out, red and hot and eat it!' says Georgia challengingly.

The spotlight is on Emmy again, like Phyllis's lighthouse beam, though she hesitates before letting Georgia see the secret little flame that she has shown her before. Nevertheless she blunders forth, 'An artist.'

Georgia adds, laughing, something Emmy had said years before, 'Mos' famous in the world.'

Emmy is encouraged by this brief notoriety to persist in her ambition. It isn't only her craving to be noticed, like Doris Day or Leslie Caron, or to be famous like Van Gogh or Utrillo, whose prints hang in the lounge, but a vague sense that painting would be a way of expressing the tragedies she feels inside – like when she can cry real tears when she looks in the mirror. She longs, too, to express some of the joys – even though they feel inexpressible – like the utter freedom of running on grassy slopes, or in fields of pastel cosmos daisies at Emmarentia Dam.

'Why're you such a dumb *kop*?' Georgia interrupts her dream.

'Hey?' she asks.

'Hay straw donkey's manure!' Georgia retorts.

Emmy nags Phyllis to join a Saturday morning drama class. Georgia already plays the piano well, so she wants to find something different. She doesn't know why she is drawn to acting.

'Em-meal-ie! I told you, I'm too busy with Alex and the baby to arrange it. *Godsake*, stop nagging!'

Emmy finds out from Cynthia and Sandra where the class is held. Eventually Phyllis makes the necessary phone call.

The focus becomes *A Midsummer Night's Dream*, another blur of words by the older children. Emmy is Mustard Seed in a diaphanous tawny tunic. Barefoot, she has to hold a long branch from the poplar tree. Amidst the babble she remembers the cue to say her one incomprehensible line – 'One aloof stand sentinel.'

She doesn't realise how apposite this line is to her feelings about herself.

The poplar staff of office comes from the tree over which she looped a horseshoe – symbol of good luck but alien metal object – gradually being incorporated in its trunk.

Holding out the branch as instructed until her aching arm becomes the centre of her universe, with a long silent groan, '*Eina!*' she resists relaxing it until the curtain is lowered.

Then she is a pawn in a scene from *Alice in Wonderland*, in a costume made by Phyllis who curses how much cotton wool is needed to stuff the tight rings around her middle. 'Just as well you're skinny!'

In another scene she plays Alice. Even though the light blue cotton dress edged with darker blue stripes around the hem, and topped with a starched white apron, is left over from another production, she feels special. The Alice band makes her long hair like the real Alice's despite not being very blonde.

But she has to sing a song. This is as impossible as getting the timing right in ballet, or that first ignominious attempt to play the triangle. She struggles at night in bed, with the help of Phyllis's croaky smoker's voice, to get the tune. She can hear it perfectly in her head, but it comes out wrong when she sings it. The drama teacher shortens the song. Emmy manages the four lines perfectly on the night.

Phyllis says, 'One thing you're not going to be is an opera singer.'

1953

Phyllis and her friend, Irene, are sitting on deckchairs, talking, and sipping tea. Bone china gold-rimmed cups, each with a lipstick imprint on the rim. Cigarette smoke swirls upwards. With thumb and middle finger Phyllis finds specks of tobacco on her tongue, and removes them.

Paul is sitting plumply on a plaid rug, as bottom-heavy as his clown-toy that always rights itself. He is surrounded by a wooden horse with a mane of real hair, a tin spinning top, wooden blocks, and Emmy's old stuffed floral giraffe. If she had been asked if he could have it, she would have said yes, because after all Paul really belongs in this family, like Alexander and Georgia, with their own mother. He is sucking one of the giraffe's horns and pulling a face as if it tastes awful. She giggles at him as she kneels on the edge of the rug, and looks up at her step-mother, but Phyllis doesn't notice. Irene is giving a litany about her 'girl' Gloria who cannot be trusted, who is always pretending to be sick, whom Irene collected from the police station yet again and for whom she paid the fine after Gloria was rounded up because she was without her Pass, yet again.

'Now tell me, Phyllis, how can anyone forget their Pass? I sign it every week, and off she goes on her free afternoon with her fancy man. And by the way, how he can afford those zooty suits I don't know.'

Irene shakes her head, while Phyllis nods with an empty look in her eyes. She has become more absentminded since Paul was born.

Emmy wanders into the house, which is full of dark-purple thundercloud light and flies as loud as bees inside the lav window.

She considers finding Georgia, but then remembers that she has gone to play with her friend, Valerie.

On her bedroom floor lies her big Croxley drawing book with crumpled corners, the strewn colouring-in books, and crayons in a Havana cigar box.

Lying on her tummy Emmy opens the big drawing book on a blank page and starts to make sweepy yellow lines at the top of the page, then using the side of the crayon because the paper has peeled off she continues dreamily, adding a few pink sweeps of colour. She imagines Georgia saying 'That's babyish! It's just scribbling!' She stops, but then continues. Lower down on the page she uses green where the ground could be, and some blue, *No, that's not right,* dark green and light green, *That's better.* She needs to add something that goes from top to bottom, that stands up, straight. Her drawing is controlled here, and strong, with this brown line; she thickens it with more brown lines. The crayon breaks. She looks at the two halves with dismay, and then at the whole picture. She doesn't know what makes her add purple and brown and black patches to the ground on top of the greens and then more orange to the sky, beneath the pink. The top area begins to look like a sunset. She draws three black birds, big 'M' shapes, above the brown upright shape. 'M' for Mommy. Her own Mommy appears in strata of blurred pictures, how Mommy used to draw with Emmy, Mommy a real artist with lots of paintings stacked up in the spare room.

She tears it out very carefully.

On the back she writes 'To Phyllis love Emmy X X'

She folds the page with the picture on the inside. And stands up, rubbing her hands on her dress to remove specks of wax crayon, before going outside.

The glare is so bright that she shades her eyes to see Phyllis and Irene exactly where they were before, still talking and drinking tea. Now Paul is in his pram. She notices the red marks on Phyllis's cup, and that one of Irene's stockings has a ladder, which Emmy imagines is for fairies to go up and up under her dress and into her *broekies*. Holding her drawing behind her back, she stands still at the edge of the rug, waiting for a pause. Irene is saying '. . . you just can't trust them. Turn your back one minute, and it's gone. The other day . . . .'

Emmy cannot bear the suspense. She slips the folded offering onto Phyllis's lap, and darts away. It's better not to appear to want anything. From a corner of the garden she watches.

Phyllis fingers the piece of paper without looking at it, puts the beaded net back over the sugar bowl, whips her tongue into the corners of her mouth, all the while nodding to Irene like a conductor beating time for an orchestra. And then she opens the paper,

'What's this then? Emmy, what's this?' She doesn't look around for the child. 'Why don't you come and tell me what you're doing? Oh, a picture. Let's see. Oh my. My goodness.' Emmy wishes she had never been so silly as to give Phyllis a picture. 'What do you think of this, then, Irene? Looks like a sunset. Very nice! What's that brown thing? A stick maybe. And why're you wearing that old *shmatte*, Emmy? I told Lizzie to give it away. Sorry to interrupt, Irene; go on, please.' The drawing slides off her lap onto the grass.

Emmy didn't think Phyllis noticed what she wore, looking down at her favourite old checked dress Grandma Gella had bought for her.

Later, when Lizzie clears the lawn of toys and the rug and chairs, the drawing is thrown into the wicker toy basket. By then Emmy is in bed after her bath, unable to fall asleep.

The world of sweets and comics is always there. Emmy goes round to the shops whenever her pocket money allows – but not across the field of course – preferably with a friend or a cousin to share or compare or swap.

Chappie's Chewing Gum – though it's really bubble gum, and if she has lots she can blow enormous bubbles that sometimes burst all over her face – are two for a penny, with a little comic under the wrapper.

Cherry suckers are on little wooden sticks, also two for a penny: red glassy spheres of perfection with a slightly sour tang and sometimes with hard black specks in them – Denise says they're dead flies – that aren't supposed to be there, but which she ignores. She sucks so hard on them even when they go jagged that sometimes the roof of her mouth and tongue bleed. She is undeterred by this, and, from time to time a sudden choking feeling.

The lucky packets and charm packets are not really satisfying if she's desperate for sweets, as they only contain a few tiny ones.

Then there are shiny liquorice pipes with red hundreds-and-thousands on the bowl so that they look alight; and of course sweet cigarettes that look real too, with red 'lit' ends. She sucks these until she has made a point as sharp as a pencil.

Nigger balls – which she can lick and sometimes black-lipstick her lips – change colour, layer upon layer, so if she smashes them in half she finds a rainbow inside. She's not allowed to call them nigger balls, although Georgia says *her* dad lets her.

Strips of Sharp's toffee, which she pulls and stretches like elastic.

Honeycomb, which goes gooey when she sucks it.

And coconut-ice, which has nothing to do with ice: layers of bright pink and white squares, which she sucks and chews until there's only coconut left.

On her way home from school she buys ice suckers – red ones are her favourite – from the boy who's really a man only everyone calls him a boy, though some people call him Sammy because he's Indian, with his cart of 'hot' ice that steams when he lifts the thick metal lid. Ice suckers stick to her lips at first when they're so cold, 'because of the hot ice,' she's been told, but she doesn't understand what that means.

Then there is popcorn, coloured pink and green and blue.

And occasionally ice-candy: big crystal lumps of hard sugar, pale blue or pink, with a wick right through like a candle, wrapped in waxy greaseproof paper.

She used to buy milk suckers: big lollipops the size of her tongue, tasting of condensed milk, but then they stopped making them.

If she is having chocolate bought for her, she chooses a Peppermint Crisp. She doesn't buy it herself as that would use up all her pocket money. Carefully unpeeling the foil decorated with red, blue and green zigzags – to play with afterwards, making goblets or animals – she sinks her teeth into the thick layer of soft (depending on how hot the weather) chocolate until they meet the crunchy airy shards of bright green peppermint crisp, and bites off a chunk. She sucks on this perfect mixture of hard yet feather-light crispy-mint and soft top-quality chocolate. Sometimes she prolongs the experience by nibbling on it until only the green middle bit is left, but she's not sure if that takes away some of the satisfaction. If, by mistake, she chews on a piece of foil stuck to the chocolate it gives her the shivers, especially if it touches her fillings.

Phyllis sometimes buys Walnut Whips as a special treat, or Eskimo Pies at the bioscope, or boring sugared almonds, which are better than nothing. After lunch every day Phyllis unlocks the cupboard and produces a silver dish of sweets and chocolates on a paper doyley and Emmy and Georgia and Alex can choose only one, or sometimes two. If there is a Black Magic *scutterbotch* (as her father calls it) chocolate she chooses that because once she has nibbled away the enveloping chocolate she can suck the butterscotch and make it last a long time.

But she can never keep sweets for later like Georgia, who keeps hers so long they go stale. When Emmy is desperate for a sweet she sometimes prowls through Georgia's desk drawers and takes a nibble that no-one would notice, never mind if it's stale and soft when it should be crisp, or hard when it should be soft, or so old that the paper won't peel off. Sometimes she sniffs out chewing gum in Georgia's pocket when they're wrestling. Georgia is so amazed at her detective skill that she gives Emmy some.

She tries to keep sweets so she can make Georgia jealous. She puts them high up in her cupboard so Lenin and Jock – and Alex when he's on the rampage – won't find them. But then she keeps finding a reason to have to go to her cupboard for something, *You're not going to have one of your sweets, are you?* And then she gets there and thinks, *Oh well, just one,* and she adds, *That's it.* But then she has to fetch something else and again she's sure she won't have a sweet. But she does. Until they're all gone.

And for absolute perfection, she goes to the Kelvinator to *fress* on condensed milk when a tin has been opened, sucking it out from one of the two little holes punctured in the lid. She goes on until she feels slightly sick and the utter richness hurts the back of her throat – only then can she know she has had enough. Her father loves condensed milk as much as she does. When he was a child, his parents couldn't afford it, so he vowed that when he grew up he would buy a whole case full. Now that he can afford it, he doesn't.

Phyllis and her father are always talking and laughing with other grown-ups and cousins at seaside holidays in Muizenberg or Durban.

Emmy loves to feel the wet, dribbly sand between her fingers and toes, almost wanting to eat it. She only wears a sun bonnet when she's forced to because it's babyish. With a pointed toe like a compass she draws a large circle, until waves ruffling like rolled-out dough wipe the circle away. Standing at the edge of the sea, feeling the sand beneath her feet being worn away, she's left on two tiny islands, which soon disappear and she topples over. She sits on the muddy edge, pat-a-caking her legs with wet sand. They feel heavy when she raises them. Then she lies back on her elbows for a wave to wash them clean, and looks at the paper-thin cut-out blue mountains in the distance. She wees, for no-one will know and it won't show on her rose pink wet crinkly *cossie*.

She thinks how the waves never ever stop, overlapping each other sort of sideways, like *pas-de-chats* in ballet. They don't even sleep at night. Why do they only appear near the sea shore? And why are those little white waves out there called white horses? Is this the same bit of water someone else has touched?

Her father says the sand is made from millions and trillions and zillions of sea shells and broken down bits of stone, all from the waves bashing them for millions and trillions and zillions of years.

Emmy taught herself to swim when she was seven, floating on her back in the Vaal River, counting how many seconds she could manage, until she could stay there for ever and never drown. But she and Georgia and Alex are not allowed to swim here (and certainly not baby Paul) without Phyllis or her father, for the waves can be ferocious.

There is talk of the dangers of what Phyllis calls an undertow, and of sharks, though Emmy has never seen either. There are shark nets. She saw a man with a scarred leg who Georgia said had been attacked by a shark. Emmy wonders what other creatures lurk in the sea. Octopuses? Whales?

She remembers the whaling station near Durban where the sea had turned red from a whale as big as a house, which lay there. Men climbed up on it and cut it open, stripping off layers. It stopped looking like a whale. And the smell, a rubbery fishy salty smell, like the *snoek* Phyllis buys, only worse. She doesn't know why it made her shiver, and reminded her of Grandpa Harry.

"'Come into the parlour," said the spider to the fly,' pops up in her mind.

Her father and Uncle Mickey buy bunches of lychees from a boy with a great big branch. She didn't know they grew like that. She rinses her hands in the sea, and runs up to the others, dashing fast so the sand doesn't burn her feet too much. Uncle Mickey gives her a twig with lots of fruit on it, so she sits down, and breaks open a rough pinky-brown shell, like cracking a hardboiled egg, to find the pure white succulent insides. Her father has taught her the word 'succulent' when he showed her a plant that stored water in its fleshy leaves. As her teeth bite around the large black shiny pip, a pip like a fat tick – that looks delicious but isn't because she's tried it – the wet beads of juice run down her arms to her elbows and dribble onto the sand. She watches the drops fall on the sand and stay as dusty blobs for a while, as perfect as raindrops on a nasturtium leaf, until they soak into the sand and leave a darker patch. Like when she weed behind one of the huts. Onto the next lychee, and the next, until they're all finished.

She buries the shells and the pips in the sand, pretending the mounds are mountains and the bare twig a tree, her hand a monster searching for treasure. She finds a sand-covered pip like a sugar *jujube* and some old cigarette *stompies* in the sand. Shadows of palm flicker like a home bioscope on the sand. Then they become hands clapping, no, crocodile jaws snapping. She looks up at the fronds. Now they're the legs of a giant *songolulu*. The wind changes. Then they become a woman's hair being blown from behind, forcing a parting.

1954

She can rely on the annual reappearance of silkworms in her life, but they can't always rely on her to keep them alive.

Emmy thinks that silkworms are aptly named, for their skin is as silky and fine as the satin lining of Phyllis's Chanel-No.5-and-mothball fur coat. She is compelled to brush her cheek along the satin of that coat – like the freshly picked rose petals which she delicately strokes along her lips, or the silky bristles of her blue Bakelite baby brush, which she won't let Phyllis throw away. And so she longs to kiss and stroke silkworms when they reach their fat prime.

The worms' life-cycle is part of the pattern of her year, like school holidays, birthdays, and the pink blossom tree in August. When she hears that this is the silkworm season, she climbs on the Dolly Varden puppet theatre (that is really a dressing table stool), to scramble among jigsaw puzzles, for the old Black Magic box with holes punched in the lid. She checks on the dried-out squirts of little eggs in once-liquid pink chalk. With luck, the tiny black creatures have not yet emerged, and she can watch for them every day, enticed by fresh mulberry leaves.

But some years the hatching has been forgotten and she is reproached by shrivelled tiny specks like commas punctuating the floor of the box. (*I did water my seeds at school, I did I did. They grew into cornflowers, they did.*)

The black specks, if given fresh mulberry leaves in time, soon grow to white recognisable worms, which in turn develop into fat and beautiful specimens with black spots and black noses – or are they mouths? – which move up and down the edges of leaves gracefully, their slowly nodding heads carving out deep indentations in the serrated leaves. The leaves become skeletal if not replenished, and the bottom of the box littered with black droppings. She strokes the worms, some as plump as her fingers, and passionately longs to squeeze them. An earthy warm green smell, like dusty soil after rain, compounds this longing.

The day comes when one of the big-to-bursting creatures starts to sway this way and that, pale golden thread endlessly emerging from its mouth, as it anchors itself to a leaf or corner of the box and surrounds itself with a cocoon, which grows thicker and denser by the hour. Finally it shuts itself into a seamless perfect egg-shape, hiding its secret transformation. She wonders how such a big worm can fit into such a small cocoon.

One day Emmy's curiosity about the hidden activities can no longer be held in check, so she carefully cuts open one of the silent shapes, to find an ugly brown hard thing inside. Cheated, she wraps it in cotton-wool and replaces it among the perfect cocoons, peeping at it from day to day. Phyllis's 'Curiosity killed the cat' comes to her mind.

She puts an untampered cocoon to her ear, and thinks she can hear some delicate movements within. A little mouth eats its way through one end, followed by comical droopy feelers, and then a damp heavy body. Wings, like a leaf-bud opening, unfurl, and the moth trembles, preening in its brand new existence. She blows gently on it. Its hairy feelers quiver, the bulging eyes look blind. She feels like stroking its wings, like she did the silkworms' skin.

Meanwhile the hard brown shape from the invaded cocoon never alters. Some mysteries, the real secrets, like how babies are really made, remain unknowable.

A few days later, a further miracle is witnessed: two moths flutter around each other, one wriggles its tail up like a bent pipe-cleaner and then they join, tail to tail, and stay like the Siamese twins she has heard about. In time they separate. One of them spurts out tiny eggs in pink liquid like calamine-lotion, which she touches. It dries so quickly.

Some moths do not seem to find partners.

Some of this season's moths have already died. She feels their hairy bodies, wings like petals, then rubs her powdery fingers together. Their solid trunks remind her of the worms, as do their little faces, making the mysterious link between them more believable.

Emmy shakes the dead moths into the bin. The egg-encrusted box is left lying on the kidney-shaped glass of the Dolly Varden dressing table. No need to close the lid now.

Weeks later she rummages for a tennis racquet and the box falls from the wardrobe. She does not question how it has been put away in its proper place.

Next Spring, when the box is rediscovered in its rightful place, she tears the battered cardboard into smaller pieces, ensconces them in a fresh new Black Magic box with its intact red ribbon anchoring the lid, still smelling tantalisingly of its contents.

Worshipping at the shrine begins again.

One day Alex needs money to go out with his friend. The only cash in the house is her savings in her Graham Crackers tin. She protests. Phyllis insists that he can borrow it, of course they will repay it, and how can she be so selfish and so silly. Selfishness is a Sin, and is equated with being like Auntie Freda, one of Phyllis's sisters. Phyllis adds that she shouldn't be causing her so much trouble. Emmy protests that it won't be the *same* six shillings and nine pennies. 'Anyway, it's *my* money!'

She lies on Phyllis and her father's bed crying, her eyes clinging to the patterns of the fancy bobbly glass in the small side windows in which in calmer moments she sees faces of old men, or witches, or peacocks. She understands that money is interchangeable, yet she's submerged in fiery outrage and injustice. Desertion, loneliness, helplessness, like all those other times before, wanting her mother, no-one understanding her isolation and hopelessness.

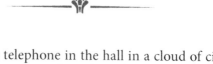

Phyllis is on the telephone in the hall in a cloud of cigarette smoke, her ears and mind stuck to the receiver, filled with someone else, for a length of time that has no end in sight and so, for Emmy, goes on for ever. The rich red Persian rug with a navy border is tufted with white: she treads round and round this path, slowly, quickly, changing direction, not stepping over the edge, 'Round and round the garden walks the teddy bear, one step, two steps, tickly under there.' Afternoon flies circle in patterns above her head accompanied by clear notes of Georgia's piano scales as interminable as the telephone conversation. A wrong note drops like a stitch in knitting, leaving a hole; sometimes re-worked, repeated, dug over, finally smoothed in an even spread of seamless rises and falls.

She goes to sit on the wide piano stool next to Georgia, its upholstered seat disguising the recess of stored indecipherable books of black dots, and names often heard – Beethoven, Chopin, Sonata, Pathetique, Mazurka, Clementi, Toccata, Fugue, Grieg, Bach, Andante – names more varied than the tunes, tunes as irritating as being stroked in the same place until it hurts. How can fingers find the correct keys, white or black, so quickly?

Emmy searches out a break from this interminable afternoon, touching the fairy high-note keys gently while Georgia plays. The piano lid crashes onto her fingers, staccato sounds clashing with the glowering room, extinguishing sunbeams of dust, before skewers of light on the piano lid shine on her fingers as they emerge. Moments of silence after the long bang, then blood and inside-flesh and bone – or is she imagining it? – and screams that she is not aware of making, and Phyllis stopping her telephone call abruptly. Georgia is slapped as suddenly as the piano lid banging down. Emmy is confused; maybe it was her fault, she knows she wanted Phyllis or Georgia to pay attention.

Mercurochrome: the red cure-all with beetle-wing glints. 'Perhaps the doctor needs to look at it,' Phyllis says. Bandages.

Pain of a dull throbbing intensity comes later, like the pain of the brick dropped once on her foot. She remembers Phyllis's concern that time, perched on her bed, and, later, her toenails going blue-black and falling off, and eventually tiny new nails beginning to traverse the battlefield. Phyllis's solicitousness when she's ill or hurt is the spotlight again. Now, sitting on the edge of her bed, tender, thoughtful suggestions about what to eat or drink or do. 'A jigsaw puzzle you haven't seen for a long time? The dinner bell by the bed in case you need me? A comic when Lizzie goes to the shops?'

'Eeny meeny miny mo,
        Catch a nigger. . . .'
    Not "nigger". "Nigger's" not allowed. My dad says. You have to say "monkey".
    '. . . . by his toe,
    If he hollers let him go,
    Eeny meeny miny mo.
    And O.U.T. spells "out",
    With a dirty dirty dishcloth wrapped round your big fat throat.'

Later, 'throat' is not allowed, and they have to say 'toe'. On and on until by elimination 'It' remains: the one who has to hide their eyes.

Are nigger *balls* allowed? Two for a penny, black outside, tongue black, pinkish when she's got through the first layer; smash them open, rainbow colours inside. 'What colour's yours? Mine's gone yellow,' as she sucks them and compares.

'Good work' in red biro in the margin of her English book, rubber-stamped with the school emblem of a linked chain under-scrolled with 'Goodwill'. The prize from the Headmaster are nigger balls. Six of them, all black, as big as ping-pong balls, in a cellophane bag. Glowing with success, on her way home she offers the sweets to the black man pick-axing the road. He takes one.

Hide and seek in and around the glow-worm studded rockery at night, the air thickly warm, silky and scented as Phyllis's fleshy upper-arms. Hiding behind the ghostly moonlit silvery fronds, the excitement of the cavorting family complete with Jock and Lenin makes her want to pee desperately.

It is always Phyllis who first says, 'Time for Emmy to go to bed.'

'What's the time? Half-past nine, hang your *broekies* on the line,' calls Georgia.

More time is snatched as Emmy side-gallops over to her father after the game is over, to stand by his side as he waters the garden under the stars.

The heavens seem wider, deeper, more vast and more thickly populated than any earthly landscape. The more her eyes search into the blackness, the more stars appear. Unsteadied by the wide firmament, she takes hold of his arm. He points out Orion's belt and the Milky Way. He talks about other galaxies, and infinity. For moments these concepts feel as elusive as grasping a shadow, at others an awareness of her smallness in the great universe buffets her like a butterfly in a gale.

Back to the emblazoned house, through the veranda where Alexander beetles lie on their backs frantically kicking their legs. When she rights them, wondering if one could be Christopher Robin's, they fly up to join the moths in a beating of the light, only to fall helplessly on their backs again. Sounds of whirring, banging, Jock crunching some down.

Into bed, watching the neon 'N' for Northcliffe on and on, her eyes open until the house is full of the sounds of others going to bed.

'Never eat elephant leaves' is a well-known family mantra. Enormous flappy elephant leaves, sometimes jagged-edged from snails' nibbling, just like battle-scarred real elephant's ears. But how do people know one mustn't eat them if they haven't tried them? Snails eat them. Unless people have died from eating them? Emmy wouldn't have thought of eating them – as unlikely as eating the crazy paving, or roses – if not warned severely not to.

Phyllis is on the telephone again when the child tears off a tiny bit, and chews on it. Knives of pain cut into her tongue. *Eina!* she yells to Phyllis, who ferociously darts around,

'I told you so! As if I haven't enough to do already! My God child!' lifting Emmy up screaming into a lilting bathroom, putting her in the empty bath. 'You'll wake Paul!'

Now Emmy knows why she must not eat elephant leaves. Red arrows pierce her tongue while Phyllis telephones the doctor.

'Drink milk! Quick!'

She does. Still, in the bath. The pain subsides.

Georgia intones, 'TruthDarePromiseorCommand?'

'Dare.'

'Dare you to eat a bit of elephant leaf.'

'Never, no, never. *Nix.*'

'Dare you to eat some canna leaf.'

'No, no way,' Emmy replies, not even if it's a way of securing Georgia's attention, possibly admiration.

'Mulberry leaf? Gowon – silkworms eat 'em.'

'No, *nix.*'

'You're *bang,* cowardy-cowardy custard, scaredy-cat.'

'Don't care. You eat it then, dumb-cluck!'

Georgia stuffs her mouth with a mulberry leaf, chews it, swallows.

'Ah-*haardy*, ah-*haardy*', Emmy retorts with big flapping movements of her elbow and wrist, watching, waiting, ready to tell on her.

At school, they're learning about the way oranges are farmed near Nelspruit: picked, sorted by being rolled down a slide with holes of increasing size. Emmy's jaw is firmly set as she makes a careful drawing of rows of orange trees on a farm. She's sitting next to Son Oosthuizen, whose tongue sticks out when he draws, making him look stupid. She draws the bright round fruit, the ladders, the ubiquitous hills in the background, paths, and as always the setting sun with radiant rays.

Mrs Viljoen holds up Emmy's drawing for the class to see, then pins it up on the notice board with shiny brass drawing pins. Emmy blushes with pride and surprise, for she hadn't thought it was that good. She wasn't even doing her very best. Not like when she and Georgia colour-in and she does shading and outlines, and doesn't go over the lines, and she can tell Georgia thinks it's good though she would never say so.

Phyllis never thinks Emmy's drawings are any good.

Her big drawing book at home is a source of frustration and pleasure. She sometimes thinks she can draw quite well, but not as well as she'd like to. She can see something in her mind, something like a beautiful ballerina, but then she can't draw it properly. She doesn't know why she draws the same female faces with long hair, over and over; sometimes the back view of a woman; often a large black woman holding a baby. She has given up drawing horses. Perfecting her signature yet again, she makes it a bit scribbly and hard to read so it looks more grown-up, like her father's. Cynthia and

Sandra's mother say she's good at drawing, yet she doesn't really know how good, or good for what. Grown-ups seem to think that drawings that look very real are good, so she tries those most of all.

Alex is another being, somehow joined to Phyllis because she is always talking to him or worrying about him, but his life is very separate out there. His friends are all boys and it's hard for Emmy to find any link with them in their khaki shorts, always jumping around or boxing or pulling each other over. Alex says he is going to be Sugar Ray Robinson when he grows up.

He is ruthless when he wants something that he thinks she has, like a ball he insists she has taken. Her incantation:

You liar you liar your pants are on fire!
Your tongue is as long as a telegraph wire

has no effect. So she lets rip with one of the forbidden words, only allowed towards dogs: '*Voetsek!*' Undeterred, Alex searches for the ball with the power that Emmy finds in his mother.

It's the summer holidays, weeks and weeks stretching out, doing nothing. Emmy is ten. The family have had their two week family holiday at Muizenberg.

Emmy lies in the garden on her back covering her face from the sun with a bent arm, opening one eye and then the other in turn, squinting at the triangle of bright sky that jumps with each blink. Phyllis is sitting in the shade with her friends, having tea. Emmy gauges they must be important guests, because the cross-stitch starched cloth and the pewter tea pot and matching milk jug are out.

She goes in to fetch a comic. As her eyes are still adjusting to the dark after the bright sun she can hardly see Stanley, Stanley Kramer, the big brother of Mikey, Alex's friend, in her room. Emmy knew he was somewhere in the house, hanging around, waiting for Alex and Mikey to return from Camp. He smiles at her, looking like a *schlemiel*, she thinks, or a *sheps*, as Granny Gella would say. He says he was also looking for comics.

'Can I lend one?' he asks.

He's much bigger than she is but he still gets 'lend' and 'borrow' wrong; she feels secretly important not only as the provider of comics for Alex's friend's big brother, but also as the greater expert on grammar.

'Sure, go ahead, Stanley.'

'Hey, why d'you call me Stanley? Everyone calls me Stan.'

Instead of taking a comic and leaving her room, he sits on her bed and begins to read *Bugs Bunny*. She looks at him, his absorption in *her* comic, and she gets that tickly feeling down her spine that she always gets if someone borrows something of hers or admires her things. It makes her want to stay in the same room. She can't also sit on the bed, so she sits on the floor cross-legged and opens a comic across her knees, trying to look grown-up even if she is on the floor, by leaning one elbow on her knee and resting her chin on her cupped hand.

They remain pleasantly companionable for a while. She begins to sense him looking at her. She goes very still. He says softly,

'Hey Emmy, Em'ly, you're pretty, y'know.'

Her heart is doing funny things now. *He's supposed to like Georgia, not me.* She swallows and gives a shy smile, mumbling 'I don't think so.'

'Emmy, why the hek don't you come and sit by me? More comfy than the floor.' He adds, 'And close the door while you're up.'

Far from nonchalant, she closes the door and sits by him on the bed.

'Oh come on, on my lap!' He's commanding and firm. She feels she doesn't have a choice. She's embarrassed that she'll be too heavy, and that sitting on laps is babyish. But she complies.

He's so much bigger than her that it feels quite nice on his lap, rather like her father's, but a bit strange, until he jigs up and down and writhes around, his hot face buried in her back, and he's pressing something big against her through her clothes. The Scarecrow Man appears like a bioscope in Technicolor in her mind. She wants to go, to get up, but he's holding her tight around her tummy and saying her name again and again as if his life depended on it. She goes behind a big thick wall in her mind where none of this is really happening, so she is only half scared and half amazed, and almost enjoying feeling so needed. He's still doing a kind of rocking under her, and then he holds her even tighter, and there's a moment of utter stillness while neither of them breathes, before he gives a stifled groan into her shoulder, and a final enormous wriggle like a snake sloughing off its skin. In her mind she sees a pot of porridge on the stove boiling over. And then he's calm, muttering 'Thank you, thank you, thank you.'

Why?

There is a pause, while she sits very still, and then he blurts out, 'You must promise never to tell anyone, that's our secret. If you tell anyone I'll tell them you started it, you sat on my lap and got my John Thomas out, I swear, I'll tell them that, and they'll believe me, 'cos I'm much older.'

She feels like crying. She was alright until he turned nasty. He needn't worry. She wouldn't dream of telling anyone. She doesn't even know who John Thomas is.

They both stand up. Perhaps he senses her unhappiness. He puts an arm on her shoulder,

'*Ag jong*, I mean it when I say you're pretty,' and he adjusts his khaki shorts as if there are crumbs down them that he has to shake out, and goes out to the lav.

She looks in the mirror and stares into her eyes. She's still half behind that thick wall, but looks the same really.

She goes into the garden. The sun is pleasantly warming. She had forgotten to bring out a comic, but has changed her mind about wanting one. Phyllis wouldn't notice if she looked different; sometimes she wishes she would notice, even about bad things. Emmy feels like sitting on her stepmother's lap, a nice comfy lap, but Phyllis would say she was disturbing her.

She asks for a slice of granadilla cake from the tea table, and sits away from the grown-ups on the grass in the sun, feeling shivery, crunching hard on the black pips. *Granadilla, granadilla. Funny word.* They always remind her of the granny who died.

That night she dreams that she's at the bioscope with Alex and one of his friends whose face she can't see. The friend makes her do what the Scarecrow Man did, but then he becomes Alex, and she's excited to have all his attention. Then she dreams she's eating sugar cane in the dark, before she realises that inside it is a really big worm. The dream changes, to bare soil with nothing growing on it. Some bricks are lying on it and are supposed to show where children have been buried.

Fragments of this dream come back to her day after day.

Emmy pictures flat fields as far as the eye can see, with a little house in the distance. The scene is like her toy farm with a mirror for the pond, except this will be real, with real calves and sheep and pigs all being fed by a woman in dungarees. She is anticipating going away to Barbara's grandfather's farm.

But on the day of departure there is a pain deep inside her jaw and a swollen lump on the gum, not unlike the day of the ballet exam when she awoke with mumps. Phyllis says,

'You *would* get toothache on the day you're going away,' as if Emmy had planned it.

Her father drives her and Phyllis and Georgia into town. Georgia is sulking because she wanted to go swimming.

Reclining in the high leather chair, Mr Stein pours something from a little indigo bottle onto cotton wool, and holds it under Emmy's nose. Phyllis smiles somewhere nearby. A pungent cloud of candyfloss-nail-polish-remover smell fills her head, she's drowning, no floating, *Nice . . . scary . . . .* The world is receding, disappearing.

She wakes with big rolls of cotton wool in her cheeks, blood from her mouth swirling into the little basin, and Phyllis standing there smiling, so it must be alright. Emmy's tongue seeks the strange bumpy hole where the tooth used to be. She's given the bad long-rooted tooth that looks quite harmless and too little to have caused all that pain. Her tongue keeps finding and stroking the little hole. Rinsing her mouth with salty water, the bloodied spit spirals around the basin like bath water gurgling down the plug hole when she's safe inside a big bath towel on Lizzie's lap.

At night, there are silhouettes thrown by the big hanging lantern on the wall, of Barbara's mother as she walks about; shadows as big as giants, black witchy and gorilla shapes in the paraffin-smelling creaky farmhouse. While the other children sleep, Emmy lies as wakeful as ever, alone in this interminable time, between bed and sleep time . . . waiting. Moths circle the lamp, to and fro, as if within a magnetic inescapable field. Outside other moths bash against the mesh on the windows. 'Mothmothmothmothmothmothmothmoth' Emmy says softly, the sound and feel of her lips perfectly evoking the furry moths she knows from her silkworms, and a new word emerges, 'Thmow thmow thmow.'

Barbara's mother's shadow crouches over an enamel pot. She pees as voluminously as a cow, making a hard, tinny sound. Emmy hides her wakefulness all the more, guilty at witnessing this private moment. Now Barbara's mother turns the little knob on the lamp and it gets dimmer and then black. All black, before she climbs into her groaning bed. Emmy hears Barbara's mother getting comfortable.

And then the house is quiet.

But, *Why does the house make cracking noises?*

Why are the dogs howling?

How long is the night?

What if it's morning time and I haven't slept? Do I tell anyone?

I want a goodnight kiss from Dad.

Barbara's mother is turning over in bed.

Barbara is snoring softly. She's so lucky.

No, it's not all black, noticing that the sky through the mosquito-mesh window is grey-blue.

The house is settling down to sleep too.

The light-darkness of the window is like my bright night light, my Northcliffe 'N'.

She dreams of a seaside place with turquoise water and a secret shore beyond the rocks, and of old buildings she mustn't forget.

Barbara banging into Emmy's bed wakes her up to the smell of porridge, the sound of cocks crowing, white-bright sun streaks darting all over the room, and Barbara's mother saying,

'Barbara, brush your hair *properly!*' Then, tossed in Emmy's direction, 'Barbara thinks she hasn't a back to her head!'

Can that be? Does Barbara really not know she has a back to her head?

Emmy is asked to help make scrambled eggs, which she's never done before. She gently stirs the egg mixture. Barbara's mother briskly takes over,

'It's sticking,' unsticking the bubbly mixture. Emmy feels useless. She watches the swift strokes of the fork – *Why does Barbara's mother always do everything so quickly?* – and remembers how to do it for next time.

Barbara's mother is called 'Pearl'. Emmy can't imagine calling her that so she doesn't call her anything. The name makes her see a pearl button in her mind because once she heard of a girl who was called Pearl Button. She looks down at her watch when Barbara's mother talks to her, fiddles with the winder, winding it even though it doesn't need winding, almost breaking the spring, pretending to check and re-check the time.

Barbara's mother says, 'Is that a new watch then?'

Emmy says 'Yes,' for how can she explain that it's not and she's only looking at it because she's shy, and needs something to do when grown-ups talk to her.

Barbara and Emmy have days of barn-hiding hay-climbing jumping running sliding sneezing itching scratchy scuffing simmering-summer-sun, amid vistas of *mealies* on dry, hard, red zig-zag-cracked earth. Horses twitch as if an electric current is running through them as they graze, their tails swishing from side to side across their flanks. Yellow weaver birds hang upside down to feed their babies in little basket-nests. Cockerels look as if they're wearing knee-length baggy trousers; chickens scratch the earth, with that clever look in their eyes, as they cock their head to one side. Emmy hears them saying what her father says they say, 'Look-what-*I*-laid! Look-what-*I*-laid!' The doves' calming call, *doo doo, du-du doo, doo doo, du-du doo,* allays the fierce heat and seems to cool her sweaty forehead, evoking Lizzie's clean white apron in the cool kitchen.

Her father and Phyllis, and Georgia, Alex and Paul, and Lizzie, seem so far away that she doesn't think of them much, in that other world of Jo'burg.

One afternoon behind the farmhouse by the pond a man chops the head off a duck. The headless creature briefly staggers, while the head, lying in prune-coloured blood, continues to open and close its beak. Rich viridian feathers on the head have the same glint as the bluebottle flies already gathering. So much movement makes Emmy freeze as she watches out of the corner of her eyes.

The duck served for supper the next night gives her a spasm of discomfort, which she buries with other irreconcilable horrors, and then she eats it. She decides that the duck she eats that day, and the chicken the next, are not the same as the alive creatures she sees on the farm.

The high *mealie* leaves clank as they bat each other in the wind, reminding her of the corner field with the Scarecrow. His face has changed now. He looks a bit like Stanley. What if the Scarecrow comes to find her here? *Don't be silly. Anyway he's probably in Jail, not collecting $200.* She desperately wants to pee. She runs and runs, and wees on the floor when she gets to the toilet. She doesn't know why. She could have weed outside, in the empty field. Or managed to get to the lav properly. But it's quite nice emptying her bladder in the cool little room on the dark red stone floor. And then she walks away from the big puddle, trying to forget about it. In her head she sees Phyllis's saying, 'Why?' and Emmy doesn't know the answer. She sees her father too, but he's not saying anything. He's slowly shaking his head, quietly clearing it up, and she feels bad, that ashamed feeling. Like when he cleaned away her snot on the wall. Something wrong inside, a black badness, the inside of the metal shiny tin with unscalable sides, herself as small and helpless as a crumb.

When two weeks have passed, Phyllis and her father come and fetch her from the farm, because it fits in with taking Alex to Camp on the way. Barbara's mother, in her flowered frock, her hair swept back on each side into big waves and held there with combs, says it's been a pleasure to have Emmy. She says it as if she means it. She reminds Emmy of Miss Jeffries at Nursery School.

It seems strange to see Phyllis and her father here – Phyllis with her usual navy-blue slacks and white wedge-heel sandals, Dad with his pipe, on this veranda, when they don't belong here. But Emmy runs to hug them, and then it all feels almost normal again.

She shows them round, but is cross that Barbara, who seems to think she knows the farm better than Emmy, comes too. When Emmy tries to deter her by scowling at her, Barbara gives her open-mouthed look, her bovine eyes looking stupid, her chicken pox scars more like craters than ever. Phyllis noticeably relaxes as she walks across the farmyard on her husband's arm, avoiding a pile of manure. Emmy holds her father's other hand. *Now Barbara can't be part of my family, she'd have to walk in the shit to be close now.*

Phyllis becomes ecstatic at the smells of the cow house, the stable, the hen house, and the odour of *vrot* apples.

Jake says, 'My, Phyl, you've got a nose on you!'

'Don't be rude about my nose, Jakey! When I was a child I stayed on a farm, but you know, Emmy, I didn't see the sea until I got married to Bernie. I can tell that the hen has laid an egg by the way it's clucking. See if I'm right!' Emmy opens a flap and reaches in for the warm egg, offering it to Phyllis to hold, who cradles it gently in her hands, puts it to her cheek, and then asks Emmy to put it back.

Emmy wipes the muck off a guinea fowl spotted feather, and gives it to Phyllis. Phyllis takes it absent-mindedly, and holds it all the way back in the car, delicately feeling the fine filaments and occasionally stroking her bare arm with it. Emmy wishes that Phyllis would stroke her arm like that. The child's face leans on the back of the Durahide front seats, watching; one cheek becomes red and sweaty.

In the car, Phyllis says something to Jake in Yiddish. Emmy knows they're talking about her. Phyllis turns her head round to tell her that Lizzie isn't with them anymore, 'She's left. Gone away.'

Emmy almost stops breathing until Phyllis finishes what she's saying.

'Lizzie had problems with her children . . . her own mother died so she couldn't look after them any more. Lizzie was getting old anyway. So she's gone to live in the country, where she can look after her children and grandchildren. We have a new nanny, called Ellen.'

Emmy doesn't say anything. Phyllis says it all so calmly. Her father keeps driving.

All the child can see, through a miasma, is Lizzie, always there, always warm and soft. Her Lizzie. Emmy never thought she'd go away. Lizzie, dozing in the scullery. Emmy didn't know she was old, *she didn't look old, not like Granny Gella. Lizzie doesn't have grey hair, or wrinkles. Why didn't anyone tell me she was old?*

Without saying goodbye.

What's the point.

I should never have gone away to the farm.

Phyllis offers her a barley sugar from the tin they always keep in the car. She takes two without Phyllis knowing, and sucks on them so hard that the roof of her mouth bleeds.

She scratches a bump on her arm, telling Phyllis about it. She says 'Don't fiddle with it. You'll start something.'

'Something's already started.'

Her father says they'll be sending Lizzie money every month, and Lizzie may come back to visit, if she manages to sort out her difficulties.

Emmy doesn't believe she ever will. She can hardly keep track of the list of all the people who have disappeared. It's more difficult than mental arithmetic. *Mommy, Miss Jeffries, Shirley, those grandparents I never knew, all my friends in Pretoria . . . .*

'Dad, what was the name of the boy, the house boy we had before John?'

'Why should you want to know that?' he asks.

And now Lizzie, who she had dared to think would be here for ever and ever.

When she gets home she rushes in to wee, and then goes into the kitchen to see Ellen.

She can't possibly be her nanny. She's thin and light brown, not at all like Lizzie. *Perhaps it's just as well – now I don't have to like her.*

1971

Emily has had her hair cut very short.

No one, except a little girl of a hairdresser in Stoke Newington, knows that she attacked it ferociously. If it hadn't been her hair it would have been her thighs again, adding to the lattice of raw raised scratches. She had hacked at the fringe until she had the look of a prisoner with a shaved head.

Later she remembered her balding doll, Wendy, left behind in South Africa. She had tied a knitted hat on the doll to hide the sparse hair, but that had not stopped Phyllis from laughing, 'You won't need *that* creature in England!' And that was that.

But in England Emily had pined for Wendy; could see, through an aura of refracted sunshine and warm tears that felt almost solid, the knitted hat enveloping Wendy's plump cheeks, her glassy green eyes beneath long lashes looking at her. *Wendy was good, she never did any harm. I left her behind.*

When the despair abated, Emily was quite shocked at what she had done, and shamefacedly went to a hairdresser in a part of town where they would never see her again and asked to have it shaped short all over.

Now she quite likes this *gamin* look, *á la* Jean Seberg. It accentuates her high cheekbones, which she inherited from her mother.

This time the provocation was Stefan going off with another woman. She had gone up to London from Suffolk specially to see him, and he wasn't there. Not that he and Emily ever really made a commitment – and if they had, it may not have made a difference to how either acted. She had seduced him in the first place, or was it the other way round? She wasn't sure. All the same, she had that sense of sexual power over him; another victory.

Now he's not here to appreciate how striking she looks.

She stares deep into her eyes in the mirror, one pupil and then the other. When she focuses on one iris the other seems to stare at her as if it's another person. She thinks she looks like a mad woman, almost laughing at herself, knowing how crazy she can be. The whites of her eyes show all around the pupils, the ceiling weighs down on her. She can imagine what she will look like when she is very old. No, dead. She feels that terrible pain in the back of her neck, a hard rod pushing down on it. Her temples throb.

She sees a knife. Again that image, cutting open her chest full of maggots, maggots which must be exposed, she's so full of them. Maggots and pus. And if it's not maggots it's a charred horseshoe in her centre instead of a heart – Phyllis always said she was heartless – like the real horseshoe she put on the branch of a poplar tree when she was six. The girth and branch gradually grew round it until it disappeared. But she knew it would always be there, and would never disappear.

Emily withdraws from the mirror and, through blurred vision, opens the brass catch to her wooden paint box.

There begins the first of a series of self-portraits.

She works with warm umber, an amethyst like the bloom of grapes, and lacquer red, smoke grey, manganese violet, Prussian blue, cadmium yellow, and white. She almost moulds the thick impasto with her fingers, then works with an urgent brush at the dark, congealed blood oozing from the mouth, overflowing, and at the tears like discharging wounds from the eyes. It hardly needs to be a face, her face – the colours and quality of the paint carry as much emotion as any face can show.

She works through the night by a single light bulb dangling from the ceiling, smoking and drinking wine straight from the bottle, dark red wine staining her mouth like the mulberries she gorged as a child.

She used to wonder if she was playing the part of the dissolute painter in a garret, or if this was genuinely her. But she has been hopelessly drunk often enough, and lived in squalor for long enough, for this to be an appalling but familiar pattern, to feel far more natural and rightful than being good to herself.

The face that emerges is barely discernible from the background: the whole surface is writhing with pain and tears and sweat.

She begins the second one. Now she paints what lies beneath the surface, scraping off the paint in places with a palette knife to reveal the canvas, the bones beneath the flesh, crumbling decay, the point of impact between life and death. She scratches with the handle of a brush the words *Hope is a lie* into the wet paint.

She can hardly look at the work by the time she drops onto a mattress and sleeps until the telephone rings at two in the afternoon. She lets it ring and ring. It stops. And starts up again with greater insistence. It might be Stefan. She stretches across to answer in a husky whisper,

'lo?'

'Emily, is that you? Dad here. *How're you?* You haven't been in touch for ages, answered my calls, or Phyllis's. Been so worried about you.'

'Christ, Dad . . . don't know.' Back in the world of bright sunlight and buzzing flies, a burnt patch on the mattress that she can't remember, the smell of turpentine from an overturned bottle, she stalls, 'What time is it now anyway? . . . not very well – hell of a headache right now; okay really. Oh God . . . ring you soon, 'nother time . . . promise.' Her efforts to sound normal don't feel successful. 'Alright? You okay, Dad?'

'Yeah, fine really. Your brother's coming down from Scotland soon – wants to see you. Alex I mean. He'll travel to Suffolk. Why don't you give him a ring?'

'Yeah, that'd be good. Sure, Dad. Okay. Can't talk now. Sorry, must go. Love to . . . Phyllis. Keep well. Bye.'

She unplugs the phone, and resolves to tell BT that she doesn't want the line.

She hangs the second canvas from a rowan tree by thick twine, wanting nature to add to the inevitable decomposition of the body. And laughs bitterly at this enactment of a gallows.

1972

Detached but emotionally charged

Emily Samuels: 'Portraits 1 – 6', Arnold and Sons Gallery, Dover Street.

Samuels's 1971 series of self-portraits convey an extraordinary development, from unprocessed primitive outpourings, almost faecal in texture and palette, with echoes of Auerbach's thick impasto, the paint almost sculpted in the first one, and something of Dubuffet's freedom and urgency in the second. The third – like looking in a fairground mirror – references Bacon's distortions. I am also reminded of the spontaneity and energy of Rauschenberg, (such as 'Bed', 1955) in this painting, whilst it, and the fourth, convey figurative mental anguish reminiscent of Munch and Nolde, where the paint is worked to a point of fatigue. Gradually, by the fifth, we see a development from the actual nightmare, to paint that blooms with a psychic bruise.

The final portrait in the series, the sixth, carries some of the weight of a Rembrandt self-portrait, the mature Rembrandt, where he is looking at the viewer – who is of course himself – looking both inwards and outwards. When we look at this painting we are the mirror, we can feel that we are looking at ourselves when we gaze at the artist.

Yet, in this portrait of Samuels's, the figure and ground share an obscurity, the face is not clearly *differentiated from the background, so that the observer has to work at reading the depths. The viewer cannot differentiate between underpainting and overpainting, yet somehow the figure is there, a part of the ground and yet separate. This is a dense, tactile painting, the paint agitated as if the brush is never still. The light glows with translucency from a hidden source: it reveals, softens, kisses, gifting that quality of young skin when bathed in candlelight. From this sixth masterpiece emanates an almost supernatural play of chiaroscuro. It is not only her technical skill that dazzles, but her ability to express human passions, which is really why Rembrandt comes to mind: her marriage of craft with emotion.*

And yet this sixth portrait in many aspects comes full circle, back to the first in the series: the same unity of subject and ground – surely Samuels's trademark – of texture and of tone, and yet, and yet how serene it is, how wise, how dark and troubled and yet restrained, in complete counterpoint to the first.

Samuels's work is a fine example of Moreau's dictum: '. . . colour has to be thought, passed through the imagination. . . . painting that has been dreamed over, reflected on, produced from the mind . . . .' She does not paint emotion; her paintings are emotions. There is no disjunction between her inner world and the external.

We can only wonder at this most painterly of painter's inner journey.

She laughs when she reads this, another of Edward Durrant's articles in *The Guardian*. He feeds off her, like a vulture. All those allusions to other artists, some of whose work she hardly knows. And the likening to Rembrandt – *he might as well say 'God'! Outrageous, I'm only a beginner,* she exclaims. *Fucking show-off, he writes as if he owns me, as if he has created me.* She mocks his thinking that he's looking at himself, when he becomes the mirror, *as if he can get inside me.* Her image of Durrant collapses into Old Man Harry, staring at her. She feels sick.

Why does she read reviews, she wonders – as she often does. She has enough of the critic in herself to not need actual others. This one confirms her stance in refusing to grant interviews, but she can't avoid the public gaze altogether because she has to sell her paintings in order to live. And she knows that having shows helps her not to feel a complete reject.

Suspicious of offers of most things, she has declined the galleries who have offered to represent her. It is safer to live this way. A dealer once told her that her paintings may be more interesting to the public, to collectors, and to critics, possibly more valuable, because she is reclusive and enigmatic.

How can she explain to anyone that painting keeps her alive – and then, at times, only barely? That she would surely have killed herself by now, although her attempts were never as determined as they could have been. Yet, she realises, the suicidal acts could have gone either way. She does not know why she doesn't shut the door to life for ever, except that somewhere the vision of her mother, *Mommy Rae*, like a ray of light, not quite warm – lemon yellow and not cadmium or chrome – weak winter sunlight streaming through a high window, more visible because of the captured dancing dust motes, drags her onwards. Sometimes the memory-in-feeling brushes her back, soft as a fledgling's feathers, or sends a gentle frisson right through her body. She cannot seek it; it seems to come upon her.

Emily worked out that Old Man Harry – she no longer gave him the title of 'Grandpa' – died when she was six and a half. He had arrived in her life when she was five. That would have given him about eighteen months to make her think she was loved, special, noticed. Did he purport to comfort her? How soon did he take her to his garden shed? Did he wait, a merciful wait, to give her time, time to elapse after her mother's death, before baiting her? Would that have allowed him to feel considerate? Or did he pounce soon, before she had begun to draw breath?

Her acerbic cackle reverberates through the still cottage.

1955

Emmy goes to a new school. Brand new. A High School, like Georgia's. She's proud of it because Georgia's never been there.

She has a really grown-up *Oxford* geometry set in a gold tin containing dividers, a protractor, a set-square, a six inch plastic ruler, and a compass into which a new little pencil is screwed.

On her first day, all the children are told that they are 'Pioneers.' That reminds her of *Voortrekkers* crossing mountains in their *ossewa,* braving all sorts of dangers. She sings the national anthem – *Die Stem* – with her chest pushed out, in the pristine hall with a floor like shiny caramel. They also have to sing the anthem in the playground, where Emmy looks up at the orange, white and blue flag, against a blue sky that looks brand new, *Uit die blou van onse hemel.* Then they all have to pick up stones in the field so that new grass can be planted. That also feels important.

She's puzzled by all the Afrikaans songs and poetry that she has to learn, and doesn't know what to make of the Afrikaans teacher with his cropped hair, bulging fat neck, Chesterfield cigarettes showing through the tight breast pocket of his thin white shirt, telling the class that '*alles sal regkom*'. Everything will come right, he says, but for who, she wonders. He says he was 'born in a Republic' and hopes to 'die in a Republic', but her father and Phyllis say that the Afrikaners are against the Blacks and they treat them very badly. When she hears the word Apartheid she thinks of Apart Hate.

Emmy is good at being good, and even if things don't make sense she pretends they do.

Her father and Phyllis don't say much about what goes on in this country – except Phyllis has talked about teaching English to the Africans in the townships. And Emmy's father fought the Black Shirts, worked for the Left Book Club, was a Communist, worked for the Communist Party, and studies what is happening in Russia. Emmy knows they'd never vote Nationalist, and that they support the United Party. Even then she gathers that the United Party and the Liberals are not really the parties that they like but they're worth voting for to try to get the Nationalists out. Phyllis and her father say they pay the servants more than the usual rate.

She can understand these politics in bold headlines, yet something clouds her mind when her father talks on and on. She cannot fully make sense of his opposition to racial hatred while condoning Phyllis and Georgia.

Meanwhile, no one had noticed what Grandpa Harry did, month after month. By now Emmy has covered all that up, tried to hide it under a blanket. She thinks she can forget about it.

'Lena, make me a fried egg!' her friend Denise commands her nanny in the middle of the afternoon. Emmy doesn't nag Ellen at home, though at breakfast time everyone else does. Ellen makes everyone laugh one morning when she says, her *doek* askew, 'What you think I am, a cockeroach with nine hands?'

Emmy shares her favourite syrup biscuits with Ellen.

When friends sleep over, they always plan a Midnight Feast. This idea comes from books about boarding-schoolgirls at Mallory Towers, and from big sisters and brothers. But the children rarely manage to wake in the middle of the night to eat the feast. They usually talk or play until late, and Phyllis threatens, 'I'll have to separate you!' Emmy thinks they may as well quietly have the feast then. Icing-sugar Zoo biscuits, raisins, apple, and sweets if they're lucky. She likes not having to clean her teeth afterwards.

One evening, she and Denise are in the bath when her father calls through the door, 'Jock is running around with some biscuits and sweets, and we're not sure where he got them from.' Later she learns he was only pretending.

Emmy enjoys lying in the dark with a friend. They put their faces very close to make 'owl's eyes': the other's eyes look like one enormous eye; or butterfly kisses, flickering eyelashes on the other's cheek; or rubbing noses for Eskimo kisses. Or they put the light on to look at each other upside down and pretend they're the right way up, and the eyes look strange and the hair looks like a beard.

They talk and talk, and tell ghost stories.

And pose choices, like what would you prefer, being cut up into tiny pieces while you're alive, or dropped into boiling water? An army of army ants walking through you while you're tied down, or being eaten by snakes? Worms eating into your ears and then your brain, and into every hole in your body, or being slowly tortured by boiling tar being dripped on you? Or rats eating you up in a tiny room full of them scurrying around and all over you, or your skin peeled off, layer by layer? Or fast-growing bamboo growing through you while you're tied down, or swarms of cockroaches going down your throat? The girls seriously consider the choices.

But afterwards Emmy doesn't always have good dreams. Usually her friend falls asleep before she does and she's left awake for hours.

Photographs of Phyllis's nieces, and of Georgia when she was a baby, and of Alex and baby Paul, are pressed under the thick glass of her kidney-shaped dressing table. And a photograph of Grandma Milly and Grandpa Harry arm in arm, smiling into the sun, Harry looking sideways, away from Milly.

This picture is in the exact spot where there used to be other snaps under the glass, Emmy notices. *Before.* It is yellow, not with age, but from spilt orange juice, which crept silently under the glass. She can't remember if she had spilt it.

Emmy kneels on the carpet, the side of her face resting on the bed, the bedspread's ridges pressing into her cheek. Watching.

Phyllis gravely applying dark lipstick, the colour of the wicked queen's in Snow White. She dips the powder-pompom, like a dandelion puff ball, into the round sweet-smelling box with Fantasia dancing seeds on it, then pats it onto her face. Some escaped grains of powder become starry dots swimming up into the funnel of afternoon-sun.

Phyllis has now 'put on' her face, and lies on the wide bed on her side so that her hips form a curvy hill. Her head is propped on a bent arm. The dark burgundy candlewick bedspread perfectly matches her lips. Phyllis's lighthouse beam dazzles Emmy.

'What would you think if we all went to live in England?' drops out of the sky like a plane crashing through the ceiling. Then solid silence of utter no-noise.

'You've already decided that we're going,' Emmy says, clutching at whatever solid ground she can find.

'Well, your Dad and I want to know what you and Georgia think. The boys are too young to really understand.'

Knowing it makes no difference what she thinks, that earthquakes just happen and that children have no control over them, she replies, 'So, when're you . . . we . . . going, then?'

'Probably in a few months' time.'

Why? How? But she doesn't say anything.

Of course, Jock, yes, that's the most important question. After a pause, 'What about Jock?'

'Oh, we'll find him a nice home on a farm in the country where he'll be very happy and have more space to run around. We can't take him with us because of quarantine laws.'

Emmy is reminded of Lizzie, who returned to the farm. It is bad enough that Lenin had been 'put down' months before, because he had become paralysed in his lower body. Jock, always by the fire in winter, in the garden in summer, always there, his big jaws and wolf teeth, which she can defy with her hand inside his mouth, Jock of the Bushfeld, Jock who followed her to school one day and ran around the playground in a frenzy of excitement. Ashamed, she had to take him home and miss some school. She knows she'll miss Cynthia and Sandra, Denise, Barbara, Lesley, Thelma, Frankie, and Ruthie and Judith, and Carl, Martin and Stevie, and, different from them, Ellen, brown Ellen, like dark Lizzie before her, Ellen who lay in bed and couldn't work only once, when she had all her teeth out. But Jock wouldn't understand. The inside of Emmy's nose stings with sadness.

'It's worse for me, you know,' says Phyllis. 'I have to leave my sisters, and Georgia has to leave her father. And I'll be leaving the graves of both my parents, in Pretoria.'

Oh God. Mommy's grave. Now a big fog to one side of Emmy's head creeps forwards until it is almost in front of her.

'Oh yes, and your Grandma, Gella. Jake, your Dad, well, Gella herself, may be going to England too, later. She's not sure.' Emmy notices how Phyllis trips over her words when she talks about her grandmother.

Almost holding her breath she decides to talk to her father later.

Dreams of big blue oceans, of ships, of being lost, of a grey London.

She knows they have to go, *because the secret police are chasing Dad, because he is against the Government.*

She has seen 'boys' – black men – hand-cuffed together and beaten with batons by white policemen, others marched off because they had been found without their Passes. She is familiar with signs which say *'nie-blankes'* and *'blankes'* (non-whites and whites) indicating which exit to use from the station, or which bus to take. Somehow the 'blacks" buses are always so crowded, whilst the 'whites" are half empty. Benches always have 'Europeans only', or *'blankes alleen'* on them, never 'non-Europeans' or *'nie-blankes'*. *Why don't black people have their own benches?* The word *'blankes'* is confusingly similar to 'blacks' anyway. *How do people get it right? What if the blacks can't read? Would they be put in jail if they sat on a* blankes *bench by mistake?*

She browses through Ellen's Pass Book on the DDT-smelling kitchen window sill amidst the drowsy flies, each sortie signed by Phyllis. The servants' squalid toilets and tiny rooms are known with a kind of acceptance that comes with familiarity of a situation from birth – and at the same time, discomfort, like when Vasco the cat's electric-in-the-sun fur was stroked the wrong way and he would become ruffled and uneasy and walk away. Like the other discomforts and injustices which have accrued without words, clogging up inside her.

Secret police phone Phyllis at odd times, their rough Afrikaans accent adding a sinister edge, 'Miss Samyewel, does yew knau weh yaw husbin is?' Emmy has images of men in beige raincoats with turned-up collars and hats, trailing her father.

'So that's why you went overseas recently! To find out if we should go and live there!' says Georgia, full of the plump confidence of rightfulness. She is told that isn't so, that they were going overseas for a holiday anyway and that only since they returned did it seem necessary to emigrate soon.

Once again, Emmy feels the helplessness of the inevitable.

The prize 'for a nicely kept Geography book' is an Autograph Book. It becomes the repository for rhymes and warnings and farewell messages which will come to carry a hollow pain of loss when she is six thousand miles away.

*If all the boys lived over the sea, what a good swimmer
Emmy would be.*

*First comes love, then comes marriage,
then comes Emmy wheeling a baby carriage.*

*When Emmy was a little girl she used to cuddle toys,
but now that she's bigger girl she loves to cuddle boys.*

The verses promise a threshold to be crossed, a plan for
the years ahead mapped out in her friends' minds, and thence
in hers. She is gratified at being so central in the rhymes, yet
dubious about the contents.

½ oz. of kissing, ¼ oz. of hugging, ¼ oz. of squeezing.

*Method: Mix well in the moonlight while Pa's not
looking.*

*Emmy likes coffee, Emmy likes tea, Emmy likes sitting
on her boyfriend's knee.*

*Fall from a steeple, fall from above, fall from a tree top,
but don't fall in love.*

And the finale is:

Will I ever discover that I can write on a cover?

The narrow confines of her life on pastel coloured paper, a
coy imitation, mockery even, of real life, like its imitation
snakeskin cover. She cannot formulate why the innuendos
and clichés leave her feeling more sad and lonely.

After school on a winter day Emmy fetches butter syrup biscuits from the kitchen when she hears an unfamiliar commotion in the servants' yard. Ellen comes in through the back door, her face a dark greenish colour – always a sign of upset – followed by a plump black woman wearing a brown coat, and a beret.

Can't be. Impossible. She is so like Lizzie that Emmy is frightened, for in her mind she thinks Lizzie has died.

'Emmy! Em'ly! My God, whata beeg gal!'

The woman beams at the child with that smile from long ago, from far, far back in the life before, from deep down inside Emmy.

'Why you look like I a ghost? Hey, man, how're you, my gal?'

'Don't know. . . . *Lizzie*?' peering through veils of time.

Lizzie moves towards her with open arms.

Emmy falls into a yielding embrace.

Ellen sweeps the floor right next to them, brushing a pile of leaves and dirt that has blown in.

The child wants to stay in this moment forever. She fears the deep sobs which rise up inside, and forces herself to gain some control.

'Lizzie, I didn't believe you'd ever come back,' trying to sound normal. She looks straight into those same eyes, now at the same height as her own.

'Yes Miss Em'ly, your ol' Lizzie have to go quick to the *plaas*, in Transkei that time, my mother she die ver' quick, all my childrens needs me. Em'ly, sorry,' shaking her head. 'I think to you every day.'

Now Lizzie's face looks dark red instead of brown, the whites of her eyes are pink, and, shaking her head again, she says she heard from the *baas* that they were all going to live in England. 'The *Baas* he ver' ver' good man, he send money every month.'

'Em'ly, you know your mommy, *ja*,' nodding her head. 'She good lady. So now I come say goodbye. You has too much peoples going away.' Lizzie sits heavily on the step-stool as if weighed down with emotion, wiping her face with a gesture that Emmy had forgotten, but which transports her right back. It doesn't matter that Ellen is clucking around.

The child offers Lizzie and Ellen her favourite biscuits. She wants to give Lizzie the spare packet in the cupboard, but not in front of Ellen.

Lizzie says something to Ellen in their language. Emmy hears the word *missus*.

'Emmy, I go see my friend, she still wok *Missus* Berman, and I come see your daddy, say goodbye, six o'clock. See you Em'ly, say bye-bye, later.'

'Oh Lizzie, come and see my bedroom,' the child says.

'You not be sad, Emmy; is better to see your ol' nanny, better to keep the spirits alive.' She laughs quietly. 'I see your room, then I comes back six o'clock, and you and me have big hug.'

While Lizzie is out for two hours, Emmy can't do her homework. She creeps into the kitchen and fetches the new packet of syrup crunchy biscuits – reminding herself to tell Phyllis so that Ellen doesn't get blamed for stealing – and wraps it in a clean page from her drawing book, which she ties with one of her hair ribbons. She makes Lizzie a drawing of a farm dotted with *rondavels*, and black families around fires and cooking pots. The sun is setting over the green hills, casting orange and pink light. The trees are all bare. It's winter in her picture.

As sudden as a clap of thunder, Djinnie, Djinnie Jensen, arrives at school from Denmark, with long hair of yellowy white, (not sickly white like Mavis McGrath,) swept up into a confident pony tail, a thick fringe curving over her forehead, older than all of them yet in Emmy's class. She is here for a while before returning to Windhoek.

Djinnie is fiercely independent and holds her head up high. She strides to and from school on her long slim legs, not caring who she's walking with. Her dresses are made of fine-looking red and blue tiny-checked material of a type that Emmy has never seen before; her leather school shoulder bag has an intriguing foreignness, like her way of speaking. Emmy catches up with her on the way home, her heart racing, and manages to talk to her. Djinnie accepts Emmy with ease. The next day, they sit together in class. Djinnie accepts the invitation to Emmy's home to play the following day. Emmy is amazed at her good fortune in interesting this attractive grown-up girl. Cynthia and Sandra look on; even Georgia seems impressed.

Soon Djinnie comes to spend the night. They play a game of Djinnie's design: Djinnie is the doctor, Emmy the patient. She has to pull her pants down and open her legs. Djinnie explains certain parts of Emmy's body, by pointing, almost touching, delicately, precisely, '. . . this is where the wee-wee comes out, and this is where babies come from,' mysterious and yet deeply familiar, strange and yet known, exciting and full of expectation, mildly dangerous and deeply secret. Djinnie demonstrates correspondingly with her own anatomy. Both bodies look much the same, except Djinnie's has a few fine hairs which she does not omit to point out. She has a way of doing and saying things that always seem just right. Emmy looks on in awe, not wanting her to stop. But Djinnie does stop, quite suddenly, with no sense of resolution. With a confident bounce of her pony tail she says, 'Let's go ride bikes.'

The game is repeated another time, only now Emmy is allowed to be the doctor. She adheres to Djinnie's unspoken code: to almost touch, and when the parts have been explained there is nothing for it but to hoist up *broekies* and go out into the garden, and join Phyllis for tea and cream-and-cherry sponge cake on the lawn. The cake looks particularly yellow to Emmy, the glacé cherries very red.

As suddenly as she arrived, Djinnie is back to Windhoek two months later.

Emmy takes an interest in this south-westerly part of Africa, finding it on her tin globe, examining the stamps –

illustrated with fruit – on the letters Djinnie sends in her grown-up writing.

Emmy returns to the old games of one-foot-in-the-water, hopscotch, charms, skipping, shipwreck, with Cynthia and Sandra, Ingrid, Denise, Lesley, and Thelma, and sometimes Arlene, each game now lacking intensity and intimacy for her.

Some of the curiosity prompted by Djinnie emerges in searches through books for anything to do with babies and how they are made. Georgia shows her – as they sit at opposite ends of Georgia's bed, their feet touching under the claret satin eiderdown like twins sharing a womb – silhouettes of foetuses: tiny chickens, pigs, and humans, all looking much the same until they grow to a certain size. Emmy stares at these ink-blot shapes. When Phyllis comes in Georgia quickly hides the big book amongst others in her pile.

'What're you two doing?'

'Oh, reading,' replies Georgia, in her dreamiest most convincing voice.

'Good girls,' says Phyllis. 'I knew you'd be real readers. But don't read in bad light, you'll ruin your eyes.' (This is one of her many strictures, like 'Don't ever put Nivea cream anywhere near your face;' 'Never leave a needle lying around, it could get into your bloodstream and travel to your heart and kill you;' 'Stop fiddling with that, you'll start something,' – meaning a spot or a lump on one's body; 'Never go to sleep on a row;' 'If you eat more than one banana you'll get terrible tummy ache;' 'Never drink water with *mealies*, or the *mealies* will swell in your stomach and give you terrible tummy ache;' 'It will end in tears' when they wrestle; 'A stitch in time saves nine;' 'It's a sin to talk like that;' 'Chew your food properly;' 'Children only need one pillow;' and 'Don't kiss the dog. He's got germs.')

Phyllis puts the main light on and goes out.

The girls wait to hear her footsteps fade down the passage. Georgia whispers, '*Lekker, man!* And that wasn't a fib – we are reading: reading pictures!'

Emmy thinks that of course Phyllis and her father can't do any longer what they had to do to make Alex and Paul, because they don't want to make any more babies. She acknowledges that they have cuddles, but that's as far as it goes.

And yet she can't reconcile that assumption with knowing, as she does, about 'contraception' from a lesson at school, which the girls had separately from the boys when they were shown a film and pictures. She has found, in one of her regular snoops, Phyllis's Dutch cap wrapped in crisp tissue paper in the middle drawer of her dressing table, under petticoats. She knows what it's for. When she checks, it's always there. She's sure it's never used.

Sometimes Emmy forgets she's getting breasts herself. At the shops one day with Georgia, she strokes her palms across her nipples through her lemon tee-shirt, because it feels nice and ticklish. She's pleasantly in a dream when Georgia hisses under her breath as only Georgia knows how, '*Stopit!*' At first Emmy is not sure what's wrong.

It must be very wrong for her to be so cross and bossy.

A few months before leaving South Africa, in her pink puff-sleeved flounced nylon party dress embossed with flock mauve harebells, sandals whitened with chalky Meltonian, white short socks, a pink angora short-sleeved bolero pinned with the edelweiss brooch her father brought back from Switzerland, freshly washed hair tied up in pink-beribboned big bunches and pink plastic slides of a row of birds, Emmy feels pretty but in a different quite grown-up way. Despite the party dress Phyllis had the dressmaker make in the same style from the same pattern as always, and the short white socks and the bunches, despite Georgia looking really grown-up in a long new emerald green party dress and wearing lipstick, Emmy feels grown up because Frankie Gavshon dances with her in the sombre light of the big *bar mitzvah* marquee, his warm cheek against hers. His skin's slight roughness yet silkiness makes her want to gently rub her lips along his cheeks. She assumes a singled-out-specialness. Frankie – who everyone says is good-looking – has dark good looks and black hair Brylcreemed back, tiny pearls of perspiration on his forehead, and is slightly taller than Emmy with a different smell and feel to him, different from anyone she's ever been close to. Except there's a shiver of a sense of her father when he wears a starched white shirt. The feel of Frankie's cool white cotton shirt, his shoulders warm and firm beneath, is gone before she can really register it.

That pure moment on the brink of grown-up shining-yet-dark time ahead, across a chasm of dislocation, heralds the departure to that strange place called *London*. The city's symmetrical two syllables seem four-square and solid, yet the 'o's are like two empty holes of nothingness.

She tastes an olive that night. They tell her it's 'an acquired taste' as she wrinkles up her nose and senses the possibility of something so strange, so grown-up, possibly desirable – or maybe disgusting. The pattern of her life, of the future unfolding according to some kind of plan, aspirations for Frankie and a teenage life, are so interrupted by emigration that she cannot think ahead. All she can do is cling to what is known, like the neat pattern of a tune she has learnt through a colour-coded way of reading music which she plays silently on an invisible piano, 'five three, five three, der der der *der*,' over and over and over, echoing Georgia's practising of scales, tormented by the interminable imprisoning notes in her head.

The train compartment is crowded with family, relatives, presents, and cellophane-wrapped fruit in baskets decorated with huge ribbons. The confusion is sorted out when the whistle blows, the relations take up their positions on the platform, and Emmy is one of the important ones left in the corridor, looking out.

Johannesburg station lights are doubly blurred through raindrops and her tears. Auntie Hilda and Barbie look fuzzy as they are swept along the platform, staring at Emmy and Phyllis – only, Emmy realises, she's moving, not them. Her knuckles are white from clenching the cold rail. Faster and fasterandfaster, like driving away from Annashirley, her best friends Anne and Shirley, when she left Pretoria when she was six-and-a-half.

That time she kneeled up in the car and watched them, turning her head to keep them in view for as long as possible, so it would not be her who let go of them. And before that . . . . *who left who?* That weak-kneed feeling, when she was four. And a half.

'What are *you* crying for?' Phyllis exclaims through her own tears. The child's knobbly familiar pain halts mid-sob, for it's not allowed and only Phyllis can have a reason to cry. The big body behind her gives her a hard hug.

All six of them – or only six, isolated, it feels – return to the brightly lit compartment, to tins of *Sharps the word for Toffees*, and to Emmy's present from Auntie Hilda of a marbled grown-up green-bakelite matching propelling-pencil-and-fountain-pen set in its green zippered case, the words *Conway Stewart* underlined in gold fancy lettering on the outside. She reads that it's made in *London, Eng.*, incredulous that that mythical place is their destination.

The next dusk they are crossing the Karoo, the train relentless in its power and purpose. Standing alone at a window, watching tall cacti and aloes silhouetted against an orange sky, it is all far too beautiful and perfect for Emmy to feel anything other than utter loss and yearning for this paradise that she may never see again. *Mommy, all alone now, Mommy, Africa, my Africa, I love you, want you.* Beyond, are Ellen and Lizzie with their solid laps and shiny dark brown faces, and her best friends, and Miss Jeffries at Nursery School from long ago, and Shirley, and somersaults on the lawn, and Jock, and firm sand at the edge of the sea that made drier patches as she stepped on it but they disappeared as she walked on, footsteps on the beach erased for ever, like her life.

She doesn't share any of this with anyone. It has that familiar desolate feeling, and Phyllis would only laugh. This time she feels the pain in a more hopeless way, like a plant that has been uprooted too often and will not grow strong again. The train whooshes into a tunnel and fills with an acrid smell. A speck of soot flies into her eye and she finds her way back to the compartment for her father to extract it. He shakes out his clean white cotton handkerchief with an embroidered blue 'J', and gently uses one of the corners to remove the speck with surgical precision. She feels momentarily comforted.

The chaotic excitement of the cabin on the *Union Castle* ship in Cape Town harbour is similar to that of the train compartment. This time the friends and relatives don't know Emmy well – many of them are Phyllis's family – and she feels less involved. The loud hooter sounds and the friends and relatives depart.

The band strikes up a tune Emmy knows but cannot name. Paper streamers stretch until last umbilical links with mother-country snap, silently springing apart and then flopping into the sea. Identifiable figures on the quay become a smudge, Table Mountain presides and then recedes beyond the two widening lines of the wake and the seagulls.

The new world here on the ship is all stranger than a dream, because Emmy cannot wake up and realise it's not happening.

Two awkward weeks aboard, in a broad space between countries, between childhood and adolescence, between 'Emmy' and 'Emily', limbo time. She feels plain and too big for her flowery dresses, changed to Viyella ones as they near their destination, her hair too short and boring. She doesn't feel that her face and body are truly her own – for if everything changes in her life at the same time, including her body, and she becomes ugly, how can she feel it's still her? Her arms are too long, her knees horrible and double. Phyllis laughs at how thin and long her legs are, and at her combinations of skirt and blouse patterns.

Perhaps Barney Bloch, her father's business partner, wasn't joking when he said that her father would have problems marrying Emmy off because of her looks. For years Barney made the same joke and Emmy had to take it on trust that he meant the opposite, but now she thinks he really means it.

While the ship creaks and hums with a strong pulse of its own, she wanders around the lounges on flamboyantly patterned carpets, amidst mahogany writing desks on which sit embossed Union Castle Line writing paper. She breathes the nauseating warm-oil-and-hairdresser-salon smells, relentlessly finger-patterning and reciting her tune, *five three, five three, da da da da, five three, five three, da da da.* It does not satisfy anything. There are English and Scottish crew whose accents are almost incomprehensible. From the various decks, she watches the powerful wake spreading behind, breaking the water open like shiny Turkish Delight. Some days the sea is almost flat, the surface softly wrinkled. The horizon is a thin band of darker blue, so far away that she can see the curve of the earth, with clouds beyond like mountain ranges. No land anywhere, and little ships glimpsed occasionally. Her father points out flying fish. The sky is so blue that she can see little floating things in it like frog-spawn. She's not sure anyone else can see them. If she told Georgia, she would laugh at her.

Madeira is a brief exotic paradise of turquoise seas and little boys diving deep, deep for coins tossed overboard by tourists. Emmy wonders about these different children, like the piccaninnies at home, who seem free and happy – but at the same time she has a sense of the deprivation that makes them go to such trouble just for a coin, any coin, even a penny.

Dinner times are awkward, for her family has to sit with other people, amongst baskets of fruit piled as high as enormous sandcastles. Georgia tells Emmy that she looks stupid when she's trying out a new grown-up look, and then Emmy doesn't know how to look. She notices Georgia dipping a spring-onion into salt, crunching it decisively with her two big beautiful front teeth, making the spring-onion seem the most delicious thing in a way that only Georgia could do, and she thinks she's going to copy that when Georgia is not looking.

Georgia is busy with the waiters and the stewards, Alex and Paul are happy playing in the playroom or chasing around with other children. Emmy doesn't want to join in the children's games, but not the grown-up or teenage games either – especially not the dancing. She plans to say that she has a sprained ankle if asked to dance. But she's not asked except by her father and that doesn't count.

She watches him and Phyllis quick-stepping, fox-trotting and waltzing, sublimely matched in their steps and bodies, gliding all over the floor with confidence. Phyllis, wearing her rosy smiley look, says that Jake is such a good leader. Emmy feels she will never be able to dance like that. The band plays as it did when the ship left Table Bay, so it's hard to feel happy about all this.

Somewhere in the hold, is a crate of the things she's allowed to bring: her Black Magic Box – still faintly smelling of chocolate – of charms, including the special, transparent, like splashy-water-in-the-sun ones; a box labelled 'Emmy's marbles'; another, 'Stamp Collection' – which will never be as good as Georgia's; the last five volumes of the ten volume set of the *Children's Book of Knowledge* because the first five were more babyish and had to be given to the cousins, and Phyllis said that they would buy more up-to-date ones for Alex and Paul; a few other books including school prizes; point shoes in the hand-stitched bag made by Phyllis even though Emmy may not want to continue to learn ballet; her autograph book; a new Solitaire set from Lesley; a gold and red brooch of a mouse from her ballet teacher; a few old school books; the little wooden dolls her father brought from overseas; a French-knitting set; the 3-D Viewmaster with its pictures of the Seven Wonders of the world; the unravelling-raffia kraal and black beaded plastic doll with eyes stuck half-closed from Auntie Hilda; the three-dimensional painted picture in a wooden frame of a South African country scene; her latest drawing book. She magnanimously gave all her proper dolls away to the cousins, even Jenny and Wendy, later regretting that premature leap to grown-upness. Eleven-and-a-half years' possessions in one small crate.

The Scottish tartan scarf, mittens, and hat Phyllis and her father brought from Scotland are waiting in the cabin until they dock.

One evening watering the garden, when no-one else was around, she had whispered to her father,

'Daddy, I know you'll think I'm silly, but, but, can we somehow, please, bring Mom's, you know . . . . What's the word . . . I mean . . . .' She pictures white bones, but she doesn't want to say that. 'I'll leave everything else here, even my charms, if we can . . . . ? You know, take . . . what's in the . . . grave?'

'No Emmy, that'd never be possible!' How quick his reply was. 'Of course we can't. 'Gainst the law. What a thought!' He added, softer now, 'The important thing is that you, we, remember her.'

She clutched his strong arm, felt the raised veins on the inside of his forearm with her fingertip, and knew that she didn't have to keep trying to remember; her mother became more real when she stopped trying hard, years ago.

On the ship she becomes 'Emily'. Phyllis suggests that she uses her 'real' name now, because she's growing up. 'Much

nicer than "Emmy."' Phyllis has a way of saying "Emmy" that has a hint of disdain about it. 'If you want people to take you seriously,' she adds with a smile. 'Changing countries is a good moment to choose, you know. New beginnings.'

Emmy looks at her father. He continues to read his book. Perhaps she was stupid not to have realised there was something wrong with 'Emmy'. But then, her thoughts meandering, nothing is very real, maybe 'Emily' would help her to know who she is.

It is more or less at this point that they cross the equator.

But 'Emily' doesn't feel part of her. It is like a new coat that is too big, the wrong material, all scratchy. Sometimes she thinks that 'Emily' is a frilly sort of name.

Even her father begins to call her 'Emily'. She is pleased when he forgets. Georgia doesn't call her anything most of the time, other than '*Hey!*' Alex now calls her 'Emmy-lee' and Paul continues to call her 'Emmy.'

She tucks 'Emmy' away in a secret fold in her mind, together with 'Mommy,' and her blue baby brush. Chewed, banged, sucked, thrown down, always returned, always there. The colour of her mother's eyes. That bakelite hairbrush, its motif of a pink rocking horse transfer embedded in a deep strata of memory, bristles almost as soft as the hair they were made for. Left behind. Somewhere.

She leans on the salt-sticky wooden rail, watching the ceaseless ocean.

PART TWO:

LIVING IN ENGLAND

1956

The weather changes from calm seas to the January turbulence of the Bay of Biscay, with days of lying on her bunk watching the ocean covering the porthole and then receding, over and over, the sky tipping, Dramamine pills not really helping the nausea, and Phyllis especially groaning more than anyone and rolling around on her bunk.

South Africa felt like it was for ever, yet it wasn't. Phyllis reminds Emily and Georgia of her parents and her father's (Jake's) parents, before they were all married, fleeing from Russia, Lithuania, and Poland, about fifty years ago, going via England to South Africa, also on big ships. Her father makes a rare mention of Emily's mother's mother, who was known as the Chocolate Lady, because 'chocolate' was the only word she knew because she was sent to buy it for her family on the ship. In the greys of a faded photograph Emily imagines this little lady in long skirts. If time was to squash together, like her toy concertina, her ship going north could meet her ancestors' boat going south.

Soon the ceremonies, sickness, no-man's sea-life is over, and they dock at Southampton. Winter coats and gloves are found. She looks over the railings at complete nothingness: a no-colour infinite yet dense end-of-the-world: no sea below, no land. They tell her this is fog.

When she descends the gang plank and walks on solid ground, she's sure it's moving.

The smell of the smoke on the train evokes a disjointed memory of the smoke on the other train in the sun, going the other way, south to Cape Town. Staring out of the train window at the invisible landscape, gaps appear in this colourless cotton-wool and white birds on green fields are revealed, lakes of puddles everywhere.

Then, vast-canopy-ceilinged Waterloo Station. Her father says something about the Battle of Waterloo. She imagines soldiers leaping from track to track, hanging onto trains like in a cowboy bioscope. Grey smoke, flat ashen sky, black and grey structures.

The dislocation increases.

So *this* is London. London of the books and films. 'Lon-don.' Nice-sounding name, sort of dignified.

'Is this fog or smoke? And what's mist?' When she exhales a cloud comes out of her mouth.

Two high black taxis like in the bioscopes take her family and their luggage to a flat in Finchley. Squashed in between the others, she peers out at identical stuck-together houses.

'What are all those spiky things . . . fences . . . for?'

'Railings,' her father says. 'People pulled lots of them down in the war, to make armaments, or . . . aeroplanes.'

Later, 'What, Dad? What did you say . . . *basements*? D'you mean cellars?'

Someone says something about Sherlock Holmes.

'Look, all the doors are painted different colours, and they've got . . . .'

'Just pipe down, Emily!' commands Georgia.

Emmy notices posters and signs in brighter than bright pinks and greens that she's never seen before – later she learns that they are 'fluorescent'. They are the only bright colours in this grey world.

Cold, such cold, waking up shivering under thin blankets, finding incredible patterns of ferns and grottoes, gnomes, mountains and fairy glens etched on the inside of the bedroom windows – until her father buys enough heaters.

Snow as white and fluffy as uncooked meringues, yet crunchy and creaky underfoot, snowflakes scurrying in all directions, some even floating upwards, dots of different sizes with no pattern or plan to their descent. No-one had told her that snowflakes can go upwards or sideways. She'd only seen rain, usually determined sheets of rain, or hail, that knew exactly how to fall straight down, or at least slanty-down. If she pokes her finger into rain it breaks open. But if she does that to snow, it sits tamely, before it melts.

The magic of a transformed world only glimpsed in books and occasionally films is now in their own garden in Finchley. Long pointy pixie hats, scarves, snowmen – so remote from the real home and friends, sunshine, sprinklers on the barefoot lawn, bright flowers, Jock, and the old school. Letters from friends compound her longing to be back there. She dreams of blue seas and, sometimes, being chased by a lion. That old place is more real, the colourful images stand out as if viewed through her 3-D Viewmaster, whilst here everything is flat.

As if overnight, the monochrome frozen world erupts into the brightest lime-green leaves. The first Spring. Birdsong with a new ebullience, daffodils which she has only seen in pictures. She spends hours alone in the verdant garden, not knowing if she is sad or happy. If there is joy it is inseparable from pain. A deep loneliness is beginning to be a part of everyday life, like the loneliness of the black-hole feelings, but now it is at the edge of everything. Emily looks at the electric green leaves but doesn't know what to do with this awareness of beauty. There are no words to describe it, no ready recourse to painting, no music to recreate and frame this heightened perception and the accompanying keen sadness – a sadness inseparable from yearning. But she begins to draw, to draw patterns and swirls and squiggles, filling big drawing books, sometimes in a controlled way, sometimes allowing her imagination to wander, to create abstractions, sometimes finding inspiration in the faces and trolls and fairies and ladies in swirls on a wet table, or a marble floor, or patterned glass, or the Jack Frost patterns on icy windows before the spring. She doesn't value these drawings, nor the compulsion to make them, especially as Phyllis calls them scribbles or doodles.

In that first shimmering Spring, a shaft of sunshine into the bathroom illuminates a brownish mark on Emily's thick white pants. It doesn't look like blood, but she wonders if it's what Georgia and Phyllis call being unwell, and what Phyllis has mentioned fleetingly – 'Oh Emily, by the way, you know about periods don't you? Oh yes, you had that lesson at school, that explained everything, didn't it?'

Emily calls to Phyllis, who frowns as she glances at the pants, 'Yes, well, now you're a young woman.' Emily feels that Phyllis disapproves somehow. Phyllis shows her how to wash them in cold water so that the blood doesn't set.

Later, her father congratulates her and also tells her that she's a young woman now. Strange. Just like that. Rather a magic transformation, to this queenly title. Heavy dragging feelings low down in her tummy tell her that it probably is what they say, and not just something she ate, because this must be the tummy ache Georgia sometimes has.

The chrysalis that becomes a moth, or butterfly. The heavy feelings about her body – her arms too long, her legs too thin, is one titty bigger than the other? – are like the damp moths she observed coming out of cocoons, droopy, furry, sad. She looks disconsolately in the mirror, staring into her eyes.

How different her body is from Phyllis's plump short shape, and Georgia's voluptuous one.

Her father is worried about earning money in England and has a slipped disc. Phyllis is worried as always. She gets really 'depressed' – a new word that Emily learns and secretly uses to describe her own state of mind. Phyllis cries and says she misses her sisters. She can't bear the cold, hates wearing thick black stockings and doing the washing-up the whole time, even though they all help her.

The final straw is when Phyllis is walking home from the shops one day and the cucumber she's bought has fallen through a gap in her string bag. She sends Emily back to look for it, but she can't find it. Phyllis lies on her bed and cries, her arm crooked over her head. All because of a lost cucumber. The child feels helpless. She cannot bear Phyllis's bleakness.

Emily finds her new friends at school so babyish – and yet they know a lot of clever facts – and are so different from friends at home. These English children wear brown old-fashioned English sandals with straps and buckles like in the *Famous Five* books, they talk of going home to 'tea' which they 'eat', say 'goodnight' at five o'clock in the afternoon, call magazines 'books', and pips 'stones'. They say 'indoors' when they mean 'inside', call *tackies* 'plimsolls', *naartjies* 'tangerines', and Eskimo Pies 'choc ices'. It all sounds so wrong, especially when they say 'roundabouts' instead of circles, 'traffic lights' instead of robots. Instead of bioscope they say 'cinema', which sounds very posh. And they say 'Saandra', when surely it's spelt and pronounced like 'sand'. They don't know what *broekies* or *goggas* are. They have Christmas trees, indeed they talk a great deal about Christmas, and get big Christmas presents.

One child asks Emily if she speaks Double Dutch. She thinks hard and says that she speaks Afrikaans, which is like Dutch. The child laughs and walks away.

But these children don't seem to know about the changes to bodies that preoccupy her, and about which she talked for hours into the night with the old friends back home. Now she envies the English girls' flat chests, while her lop-sided breasts are kept as hidden as possible. In her bedroom she ties a strip of material tightly around her chest. But it won't stay there.

She and her South African friends had planned to write a code word – 'Bluebell' – at the bottom of a letter if one of them 'started', but their correspondence becomes desultory, and she doesn't bother to tell them about her periods. Finally, like the paper streamers which strained to connect the ship with the land, the contacts stretch and snap.

1957

Emily longs for a pale blue polo-neck jumper with short sleeves that she has seen in a shop window. It costs ten shillings. The jumper makes the model's breasts look beautiful. She thinks that if she had this sweater, she'd be grown-up in the right way, like Leslie Caron, or Audrey Hepburn, or Doris Day . . . or Georgia. She beseeches Phyllis and her father for the money, but they say no, they're worried about income as her father doesn't have a job yet, 'And anyway, you don't need it.' She can't get the song, *Loretta, Loretta, what she does for a sweater; Loretta's a sweater girl now* out of her head. She returns to the shop on her bike, stares at the transparent plastic model, loves it all the more. The colour is perfect. Pale blue, baby-brush blue; distant blue, out there, behind glass, beyond reach.

She thinks she will never be properly grown-up or attractive. She doesn't belong here with these English people, and her friends in South Africa are managing without her as if she never existed. Esther's Head Girl instead of her now, Frankie's probably got another girlfriend. *It's not fair, I might as well be dead. Then they'd be sorry. Then they'd wish they'd bought me that jumper.*

Emily is sure that it's because Phyllis is not her real mother that she doesn't care how she looks. If she still wore baby dresses Phyllis would be happy. *I'm nearly thirteen now! Why can't I be allowed to be grown-up, like Georgia?*

Looking up at the black sky of the Planetarium, with its stars and planets and reassuring voice over the loudspeaker, Neil's hand moves from holding hers to stroking her thighs under her skirt and then stroking her between her legs through her Marks and Spencer thick winter pants. She can hardly believe what he's doing, the daring of him. *Is* this *what boys do to girls?* This unspeakable event cannot be halted for it feels good in a new yet vaguely familiar way, hearkening back to that moment in the bath and other abstract moments moving invisibly within. Neil's mother is sitting on his other side, impervious, her head craned upwards while Emily's universe vortexes downwards.

She's not sure she likes Neil. She doesn't dislike him, but he's not really attractive. His fingers are soft and curvy when he plays the guitar, and he makes stupid jokes and imitates the *Goon Show* all the time, which isn't at all funny. But as their parents are old friends from South Africa, this alliance feels like a natural development, and yet at the same time has to be kept deeply secret.

The next time his parents invite her family to supper, he suggests they play chess in his bedroom. The chess board tilts, and chess pieces are suddenly arrested by the sight of Neil's enormous penis on display, dwarfing the King and Queen.

'Touch it, would you like to touch it?' he says.

She hides her shock and calmly looks on at this extraordinary happening, the first of its kind in a way, and yet she knows she has seen it before in the corner field, and before that too. She wants to look at this one, though. This is nice, she tells herself, even if it is so big and so like the Scarecrow's. Again, she feels special: this is specially for her, perhaps because of her. She knows he thinks she's pretty.

She does touch it, delicately, as if fingering a precious musical instrument that she has no idea how to play.

'*Kos is op die tafel!*' – using Afrikaans more than if she were still in the mother country – Neil's mother calls up the stairs. And that's that, he puts it away (like Djinnie, back in South Africa, hoisting up her pants) with difficulty, for there doesn't seem enough space in his trousers. Emily feels a little sorry for him – it must be so uncomfortable.

Downstairs to the grownup's chatter and chopped liver with its decoration of reassuring separated areas of white and yellow mashed hardboiled egg, her father making a joke about 'Apartheid for eggs', served inconsequentially after that tipping of the universe. She doesn't look at Neil over supper.

That sight remains the focus, eclipsing the bad ones, for future fantasies for years to come. Later more intimacies take place between the two of them, Neil always initiating, gently but firmly, under the red-and-blue tartan rug to keep them warm as they watch black and white television for the first time – Emily looks round for the projector – in his lounge.

That cough does upset her, what shall mother get her? Do the parents know what is going on under the rug? *Wise mother says Veno's, it's the best mixture she knows.* Emily chooses to believe that others are oblivious to their gropings. *The cough quickly goooes, when she takes Venooo's.* Tickly warm flickering-light and fingers, *Murray Mints, Murray Mints*, smooth, silky, secret shapes, *the too-good-to-hurry mint,* you-and-me, you-or-me, you, me, I, together, *why make haste,* intermingling, voices, parents, *when you can taste,* South Africa, BBC Nine O'clock News, Lady Isobel Barnett, Face-to-Face, John Freeman, Gilbert Harding, cosy, if-only, more, *the hint of mint,* dreamy, sleepy, muddled, far-and-near, Finchley, Jo'burg, *in Murray Mints,* dark, blue-grey eyes, blank eyes, teeming head.

Neil introduces her to *The Complete Psychological Works of Sigmund Freud* (for his father is a psychoanalyst). He knows where to find some of the sexy chapters, which they can both more or less decipher, whilst he shows the same skill in finding parts of her body.

Yet she continues to find Neil irritatingly unfunny in his impersonations of Bluebottle and Neddy and unattractive in his strumming of the guitar with soft and curvy fingers, his smell not always appealing. She cannot say 'No' to him because that would be hurtful, and because she feels specially chosen, she doesn't feel she has a choice.

Her own secret world develops with him and on her own, reinforced by a 'parents can't stop me' defiance – a world of pleasures and deep night-time longings for Lawrence, a teacher at school, who is married. With Neil and others after him, she has this power and possession of the treasure – she can make it respond, can feel wanted. When Lawrence's marriage breaks up, she is deeply shocked yet fearful and pleased, for her fantasies become dangerously realisable.

1958

Amongst ramshackle unremarkable buildings, wild grounds, classrooms so cold in winter that she has chilblains, she begins to find some joy and deeper meaning to being alive. Her nourishment is in this 'progressive' school of her growing-up years, the years from twelve to eighteen.

Yet she is tainted by feeling 'the new girl' for years, not fully rightful, despite others joining the small class of boys and girls after her. Her narrow education is emphasised by Charlotte, the cleverest in the class: 'You don't *know* who the Picts are!' Emily had studied The Great Trek every year; endured so many years of daily Afrikaans lessons, and knows where the Orange River, the Limpopo and the Vaal are. She is not expected to be as clever as Georgia, who is now at a prestigious private girl's school.

Patricia, who has become her best friend, seems lacklustre. Still unsure of her identity, when she changes her hairstyle, she fears that others will not recognise her. Despite her fragility, she becomes completely enraptured by *Jane Eyre*, Dylan Thomas, Wordsworth, Keats, T.S. Eliot, Hardy, in ways she has never before experienced, and inspires herself with her own ability to conjure up images with words or painting by closing her eyes and simply imagining whatever the class is told to write about or paint. The lines from Wordsworth,[1]* 'the light that never was, on sea or land', give her a shiver of connection with her mother, invisible but somewhere there.

The lofty art room is always open, and in the afternoons the children can choose what they do, so she is

---

1 *'Elegiac Stanzas', l. 15.

often there while the madrigal group sings and she paints, voices mingling with the sunshine and the colours of her palette. Musical phrases overlap, are repeated, sometimes competing for prominence, sometimes subversive or perfectly harmonious, in parallel to her attention to colour, pattern, tone, depth, and tension. She stays after school to paint scenery for the play, or to make murals of a French scene for the school party.

Teachers see the potential in Emily, take her seriously, inspire her, treat her equally with the others while recognising her particular talents and weaknesses. One teacher tells her to learn 'to blow her own trumpet.'

Her right to life is re-claimed, gradually, day by day, in that big scuffed family of a school, a school like a leather-bound Treasury of Poetry that has been loved by generations, the words within still crystal clear on fine paper, even though the binding has worn through on the spine and edges. There would be a few damaged pages within: some irrevocably torn, some missing forever, some mended, some spoilt by a child who has scribbled with a pencil. Preserved between the pages, you could find a few exquisite faded flowers, some blue, some white, called 'Yesterday, today and tomorrow', their perfume now a memory. They leave a timorous yellow stain on Keats' *Ode to Melancholy.*

Teachers, unlike parents, are the purveyors of inspiration, especially those she falls in love with. First there's Maya, (for they all call the teachers by their first names in this spirited school), her English teacher when she is twelve. Maya is the epitome of grown-upness with her high cheekbones, shapely figure, dark Indian skin, husky voice, and gentle encouragement of Emily's early forays into literature. There is something familiar about her. Emily sucks in her cheeks, hoping to look like Maya.

But then Maya gets married, is going to have a baby, and leaves. Emily and Patricia feel a frisson of excitement when their calculations reveal that the baby was conceived before Maya was married.

When Maya talks to her on her own one day in the Hall, Emily closes her eyes for an inexplicable reason. When she opens them Maya's attention is elsewhere. For years she regrets her lapse, wondering what Maya made of it. Did she think she was idiotic?

An obsession with Lawrence begins to eclipse that of Maya. It is hard to know if Yeats or MacNiece or Owen or Dylan Thomas would have had such appeal if not read aloud by Lawrence. She takes to wearing red because she knows it's his favourite colour, can spot him instantly amidst vast crowds on the other side of Centre Court at Wimbledon, and runs faster than on Sports Day to catch up with him on his way to the station. Although he may have preferred to travel alone or read a book, he is never impatient with her or rejects her. She lies awake at night longing for him: a sense of a physical absence in her body that needs to be filled. He is felt to be more than perfect; she thinks that the reservations that hold her back from having a full sexual relationship with boys would not stop her with him.

Early morning fine mist hovers above the ground when she opens the tent flap and gazes up at morning sunshine, and Lawrence making a big pot of porridge – like her father in the Game Reserve. Fresh sliced white bread as soft as marshmallow, with butter, and a choice of treacle or Marmite on hungry walks.

She is camping in the New Forest with her class, including Carol the Barrel, and Biscuit (because his surname is Jacobs), and Birdcage (no-one seems to know why Nicky Beresford is called that), and Moley, who digs long deep tunnels in the school grounds. She doesn't mind when the others call her Sammy from her surname: it feels affectionate and a sign of belonging to this carefree family, now headed by Lawrence, and Trishia the art teacher who looks like a windswept New Forest pony with her mane of blonde hair, big nose and teeth. Without realising it, Emily is happy: her happiness is not always registered in the way that her unhappiness is.

She loves that still time at dusk when the trees and grass and whole forest hold their breath before the night sounds take over. At night, she skips and runs through knee-high wet grass that looks black, so as not to feel the cold dampness. The moon, as white as a paper plate, darts out from behind a cloud, and tiny white daisies are like bright stars.

All her activities keep Lawrence in mind if not in sight. When he sits to write the holiday diary at night by the light of a lantern, she stares at his Byronic profile. Typically, while everyone else is asleep, she lies awake. And yet there is something shameful about being awake for hours, so she doesn't tell anyone.

On the next skiing holiday, when Lawrence really goes off with Jilly – younger than Emily and even taller, with a husky voice and long slim fingers, who smokes – she is devastated. Lawrence and Jilly lock themselves in a bedroom in the chalet with a bottle of *Cinzano*. Emily feels that he didn't choose her because Phyllis and her father would have caused such an uproar if they found out, whereas Jilly's parents are divorced, 'Bohemian,' and permissive. This seems an easier explanation than the possibility that he prefers Jilly.

That evening, wearing more eye makeup than usual, Emily throws herself into flirting with the boys, smooches closer to them when she dances, and drinks more than she normally does. She tries to smoke a cigarette but hates it. The boys know how upset she is. Lawrence's action feels like a terrible betrayal – but then for a while she imagines it increases the possibility of him having an affair with her.

Emily hears, months later, that he is still involved with Jilly. By then Jilly has left school – unlike Emily, who stays on to do A-levels.

She speaks fluent French after spending two weeks, and, later, several more, staying with a French family. After the initial impossibility of understanding the gabble, some words and then phrases take on meaning, like the noise of her father's classical music evolving into a shape and a beauty. The enthusiastic delight of the French family at her progress is no small part of the development. It becomes easy and satisfying to speak this language, which she heard consciously for the first time standing with her father at a bus-stop outside the Albert Hall when she was eleven.

The sounds have the same appeal that she later feels for Italian as sung in opera; and, in deep sub-strata, a connection with the pattering of leaves in the row of poplar trees framed by her pram hood – dark shady nook, golden light beyond – bundled warm on a winter's day, visited by a face with a radiant smile and two lustrous eyes.

Early memories mingle with later ones. The poplars grew, their leaves glinted and danced in the breeze. The swooshing sound filled her mind with an un-nameable memory of tidal surges in and around and everywhere.

Madame Fournier knows nothing about the snatched passionate embrace with Jean-Pierre whom Emily had only just met at Vittel swimming pool, in the subterranean chamber for viewing swimmers under water through glass panels. He has a tanned, grown-up, slim body. Their swimming-costumed bodies feel almost naked. Brief moments of avowal, skin on skin, where she, with dawn-freshness, is Eve to his Adam.

She continues to perceive a naïveté or even a lack of interest in sex on the part of many of her girlfriends. Indeed, she keeps these passions private from all, except from the boys with whom she becomes involved. Georgia has to be kept firmly out of her confidence, especially as she is sent by Phyllis from time to time as an emissary to find out what she is up to. Emily can see through this ploy.

1959

The keen Austrian air stings Emily's cheeks. The fairy-chimes of cattle bells, dwellings built into hillsides housing families and their livestock, are all so different from anything she has ever known in South Africa. She notices the delicate, almost imperceptible smell of snow, which has a hint of flowers and pine trees and grass, and the penetrating odour of resin.

One afternoon Phyllis stops to scoop up snow in her bare hands, pats it into a shape as if she's making *matzo* balls, and then manages to hit Jake smack on the back of his head. Pretending to cuddle her, he delicately puts a lump of snow down her back. Phyllis's shrieks, like splinters of ice, pierce the clear air, and her cheeks glow without the help of rouge. Emily can see what a beautiful young woman she must have been, and why her father loves her. *But where is my Mommy? He doesn't remember her at all,* quickly comes to her mind.

One day Phyllis wants Emily, her friend Miriam, Georgia, and Jake to leave her alone in the mountains and come back for her in an hour. Alex and Paul are away at camp. Emily can understand that need to be alone sometimes, especially in this place. When they return after tobogganing to the path where they left Phyllis, she is nowhere to be seen. Emily thinks that she could have got completely lost, or fallen in a snow drift.

She feels excited and frightened at the same time. The others do not seem perturbed. She tries to follow footprints, her boots crunching and squeaking through crisp snow. *Why aren't the others worried? No even Dad.*

'*Jake-ey!*' rings out from higher up the mountain.

Phyllis is sitting on a rock, half hidden behind trees, in her dark glasses, fur coat and fur boots, her head wrapped in a woollen shawl the colour of the bright cobalt sky. Emily stamps uphill through snow to get to her, feeling proud that Phyllis is her step-mother. Phyllis is ecstatic about the silence, although her words shatter it, 'It's white and luminous, and I can hear strange creakings. Reminds me of my favourite line from Rousseau. How does it go? Something like, "The spectacle of Nature is in the heart of man: in order to see it, one must feel it".'

This makes Emily go quiet. Phyllis's feelings are so big that there's no space for anyone else's.

They are all staying in a little inn. A trio strikes up after dinner one night; the violin giving a light rendition of a waltz, accompanied by a piano and a cello. As Emily sits watching the old men and women – even older than Phyllis and her father – she imagines them here in this inn, year-in, year-out, dancing like clockwork figures, waltzing away time until death.

Amidst the cigar smoke and glowing from the *glühwein* and sunburn, a tall much older man, but not nearly as old as the *old* ones, asks Emily to dance. He seems as old as her father. He's very polite, his wavy dark hair greying at the temples, his clear-cut bone-structure giving him an aristocratic look. He tells her his name is Roman. (How romantic, she thinks.) During the next slow dance, he gently presses close to her, and she can feel a taut ridge that she finds utterly irresistible. She doesn't want to move away. The music gives them both a perfect excuse to carry on and on like that. The dance floor is crowded and she's on the other side from her family; her father can't possibly notice. Roman looks down at her with a gentle smile,

'How old you are?' in his Austrian accent.

'Sixteen', she lies, adding on a year. She knows she looks more like sixteen. She asks him his age.

'Surty-six', he replies, probably lying in the opposite direction.

Georgia is dancing with a young Italian man. Miriam is looking fed up, so her father dances with her, and then he and Phyllis twirl round the dance floor to a foxtrot.

Emily decides to allay suspicion by having a break and a drink with the others, but she feels a wrench leaving Roman in that state. Soon he reclaims her.

They dance across to the other side of the room again, and she feels shiveringly beautiful as he holds her tightly round her waist and gently kisses her right ear. His body is back on form. The movement of their bodies and the knowledge of what is there through a few layers of clothing as they press together cause unstoppable waves of pleasure through her body. She clings onto him like a hurricane survivor, and then, embarrassed at her powerful experience – *What would he think? Did he notice?* – she relaxes, feeling supremely grateful to him.

Her father comes over to her, looking stern.

'Time to go to bed, don't you think, Emily? You'll be getting up early tomorrow for your ski lesson. Miriam's already gone to bed, Georgia's going up now, Phyllis is tired.'

Emily wonders what he thinks of Roman.

'Okay. I'll come up soon.'

Roman, still full of desire, asks her if she'll go for a walk tomorrow afternoon. She cannot possibly say no.

The next morning Emily sees her father walking towards her in the breakfast room looking very grim. She is sure he's cross because of Roman – perhaps he noticed more than she thought. He tells her that Phyllis is ill, suffering from a migraine. She is momentarily relieved.

That afternoon, she meets Roman. In a pine forest below the snow-line, with serried lines of yellow sunlight funnelling through the trees, like her father's record cover of The Brandenburg Concertos. There is a stillness except for a distant high screech of birds, the dry snap of twigs underfoot, and her heart pounding. He gently kisses her. No-one can see them as they stand, repeating some of the experience of the previous night, only now it's quiet, and she has time, and doesn't have to dance – though in some ways she'd like to. Roman's skin, his smell, his height, his body, all feel right for her. She follows his respectful and gentle lead in his explorations and pacing. Her hand strokes the outside of his beautiful brown corduroy trousers covering that most wondrous thing that again has made its presence felt. She pauses, as if a question has been posed and she awaits an answer. He takes her hand and gently places it higher, at the waistband of his trousers. The hand knows where to go, to gradually delve down. Hidden, warm, silky, squashed against his stomach. While he explores and kisses her breasts.

They form a perfect duet, or is it a whole symphony, of light and dark, soft and bright, strong and yielding, gentle and hard, fast and slow, harmonious and yet contrapuntal – except symphonies come to some resolution, and this couple doesn't. In her easily-led way she might, if he initiated it, but perhaps he senses how young she is. She doesn't want to appear 'cheap', as Phyllis would call it, so she does not go beyond the reaching down, and his gasping, and the kisses.

Men can be so grateful, she thinks, and yet she's enjoying it as much as he. Somehow, she feels this is different from the urgency with which some boys have expressed their desire, the imperative that makes her feel they have to be gratified – like the book she read that talked about boys' urges being difficult to control, and how easily they 'go too far', unlike girls. Not with proper sex, of course, but with other things that she usually – but not always – enjoys. But with Roman, the powerful urges are Emily's, and because he's so much older, it feels dangerous and illicit.

She begins to feel she ought to get back. She'd told her father she was going for a walk with Roman. He disapproved but not enough to stop her. She hopes her red cheeks from Roman's bristly yet clean-shaven cheeks and upper lip won't show.

Roman asks for her address, and gives her his. Out of his back pocket he takes a little water colour painting in a cellophane packet, of an intertwined 'R' and 'E' that he made late the previous night, as a present. The curved foot of the 'R' forms the centre horizontal line of the 'E'.

She keeps it secretly for years, with the lavender bag under her pants in her wardrobe.

Back in London she can't get him out of her mind, amid images of the striated sunshine.

In Roman's cleanly shaved yet slightly bristly cheeks she sensed her father's cheeks, and a sliver of recall of Frankie, Frankie in the *bar mitzvah* marquee, the night she tasted her first olive.

Roman and Emily write awkward letters to each other and exchange photographs, but the distance in miles, age, language, and culture, gradually attenuates, until it is as fragile as a spider's thread.

She never forgets him, wonders what his life is like, and if he is married.

1960

Despite 3 a.m. trysts of Romeo and Juliet intensity, of extraordinary beauty, when Emily marvels at a sword that is not hurtful, that she longs to incorporate – and that can hold up a sheet as Steve modestly tries to hide his nakedness – despite necking at parties and fumblings in sleeping bags on Aldermaston marches, despite the brief relationship with old-enough-to-be-her-father Roman, despite all this and more, she keeps to Phyllis's dictum not to 'go all the way' until she is married, or at least until she is with someone she knows she is going to marry. Despite overwhelming heavy longings, young skin, silky lips, tautness breaking through uncontrollable waves into slackness, a feeling of completeness yet an ache for an indefinable 'more', she keeps to this pronouncement, because she feels that none of these boys are quite right for her.

Her father seems more remote and even slightly embarrassing (though not nearly as embarrassing as Phyllis when they are out together) and his answers to her questions are so long and boring that she forgets what she has asked him in the first place.

1961

Steve strokes her arms sensually, but she is ashamed of his plump babyishness and shyness when out with him.

Chris is brilliant at cricket, but there is something strangely inhibited about his sexuality that does not intrigue Emily.

Anthony is a non-starter because he has spots, sweaty palms, bad breath, and a face that reminds her of a rubber mask, but somehow she lets him kiss her in the back row of the Golders Green Ionic. Later, at home, she vomits. She decides that she will never go out with him again even if it hurts his feelings.

Then there's Mike. In a brief liaison at a party, his groans of pleasure seep deep into her body as he touches the tops of her breasts in her underwired bra. Gratified at being the purveyor of so much pleasure, she carries the illusion that she owns this power.

Nicky is fine, good looking and confident, but kissing and fondling is enough for him. After all, Nicky is in her class, and people get to know who has 'gone all the way'. She regards those who are on the other side of this big divide with awe and curiosity, some discomfort bordering on disapproval towards the girls, and imbues them with a grown-upness she can only dream about.

Emily lies down on the floor with Nicky at a party, in a dark room amidst other couples doing the same, and the plastic hoop of her petticoat lifts her gingham skirt up like a cave. She hadn't foreseen this problem. This year can-can petticoats – layers of netting soaked in starch – have been replaced by these crinoline hoops, in imitation of American

Rock 'n Roll film stars, worn with bobby socks or white pointed high-heeled shoes called winkle-pickers.

She is fearful of getting pregnant. Condoms are not yet a part of her culture, and despite that Dutch cap in Phyllis's drawer, she has no idea how to, nor indeed wish to, procure contraceptives.

Then there's Neil who resurfaces occasionally – Neil of the curvy fingers that she now thinks of as feminine – and again she feels she has to satisfy his urgent requests. *Malt-esers, honeycomb crisp as light as a whisper.* After all, it's quite pleasurable for her, even though her arm aches, *Mmn mmn Malt-esers,* to be the focus of his desire and the purveyor of such relief and gratitude. Her own pleasure is not sought with him. Somehow Neil's smell is not right, and never has been.

And Greg, remote tall Greg, a champion tennis player with muscular legs that look tanned all year round in his white shorts, whose persistent wooden smile beneath his non-smiling eyes becomes disquieting.

Rick, who she brings to the new house in Hampstead under the lime tree, shares her pride in it. He too, though intelligent and kind, and powerfully responsive sexually, is not really 'it', the 'all' that would tempt her beyond the ways in which they already gain satisfaction from each other's bodies. His small, hairless chest and narrow shoulders epitomise his incapacity to be big and strong enough for her.

On a summer night, Emily stands under this huge tree, under leaves that look black, holding Rick's hand. The big house and this vast garden will soon belong to her family. She feels immensely rich and blessed. Only a magisterial house such as this could have such a tree in its garden. On the lawn, tiny white daisies have closed their faces for the night, appearing as surreal dots in the moonlight. The couple lie down under the tree, their bodies blessing each other, anointing the ground and the new house in an ancient rite.

A distant whooshing of leaves becomes louder until the breeze reaches and cools her damp brows. An owl's cry is followed by another – its mate, she thinks. The lines of Keats, who once lived near this house, come to her mind:

Beauty is truth, truth beauty,
That is all ye know on earth and all ye need to know.

The beauty she once perceived, the poetry of the voice, of leaves in the breeze or of birdsong, reverberations of that dance between that first smooth voice partnered by a rich sandpaper one, lies beyond a chasm and yet stirs within.

Movement and dance of the leaves on the trees, of branches on boughs, of daisies in groves, of clouds and of crows, of grasses in swathes and meadows in waves: a whole world of this movement, all dancing the same dance.

But also stillness, such stillness.

The fine balance of the universe poised on that blessed place.

A dislocated life – that early life of heart-stopping moments of bliss, and equally life-stopping moments of hopelessness – have all been pushed beneath the surface, like a tuber that has to wait for its season. Within the tuber is that steely foreign body, the horseshoe within the tree trunk – not killing it, but sometimes, when the tuber is withered, the balance of alive matter is dangerously threatened by this lifeless thing. For years the tuber lies dormant, waiting for the earth to receive enough water for it to plump up, send up new shoots and drive down new roots – like the big dried butter beans, which Phyllis called *bebelach*, which Emmy used to put in a jam jar covered with damp blotting paper, and wait for that luminous green vigour, sprouting and splendid.

The dead bit inside becomes less significant, but it never goes away.

1962

The name of the shop first catches her attention. *Roma*. Emily notices a skirt in the window on her way home from school. She stares at the mustard woven fabric, the grown-up long length, the heavy white cotton embroidery, the appealing 'foreign' look that years later she would say looked Greek. (Or Austrian, like Roman?)

At home she describes the skirt as attractively as possible, asking Phyllis if she can have it. Phyllis and Georgia return with Emily to the shop that afternoon. Georgia tries it on, and Phyllis buys it for her. Phyllis says that Georgia needs it more than Emily. How stupid of Emily to have presumed that she was rightful, allowed to be attractive, to grow up, to find a way of looking good. Georgia will always be the one who gets what she wants. Despite Emily's rationalisation that it's because Georgia goes out with boys, while she doesn't officially, her rageful frustration about the skirt turns to self-pity. Her sense of being a second-class citizen, an outsider, digs more deeply into her.

Even if it means having to manage on very little money, she chooses to have a clothes allowance, to shop for herself. C&A sales excite her with what she can now afford.

Although there is still, in the back of her wardrobe, the unfinished baby's Viyella nightdress from Mrs Salkinder's desultory sewing lessons years ago in South Africa, she is keen to learn to sew from Phyllis. The abundance of styles and fabrics as she browses through pattern books in haberdashery departments gives her a sense of untold wealth. She can make a dress that no-one in the world has. On the dining room table, she lays out new fabric that smells as fresh as new-mown grass, pinning the pattern down economically. Sometimes, managing on less fabric than the pattern says, she conserves some for something else as a bonus. The pinking shears scrunch satisfyingly through paper and material. Cutting out notches, interfacing, avoiding the boring tacking (or 'basting' as the instructions call it) as much as possible, she reaches the rewarding machining. The cautionary tale of Michelle's uncle who machined through his finger stays in her mind. And then she tries on the rough garment for size, holding her breath to avoid pins lurking in seams, and imagines how it will look when finished.

This becomes Emily's own activity, tinged with a sense of 'in spite of' her step-mother not buying her things. She begins to feel less babyish than she did in the styles Phyllis would have her wear: less plain and ordinary, more striking in *Liberty* fabric remnants, or Swedish-stripe curtain fabric.

But she has to bear Phyllis and Georgia's mockery of her creations.

1964

Emily is a child at her own wedding, pretending to be grown-up. She looks like a wedding cake in a large-rimmed candyfloss-pink hat and a white linen suit from Fifth Avenue in London – for once not the cheapest of shops, but still reasonable. No-one comes shopping with her. She suffers the discomfort of wearing a 'roll-on' underneath – the young person's corset which she thinks all women wear – for a slightly slimmer silhouette, her stockings held up by tiny awkward suspenders.

Emily has rushed into being 'grown-up'. She is at art school, straight from school. Marcus, six years older, is happy to marry her.

Marcus looks boyish and fresh faced, his soft, just-washed hair flopping in the confetti breeze. The guests are mainly Phyllis's and her father's friends and relatives, and Marcus's parents and their close relatives, at a formal lunch party at her family home. She does not think of protesting, of having more of her few friends and Marcus's – for this public statement to the parents and their friends is the main point.

And, of course, Alex and Paul are there, playing chase in the street, and later, catch in the garden. Emily hardly notices them.

But she senses that the registry office ceremony will not alter her position in the family, as the one who is not really legitimate, the only one without a mother. She did manage to marry before Georgia, though. There Georgia is at the party, presumptuous as ever, sitting plumply on her fiancé Dick's lap, stroking his hair, playing with his tie. No matter that Dick works in advertising, and is not an academic like

Marcus. For Dick is Jewish and Marcus is not. Dick's status in the family was assured from the moment he and Georgia became engaged.

Tables are decked with pink roses and gypsophila. Marcus makes an eloquent and humorous speech, as Emily knew he would. She could never do that. Phyllis wears her shiny face, her cheeks perfectly matching the salmon-pink orchid pinned to her georgette dress, drinks sweet white wine and goes with the flow, while graciously talking to the guests. She has told Marcus that he couldn't be nicer even if he was Jewish. Jake takes photographs. As usual, he is the foil to Phyllis's main part in the play.

Emily's first married night is in a hotel in Dover under the white cliffs. The flushing toilet next to their room repeatedly wakes her with a start in the night, with terror of being found by Phyllis to be illicitly in bed with Marcus. The next morning, she sends a postcard to her father and step-mother, before she's crossed the Channel. Writing as a married woman, not quite twenty years old, she tries to substantiate the marriage.

She married Marcus because she liked his solidity, his deep-set grey eyes, his broad shoulders, his sexual responsiveness. The fact that he was as tall as she, even an inch taller. His wide knowledge of the world. Perhaps his very different safe English family was also an attraction – she was never sure. His childhood, compared with hers, was uneventful.

She first met him on an Aldermaston CND march when she was going out with Rick. Marcus boldly asked her for her phone number when she was waiting outside the school where hundreds of people would be sleeping that night.

Rick had gone for a drink with others. Her feet were blistered, and she could not contemplate the walk to the pub. Her and Rick's sleeping bags were unrolled next to each other, waiting for the usual night-time fondles.

Sitting back against a pillar, wearing tight blue jeans, her feet bare, her hair in a long thick plait over one shoulder, she was reading Golding's *Free Fall*. The novel led her to wonder whether she was with Rick because it was her choice, or because it avoided being 'single'. Marcus crouched down next to her, to ask what she thought of the book. She found it hard to come up with anything that seemed intelligent enough.

'Does it make you think there really is such a thing as free will?' he went on. 'I mean, even if we think we are making a choice, maybe we aren't, maybe we are still constrained by things we aren't conscious of.'

She struggled to think. All she could say was, 'I don't know, really. I think there are times when one, when people, do make real choices, where they are free . . . .' Her voice trailed off; for her mind was focussing on the worn York stone of the steps, the way that much use had softly dented them.

'That's the beginning of an interesting discussion. I've only read Golding's *The Inheritors*.' He seemed so grown up, so confident; she soon gathered that he was completing his PhD at Manchester University, in Sociology.

'I guess you're with . . . people?'

'Yes – a group.' She gave a shy smile, 'And my boyfriend.'

That did not inhibit him from saying that he was coming to London in the autumn and wanted to meet her. Flattered, she saw it as a way out of the relationship with Rick.

So they met in October. She was impressed by his having his own flat in Islington. There they shared tinned minced meat on toast and drank cider, in a small room heated by a hissing gas fire. They played Beatles and Stones LPs, and sometimes the Modern Jazz Quartet, on Marcus's red leatherette record player, while lying on the narrow bed covered in an Indian bedspread.

She ignored Marcus's homosexual history of which she had intimations, his change of tone to faintly lascivious – lowering his voice, speaking almost in a lisp – when he spoke of homosexuals. She tried to overlook his interest in her bottom and her mouth to the exclusion of her vagina and her breasts. She could be as selective in what she saw in Marcus as he was in what he saw in her.

When they made love, each was in their own private world. She never knew his fantasies, but sensed what they were. She could please him by providing some of the things he craved, but as the months went by, she felt like crying that he did not really want her as a woman in her own right. She felt her breasts were not up to much anyway, but with Marcus she might as well not have any. She began to feel that if she had her vagina stitched up, he'd be pleased. With deep distaste that she hardly dared acknowledge, she sensed a repetition of being used by Harry, and other men, for years before meeting Marcus. And how desperate she had been to escape from Phyllis and her father.

She survived by finding a range of fantasies of her own, separate from Marcus. His potency seemed directly affected by the extent to which she played into what he desired, and if she wanted a more sustained union, his potency suffered. Emily knew she was not tolerant of frustration at the best of times: it carried terrible associations to that *no-Mommy* time.

1965

She sits day after day in a large studio where the old dark wooden floor is permanently spattered with paint and on which a forest of wooden easels seems to grow randomly. Models pose nakedly and variously in the middle of the room – sometimes sitting, sometimes lying on draped couches, occasionally standing. They come in all shapes, sizes, ages, races and personalities, and she and the other students join the tradition of sitting on stools – or 'donkeys' as they are called – and look, and make marks on paper or board, and draw, or paint. Emily learns about plumb lines, and to recognise and respect the horizontal and the vertical, and holds up a pencil to measure the proportions. Absorbed in the task – it could be a bowl of apples or an old woman before her – her objectivity is such that the nakedness or vulnerability of the model becomes immaterial.

Or so she thought. The male models are generally not a problem: she can look and feel and draw – except for one, a muscular man of about sixty who refuses to remove his loin cloth and will only pose standing up. He favours positions with his legs apart and an arm raised, like a warrior. Anton Schwartz, the life drawing teacher, tries to cajole him into a more relaxed pose, but the man resists with such ferocity that Anton, with an almost private smile, allows him his own way. Emily chooses to draw this model from behind, where his sinister particularity is diluted. But she cannot relax into the task. He has scars on his back and buttocks, and she senses a brutality within him that makes her feel confusing waves of fear and anger. One afternoon she decides to skip the rest of the session and to leave college early.

Many times the students are told by Anton to feel their way across the body with their pencils or charcoal, to imagine what is round the corner, for there are no *lines,* and what we think of as lines are informed by the tension between the object and the space around it.

It is the women's flesh, their breasts, their lolling stomachs, their clumps of hair, their skin texture, that is all too real for Emily. She knows that for most of her life she has avoided, or searched for, this soft fleshiness, and now she wants to touch it, stroke it, rest her head on that lap or that bosom.

It's a wonder I'm not a lesbian, she thinks on more than one occasion. *Perhaps I am, and have just denied it?*

One Wednesday afternoon in November, in her first term at the Slade, she begins to feel faint while trying to draw a large woman whose pubic hair is as red as the long wavy hair on her head. Emily tries to focus on the body as if it were simply a boulder, or a tree trunk, or a cloud, to marvel at the tones of violet and green in the shadows, the ochres and pinks in the light. But her heart races and she knows she will have to leave the room if she is not to collapse. She dreads drawing attention to herself.

Stumbling over feet and bags and splaying easel legs to reach the door, she is too ill now to care if anyone notices. The room tips and sways and Emily finds herself on the floor, sure she is dying, *No choice now. . . .*

She awakes in the corridor to the anxious face of Anton above her, and Merielle, the French student, fanning her with a large sheet of paper. Merielle's pale pink lipstick gives her something to focus on.

'Oh silly me! What happened? Oh I'm sorry! Alright now, really!' She raises her head.

'Oh no, Emily. You must rest, you are the *couleur* of a putty rubber,' says Merielle. 'But your *couleur* is coming back now into your chicks. 'ave a drink of wateur.'

Someone has bundled drapery under her head.

'No really, I hate causing a commotion, I'm okay now.' She recalls, at this moment, how as a child she nearly drowned because she was too shy to call for help.

'Is your husband around?' Anton asks. 'Shall I phone him to fetch you?'

Emily sits up, determined to stop the fuss. She wants to leap up to show them she is fine, but feels too shaky. Sipping water, she musters a confident smile.

'I didn't have breakfast, that's all. And I think I had my head down for a long time, and then stood up – that's all. Really!'

Merielle looks penetratingly at Emily, a look women reserve for other women who they think might be pregnant. She recognises the look, and thinks *I hope not!*

Managing the two paces to sit on a bench, she implores, 'Now please you two – you'd think I'd nearly died or something! Let me just sit here.'

'*D'accord,* but promise me you won't move 'til I buy you some *biscottes.*'

Emily smiles and nods.

Merielle trots off in her short Biba dress, her Vidal Sassoon hair bobbing.

'I'd better tend my flock then,' Anton remarks, trying to sound matter-of-fact.

Anton has been intrigued by Emily since he first saw her, her tall shapely body, her wavy long hair, her almost ethereal remoteness, her untapped talent hiding there like a Spring flower waiting for sun before it will open. Unobserved, he liked to watch her draw, standing at the back of the studio. How like a gazelle she is, her way of silently observing, as if ready to flee at any moment, and then when she did make marks on the paper – like some of Giacometti's sketches – delicate flecks gradually mapped out the object in sculptural corporeality. He felt he could not teach her very much, and did not want to shape her vision to his own when he felt that he could learn from her.

He knew Emily was married, because the forms in the office registered her as 'Mrs Emily Clarke'. He sensed something very unhappy about her.

Now he returns to the studio, notices how hot it has become with the radiators full blast. He asks the buxom model if he could cool the room. She nods. Swivelling the little radiant bars more towards her he opens a fanlight with a brass-hooked long rod and turns down the cast iron radiators.

And looks at his watch. Another ten minutes until there is a break. Dutifully, he looks at one of the student's drawings before walking up to Emily's easel. He stands and stares, stares at feather-light spidery marks from what must be a 4B pencil, on soft cream paper. The marks both construct the form, and interpret it. Those monumental breasts are as surely there as *Mont Sainte Victoire*. Despite their weight the eye is drawn into the dense hair between the legs, darker than any other part of the drawing, and beyond, imaginatively, into the womb. Emily must have positioned herself today with this view. No wonder she fainted, he thinks – not only the heat, but a vortex, sucking her in.

A policeman stands outside the wrought iron gate to Emily and Marcus's little flat in Battersea late at night, waiting for the person who answers to the name of Marcus Clarke to return. The street-lights reflected in a large puddle illuminate his features from below. His skin is stretched tightly – as if there isn't enough of it – over his face. This, added to the fact that he has a very flat, almost unformed nose, gives the appearance of a skull.

A man of twenty-six with light brown hair that looks dark in the gloom attempts to brush past the policeman, through the gate.

'Mr Clarke?'

'Ye-es?' Marcus's answer gives the word a second syllable that floats upwards, his foreboding compounded by the policeman's face.

'You live 'ere?'

'Yes, Officer,' always polite.

'Your, *ehrm,* wife's name, sir?'

'My wife's name? Why? Oh, Emily, Emily Clarke.' His voice begins to quaver. 'Anything the matter?'

'Well, sir, your, *ehrm* wife, Mrs Clarke, took . . . an overdose. She's back now,' his head gesturing over his shoulder, 'and I'm jus' checkin' to make sure that someone came, comes, home. She's alright now, I have been informed,' he adds, his tone now kindly.

The puddle fractures into splinters of light as he saunters off, his heavy shoes squeaking with each step. Straight out of *Dixon of Dock Green,* Marcus thinks, as he breaks out in a fine sweat and bounds up the front steps two at a time.

She is lying in bed, in a dressing gown with vomit-matted lapels, waiting for, yet fearing, Marcus's return. He switches on the bedroom light, comes in hurriedly, sits on the edge of the bed, gently asks what happened.

'How d'you know? Why d'you ask?' trying to suspend time, to stay in this moment that recaptures her father coming to comfort her after yet another storm with Phyllis.

'A policeman was waiting outside, at our gate. I got quite a fright. He told me you'd . . . you'd taken an overdose. Well?'

Cover up, lie, evade? But no, she has to tell him, to explain, to grasp at a more honest relationship if she can, to begin to make sense of the step she took.

Marcus seems more shaken than Emily. She is in an unreal twilight, sharpened by pinpoints of insight: the attempt has to be a way of confronting difficulties, or of leaving the marriage; not wanting a half-dead husband as well as a dead mother.

So she tells him, not looking at him, her words spewing out like the salt water and pills she'd just vomited up in the hospital, '. . . not wanting to live taking lots of pills then changing my mind calling an ambulance made to drink lots of salt water in the ambulance or was it when I got to hospital – can't remember . . . .' She pauses, a weight of despair pressing down on her.

'Ambulance' always reminds her of her mother, all those years ago, how could she . . . .

Then, breathlessly, resolutely, to keep all that at bay, but not fully in the moment, looking away into the corner of the room, she relates, like a runaway train,

'I've-been-having-an-affair-with-Stefan-Wilson-and-it's-ended-and-this-was-is-a-way-of-telling-you-about-it.' She draws breath, 'And ending it.'

Marcus's solicitousness changes to fury as rapidly as Phyllis's moods. Hauling Emily out of bed, he throws her down again, Othello to her Desdemona, only with more substance to his jealous rage. Her unbalanced state is hidden behind a quickly erected wall, letting him vent his outrage as much as he likes on a body that's no longer hers.

Of course she can't tell him about her utterly bereft feelings as Stefan went off on a skiing holiday with his ex-girlfriend, how she wandered up a street near the Slade, took a taxi, bought over-the-counter sleeping pills in three different chemists, changed into her nightdress to go to bed, took all the pills without thinking or feeling much except that this was something she'd wanted to do so often and now she was doing it and she'd go to sleep and never wake up.

Nor does she tell him how she ate a banana, half knowing it was strange to do so, and then felt a wave of fear at what she had done. How she put her finger down her throat. Some banana came up, but no pills. She tried again. And began to panic, like a flailing beetle desperate to right itself. She dialled 999: 'I've taken lots of pills and now I regret it.' How feeble that last phrase sounded, she thought at the time: something so deadly simply negated, as if led by fickle whims. She had the foresight to open the front door before flopping onto her bed.

The two ambulance men soon arrived, asked her for any bottles or packaging from whatever she had taken. 'Under the jumpers in the bottom drawer,' she obligingly told them, soon to walk out to the ambulance, stabilised by a man on each arm. Her shift from being on the side of death to grasping the cable of life was dramatic.

The half-light in the ambulance added to her increasingly unreal state, or was it just the drugs? She felt churlish for being unable to respond to the paramedic's kindly attempt to chat.

It was clearly just another 'case' on a busy night for the team in St Stephen's casualty department. She dutifully swallowed what felt like gallons of salty water, and dutifully brought up the contents of her stomach. As always, forms had to be filled in. If she was dying, she thought, they'd make her hold on until they had all the required information. They asked where her husband was, and what his job was. She told them he was a lecturer, and was taking an evening class. 'Letcherer', one bright-spark nurse said, out of her line of vision.

Soon she was despatched home, with no mention of a psychiatric follow-up, nor a letter to her GP. She wondered if she had impressed them with her clarity and sensibleness, and quick change-of-mind. Was this not considered 'a cry for help'? At least they'd bothered to put a policeman outside.

'Unless the main-spring is broken,' was her father's proviso when it came to being able to fix a watch.

Under the light of an angle poise lamp, at the kitchen table topped with blood-red Formica patterned in tiny squiggles like the veins on the whites of Lizzie's eyes, he would fiddle, adjust, blow out dust, and add oil, all with delicious precision, using doll-sized minute screwdrivers and sharp instruments, until her watch worked again. How easily the main-spring could have broken, she knew, when she wound her watch.

It always made her think of her mother. How her mother's main-spring did break, how she must have been over-wound.

And how her spring stretched gossamer fine and almost snapped when her mother died, when Harry came and plundered, when her father wasn't really there, when the pale ray of high-up light faded and the tissue-thin world of surfaces lost all depth, time and time again.

1966

Marcus becomes increasingly impatient with her depression, her crying into the night, her jealousy, her love affairs. Not that he doesn't have affairs too, but he did not choose to marry such a bundle of contradictions: a woman who wants independence and yet needs him so much; who is talented but thinks she is hopeless; who is beautiful but does not believe him when he tells her. Above all he cannot understand her wish to die, which occasionally he glimpses, though she tries to hide it from him.

'Emily, come on, you can't lie there all afternoon. Would you like a cup of tea?' His attempts to reach her feel half-hearted; she cries all the more. It reminds her of her father's attempts to assuage her after the battles with Phyllis, yet without the power of love she felt for her father. Sometimes she wants to show Marcus how distraught she is, to burden him with it: she howls and sobs, not knowing any more if she is genuinely beside herself or if she is being histrionic.

'Stop it, Emily! Stop it. You're crazy.'

'I know I am, 'course I am! I'm mad, crazy, deranged!' she screams. 'Get out! Get out! Leave me alone!'

This acknowledgement of madness is lobbed back to her when they row.

In the small ads in the local newspaper, between 'Conservatories' and 'Curtains', she notices 'Counselling'. One entry runs:

Wandsworth Counselling and Psychotherapy
Experienced practitioner offers safe place to explore emotional difficulties, such as trauma, sexual abuse, depression. Sliding scale of fees.

She is unsure about the psychotherapist, a quiet woman in a top floor flat in Wandsworth. She seems austere, but Emily senses that this may be more to do with her own perception, and that it may be a necessary stance. She tries to appear rational in her résumé of her life, but her account feels so inadequate, like trying to play music without any attention to the pauses between the notes, everything coming out as noise. The therapist says little, but comments on Emily's difficulty in putting herself directly forward, how she hides behind an anonymous 'one', instead of saying 'I'. She feels criticised, and surprised at the tears that roll down her cheeks, unbidden and uncontrollable.

The woman offers her a time once a week.

She is almost relieved that she would find it difficult to afford the fee, even a reduced one. She does not want to discuss it with Marcus, who she knows would say all the more that she was disturbed. But she realises that this is the wrong reason for not having therapy.

Marcus is very scathing about therapy, as is Phyllis. Phyllis's attitude is 'Just pull your socks up!' about emotional difficulties. Emily knows her father is more open to the idea, and she wonders about asking him to pay half of her therapy. But the therapist has said that it would be better for the process if she paid for it herself.

She stores away the possibility of this eyrie in Wandsworth, but is too depressed to do much about it, let alone find a part-time job to fit in around her art degree.

Marcus gets a full-time post as a lecturer in sociology at a polytechnic in East London.

They move to a small flat in West Hampstead, where she has a tiny room on the top floor for a studio, with a strong northern light. It is hard for her to feel rightful about a dedicated room, so she does not use it much at the beginning.

He wants to have children. She discusses it discursively, if she sees a baby in the park, or a film where there is a baby.

'I'm really not sure, Marcus. Such a commitment. You know, so much can go wrong.'

Another day, 'It's frightening to think that a baby is totally dependent on its mother – and father, ideally.' And then, as if thinking aloud, 'Such a small life . . . a whole life . . . a new life, so so dependent. And fragile.'

Marcus says little. She doesn't know what he is thinking.

A few weeks later she bravely says, 'Anyway, you know I get depressed. I can't risk infecting a baby with that. No, it wouldn't work.' Secretly she knows that having a baby would make it much harder for her to believe that suicide was a way out.

A few times Emily catches a hateful expression on Marcus's face which disappears as rapidly as it appears.

'What's the matter?' she asks one day.

'Nothing.'

'Sure?'

'Fine – yes.'

He does not enquire why she asks.

Puzzled, she ponders if he harbours such negative feelings towards her, and why.

In rows his contempt escapes, 'You went to the wrong school.'

She knows her capacity to think is flawed. Perhaps she really is unintelligent.

Sometimes she has the thought that when she finishes her degree at the Slade she may want to teach in order to be financially independent, and to continue to paint.

The couple are shopping in Liberty's for a present for Marcus's 28th birthday. She shows him a silk tie in a patchwork of subtle blues, greens and greys.

'Don't look at the price. Do you like it? Want it?'

'Ye-es, lovely. Not sure I need another tie.' His reply is lacklustre.

'Oh come on. It's not a question of need. What would you really like, then?'

'Do you really mean that – that I can have anything I like?'

She senses which way this is going, and is right, for he comes closer to her and whispers in her ear. His face flushes, fuelled by a surge of desire.

She half smiles and ignores him, but feels upset, wrong-footed and angry, for she is, again, in a position of having to withhold what he longs for, or to grant it and feel uncomfortable. She doesn't want this outing to be spoiled, although now it has been.

As she half-heartedly looks at the piles of shirts, as neat as stacks of envelopes, she thinks that if Marcus didn't want certain things in such an exclusive way she might want to give them, as she has with other men.

She had agreed to that at the beginning, occasionally – it would 'happen', as if by accident, she had allowed him there, and he showed much greater rapture than at any other time – but over the years she knew that it led to her feeling too hurt, too humiliated.

Oral sex was different. It was something she could offer – she sensed that the marriage would not have survived if she had not – by shutting off her feelings and thinking of other things. The choking and gagging reactions now rarely arose. And yet, she knew, that was not the be-all and end-all, that his passion was extreme when she allowed him the dead-end, the back door.

The problem remained of his great emphasis on this, his assumption that that was the summit of sexual contact.

Marcus becomes more controlling even when she is agreeing to oral sex. 'Move round a bit, let me see you in the mirror . . . move up a bit, stop . . . slower, when I'm near will you . . . .' Her own creativity dwindles, and she becomes more of a puppet. Hate and disgust begin to eclipse any love there may have been. *This cannot go on*, she thinks in a thin voice.

Her own fantasies involve scenarios she had read about in a friend's book; or of being with some of the men she has known previously or in the course of her affairs: with boys and men who want her and are aroused by her. But when these fantasies lose some of their power, she begins to imagine that she is a man, with a penis: that she has a wonderful penis that is potent – for then she does not need Marcus. If his penis comes into her fantasy world, she imagines that she is a man with a man. That is arousing too, and strangely may be exactly what Marcus is secretly imagining. She has bypassed being a woman, but in the moments towards orgasm she always finds herself magically transported back to being herself, a woman.

She feels uneasy about the state of her sexual mind, unhappy at the way she manages to triumph over Marcus, or to dispense with him.

1967

Emily feels tired and lonely as she undresses for bed one February night. Some days, time seems to pass so slowly that she thinks her watch is faulty.

Pulling her tent-like winter nightdress over her head, she knows that she can't blame Marcus for not finding her sexy. She has hardly really looked at him for weeks. He is lying on the bed reading a journal. So she peels off the nightdress, sits on his side of the bed and hugs him, and finds the energy to kiss him more passionately than usual.

'Goodness, Emily! How lovely you are.' She is not surprised that he seems startled. She feels like laughing. He continues, 'I know I've not been very sexy lately, but I have to tell you, I caught my willy in my fly, in my zip, the other day, and it's quite sore. But let me look after you tonight, give you a lovely time. And maybe you could just rub me.'

'Oh no, it's okay. No, I'm fine . . . quite tired. Let's see, what happened? Show me.'

He shows her two scabs on the side of his penis. He says he was going to tell her, but kept forgetting. He has some ointment that he got from the doctor, because he was worried that it was getting infected.

Two days later, in the bedroom, he says 'I'm sorry, Emmy, but I have to tell you something. You know those sores . . . well, I think you should get checked at a VD Clinic – I'm sure it's nothing serious – but a couple of months ago, you know, when you went to Barcelona with Felicity, I did have a little fling with one of my ex-students, who seduced me.' She puts down her hairbrush, maintaining her position with her back to him, but scrutinises him in the mirror. 'I'm very, very sorry,' he continues, 'but I think I may have caught something.'

'What do she mean, "may have"? You mean, you have *VD*?'

'Well yes, s'pose so. They say you should get some pills or cream or something. The clinic at Charing Cross Hospital is very good – you can just walk in.'

'Oh God Marcus.' She turns round now to face him. 'Thanks for telling me! So now I have to go through all that, *and* take in the fact that you slept with someone . . . someone who's infected. What kind of VD anyway?' Not waiting for a reply, she rushes on, 'You always make out that you're so passive – someone just seduced you. Poor you! As if you have no say in the matter. That's what makes me furious. I think I'd mind less if you were more . . . more responsible for your part in these things.' She feels like crying, but is loath to expend the energy it takes. Only later does she question her assumption that the fling was with a woman and not a man.

Marcus sits on his side of the bed, his head in his hands. She almost feels sorry for him, he looks so pathetic. She doesn't want to slide into despair herself, so she takes a sleeping pill and reads in the hope of falling asleep.

She becomes more suspicious now: a sleuth, rummaging in his pockets and briefcase, even delving into his drawers and filing cabinet, examining his credit card statements. She asks him to tell her if he's having an affair – she would rather know than not know; she says she won't be angry.

One day when he is at work she finds, in an inner pocket of his old green raincoat, a card of a bare voluptuous nymphet with large breasts and long blonde hair, with a telephone number. She almost laughs at this parody of womanhood, a depiction so different from her own femininity. The caption reads,

> *Curious?* Visit Naughty Nina for 'every' thing
> You've dreamed of !!

She is unsure how to proceed: whether to uncover more by stealth and maybe trickiness on her part, or to be direct and confrontational. Or to ignore it. Finding the anxiety intolerable, when Marcus returns that evening she says she needs to talk to him, and suggests they both go into the kitchen. Gesturing towards the prostitute's card in the centre of the table, she says as calmly as possible,

'Found this. What am I to make of it?'

He frowns, says he doesn't know where it came from. Then he opts for greater honesty, as if he senses that there is no way out,

'Oh yes! Where did you find that!' He gives a little laugh. For a moment she hopes that he really is innocent. 'I think I must have picked it up in a telephone booth ages ago . . . .'

She bites her tongue, resisting a sharp comment, *Oh, by chance, just like you picked up VD!* She allows him to continue:

'I wanted something to jot down a number.' He grabs the card and turns it over. The rescue of a scrawled number isn't there. He shrugs, trying to look nonchalant. 'Oh well, so I didn't write a number on the back. So what. What are you saying? What are you accusing me of then?'

'No Marcus, it's not me "accusing" you of anything. Is there anything you want to tell me? I promise I'll try and understand.' She pauses to take a deep breath, wishing that there wouldn't be a big disclosure, that it's all her imagination. 'I just wondered if this is really the cause of the VD?'

'Okay then. Let me pour myself a drink. Want one?' She shakes her head. He pours a large whiskey. Ice cubes crackle loudly in the tumbler. His hands are trembling.

Emily wonders if Marcus wishes to relieve himself of guilt, for he tells her more than she bargained for, about going to prostitutes regularly since before they were married. She feels frightened. He says that he has tried to give it up, and often succeeds for weeks on end, but then succumbs, whenever he finds himself near Kings Cross.

He looks at her with his little boy expression, 'You know, darling, I did want to tell you. Really. Because now that you know, I think I can give it up. I'm really ashamed of it.'

He looks down. She thinks he's going to cry. She knows that she cannot comfort him.

She becomes calm, and even somewhat relieved, because it makes sense of much of his behaviour. She wasn't imagining his predilections: the great urgency surrounding them, despite having recourse to prostitutes. His ritualised ways of going about things. Would things have been different if she'd provided him with whatever he wanted? Now she simply nods at his revelations, while focussing on the pattern on her tiered gypsy skirt – the way the purple and mauve stripes condense in the gathers so that they look solid in colour.

Looking in the mirror, she sees a grimness about her mouth that used not to be there. She no longer loves, maybe does not even like, Marcus. Even if a break-up gratifies Georgia, and Alex and Paul and Phyllis don't understand, and even if her father thinks that she should 'work at it', that all marriages need to be worked at, and that Marcus is a 'good chap' – if only he really knew! – she decides that she will summon all her courage, and leave. She knows it will be hard to admit to everyone that she has failed, but thinks with relief of being on her own, painting when she wants to, and not having to try to please Marcus sexually.

Maybe I'm not cut out to live with anyone, she thinks gravely.

She imagines finding a cottage in a remote country place, and painting, and living a very quiet life. For a while anyway. To get away from London and from Marcus. Perhaps the Slade would let her back on the course at a later stage.

PART THREE:

LEARNING TO LIVE ALONE

1970

The sun streams through the small open window onto a scrubbed pine table, lighting up cow parsley, ragged robin, and dog roses in an old earthenware jug. Petals drop from the roses, as soft as a kitten's footsteps. A bowl of plums lie duskily in an azure bowl, in the shadow of the jug. She lifts one, polishes it on her skirt, and places it in the sunbeam, to observe the colour change from mauve to claret, a reflected golden sun now highlighting the globe.

She peels off her blouse to wash at the stone sink. Her arms and neck are brown from working outside, her body white. Sponging her breasts and underarms, and then her face, before she blots herself dry with a soft pink towel – like a model for a Renoir pastel of a bather, she thinks: where the nude's skin tones are lavender and apple-green and roseate. Peering in the little speckled mirror at her tanned and healthy face, she looks much younger than her twenty-six years.

This Spring and Summer carry abundance to the point of profligacy. There is a palpable warmth rising from the ferns and the long grass, even the butterflies are ecstatic in their swirling dances, the bees frantic in their search for pollen, the birds raucous in their cries. As if all living creatures and plants and trees are making up for the months of static winter and cannot trust that there will be other summers.

Emily has never lived alone for long.

Sleeping on her own was lonely at first, and she would clutch a rolled eiderdown to her body, but gradually sensed where her own body began and where it ended, to find its energy source within. It was possible to find contentment in a way that she had rarely known before, having needed others to affirm her in particular ways – and they nearly always fell short of the mark. She laughed at her phrase – yes, how much Marcus fell short of. When she thought of him, she hoped he would find someone else, someone who would give him what he craved. She realised how little she was plagued by the jealousies she used to feel.

This evolution followed a period of terrible desolation when she first moved, just over two years ago, here, to Suffolk, to a dilapidated cottage crouching in a wood near Westleton. Blackthorn and birch crowded round the sides of the cottage, as if to protect it.

It belonged to a tutor at the Slade who admired her work and had asked for a nominal rent – and possibly a painting or two, though that was not a requirement.

The whitewashed exterior was faded to grey, except for lichen-green patches beyond the sun's reach. The thatched roof, so thick with moss that it too was mostly green, was tucked beneath a layer of chicken wire. On most days, water dripped from the overhanging thatch, for even if it had not rained there was pervasive damp. A tiny lunette window high on one triangle of wall allowed a smudge of light to enter an attic room through grimy glass. The front door was unpainted dark wood, cracked in places. The letter box, which may have been of brass, was as black as iron. The back door, painted dark nondescript green, revealed through cracks a brighter turquoise from more optimistic times. Crude white paint on window frames crept over the glass. The front path was of irregular stone slabs, each one outlined by vivid moss – bright even when the sun was not shining – and made a welcoming carpet for her sojourn, which began in January. Sometimes she silently laughed at this ridiculous jollity in the face of so much cold and wet.

During that early phase, she made wood and coal fires to find warmth and to wage war on the damp. Labouring and lumbering heavily, Emily was unsure if she would or could continue this struggle to live. She drank wine to buoy herself up or drown her despair, so that her moods swung drastically and she suffered bad headaches. She slept in her clothes some nights because it was too cold to change. And dropped back into the *no-nothing-no-Mummy* world, more than once staring at the oak beam in her tiny parlour. And imagined hanging from it. Habitually, she thought of overdosing on pills and alcohol, and had studied the ingredients of rat poison in a hardware shop. Hanging seemed so quick and . . . maybe not easy. But the peace it would bring, at last.

One day, searching for some boots she had left in the roof space, she noticed a yellowing 1921 newspaper – *The Suffolk Chronicle and Mercury* – lining the recess. An article, *Westleton's Farmer's Suicide*, caught her eye. Sitting cross-legged on the floor she read how Montague Faulkner had bought cyanide of potassium from a chemist, ostensibly to destroy wasps' nests. Only twenty-nine, almost the same age as me, she registered. The man had been worried about the dry weather and the poor state of his farm. Poor man, poor, poor man, she found herself thinking. The article said that his wife had recently been confined and slept with the nurse. No doubt he worried about all those mouths to feed. The subsequent investigation deemed him 'temporarily of unsound mind'.

Crazy, bonkers, insane, she thought. Staring at the now out-of-focus newsprint she thought of Marcus, and Phyllis, and Georgia, all accusing her of being mad, and how, beneath her rejection of this label, she agreed with them deep down. Is it mad to kill yourself? If there really is no way out of hell . . . . But, how do you know if there's a way out? She did not understand why some people tipped over into hopelessness while others struggled on, as she folded the newspaper carefully and placed it back in its dark recess.

Despite herself, she began to find some satisfaction in the simplicity and hardship of this life, cut off from a telephone or radio or television, and mostly, from people: her walks every day, dragging wood home for the fire, the wind whipping tresses of hair across her chapped face, her ambles across heathland to the nearest village for basic supplies, listening to the cries of birds that she could not identify, the creaking of branches, the roar in the trees. A steely resoluteness, defiance even, subtly changed to a delicate awakening to the gulls in the sky, to the whisper of blue-grey appearing from behind thick clouds. That colour again, somewhere on distant shores of memory.

She began to feel she was everywoman, connecting with men and women through the ages. Even the lost fiery flowers of her remote South Africa were evoked here in this hearth with its glowing orange coal and wood fires: the labyrinthine depths as expressive as the Beethoven *Razumovsky* Quartet she played on an old long-playing record.

Gradually, her ability to observe and to draw returned. Running around intermittently to regain sensation in her feet, blowing into her thick woollen gloves, she drew the trunks of trees, finding grotesque faces, bodies, animals and ogres; she saw eyes staring out of the trunks: sometimes they were blind, sometimes there were holes or sockets and no eyes; she sketched the lattice and depth of branches; the shapes of the no-colour sky competing with the evergreen leaves or bare branches that defined it; the dead leaves of oak and beech at her feet, peppered with beech nuts; the hoar frosts exaggerating and emphasising fronds of fern and every blade of grass, each one glistening in its sugary particularity. The frozen ground beneath her boots crackled as she walked, and one March afternoon when she returned from a walk, rosy-cheeked, the sunlight set her cottage windows so ablaze that she was sure she had left the lights on.

Yet another day, she smiled to see a packed row of starlings along the ridge of her roof, like a wrought iron decoration.

Her special vision of the world had not deserted her. Satisfaction changed to pleasure as gradually as a ripening apple changes from green to red.

Now, she sees a creek as a primeval swamp, its surface as smooth and still as a billiard table, beneath geese coughing overhead. She wonders, but knows it is idle speculation, if this would be the perfect place to die, because no-one would find her. The reeds take on the look of a mangy lion's winter coat; unable to focus on every blade, they become a blur, like a smudged pastel depiction. The pallid masquerading skin of silver birch splits open, revealing scabby brown bark. A barn owl shocks her with its sudden appearance, its dark eyes like holes in facets of ice. A toadstool the colour of tangerines pierces this mainly monochromatic world.

Then a cock pheasant, with his urgent clanking cry, startles her as she startles him. He glides away rapidly, his red eye a beacon in the grey on brown plainfield of stubble.

She crests the hill. It can't always delight – but then, soft and immense, the world opens up in the silvering sun. *Dear God*, shading her eyes the better to see, to see the white waving grasses, the waterways blue, blue the sea, blue today, (not the gunmetal of yesterday). And a powder-soft pale orange mist – can it be? – towards Dunwich. She hardly dares look towards the ridge of high land by the sea, for always there are silhouettes of people, or dogs, to crown it all. Yes they are there, but superfluous today, super-numerous to the life of the marshes, the swathes of grasses with a vigour like the sea beyond, pounding and swaying and rising and falling. The reeds whisper soft and then loud, urgent, like a Bach Partita sweeping everything along with its pace, the wind making Mexican waves in the tall grasses.

She keeps returning to this spot. And it never disappoints. The lump in her throat swells and the reeds ripple under her skin.

Early Spring leaves hang damply like newly-hatched unfurled butterflies, and a cracked glimmer of a smile is cast across her heart.

With the sun on her back in April, the first spring of her sojourn in Suffolk, standing in a clearing amongst the trees, she closes her eyes before she can begin to paint, and through tears and a tightening in her throat she paints the blood pumping through her body, the sun making orange and purple explosions under her eyelids, the sap rising in the trees and the warming ground driving up the green shoots beneath her feet, all turning on the earth's axis.

She is finding her beginnings, and not clinging to pictures of everything, although they are there still, illuminating everything. Instead of a flat patina of images, she is in a moment that carries all the past, present and future pictures in her mind – like minute cells to give meaning to pulsating life. Her earliest memory – bundled warm in her pram, the row of poplar trees framed by the pram hood, dark shady nook, golden light beyond – is here, beneath layer upon layer, all stored like the annual rings in the vast beech at her side. Now the oak, beech, hazel and chestnut whoosh and whisper, like the leaves of the babyhood poplars glinted and pattered in the breeze.

When her mother died, it was as if the poplars stopped growing, became frozen in time, and all she could do was accumulate more and more bright details, like a magpie. Until details were everything. That did not stop her sliding into nothingness.

Her thaw here in Suffolk melts into an orgiastic omnipotence, a wild freedom, a way of letting go of the control over details and pictorial facts.

When she paints, she realises what she has been missing. She calls this 'repainting' which reminds her of 'repairing'. Her paintings are in thick oils into which she mixes sand, or gel, or resin, and, one day, soil – for she wants them to be of the ground that inspires her – on large canvases propped on bricks that take up almost a whole wall of her cottage. Each canvas teeters on the brink between disaster and hope. She stands on newspaper spread on the flagstones, and paints without any sense of time or date, playing old records of Mahler's Fourth and Fifth Symphonies, and sometimes the First and Second, over and over again. And, when she can bear the pain and the beauty, his *Kindertotenlieder.*

One night, she falls asleep in an old armchair whose springs poke through the ticking, drunk from white wine, and is awoken by the smell of burning. A corner of the canvas is on fire, the wooden frame almost burnt through, flames hungrily licking the newspaper beneath. She stares at the spectre, intrigued. And then a fear of how it could end jolts her into action. She douses it with buckets of water.

Drawing breath she realises that for once death was not a welcome escape. It would snatch away the hope she is beginning to find: excitement at ways of capturing transparent light in all the gloom, the glimmerings of meaning and beauty. Yes, to be burnt is too literal: no symbolism in that, she laughs.

Day by day, she feels herself expanding, growing taller and plumper, in her reaching up and out towards life. Now she senses how she had shrunk, reduced herself and her world to a diseased state.

Years of bleakness, vagueness, mindlessness, pocked by abscesses of fear and despoiling, come into these paintings, but now they are transformed into a kind of cruel beauty: drab flat areas of teal, of violet and russet whorls, dripping sepia or ruby, competing with rays or pools of opalescent light. She knows she cannot paint light – light and its mate, air – that its ephemeral nature can only be known in the way it gifts objects that it rests on or glances at, or in the shadows it casts. Yet fragile light, in all its elusiveness, is driving the darkness away.

She struggles with her attempts to do the impossible: to paint the second that is different to the next, is a moment in time, that can never be repeated. She realises that her paintings can never be more than that: *a* moment, not *the* moment.

And woven into her study of light is her effort to observe the complexity of nature. Burdened by her over-attention to detail, her years of acute visual perception, she tries to forget everything she has seen before, and see, as if for the first time, the truth before her: to perceive the thing before her with an intense life of its own, its own logic and coherence, and its many secrets. Struggling to find the sensations within her mind and her body that are as sincere as possible to the object, she looks long and hard, sometimes not touching the canvas for minutes on end. She has to figure it out. Every mark is related to the whole.

She tries to forget what she learned at the Slade – when she tried to draw what was out there with a detached objectivity, when she learnt, to her peril, that that could break down. Now she tries to marry the magnificence of the universe with her inner storms and elation.

> *What I see is in a way abstract, unreal. Matter exists, but has no intrinsic meaning. I want to look at things with the wonder of a baby, and if people give my work meaning that's fine.*

she writes in her sketchbook. Reading it through, she crosses out 'in a way' in the first sentence.

Another day,

> *Why do I write at all? Words can't express what I feel with my eyes and with my hands. Words distort thoughts, writing perverts thoughts.*

There are times when the thought pushes through, like a strong weed through cracks in concrete, that someone looking at her paintings may feel similarly to herself, and that way she would be understood. Yet she tries to make work for work's sake, for her own needs, and to exclude others' views. Phyllis's incredulity, mockery, rejection at times, of her drawings and offerings are still like a deep sharp hook inside her.

Now she knows that she is living from second to second until she dies, and that is alright, because each second is alive.

She wakes in the middle of the night excited about all the paintings in her head waiting to be born.

> *What have I been doing these last twenty-six years?*
she jots down.

One particular day in May, her imperial size sheet of drawing paper has marks on it in soft oil pastels – lots of shades, mainly blues. Some warm, some cold, some joyful, some deadly: from palest baby brush blue – the colour of a sleeping baby's eyelids – through to serene sky blue, to deep cobalt, strident royal, sombre dark, ultramarine, deepest Prussian, navy, deadly nightshade – with tributaries of purple and indigo.

She has realised the unnaturalness of naturalism, and now plays with making the invisible visible.

She began this picture with the faintest smudge of charcoal for a nebulous, diffused sense of loss, as delicate as an embryo, soft, and even with some degree of comfort and familiarity, like an angora cardigan on a winter's night, but no, that's too easy, she thought, it's more the scratchy lines made at random by a branch etching a window pane, repeatedly, in the wind. Or the dark lines on a pear's skin, as it hangs on a tree, from a twig rubbing it. She was thinking then of the rightness of the seasons – imbued with loss but on a scale that she can respect. Unlike violent losses that upturn the universe.

An area of her picture is the purplish scab of a healing wound, different from the raw seeping pale watery-orange puss from a recent one.

Another day she observes clouds that evoke watercolour on wet paper, nature imitating art.

Images used to weigh her down in her centre, coalesced into an amorphous lump, like petrified larva. Like the horseshoe in the tree. A rotting peach, once honeyed, crawling with maggots. A *thud-thud*, like a heart beating, only it hadn't a rational explanation, and felt like deep indigestion. Oily slurry washed up on a beach. The look behind a child's brave smile, which she wore like a mask. The ticking of a clock that went on and on and on – while some things stopped. The dripping of a tap, so pointless, timeless, unthinking. Like Sundays.

Some of those associations bypass any conscious control and emerge in her paintings.

Her heart feels lighter, and she has fewer headaches.

Despite her distrust of words she continues to make jottings in her sketchbook.

Things, objects, space. Painting: trying to do justice to the things – myself probably – and the space around. Space is created by the thing and the thing creates space.

She draws an arrow pointing to the last sentence, and writes,

profound? superficial? Sometimes I know nothing.

When she returns to the cottage after a walk, she does not like everything to be exactly as she left it: a tea towel over the back of a chair, a mug by the sink, crumbs on the floor. Without signs of another, she wonders if she exists. Like staring into her eyes in a mirror for a long time: no-one to reflect back and affirm her existence. Sometimes she almost panics at the lack of anyone.

She tries to trick herself by leaving a jumble of mess in the sink, or books pulled off a shelf, cupboard doors open, or clothes in a bundle, or the bin overturned, so that when she returns she can pretend that someone else has been here. Her subterfuge makes her smile.

Emily writes in her sketchbook, on a page where she has delineated landscape with bands of wash in pale ochre, umber, a fine stripe of leaf green:

Must go back to <u>drawing</u>. There's a danger that my painting competes with nature, that it's too caught up with colour, and tone, and the past. <u>Drawings</u> are more like diagrams: the paper and the lines can play with the illusion of what is drawn. Like the sculptor's maquette which can be more alive than the finished piece. Less danger of drawings attempting the reality (?) and yet, paradoxically, more likely to capture it. Yes: more breath, more space, more air.

She rereads this note later, and jots down: *<u>Chinese drawings</u>: British Museum? V&A?*

1971

Some nights Emily lies awake listening to the wind, grateful that she is not afraid; that she has no fears of anything supernatural, nor is she plagued by her erstwhile undefined fears of men, men creeping up on her or leaping out at her. She smiles at the richness, fullness even, of solitude. Teeming with ideas and impressions, and sometimes a relaxed drowsiness after a full day, she welcomes her journey along the corridors of her mind as she falls into sleep and into dreams.

Many nights the windows rattle, the whole cottage groans and moans, while branches crash all around. She imagines the place could become untethered from its moorings like the house in *The Wizard of Oz*, and whirl into the air. But this stone dwelling has survived three hundred years, so another few hundred are possible. Sometimes she hears voices in the groans, sometimes persistent banging that she briefly thinks could be someone at her door, but she tells herself that it can probably wait. She lies warmly under a feather eiderdown pulled up to her eyes, excited at her survival, her life continuing, against the odds.

Her expectations on each walk in her Suffolk woods are never disappointed. The astonishing capacity of nature for renewal: ancient trees strain to reach the sky, or have toppled, exposing huge root balls which shoot new vertical branches, resisting the horizontality of death.

From time to time, she stops and sits on a log, or a mossy outcrop, and listens. The wind from afar gathers strength, closer and closer – the trees roaring like the sea – until it crashes all around. At other times a perfect stillness, except for remarkable tiny movements of a few leaves, frenzied, in a precise funnel of wind. Or the odd rattle and skitter of a few dead leaves, only to cease, as if they had never stirred. As if she had imagined it. Layers of dead oak leaves, and beech and chestnut and ash, form a flat stone-coloured patina on the loamy ground, season upon season, the earth endlessly nourished. Brambles, ivy, deadly nightshade, nettle, fern, wild mint and oregano, grasses, heather, broom, gorse, hawthorn, honeysuckle, sloe, dog rose, wild clematis, dandelion, thistle, small saplings – all competing for space. She is moved by such abundance. When the weather has been dry, the sandy ground is pale; when it has rained, it is transformed to a rich chocolate brown. Her focus zooms in, a detail becoming an abstraction, scale-less. Or reveals unexpected miracles: the mud transforms into mountain ranges; a tiny shoot is a giant Scots pine; a moment later, she sees a rich canvas of linseed oil and varnish-rich viridian, as if worked with a palette-knife.

Another day, walking in rain that whispers loudly on leaves above her forest path, she doesn't mind the wet seeping through her thin woollen coat. She crouches down to see more closely the *pointillist* dots of green water-weeds covering a marshy inlet, pierced by black circles from droplets of rain which appear and disappear with a Bach-like rhythm. And inhales the mushroom smell as if her lungs require it. Hanging from an overhanging branch for a moment, she tries to recapture the feeling of being a child, but her body feels heavy, unyielding.

She notices some over-ripe blackberries, amidst hard pink ones that seem never to have ripened properly. And yet there are still some white blossoms with a hint of pink, now, in October, on some stems. The whole life cycle of the blackberry on one branch: buds, blossoms, small fruit like a young girl's new tight breasts, plumping to fuller fruit, through to swollen wine-dark berries. Some have begun to rot. And then there are the fruits that have died and withered to desiccated brownness.

Above all, it is the light, the sunlight, that provides endless play for her eyes: its illumination from beneath or behind or beyond some leaves, sepulchral as stained glass. The golden shafts dive deep into the forest, beyond obstacles, always finding a way of beaming onwards as if for ever; sometimes in thin streaks, sometimes as bright as tinfoil, sometimes diluted, granting colour to everything. The family of green – emerald, jade, sap, olive, lime, slime, grass, mould, hazel, moss, teal, bottle, forest, sea, viridian, acid, shocking, verdurous, verdigris, verdant, leaf, milky, all the adjectives she can think of, and yet there are even more nuances before her eyes, even before recourse to the blue-green or brown-green ranges.

'Green'. She wonders if it can ever be fully blessed and rich, or if the association to Harry Green will always discolour it.

To try to erase him she turns to a recently discovered quote by Flaubert in a book on Cézanne, which she has copied into her sketchbook,

> *. . . there is a part of everything which is unexplored, because we are accustomed to using our eyes only in association with the memory of what people before us have thought of the things we are looking at. Even the smallest thing has something in it which is unknown. We must find it.*

She tries to see the world afresh, uncontaminated.

And closes her eyes.

But there he is again, popping up uninvited when she least expects it, surrounded by beauty. She doesn't know if her painting will ever fully expunge him, his violation of her when she was as vulnerable as a barely formed bud. She kicks at leaf mould with her boot, uncovering rich moist loam beneath.

Sitting on a log, her head in her hands, Emily knows how, as a child, she stayed mostly in a dream, a numb place – to not register an old man with leathery hands as hard as the pads of Lenin's paws, in a darkish place with a curtain drawn across a doorway, patterns of trailing ivy on the fabric. Her head the height of the table. And the promise of sweets on his thick breath snarled up with *If you tell anyone I'll tell them you started it, and . . . I'll take away your doggie. But you won't tell will you, because Grandpa loves you, so no harm in that is there,* his lips tickling her ear, his heart thumping or is it hers. *You're going to forget all this, aren't you . . . forget it ever happened.* Sunlight fires through a hole in the ivy material, her mouth filled with she doesn't know what instead of sweets, something like a big rubber toy, and he heaves like he's vomiting . . . and something else . . . like snot.

You're the best girl in the world.

And of course she wants to vomit, but tries not to.

And now she cries, angry despairing sobs, that could lead her back to the familiar inside of the metal tin with unscalable sides. She knows the dead-end of all that, so she clutches at something she has considered since her retreat to Suffolk: that she will have to talk to Phyllis and her father about what happened. To try at least to gain their understanding, their endorsement of what she went through. She senses how careful she will have to be in how she raises it, or they will be defensive. She imagines saying that she just wants them to know, to know if they suspected . . . to help her to recover.

A mild November morning. Emily is walking on a track through the woods, her thoughts swift and intense.

With no forewarning, no crackle of sticks or rustle of leaves, a man stands before her. She stops still. The sunlight is behind him, she cannot see his face easily. He seems stocky and small. She smiles to placate him if he should need appeasing, to let him know that she is not afraid, while deciding whether or not to run away.

'Well, what you looking at then?' he asks in a voice that is surprisingly high-pitched.

'I wasn't looking at anything,' she says. And worries about contradicting him.

Stepping towards her, 'Why do you keep stopping, then, and peering at things, like this ground, for instance?'

The realisation that she has been watched unnerves her further. Emily gauges from his accent that he is not from this part of the world. His hair is long and matted. His chest is bare though he wears a loose open overcoat with missing buttons, and baggy trousers. Also something like a bag is slung across his shoulders.

'Oh well, yes – I'm a . . . a botanist, I always look at things. I didn't know anyone else was around . . . .'

When he stares at her she finds his silence more disturbing than his talk.

'Well, bye then,' she says as breezily as possible, beginning to walk on past him. She doesn't want him to see her fear if she were to back the way she came, or head off into the thick undergrowth.

'Live near here then?' he asks.

She looks at him, closer now. She sees his cold grey eyes, and notices a large rifle slung across his back. *He must be a hunter.* She knows she cannot take risks with this man.

So she replies with forced calm, 'No, I live in Southwold. You know Southwold, of course?'

'What's the "of course"?' His tone sounds menacing. 'Posh place like that? Wouldn't go there if it was the last place on earth that sold Fray Bentos.' His words tumble out without pause, ''Course I know it, know *of* it, *knew* it, once, "South-*wold*", emphasising the 'wold' in a parody of an upper class accent. 'Oh yes, when I was on the concert rep-er-toire. Recognise me then?' He holds his chin aloft, turning to show his profile.

'Well, I think maybe you are familiar,' she dissembles, trying to sound puzzled, wanting him to assist her memory.

'Patrick Fuller, call me Pat if you like. Pianist. Studied with Nadia Boulanger, Paris *Conservatoire* and *Ecole Normale de Musique*. And then in Moscow . . . , before, before . . . .'

He is losing himself in incoherence. The longer she talks to him, the more she is in danger of being caught in his web. She should just walk away, but that would hurt his vulnerable pride. If not for the gun . . . . She begins to feel angry that a stranger should so invade her privacy, her sense of security.

'Well, Patrick. It's an honour to meet you,' smiling at him in as impersonal a way as she can muster. 'And I'm Annie, and I promised my father and my brother that I'd be back by lunch-time. Going to London this afternoon. They'll be coming after me soon if I don't go now.'

'But I never showed you the reviews. Reviews of my concerts. Testimonials, references.' He scrabbles in his coat pockets. 'Articles, listings, personal letters, reports, programmes, you name it, the lot.' Rummaging in his trouser pockets and his inside-coat pockets, he extracts a crumpled piece of paper while pulling his rifle round to his front in the process. 'It's not far from here, my place, Tinker's Cottage; won't take long . . . .' He falls silent as he sees her looking at the gun.

'Don't you worry about this, love! Look at my hands, my fingers. See the span? Glenn Gould, Sviatoslav Richter, couldn't reach more notes than I, so what would I be doing with a gun? Though, you never know . . . . No no, Anne, Annie, *Annie Get Your Gun*!' His laugh sounds like a hooter. 'Remember that? But if it worries you, I'll put the thing down.' Now he sounds more like a boy who has inadvertently scared a small girl. She is wondering if it's loaded.

'It's okay, Patrick, but I'd better be off soon – maybe another time: your . . . testimonials.'

Walking past him, her heart hammering, she rounds a bend and runs. Her cottage is in the opposite direction, but she wants to put as much distance as possible between herself and this stranger. She decides to look up Tinker's Cottage and avoid it at all cost.

Later she thinks he was probably harmless, crazy but harmless. *There but for the grace of God go I, a mad woman, one day, talking about my greatness as a painter . . . .*

She knows she did well with this Patrick, knows she has come a very long way from the Scarecrow in the field, or Stanley, or Old Man Harry, or even Marcus.

That evening, she locks the cottage more carefully than usual, draws the curtains meticulously, and cannot sleep well. Waking dreams torment her, dreams of maggots, maggots and pus, sometimes in her chest, sometimes in her throat. A bizarre image comes to her, of curtains – maybe a concept for a piece of work she might make – curtains made of fishhooks and apple peel. And then she imagines curtains made of many small pieces of tissue paper joined together with sticking plaster.

She gets up, puts on an old record of Mozart piano sonatas, and makes herself a bowl of porridge which she eats with honey. The lamp is still alight as she falls asleep on the bumpy sofa downstairs, wearing her coat.

The next day she tries to draw, to draw woodland reduced to a basic play of dark and light, patterns of leaves and of branches, remembering a Van Gogh drawing of trees. But she remains unsatisfied.

Why fishhooks? she wonders, returning to her night-time images. She senses something that is so deeply hooked into her within her layers of apple peel skin, something that seems impossible to extract without tearing it. The hurt fragility of the tissue paper curtains disturbs her further.

When she ventures out to collect wood for the fire she looks over her shoulder, sensing someone following her. She worries about having left the cottage unlocked.

She tells herself to stop it, determined not to let this get to her.

Marching across heathland, scrambling through a forest, creeping through high reeds, or watching the clouds, she re-finds her love of nature, her place in this marvellous world, but a pervasive fear still haunts her.

Waking at three or four in the morning becomes habitual.

No, she tells herself, I can't live like this. *Maybe I'm crazy. Maybe so scarred that I will never recover.*

She works at her paintings, struggling to bring together something hard and sharp on the one side of the canvas with something soft and nebulous on the other. The centre of the canvas is a problem. She produces a series of unfinished work with this strange empty space in the middle.

Jacob Samuels pours himself another whisky. No point in adding ice; it's the neat stuff he needs. He doesn't know how much he drinks – why count? When Phyllis challenges him on the amount he laughs dismissively.

His features have coarsened over the years: his nose is fleshier, his face bloodshot. He is less attentive to Emily, Alex and Paul. His relationship with Georgia is as strained as it has always been.

His heart has developed arrhythmia whenever he exerts himself or is anxious. Phyllis dismisses this as Jake being 'hypo'.

She plays tennis and golf and bridge whenever she can, in her comfortable life in Hampstead. She has joined a book group, but finds that she hasn't as much to say as she would like, and resents those who contribute with passion.

Phyllis has lightened the colour of her hair, and wears it shorter, but continues to favour dull shades of unremarkable garments. 'You cannot tell a person by their clothes,' she tells her flamboyant friend Leah with barely disguised smugness. Her face has become noticeably more lined in recent years, particularly her forehead which carries a deep upside-down V.

She worries about the contents of Jake's will, and whether it is clear about leaving everything to her in the first instance. She is quite confident that she will outlive him, although he jokes that the creaking gate usually lasts longest. He is secretive about the purpose of a recent visit to his lawyer.

The distance between them increases. They have slept in separate bedrooms for two years now. Neither really acknowledge this drift. It feels as inevitable as winter following autumn, though without the promise of a spring.

He retreats to smoking, drinking, managing his business properties. And photography. He turns a box room at the top of the house into a darkroom. Jake has always been serious about taking black and white photographs, enjoying the technicalities of depth of field, focus, aperture, film speed, gradation of paper, as much as the composition and choice of subject. This is the one area of his life where he enjoys degrees of control, but with elements of fortuitous surprise. He finds comfort in the red glow of the light in his only private space, and in the images which emerge magically in the liquid solution.

From time to time, he makes prints from old negatives of Rae, staring at her soft smile, her gentle beauty, like an archaeologist uncovering another world that he has dreamed about. Indeed, he has had recurrent dreams of being in a wilderness and reaching out for an astonishingly beautiful sphinx-head in azure and terracotta, which always recedes beyond reach. Now his uninhibited tears roll into the developing fluid.

Phyllis calls photography his 'hobby' and the darkroom 'Jakey's little playroom.' But in the company of others who are appreciative she talks knowingly, as if Jake is her protégée, and acknowledges the power of his stark black and white landscapes, prints of Hampstead Heath taken at dawn in the frost, or trees semi-veiled in fog. Jake is becoming a master of the austere, the bleak, the cold.

He keeps his photographs of his first wife tucked away in a filing cabinet.

Phyllis ventures into the darkroom one day, while Jake is out. She is not sure what motivates her, other than a suspicion that there is something secretive about him that she needs to know in order to wage battle. She pounces on pictures of a woman smiling shyly, pegged on a line to dry, confirming her fantasies that he is having an affair. She smuggles them out of the darkroom to see them in daylight before realising that they look like Rae. She is not sure what is worse, Jake still thinking about Rae, or having an affair. She resists tearing them up and hides them under the jumpers in her wardrobe.

Withdrawing further from Jake over the next few days, she plans to go on another golfing holiday with Leah.

'Phyllis, have you seen some prints I made for Emily, of her mother?' he calls from the top of the stairs.

To acknowledge jealousy would be to acknowledge weakness, to acknowledge caring at all. 'What's all this about Rae?' Phyllis shouts. 'For heaven's sake, she's been dead now for, what is it, over twenty years,' and mutters '. . . in case you hadn't realised.' She raises her voice, 'And if you gave Georgia half as much attention as you do Emily . . . .'

The couple are better at having rows when in separate rooms or different floors of the house than face to face.

Phyllis goes into the kitchen, snaps off a row of *Lindt* chocolate from a slab, and decides she will say she is not hungry. Jake will have to cook for himself.

He pours himself another drink, and vows to hide all his old negatives for safekeeping.

1972

One evening Emily drafts a letter in pencil, and then, on her big block of good quality white smooth paper – with the fountain pen she has spent years searching for, and found – she writes:

Dingle Cottage,
Wooton Wood,
Nr Westleton,
Suffolk
March 15ᵗʰ 1972

Dear Phyllis,

I'm writing to you about something that I'm sure will be very difficult for you, but I need to share it as it is vital to me, and maybe to you too. I have struggled with the idea of writing for months now. I hope I have the courage to finish this letter!

(Since you and my father are estranged, I'm writing to him separately; sending him a copy of this.)

Well, straight to the point then.

I have become increasingly sure that Grandpa Harry abused me, sexually, when I was little. It must have been – more or less – from when he came into my life, until he died. That is, from when I was about five and a quarter, until I was about six and a half. I could go into details of what he did, and how I now know about it – from memories, dreams, fears, and physical sensations that I have – but perhaps that's not necessary.

I need to share this with you because I feel that you may have some idea about it; any details, even if painful, which you might be able to add to the story would be helpful to me in my recovery. Things like this are better acknowledged. If you were unaware, I'm really not blaming you now – it's not all that unusual . . . .

I don't want to upset you; I appreciate your life is quite difficult these days, and you won't welcome this now. But you see, I feel I can't quite move on until that awful phase is acknowledged in some way by you and by my father. I may write to Georgia separately – I wonder if, perhaps, she too was abused by him. I won't worry the boys about it.

I'm writing rather than ringing because it's easier to be clear. And, as you probably know, I don't have a phone here.

I hope you're well, and that I'll hear from you soon.

Love,

Emily

She re-reads it twice, deleting the sentence in the first paragraph about courage to finish the letter, corrects the odd word, and makes two copies, before rapidly sealing one in an envelope as if her courage was time-limited.

She adds a note to her father's copy:

Dear Dad,

The enclosed is, I hope, self-explanatory.

I'm sorry not to have been in touch lately. I think of you and hope you're okay. I'm working away at my painting (what's news!) and feel well – you may have been to my show in London (Arnold and Sons Gallery) recently. Sorry I didn't get in touch, didn't feel up to it.

Yes, I'm OK, <u>but</u> for the stuff detailed in the copy of the letter I'm enclosing.

I'd be grateful for a response. You know I don't have a phone, but if you'd rather we spoke drop me a card and I'll ring from a call box.

Lots of love,

Emily X

She walks the three-quarters of a mile to post both letters in Wooton Wood.

At the little shop that is also a sub-Post Office the wares are reassuring in their predictability and normality, almost obscuring the little woman behind the counter. Packets of pink blancmange, butterscotch *Instant Whip*, *Liquorice Allsorts* sporting the man made of sweets, *Jacob's* Cream Crackers, tins of *Bird's* Custard, *Heinz* Tomato Soup, *Kellogg's* Corn Flakes, *Nescafe*, *Bengers* night-time drink, neat balls of string, wooden clothes pegs on cards, *Bryant and May* matches, *Rowntree's* fruit gums, *Maynard's* wine gums, *Spangles*, a jar of sherbet lemons and another of *Winter Warmers*, against a backdrop of *Wills Woodbine*, *Craven A*, *Mac* sweets and *Kirby* grips on cards.

Emily asks the shop keeper about the whereabouts of Tinker's Cottage.

'Tinker's Cottage? It's over Wenhestan way, near the pig farm – the new one not the old one. They closed the old one down didn't they. Now you go down past the Cross Tree, you know, where that man was 'anged they say. But it's half fallen in now, the cottage, roof just about gone, my 'usband tells me.' She smiles at Emily enquiringly, her head cocked to one side.

'Oh thanks. I think I know more or less where you mean. Just wondered. I think I saw it on a large-scale map, and then couldn't find it. Weather's improving, isn't it? Looks like a mild stretch now.'

'Never can tell for long hereabouts. Sunshine one minute, rain the next. Grass very dooey early in the day. Never know when to put the washing out.'

'Yes,' Emily says, running out of small talk. 'Thanks. Bye then.'

Three weeks elapse with no response from Phyllis or her father. She worries if she has done more harm than good by broaching all this. From time to time she wonders if she has made it all up, and if she's crazy.

She stops expecting a letter.

Perhaps Phyllis is away on holiday. Should she write again? What if she never received it?

Her sleep is more troubled. She begins to hear deep threatening voices in the groans of the branches outside. One day she chokes on a piece of apple, and thinks of the wicked queen in *Snow White* disguised as a peasant woman. How that book intrigued her as a child. It occurs to Emily that this cottage is rather like the seven dwarves' cottage.

Her painting reverts to swirls and abstractions, in which she sees nightmarish phantasmagoria, the palette changing to umber and ochre, ultramarine, splatters of carmine. She had given up black, but now it rears up again. Black, she always thinks, is such a dead colour, like a hole in the canvas.

Her letter flap clatters loudly one morning. She rushes to the envelope on the mat, the postman already disappearing towards the gate.

But the italic bold writing in sepia ink is unfamiliar. Tearing it open she finds a letter from Elizabeth Fell, the tutor who has loaned her this cottage.

Emily washes the dishes and makes herself a cup of tea before sitting down at the kitchen table to read.

April 11th 1972
London

Dear Emily,

> *I hope this finds you well in little Dingle Cottage. (If it was called 'Dingle Dell' my opening line would rhyme!)*
>
> *I often think of you there, and am so pleased to know that the hideaway is being used and enjoyed by you.*
>
> *Thank you for your letter in January – it meant a lot to me to know you're fine. I dropped you a card from Florence, acknowledging your letter. Good to know that you're really painting. Well, that was the whole idea, wasn't it? Away from distractions. I look forward to seeing your output in due course – if and when you want to show it to me. (Don't think that 'production' is a condition of tenure! It's a possible bonus, that's all. Although, as you know, I would love a painting of yours – if possible.) By the way, sorry for the delay in replying properly – I was away with a friend in India.*

She skims the rest of the letter to see if Elizabeth is asking to have Dingle Cottage back. When it seems not to carry that sting, she reads it through slowly, with enjoyment.

> *Don't worry what they think in the village! (– your last letter.) I think they were used to me in my shawls and hats, long dresses over trousers, paint under my fingernails. Especially when I spent months painting outdoors in all weathers – mostly under plastic macks – and if a bold person came up to see my brown and grey earthy washes I think they wished they'd never bothered because they couldn't find the words to comment.*
>
> *As I'm now hooked on the Dales – where as you know I use my cousin's house – I don't foresee reclaiming Dingle Cottage in the near future. Somehow the loftiness and airiness, greenness in places, and above all the hills of the Dales, suit my mood more*

*these days. But I don't want to put you off lil' ol' damp
Dingly Dell!*

*However: I would love to come and visit, maybe
just for a couple of days, during the Easter holidays –
when the Slade is on holiday and I'll be in Peterborough
at a friend's for a week or two. Suffolk isn't that far. But
not if it will disturb your equilibrium . . . . Or your
output?*

Do drop me a line.

Yours,

Liz

She rereads the letter twice, smiling at the picture of
Elizabeth as an outdoor artist. Emily is not sure about a visit,
though. She would have to clean and tidy a great deal, and the
pattern of her days would have to alter. But no, she realises, her
reluctance is deeper than the inconvenience. It is because this
is the first place where she has really felt a sense of belonging,
even of ownership. And where hope has been risked.

Taking a brisk walk, her hands deep in her pockets, for
once she does not really look around her. Striding across
heather, she trips and falls on a branch of gorse. The sudden
jerk to her body shocks her into realising she has begun
to feel too confident, too powerfully in her stride. She has
sensed that lately her paintings are too full of life – that
they lack an edge of fear, of risk, of . . . . *Have I become
presumptuous, like Georgia?* As soon as she dares to trust the
world, she seems to rush to the extreme of being too full of
herself. In the background of this boldness, like someone
whistling in the dark, is the non-response from Phyllis and
her father. Returning to the cottage she knows that she and
this older artist share a language, a licence to be scruffy and
spontaneous and eccentric; and much more than that, she
hopes they are both searching for understanding.

Trapped bubbles glisten like mercury on the thick stems
of sticky chestnut buds in a heavy glass jar on the kitchen

window sill. Emily's vision is sharpened by the prospect of someone else seeing them, as she steps back to admire their promise. She places sprigs of pussy willow and catkins in an earthenware jug by the sink. To complete the festive look, she arranges a bunch of wild primroses – a small bunch, not wanting to denude the banks of nature's displays – in a blue and white china teacup on the table.

Next to the bed in the one bedroom, at the top of the small spiral staircase, she places violets – their stems as delicate as their smell – in a tiny glass bottle, with trailing new shoots of ivy. In the milky light streaming into the little loft she makes up the bed with sheets smelling of fresh air, and piles on blankets, over which she throws an Indian bedspread. And neatly folds the eiderdown she found in a charity shop across the foot of the bed. Preparing a bed for someone else feels so intimate, even exhilarating, after two years of isolation.

She will sleep on the sofa.

Scrubbing the flagstones requires four bucketfuls of soapy water. This, like cleaning the lunette window, she thinks she should have done months ago.

But showing her canvases to anyone is more of a problem. They all look unfinished, all 'work in progress'. She turns them to face the wall, behind the sofa, even a wet one for the time being, muttering 'Sorry'.

She had sent a postcard to Elizabeth the day after she heard from her, welcoming her, and suggested a date a week before Easter. She added that unless she heard to the contrary she'd expect her then, as she didn't have a phone. She knew her propensity to postpone this sort of thing if she did not act immediately.

On the morning of the appointed day Emily is unsure how to spend her time, whether to venture out or wait. She dusts the windowsills and cleans the sink taps, then decides to stay in and read as the weather is wet and cold. She puts on Mahler's First Symphony, knowing she is in need of its fresh optimism and lyricism.

The letter flap startles her as it always does. This must be a late cancellation from Elizabeth. How could she believe in a visit, in Elizabeth – or anyone – wanting to see her. *Anyway, life is better without visitors . . . .*

Phyllis's writing, with those curvy loops that still seem so grownup, on a blue Basildon Bond envelope, disturbs Emily's peace.

She sits on a kitchen chair, trembling, to read.

Dear Emily,

Your letter troubled me, as it did your father. I didn't know how to reply, because I was so upset by the contents.

I will come straight to the point. What you say simply could not have happened. I think you are suffering from a False Memory, it can't be anything other than that. Quite what or who put those ideas into your head I do not know.

Quickly reading the final paragraph, needing to know the conclusion, she then returns to a careful reading.

My late father always loved you, and would never have done anything to upset you, or, God forbid, hurt you in any way. And if he had, we'd have noticed, surely. I'm only grateful he (and my dear mother, Milly,) is no longer with us to hear your accusations.

I have discussed your letter with Georgia and she thinks it's outrageous. We wondered if living alone like that is driving you to these thoughts – whether it's not healthy.

You know, Emily, you have always had a chip on your shoulder, and now there seems to be a big block of wood! It can only weigh you down. I thought at first when I read your letter that you should apologise to me for troubling me with such crazy ideas – your letter reminded me of our old dog Boetjie, in S. A., who'd drop a dead rabbit at our feet – but now I think that you must be troubled, and I feel sorry for you.

So think nothing more of what you wrote, and I won't either.

Your father isn't in very good shape* these days, as I think you must know, and so I'm not sure what he really thinks about your letter. I did try to discuss it. I think he thinks as I do – how could he think otherwise! But we don't communicate much, I'm sorry to say. Not that I don't try.

Bye for now,

Look after yourself, my dear.

Phyllis

* I don't mean your Dad is ill – he's well, I think – but I cannot fathom his mind these days.

Now the Mahler sounds too insistent in its joyousness, too exultant. But she doesn't stop the tape. She stares at the primroses radiating their own splash of weak sunlight on this grey day, the windows pummelled by rain at this moment, and almost smiles at the way Mahler keeps trying to lift her spirits. She is reminded of Jock, and before him, Lenin – it isn't only Phyllis who can invoke lost pets – who would sense her sadness sometimes, lick her hand, and lie by her side. Perhaps she should get a puppy. The thought leads to a brilliant apparition of a Border collie puppy, black and white. In unison with a triumphant wind instrument in the symphony at that moment, her thoughts erupt, *Why let Phyllis the Philistine get me down? Does it matter if she doesn't believe me? Isn't that to be expected?*

But when she thinks of her father not being in 'good shape' she feels heavy.

Wondering if she'll tell Elizabeth any of this, she pushes the letter under a pile of books.

Right now the music's folksy fourth movement connects her with people all over the world, searching for meaning when struggling with loss, as she knows Mahler did. The sound of a cuckoo in the next passage signals spring. *That's all we can do,* she thinks, with flat resignation.

At mid-day, a car pulls up the lane and stops beyond the front grassy area. Peering through the window with some dread Emily sees an old Austin of an indiscriminate colour between grey and cream. The rain has stopped.

She watches shyly, hardly having spoken to anyone for weeks. She sees Elizabeth Fell climb out and squint at the cottage. Emily tells herself not to hesitate too long. She emerges from the front door, unsure how enthusiastic to be.

Elizabeth dictates the mood, 'Emily! Lovely to see you!' as she hugs the young woman. Emily had forgotten how small Elizabeth was and feels embarrassed by her own height.

'Don't know if I can say "welcome" when it's your place.'

'Don't be silly, Emily! It's much more your place now. Great to be here. Let's get some stuff out the boot.'

Elizabeth is encumbered by a voluminous black velvet skirt, a knitted poncho, and a violet woollen brimmed hat framing her round face, as she unloads a battered small leather suitcase and carrier bags from the boot. Her dramatic mauve eye makeup accentuates the whiteness of her face.

Uncertainty about offering tea or coffee, or wine, or the sherry she has bought specially, is eased by Elizabeth's way of making herself at home, with the occasional 'I hope you don't mind . . . .' The visitor has brought a bottle of good red wine, Swiss chocolates, a pile of old issues of *l'Oeil,* and a gift of a bumpy woollen scarf found in a jumble sale in subtle stripes of lilac, grey, brown and olive. Emily is touched almost to the point of tears.

As they both sip sherry that evening Emily smiles to herself at her flash of inspiration and even premonition about a puppy, realising that Elizabeth looks like an overweight sheep dog, all black and white and bouncy. Now her brown eyes, framed by almost black hennaed hair and a white face, have that particularly intelligent and kindly expression that she associates with sheep dogs. Elizabeth is particularly animated, her cheeks glowing, revived by a rest and a sleep after lunch.

In the background is a sizzle from the oven of a fat chicken pierced with garlic, smothered in olive oil, herbs and chopped mild chillies. Emily guesses that Elizabeth, in keeping with her big personality, would like flavours that are strong.

They had gone for a walk between showers in the afternoon, picked wild mint down by the stream, and, while peeling potatoes and garlic, chatted about the locality and Emily's discoveries. But all afternoon they circled round each other politely, despite the older woman's efforts at heartiness and spontaneity. Emily felt cross with herself for her old pattern of reserve, especially with Elizabeth, towards whom she longed to show warmth.

'Come on then, Emmy – can I call you that? – what about the paintings, then? Why've you turned their faces to the wall, poor things! Like flowers when the sun goes down. What've they done to deserve that. You know I won't let you get away with such reticence.'

Emily blushes but says nothing, gulping her sherry. She throws a log onto the fire, causing sparks to fly.

Elizabeth continues, 'Now if this was the painting studio at the Slade, and I was teaching, you'd have to expose yourself. And in front of all the other students. Hopefully I'm not a dragon. Well?'

'I don't know. Sorry, Liz – can I call you that? I guess it's that I don't know myself . . . . I've been such a recluse here . . . . Whether to, you know, show the work, when I haven't a clue myself if it's good or . . . rubbish.'

'You nincompoop!' she exclaims. 'How does one ever *know?* How do you think . . . Cézanne knew, or Monet, or Joe Bloggs? Or I? Or whoever? You know we have to expose ourselves to the light from time to time, otherwise the shoots we send out are pale and sickly. No photosynthesis. Come on my girl!'

'Well in that case,' she says, summoning courage, 'mine, my paintings, probably are sickly. Haven't shown them to anyone for ages. But yes, you're right about *light*. Funnily enough that's what I've been obsessed with here. Okay then, let's go.' She is grateful to the sherry for the light-headedness she feels. 'Before supper?'

Elizabeth nods, her face grave.

So Emily pushes the sofa aside and heaves out four large canvases, three smaller ones, and six rectangular small paintings on wooden boards. Like shy strippers, they still keep their backs to the audience. Draining her glass of sherry, she offers Elizabeth more – who scowls, 'Not now!' – and turns round one of the large paintings.

A vast mysterious canvas in Prussian blue and brown emerges, with whitish areas painted onto the navy when it was wet, making some white and pale blue patches. The brushstrokes are vigorous, the whole like a universe of swirling cosmic explosions. But the eye is drawn to a place in the bottom left: not as if it is falling off the canvas, but firmly there, an area which is dark and deep and tinged with thick carmine.

'Goodness, Emily. Where did that come from? But come on, show me the others. All of them. I want to see them all, even if you don't think they're a series. It doesn't matter what order you did them in.' She is quite commanding. Emily obeys without thinking. Her fear has vanished, but her heart is racing with excitement.

She positions the paintings around the small room and on the sofa, props one on a wooden chair across its arms, and others on the deep window sills blocking the evening light. She switches on the ceiling light and a lamp, and places the self-portraits in a row along the floor of the remaining wall, beneath the window. These she rearranges to correct their order.

Elizabeth swirls around, taking them all in, and then stops at each painting, singularly, before moving onto the next. She allows her poncho to drop to the ground and tramples over it. Scrutinising one work closely, she then steps as far back as the small room allows. She glances at the young artist. And then returns to her perusal. Emily's heart is banging in her ribcage. She feels utterly naked, but not at the mercy of a predator.

'Well, my girl,' is all Elizabeth says at first. Then, 'What happened to you, what must have happened? These paintings are like, are like . . . the cross-section of a tree, no, worse, like a . . . .' Emily shakes her head. And begins to panic. Elizabeth senses her anxiety, and seems to force herself to say what she is thinking.

'No, Emily, don't worry. I think they're . . . wonderful. Superb. Really. But I can see something of what you've been through. I get a strong sense of some expunging of something dreadful, something from . . . possibly ages ago? What I was going to say just now, but then you went so white, was that it's like a tree that has been burnt, and yet there's new growth . . . .'

Emily begins to shake so violently that she has to take a painting off a chair to sit down.

'Oh my God! You poor girl! Poor child!' Elizabeth hugs her, enveloping Emily's face in her bosom.

Elizabeth's warmth makes her sob uncontrollably. She tries to stop, 'Oh God, how silly . . . ,' but again she is racked by cries from her depths. 'Sorry, Liz, sorry. Oh my God, you know, I had a nanny – just realised – called Lizzie, when I was little . . . . But that's not why I'm crying . . . .'

'It's alright. You can tell me about it. In due course. There's plenty of time.'

Elizabeth continues to hold her, and Emily is taken right back to that sunless flypaper kitchen and Lizzie's arms and the sound of her voice and the rocking of her body.

'No, Liz, it's too much. Really. I daren't go there – any more than I just have. Really. No. I must try and be here with you now, to find my . . . rational self, my . . . my grown-up self. Don't be too kind; it makes me . . . cry all the more.' With great effort, she makes herself think of something ordinary, noticing the dark flagstones and the way they are shiny in places. 'I know there's all that stuff, but . . . it's not fair on you, and kind of scary for me.'

Yet they remain in a silent embrace.

In a muffled voice, 'What were you seeing in the paintings, Liz? Can you try and tell me?' She begins to pull away. Now she feels a twinge of embarrassment at this degree of intimacy with someone she hardly knows.

'I think you know. Something very grim. Something that tore away your skin. You know, the sort of "skin" that keeps us safe in the world. Very brave to revisit it in painting.' She pauses. 'But, perhaps you had to.'

Emily disentangles her arms and struggles to focus, swallowing hard, and nods almost imperceptibly. She sees love in the other's eyes, and warmth, and acceptance.

She takes a deep breath.

And nods again. 'So, you do believe me?'

'What?' says Elizabeth.

'Well, believe that it happened.'

'How could I not! The evidence is before my eyes. But, Emmy, you have begun to make something of it, whatever it was, or is. It isn't just shit, or pain. There's real life, and light, yes – I see what you meant about light and, I guess this one is recent' – pointing to a small canvas inspired by the forest and the abundance of nature, the rich tapestry of earthen hues. 'And, dare I say, redemption?'

Emily shakes her head. The older woman is puzzled. 'What then? Do you mean, you're still . . . tortured?'

Emily replies that it isn't the paintings as such that are finding a way through the shit, although that's true, of course, but . . . . She struggles to continue to talk, to ride the knots of anguish in her throat, 'It's the fact that you believe me.' She begins to cry again. 'Can't explain . . . .'

'Well well, don't worry. Whatever it is, the main thing, you are getting there my girl.'

'My goodness, the chicken!' Emily shrieks, rushing to the oven. She turns it down, takes out the dish of potatoes, onions, and chicken, bastes them hurriedly, and puts them back.

She knows that Elizabeth cannot understand why it is so important for her to be believed.

'Okay then, after supper, if you want to tell me the details, or whatever, you can. That's up to you. I can take it.'

'I know,' she says, with an inner smile of relief.

Elizabeth closes the gingham curtains, pours the Burgundy and carves the chicken, while Emily dishes up onto Edwardian blue and white plates she bought in a jumble sale. She is pleased that she has made the kitchen look beautiful, pleased she has used as a tablecloth one of the ancient textiles that she keeps for backdrops of still-lives, grateful for the primroses on the table, and the candles.

Before she sits down she rushes into the adjoining room, and dashes back.

'I was going to put them away you know. The paintings. They're so exposed, while we eat. Like faces, looking out. But it's okay. They'll survive.'

Her cheeks flush. 'You know, Liz, I've been such a hermit. Some days I forget the sound of my own voice. Like the old biddies in the village, I sometimes trek all the way to the shop just to hear myself speak.'

'Ah well, that sounds familiar. Had periods of my life like that. When I split up from Nat, my partner.' Elizabeth fills their glasses.

Emily is relieved to hear she had a partner, she knows so little about this woman who has become so important to her.

'Oh, when was that?'

'1968. Terrible time. Nat, Natalie,' staring at the candlelight's fuchsia patterns in her glass of wine. 'She was having a relationship with someone else, another woman. She's a writer, gathers an entourage of admirers, secretaries, managers etc. You've probably heard of her – Natalie Burlingham. So much temptation I guess.'

Smacking her lips from the wine, and unsure how to proceed, Emily perceives Elizabeth withering and shrinking. This older woman has already given her far more than she can ever repay, and now she feels helpless when an ordinary comment is called for. Cowardice and naiveté about Elizabeth's sexuality, and the fame of her ex-partner, is getting in the way of her responses. Just because she is a lesbian, or maybe bi-sexual, doesn't mean she has designs on me, she tells herself. She briefly wonders if she would like that closeness with her.

Elizabeth's intuition about the paintings, how she zoomed into what they were about, now enables Emily to respond. 'Liz, I'm sorry. Sorry you suffered what seems, seemed, such a . . . a betrayal. Sounds like you felt used. All those other women were allowed to be close to Nat, Natalie, and your part in it all was overlooked.'

'In a way, yes. But that's not quite it. No. I think that for ages I was duped. Nat denied my suspicions, said I was ridiculous, possessive, insanely jealous, and all the time I was right. But even that isn't quite "it". No, I think . . . I think it was that she was the only woman I'd had a sexual relationship with.' Elizabeth becomes dreamy, 'She seduced me, ages before that, when I was married, married to Howard, in Leeds.' Now she fiddles with the chicken on her plate, dissecting it, not eating.

'He was a painter too. We used to paint in the Dales. That's when I fell in love with the Dales. Then, along came Nat, in a pub – sounds corny – and she asked to see my paintings, and somehow understood them, understood the struggles and . . . .' Elizabeth becomes quiet. Emily is aware of the similarity with the situation that occurred between both of them less than an hour ago.

'Silly me, Emmy! Going on like that! Sor . . .'

'No, Liz!' she interrupts, 'No. You're not "going on". It feels better that you've told me something about yourself – you know, now it's not so one-sided. I mean, of course I'm not pleased you had such a hard time, but pleased you told me.'

'Fair enough. But you've just exposed your guts in those paintings, and here I am a few minutes later chirping on about my stuff. My old stuff. Bad taste, to say the least.' She looks hard at Emily. 'But I can see what you mean. Perhaps I should just say, that by the time Nat had finished with me, Howard was in another relationship and had a kid.' Now Elizabeth attacks her chicken with vigour, and takes a large mouthful. 'I'd always wanted children,' holding the food in her mouth. 'Missed the boat. How about you? Children? Want kids?'

Emily shakes her head, but her utterance is, 'Don't know. So much has happened in my life, as you've guessed, that bringing kids into the world might be a selfish or short-sighted venture. And I don't know if I'd have the . . . you know, maternal resources . . . .'

Elizabeth seems to be taking this in as she sips her wine, minutely nodding her head.

'We've covered quite a lot of ground, haven't we, Emmy? And I'm going tomorrow afternoon, back to the spires of Peterborough,' with a moan in her voice. 'Well, do you want to tell me more about what you've been through? After pud?'

They both laugh at this mention of pudding, knowing Elizabeth's love of puddings. A treacle pudding is steaming on the cooker, with extra maple syrup and custard.

But it gives Emily time to think, to think that she does want to tell her about the abuse, and about her step-mother's response. She senses that it won't take much explaining, given Elizabeth's intuition.

'But what do you think I should do about Phyllis's letter, Liz?' her eyes glinting in the firelight.

'Well, let her stew for a while. She didn't get back to you for ages. How about going to see your father? Sounds like you want to do that anyway, to see how he is? To see what he really makes of your . . . your disclosure?'

Emily nods. Phyllis's recent letter, its blue ballpoint writing indenting the thin paper, is lying on the rug between them. Both women are reclining on cushions on the carpet, each with a glass of wine. Elizabeth is looking particularly flushed.

She continues, 'And your step-sister – what's her name, Georgie, Georgia – do you think she was abused too, despite her denial?'

'I don't know. In many ways I don't think so. You know, her own grandfather, Phyllis's father, no . . . . I think I was a sitting target, desperate for love, perhaps I even encouraged him. Doesn't matter that much to me, about Georgia. She and I have never been close, never got on well. Maybe briefly it wasn't too bad when I was about nine or ten. Or eleven.

So, it's not as if we'd try and help each other, if we were in the same boat. No, it's just that if she was, it makes my story much more credible, of course.'

While she talks, she is taking in the way Liz strokes the base of her empty glass, the way the firelight is refracted through that glass, the way Liz's skirt, which she has changed this evening for a russet velvet – made from an old curtain which, she pointed out, has faded in sections from the sun – stretches over her full thighs, like soft hills. And the way her plump pink toes peep out beneath the hem so innocently, like a small child's. As usual her visual inventory is all-embracing, as if her life depends on it.

'You seem far away, Emmy. What're you thinking?'

'Nothing much.' But she feels churlish for not sharing her thoughts. 'Well, actually, I was thinking about a habit of mine: the way I always notice things about people, and things, all the time. Sounds crazy – but I can recall every detail of every visual thing: every juxtaposition of speech, and my thoughts, with the simultaneous visual perception, during our time together – and for that matter in almost everything I do. My thinking can get a bit all over the place, because of it. So, just now I was doing my usual visual inventory, but more than that, I was beginning to wonder if I'll always be compelled to do that, even when I feel that the stuff I went through as a child is more in the past, less present.'

'Well, I wonder how it affects you as an artist. I mean, it seems central to your vision as an artist, your particular way of seeing subject and object, object and ground – the way you don't privilege the one over the other. I mean, if you gave up your incredible attention to detail, what some might call indiscriminate attention, I wonder what would emerge.'

'I'm surprised you recognise that about my painting. This lot' – tossing her head in their direction – 'is more fluid, more spontaneous, more abstract. I think when I first came to Suffolk I had to start from a much deeper place within me, after nearly dying – well, nearly . . . killing myself. Twice, actually. Oh God, I've never told anyone that before, except a psychotherapist I saw once. Yes, really, but I don't want to go into all that now. I feel sort of ashamed of it, of having been suicidal. Maybe later.

'I know, at college my work was more intricate, more detailed: the microcosm, rather than the macro picture. But in the end it's all the same: whether we focus on a corner of the universe – you know, as Blake wrote, about a grain of sand – or try to encompass the whole mystery, it doesn't really matter: the details in the wings of a moth, or the mountains on the moon. The magma underlies it all until we discover something underlying that. But, more than that . . .' she pauses, to look at Elizabeth, to make sure she has her attention, before continuing, 'I'm fascinated by everything defining everything else, you know, how the space inside this glass is as present as the glass itself, the tension between insides and outsides not only in the world around us but within ourselves. The play between the inner and outer,' placing her palms on her cheeks. 'Oh, I'm going on too much. Not used to talking to anyone these days, and now I can't stop.'

Elizabeth remains silent, and then says, with a frown, 'You have . . . wounds, don't you . . . Well, we all do, but I think that when yours have healed, healed more, you'll move on to even bigger things in your work. Or perhaps the healing will be through the bigger things.

'And we still haven't decided about Phyllis's reply!' Elizabeth says now.

Emily is relieved, but registers a vestige of hurt that Elizabeth so easily left aside her excitement with the universe. 'Yes. Good thinking. I like the "we." But, before we leave my preoccupation with visual stuff, I wish I wasn't so caught up in it, you know, because I think it stops me thinking, and feeling. I've managed to shake off some of it, but it still stops me getting beneath the skin, to use your earlier metaphor, though in a different context.'

Elizabeth beams a warm smile at her, and says, 'You know what Brancusi said, about his relationship with Rodin? "Nothing grows well in the shade of a big tree." Well, I think you are already overtaking me in vision and output; other tutors at the Slade were similarly impressed, you know.'

Emily is not sure what to make of this, which seems like a *non sequitur.* And even without trying to follow the context, it feels far too big and unwieldy a statement.

Sitting cross-legged on the floor, propping her paper on a book, Emily suggests she draft a letter and then shows it to Elizabeth.

Elizabeth browses through tapes on a shelf. 'Mind if I put this on? Glenn Gould – my favourite version.'

Soon the precise notes of the Goldberg Variations fill the room with an inevitability, the spaces between the notes as clear and significant as the sounds.

'Oh God, this music . . . so . . . inventive. Mustn't let it stop me in my task,' Emily says, more to herself than to Elizabeth.

Within minutes she passes the letter to Elizabeth.

Dear Phyllis,

I'm sorry, and disappointed, that you can't believe me. I'm afraid that does not make me change my mind about what my body and my mind remember. If only I could just forget!

Perhaps there's not much more I can say on this subject.

Emily

'Perfect! I'm glad you've kept it simple; not engaged in a debate. That wouldn't get you anywhere, from what I gather about the woman.'

'Perhaps I'll just add "love" before the "Emily"?' She notices the Bach going back over itself at that moment, as if hesitating. 'Oh, I'm not sure. But no need to hurt the old woman. I know "love" is often a convention. I'll see what I feel in a week or so.'

They agree she shouldn't post the letter for two weeks.

1976

His hairless chest is like a boy's; his white belly hollow and vulnerable, half hiding shyly beneath his jeans. And yet, he is not like Rick all those years ago, before Marcus, despite some physical similarities. His hair is long, longer than hers, baby-fine and bleached by the sun in golden streaks. His lean, long limbs are rather like hers. Soft bristles on his upper lip and chin indicate that he hasn't shaved for days. But it is his eyes, the most sapphire eyes she has ever seen, deep and crystal clear with navy specks, that make her stomach sink as he puts an arm around her and kisses her. He kisses as if it is an end in itself with no further requirement. She smells his burnt coffee smell; his taste, like nectarines. She has never been kissed like this. Their tongues nuzzle each other, two primeval organisms seeking fusion.

He withdraws and takes a deep breath, muttering 'Thank you, Em'ly,' his eyes closed.

She has melted in his arms, so when he pulls away slightly she feels a knot of sadness in her throat. She wanted the kiss to go on for ever, wanted him to make love to her, while he seems content to just lie here with her now, facing the deserted sea beyond. The Aegean, cradle of myth, could be her beginning, she thinks – his eyes the colour of that sea.

She loops an arm around his shoulder, gently. And strokes his sunburn. She knows how hypersensitive her own skin can be when it's burnt, how fine the line between pleasure and pain. He looks skywards and smiles; his eyes close again.

She tries to follow his mood, for she is fearful of upsetting his equilibrium and the precious moment. She is watchful; he simply *is*.

Emily breathes deeply. An image of her mother, shining, resplendent, surprises her: eyes as blue-grey as Peter's are blue. Maybe that's it, she thinks; maybe . . . that's what I need, what I'm finding. Beauty, beauty that's bigger than me, that I don't have to worry about, maybe I can bask in it, and relax, and worship. The French word *'étonner'* – to be astonished – comes to her mind.

> *In a deep strata, the contentment of dappled sunlight on grass, a soft fleecy blanket bundling her in. The starched edge of her mother's open blouse endlessly stroked whilst she lolls at the breast, plump fingers and palm yielding varying degrees of sensitivity and bliss. The red lips smile and the sparkly blue-grey eyes reflect her own.*
>
> *But sometimes those eyes are empty, or are full of another, so she takes in the milk in a small empty bubble, her eyes rebounding from grey nothingness. And sometimes the other is too late anyway, she is all bad, everything is poisonous.*

She glances down at his thin jeans. The unmistakable bulge, and more than that, for the trousers are low-slung; the dark pink dome appearing at the waistband. How can he be so desirous, and yet not proceed? It makes her melt further, makes her want to stroke the denim gently, to feel that fat shape through the fabric, to arouse her hands in expectation of the place between her legs. Perhaps he does not like her enough, perhaps in their brief contact she has said or done something that disturbs him. No, she tells herself, perhaps there isn't always one outcome, one path. She tries to let him guide her.

She too closes her eyes, her arm still around his shoulder, her fingers stroking his shoulder from time to time.

The sun makes purple and red cosmic explosions behind her eyelids. A slight breeze cools her perspiration; she feels a prickle on her skin from dried salt, from her bathe earlier.

Having left the Jeep higher up on solid ground, like two children they had run down to the soft white sand, pulled off their few clothes, and galloped shrieking as if it were a race into the clear water. Peter looped in a shallow dolphin dive, while Emily ran and ran until the water tripped her up and she fell into a swim. The droplets of water as she splashed were like pearls, white sand below like moonlit snow, the small waves plump cushions on which to sway and float until she was almost dizzy with pleasure.

Neither had acknowledged the other's nakedness, though she had registered his almost hairless body and his heavy penis. She hoped that her small breasts did not disappoint him, but then he'd have noticed them anyway through her tee-shirt. Her shyness about her lower half, her thick hair and full bottom and thighs, compelled her faster into the sea.

Floating on her back, she welcomed the sun pounding down as she lay on the cool sea. She opened one eye a fraction to locate her new friend. He was nowhere to be seen. Treading water, she looked harder, called his name. Her voice evaporated in the vast space. 'Peeee-ter!' again. It was easy for someone to be obscured by the swell of waves. Perhaps he was playing a joke; she half expected him to surprise her by swimming underwater a long way. So she returned to floating on the water, to play a double-bluff by appearing not to notice his absence.

After a few minutes, she looked around again. He did not seem to be back on the beach. Perhaps she had been carried along the shore by the current. But no, the Jeep was directly in line, like a monument, up on the cliff. She began to think he was ridiculous to disappear like this. This was going too far, not funny at all. Perhaps he was a figment of her imagination, she joked to herself.

How easily an idyllic moment could turn bad. She knew how susceptible she was to things going bad, in a second. Drowned? What should she do?

She swam back to shore as fast as she could in a furious crawl, hardly drawing breath.

Pulling on the pants and tee-shirt she had discarded, she scanned the sea for him, the wind whipping her wet hair across her face. Climbing on a rock, she thought she could see a small shape far out, maybe a sea bird.

Watching beneath the shade of her cupped hand, she discerned someone swimming parallel with the coast. She was sure it was Peter. So few people found this bay. But why hadn't he told her? He was still between the two headlands, but wasn't it dangerous? She had realised he was a free spirit, but had no idea he was as liberated as this.

She felt relief, and then anger that he put her through this anxiety, regardless. Well, he wasn't to know that she was obsessed by death, was he? One minute she envied his sense of freedom, his ability to feel at one with the elements, to be true to himself. And the next, that he was thoughtlessly selfish. What would it feel like, to swim and swim, to see how much ground – well, sea – she covered through her own efforts, to see the shore recede, to know that she could decide to return when she wanted to. She knew she wouldn't chide him.

She pulled on her faded pink shorts and stretched out on the sand on her stomach, enjoying the late afternoon sun.

Awoken by a gentle stroke along the back of her neck, she lay still, amused at this stranger's ways, wondering what would happen next.

Through one eye, she observed him pulling up his jeans – he clearly did not wear underpants – facing away from her. His back was long and slim, his buttocks well formed. She felt a strong current running through her – maybe it was the firm sand beneath her *mons venus* – that made her long for him. She wondered what men felt about their own genitals. It occurred to her that he could be embarrassed, that he feared that some women might think it was too much.

Then Peter, too, lay on his stomach on the sand, not quite at right angles to Emily. His eyes were closed and he breathed deeply. She was faintly amused at his positioning, like hands of a clock stating a quarter of an hour. Their heads almost touched. She envied the sand receiving the imprint of his whole body.

Lying still, she pretended to be asleep. But her mischievousness broke through and she licked his shoulder with the tip of her tongue. Although the saltiness aroused her more, she tried to let this newcomer just be. He seemed to have such a strong sense of rightfulness that she wanted to let him rule, to dictate – so that, paradoxically, she was not the supplicant. She was weary of trying to give men what she thought they wanted, weary of trying to ensnare them, to have power over them. Now she wanted this man – who was almost feminine in his beauty – to teach her how to be.

And that was the moment when he edged sideways towards her, his body like the second hand of a clock moving rapidly until both hands touched, and, lying on his side facing her, this was when he first kissed her.

Later, on the evening of the bathe, they stroll along the harbour to choose a *taverna*. He holds her index finger as they walk, almost as if he were a child clinging onto a parent's finger. Except that his six foot height exceeds hers. She feels soft and glowing from the sea and his delicate touches earlier, in this, her favourite time of day, when the sun drops down towards the horizon, casting long shadows of their tentatively linked bodies.

Peter stops at a café that is less crowded than the others, chooses a table at the end of the terrace. She likes his certainty, his way of deciding what to do. He pulls out a chair for her, and when they are both seated he pops a shiny *kalamata* olive into her mouth, just like that, no questions asked. This is one of the most intimate things anyone has done to her for a long time. Other than that kiss. She is slightly shocked, but she eats the olive enthusiastically. While reading the menu she feels his eyes looking at her breasts, through her thin tee-shirt. Sensing her nipples' reaction, she resists hiding behind the menu, and states,

'Grilled sardines, with chips.'

'Me too,' he says, ordering a bottle of white Boutari when he gives the order. She hears the waiter asking 'Peanuts?'

'Peanuts?' she asks.

'He's asking if you want spinach,' Peter interprets quietly, his aquamarine eyes smiling.

'Oh, in that case, yes please!'

She adds, quietly, 'It's amazing that "spinach" can sound exactly like "peanuts".'

The waiter brings the food with a flourish as if it is a gastronomic feast. Peter squeezes lemon over her fish, pours the wine. She feels cared for. He passes her raw onion from his plate. She laughs that she'd better not be the only one to eat it. He looks out at the sea.

'"Wine-dark sea." Isn't that what Homer called it? Good description,' he says, almost as if talking to himself.

Unused to feeling so awkward with a man, she knows it is because she likes him so much. And because she has been out of the world of relationships for seven years. Perhaps she was never really in it. She fears that whatever she says will sound mundane, but she risks saying that it's amazing how quickly the sun sets, and how the sky is often more dramatic after sundown. He takes a gulp of the cold wine and looks at Emily, but does not say anything. She is learning that this man does not speak unless he has something to say.

He eats his fish with delicacy, dissecting with a surgeon's skill. What a mess her plate is compared with his. His long thin fingers are similar to hers.

Because it is making her light-headed, she decides to slow down on the wine. Sitting back to relax, eating chips with her fingers, she pours water for both of them from a carafe.

She wants this to be different, to continue to be different, in the way she feels it could be. So, perhaps, they won't sleep together. Maybe not yet. Maybe never. Even though she wants to. She must not try to lead him in that direction, but to see what evolves.

Over *baklava* and Turkish coffee, Peter puts a hand over hers on the white paper tablecloth. His large hand reminds her of the paw of a big dog, the way he rests it there, nonchalantly, almost as if he's not particular about where or how, but it's just a way of making contact. She's pleased that his hand is broader than hers, that hers feels pinned to the table. She smiles inwardly.

He takes care of the bill, writes in careful handwriting the amount of the tip, and frowns at her when she says she wants to pay.

On the walk back to her hotel up on the cliffside – or to his room in a house, up a lane into the village, she doesn't know yet – a few ragged clouds over the half-moon give it the look of a profile in a child's picture book. Its silvery gleam on the sea follows them on their promenade, seeking them out, in a way that used to intrigue her as a child. She doesn't know whether to share this thought with him. Being with Peter is like holding her breath, like having a marvellous present to unwrap, and she doesn't want to spoil the excitement and the potential.

In the *taverna* he had talked about his job as a town planner in Sydney. And how he had lived in north London for the past five years, settling in Chalk Farm, on the top floor of a Victorian house with views across Primrose Hill to the zoo, and iconic landmarks like St Paul's that he still could not believe were *his* view. He spoke of how he worked as a draftsman in a local authority office, but did not know what he wanted to do with his life. Maybe travel, to northern Canada, Alaska, perhaps Greenland, maybe Lapland – his grandfather was from Iceland – and then see.

He briefly mentioned the months he had spent in Japan soon after leaving university, 'Y'know, that was the beginning of my interest in architecture. I realised something that may seem quite obvious, but I appreciated their use of sliding screens or moveable room dividers – the basis for "open plan" – but, more than that, how porous their rooms are. You can hear everything, including what's outside – they don't often use glass, but sort of waxed paper instead – and so each room connects with the next. I found that very exciting: as if the dwellings were far more organic, and more connected with nature. I began to think more seriously about the necessity of architecture developing the essence of . . . the geography, or the spirit of the place. Oh God, Emily, don't get me started on all this!

'I want to open doors . . . in my life; not close them.' He was momentarily wistful, before re-finding his enthusiasm, 'Nowadays I'm intrigued by what people in flat landscapes make of the vertical, the high, the tall – when it's not a part of their everyday. I've read that there are even differences in the brains of people from different landscapes. Maybe I'll do some research into this, but it would be more like anthropology, or neuroscience, than town planning. Or, maybe I'll take another degree.'

She wondered if he was too dilettante, one of those people who are always onto some new thing, who never find satisfaction or depth.

'But why town planning in the first place? What led you to that?'

'Not sure really. I had a lot of freedom as a child, and as a teenager – liberal parents who gave me a sense that I could do whatever I wanted in life. My father was a chemist – a pharmacist – with his own shop, and my mother was mainly a housewife though she had worked as a secretary when she was younger. Perhaps they were too unconditional in their love for me and my sister.

'But, town planning. Well, I think I always knew I'd travel, leave the suburban life we led, leave Australia one day. And y'know, maybe working on plans for towns and cities was a way of always creating "home": a place in my imagination where I belonged, where I was rooted, even if I travelled. Don't know if this makes sense. Funnily enough, I suffered from extreme homesickness when I was sent to boarding school for a while, when I was twelve or thirteen. It was my idea, I wanted the life of sport and fun and companionship – but I became ill.'

He did not appear to notice the waiter clearing the plates and placing more water on the table.

'Perhaps I did bring a sort of idealism to the job at the beginning,' he continued.

Although she was interested in his analyses of what he said, she was more struck by his telling her so much. His ability to talk and talk, his assumption that he had her interest, was so different from her fear of boring people, or imposing on them.

'You know, ideas about ideal environments,' he continued. 'Townscapes that combined town and country, the natural with the man-made, the wild with the tame. Something quite formative for me was staying in Hellerau, near Dresden. It's a really interesting example of an early Garden City.'

'When was that?' she asked, although the date was not important to her. She wanted him to think she was latching on to his flow. 'When was it built?'

'Oh, it was begun in about 1909.' He looked at her. She did not understand his poignant tone, for it seemed to have nothing to do with what he was talking about: 'But I wanted to develop that cosy kind of suburb, to make it more exciting . . . to combine the vast and the tiny in scale, general areas juxtaposed with specific areas – you know, like, well, inspired by the way a complicated succulent plant with its rows of concentric leaves and spikes grows in a circular fashion, in a desert; or, rusted iron alongside smooth steel. So every walk through the district would give people the chance to marvel – if they had a mind to. Y'know, those details with which people orient themselves, rather than relying on street names and numbers. The opposite of the layout and feel of New York, I suppose.' He paused, and added with an unexpected weariness, 'If the plans were to pass the various committees.'

During the silence that followed Peter gulped his wine as if it was water, fiddled with a piece of bread, smoothed crumbs off the paper tablecloth. She watched, and waited, and took in what he had been saying. She wondered if the sadness she had perceived arose out of a sense that many of his ideas were not considered practical, or realisable – as if his talent was wasted.

He looked at her as if from afar, and said, 'What about you, then? I don't know much about you.'

'But we're talking about you now, Peter,' she replied, leaning forward, her elbows on the table.

He nodded, and gave a wry smile. 'Done me, haven't we?'

'No! Not by any means. Only just begun. It's interesting, about your ideals, and if they'll evolve into some other form now . . . in your work. Some of what you say is exciting, links in some way with how I see the world, you know. Isn't what you observe really another way of describing nature: the contrasts, the variety, the beauty certainly, as well as maybe ugliness, like the way things rot, or erode, or decay. And you want, partly, to introduce that in a man-made way, into a town?'

She noticed how he swept back the hair from his forehead, and looked burdened. Fearful that she was being superficial, trying too hard to respond to his ideas, she changed direction, 'But, but we can come back to all that, can't we. I want to ask you about . . . been wondering, about relationships – you know?'

'Oh, nothing like that!' he said light-heartedly, with a little laugh that sounded like a bark. 'No, I just do my own thing, a bit of a recluse.'

She didn't know whether to believe him, or if he was joking, or lying, or testing her reaction. Or keeping her out. Especially as he was so beautiful.

'Have you always been like that? You know, what you say: solitary?'

He looked at her in a way she was beginning to recognise, out of the corner of narrowed eyes, as if caught in his own thoughts and could only encompass her fleetingly. It made sense of their previous hours together. She began to feel that this relationship may bring more pain than pleasure, especially if he was not going to recognise her.

'I was quite young when I got spliced. We had a son – who's nine now. He's in Australia, with his mother, Stella, and her partner, and now, two half-sisters.' He drained his wine glass. 'I see him as often as I can, which isn't often enough by any means.'

'What's his name – your son?' she asked tentatively, fearing that she was getting into territory that he wanted to guard.

'Adam. Straightforward Adam. And he is a straightforward boy, actually. Never thought about him in quite that way. You know, his mother's brown eyes and thick dark hair, a gaze that's direct and engaging, a swift and sure muscular body. Clever, funny. Oh dear, but don't get me started on this, or I'll start crying!'

She took a deep breath, realising how much there was to this slip of a man who she'd thought of as not much more than a boy himself. She wondered if the swift and muscular body and thick dark hair, and the direct gaze, were also Stella's, and if that was what Peter had loved. She felt jealous.

This is when he put his paw of a hand over hers, and said that he was glad she wasn't one of those people who believed everything had to be about taking turns.

She was pleased he was pleased, but didn't quite understand what he meant. She felt sure however, that he'd be pleased if she didn't probe into everything, though, so she left his comment hanging in the air like a dead leaf suspended from a cobweb – or maybe, like a seed that would find fertile soil and grow, in its own time.

Near the nodding fishing boats, the tangle of nets on the shiny stones on the quay, the metallic *tick-tick* of taut wires and a faint smell of dead fish and diesel oil, away from the well-groomed yachts by the harbour wall, he puts his long arm heavily on her shoulder and gently strokes her skin. A current runs through her, down her spine.

She is noticing the whorls of colours, cerulean and chrome and magenta, reflected on the oily surface of the navy water, where it lies heavy and undisturbed between the boats; and the wiggly lines of the masts' reflections on less protected water. She feels like telling him about herself, about some of her pent up feelings that lead her to be here alone. At the thought of really talking she becomes slightly dizzy, yet she knows that not talking may play into the non-being that she is fearful of being with him.

She surprises herself with where she starts her story.

'You know, Peter – I like your name, it's a serious sort of name – don't like "Pete."'

He gives that bark of a laugh again, more like an exclamation of '*Hah!*'

'You know,' she goes on, 'when you talk I see things the whole time, alongside, wrapped up in your words. I see things before me, that make everything like a film that I can replay easily. Do you know what I mean?' Knowing he cannot possibly know what she means, she glances at him and thinks his expression in the half-light says, 'Go on,' so she does.

'You know I'm a painter. Yes? I did tell you, when we met this morning at the market. Took me years to be able to own being a painter, to feel I had the right to call myself that. Once, years ago, when I tried it out, I immediately spilt a hot cup of coffee over my silk skirt – jade silk it was, with a carmine silk sash. Ruined!' Peter laughs kindly and ruffles her hair.

She tries not to stop in her story, although she's distracted by his action, the unfamiliarity of it, the way it is both endearing and yet has echoes of not being taken seriously.

'I think I find my voice in my way of making art. I have to. If I don't I think I'm going mad. Well no, not exactly. That's a cliché. I think I fear, no, I know, that if I stop, if I don't paint, then everything will become amorphous, chaotic, meaningless. Not necessarily bad, but sort of blurred. A what's-the-point world.'

They are walking slowly now, his arm still round her shoulder, her arm looping gently around his waist.

She hates the silence that follows because she doesn't know if he's waiting to see if she wants to go on, or if he's disinterested.

Then he says, 'That's wonderful, that you have that. That you feel that. Marvellous, that you keep at it. Really.'

He doesn't understand, she thinks; he thinks it's just my hobby. But she perseveres, fuelled by the past twelve hours.

'Sometimes I don't know if I'm deluded, though,' she says. 'Don't know if it's a type of madness, this relentless need to

make pictures. And what's more, if my way of seeing things
and storing details all the time is crazy. You don't know half
of it . . . . For example, just now, in the *taverna*, I can tell
you exactly what my eyes took in while you were talking,
sentence by sentence. I don't just mean that I could imagine
obvious things, like the London skyline you described, but,
for example,' and now her speech gathers speed, 'when you
talked about those arctic places I saw mauve and purple
shadows on ice, craggy ice and smooth ice, sculptural ice
with holes in it, ice yellowed by the sun, grey and ominous
ice, horizons so far away because of the flatness, blue, blue
sky like your eyes and I thought maybe that's why you're
attracted to that part of the world, because of your genes.
And then, when you talked of Sydney, I saw the harbour
– bright blue with glints of silver – and the boats and the
Opera House, though I've never been there. I saw the offices
you've worked in, the big sheets of blueprints on thin paper,
the angled drawing tables, the angle poise lamps, the set-
squares and T-squares, the Rotring drawing instruments,
you wearing respectable work clothes – I imagined you in
a Fair Isle sleeveless jumper, predominantly grey. But no,
I mean something even more basket-case than all that, I
mean that when you said what your ideals were for a town,
I have a snapshot in my head of the plate on our table that
I was looking at, at that moment, with half a green chilli –
a particular green that I would make with chrome yellow,
white and a speck of Prussian blue – yes, half a chilli, and
one black – well, more purple than black – olive, catching
the light – an olive with a pointed shape at one end – and a
flake of pickled onion, all on that little oval yellow plate with
crimped edges. And some brine or oil in it.

'And you know, now, when I talk, I think I'm going on too
much, but still, the trouble is, I've given a plausible account
of something you may think is a typical painter's way, but it
isn't – it's more than that, it's crazier. My head is so full of
visuals, and they stop me thinking or feeling what's going
on. They're like. . . like, I'm beginning to realise, like blotting
paper that soaks up feelings and real thinking and provides

a web, or maybe a surface crust, of safe images that keep me secure in the world. Well, sort of. Now I've really gone on much too long.' Blown it, she says to herself.

He seems to be looking at the ground, at the flat smooth cobbles of the pavement. They have stopped walking, and are leaning against a heavy chain that blocks a road.

Then he says, 'Yes, but how come? Why? Do you know why? You probably do.'

She almost laughs with relief at his staying with her madness. 'Well, yes, by now, one failed marriage and several relationships later, and more . . . .' She's thinking of her suicide attempt and suicidal thoughts that were as second nature to her as sighing when things got rough.

'Lots really, lots of reasons. I'll try and be concise. Well, my mother died suddenly when I was four. I was alone in the house with her.' Emily sees a red-grey cloud, a smudge of overwhelming feelings that she can unpack into details, minute details, details that avoid all feelings, but she won't do that now. She goes on, fairly mechanically, 'In South Africa. Yes, we're both antipodeans. You didn't seem to pick up my accent.' She tries to see his face – he is still looking at the ground – before continuing. 'But yes, so, well, that in itself was the beginning of the end – my mother's death. My father then married a proverbially wicked step-mother, Phyllis. She's still alive. She brought Georgia with her – her daughter – who was, is, two years older than me. All that was bad enough, you know, because my Dad sort of lost the plot when my mother died, I think; I know I lost him too, at the beginning anyway. My mother was hardly talked about, hardly acknowledged. That was twenty-seven or so years ago, and maybe then people weren't that clued up about psychology. But still, I think my father was so grief-stricken that he couldn't help me at all.' She pauses. 'Should I go on?' looking at Peter. 'All too much?'

'No, Emily, no. I mean yes, do go on. That was all too much for you, you really mean. But why was it the "beginning of the *end*"? I mean, I can see it was unbelievably awful, but you seem to hint at something even more, even worse? Or am I being naïve?'

'You didn't realise what a ragbag of complications I am, did you!' trying to sound light-hearted. 'Better to find out sooner rather than later, I guess.' He smiles in a serious way that seems to invite her to continue.

'I really will conclude my monologue soon. But, yes, just to say, when my mother died, Phyllis brought her scummy father, Harry, into the family. He seemed nice enough – you know, into dogs and gardening and chain-smoking and betting on horses. But also into abusing little girls.'

She feels a tightening in her throat. 'And after all these years, I still feel . . . . He died when I was about six, so I only had to . . . was only abused for less than two years.'

She's angry with herself for the tears now, for the tension in her throat and her jaw, for all that spoiling this beautiful evening. Again.

Peter strokes her arm gently, then grips her firmly by the shoulder. 'I'm sorry, Emily. Sorry about all that. Yes, what a bugger, well, you know . . . !'

They both laugh at his choice phrase. 'Actually, I think he didn't do that to me, it was only my mouth! Only.'

'Perhaps you're grateful for small mercies,' he responded. 'No, we shouldn't joke about all that. Or perhaps that's all we can do now.'

She feels touched by his use of 'we', especially over all this.

'After all that, I don't think I've explained why I'm obsessively caught up in appearances, have I? But you've probably understood enough by now to see, to understand, that I clung – afraid I still do, though much less, believe it or not – to surfaces, to things, so that I was, am, sort of held by them, almost cocooned. No that's not the right word, that's too enveloping, because my obsession is more two-dimensional, more about surfaces which don't even have an interior. I'm both distracted and comforted by them. And then I used to draw a lot as a child . . . . Enough of me! Really. Shut up Emily Samuels!'

'Do you like the sound of "Emily Johansson"?'

There is a moment of silence while she holds her breath, and then, 'What! You're crazy! God, Peter, you do come out with some things. I don't know what to make of you,' shaking her head and smiling, glad that he probably can't see her blushing. 'I think you say things to test me, to see my reaction. Maybe it's a bit cruel. What if I took you seriously and you were only joking?'

'You're right, serious one. I shouldn't. Okay, no more jokes. But maybe it wasn't a joke. Y'know, I don't know myself. Was just sharing my thoughts. And you've got lovely skin,' feeling her upper arms with the backs of his fingers.

She registers that his spontaneous question, or joke, follows her outpouring. So perhaps she hadn't put him off.

Her grief-blurred face watches after he has disappeared from sight, as if to gain the last ounce of sustenance.

He had waved her off as she stepped onto the ferry, before he had to turn and run to catch the only bus back to the village.

She wanders around the cottage back in Suffolk in her overcoat. It is not particularly cold, but Emily feels a deep chill in her bones. A hot shower warms her, but then she has to brave leaving the cubicle. Soon she feels cold again.

And empty. She eats a bread roll ravenously. But it doesn't fill her up. And then she feels slightly sick.

In the evening glow of the lamp, she looks at her breasts in the speckled mirror, and caresses them. They feel cool and silky-soft. She imagines that her hands are his.

And all the time her heart seems to flutter like a trapped bird, she can almost hear the feathery whirr of wings. Crumbling the pocketed lavender that he had picked and given her on a dusty hillside, she extracts some grains and sniffs them, though they are almost fragrantless. She turns her pocket inside out and scatters the chafing seeds.

1977

'Peter, hi!' dissembling a calm appearance.

'So this is where you hang out? Wild woman of the woods!' as he brushes back hair from his forehead. She had almost forgotten those boyish good looks, his sapphire eyes.

'Yes, it is a bit like that. Remote, hey? – the place . . . . And me too, I guess,' looking down now, her last phrase emerging as a mutter. 'Sorry if I don't make sense . . .' *Here I am, apologising already – the last thing I want to do,* she thinks. 'Hardly speak to a soul. Thank goodness the taxi found this place. Must've cost a fortune. Drink? Toilet's through there. How was the journey?'

With a smile, Peter looks at her as if his vision is blurred, breathes deeply, before casting his eyes round the small space.

She hangs his jacket in the hall. All of a sudden the row of iron hooks looks so different, his big checked jacket rightfully there.

As nervous as a girl in front of a big assembly, she pours him a whisky, and one for herself, hoping it will have the desired effect. Gulping it down like medicine,

'Well? How . . . .'

Before she can finish her sentence, he pulls her to him and hugs her, tightly, so hard that she feels her ribs will crack, and kisses her roughly with a great hunger, kisses her neck and lips, not deeply, but like a blind man skimming the surface, reacquainting himself with what he has been missing, breathing in her smell, her warmth, her beauty. She is overwhelmed by his way of taking possession of her, and almost laughs with the pleasure, the outrageousness of his behaviour, when she feels they hardly know each other.

'What are you laughing at?' he says, eyes closed. 'You alright? What's the matter?'

'No, yes, I'm laughing with pleasure!' And she meets his passion with her own, allowing it to surge from her depths, allowing herself to find what she has been missing, too – her energy, her inspiration, to stoke the fire with him.

He pulls back, and then she does too. They look at each other properly for the first time today. He looks at her through slightly closed eyes, as she remembers from before, as if from afar. And she gazes deep into those clear eyes, and notices how sculptured his lips are, how naked they seem, and how his teeth felt hard just now although their tongues did not meet. She wants to kiss him again, but waits, to see what he wants.

He seems to want to savour her, to take his time. 'So this is where you've been hiding! Ah ha! Found you!' and begins to kiss her all over again. She goes with it again, and this time he finds his way into her mouth strongly with his tongue, and she knows that she could find this appalling, but she doesn't. Relieved and moved by the connection between them, tears come to her eyes at what is being expunged. Like a river that can flow at last, she is without fear of being pulled into a vortex, or of crashing and fragmenting over weirs and boulders.

He steers her towards the sofa, and presses himself against her. Finding her beneath her layers of clothing, in a few seconds he is beginning to transport her to pleasure that she cannot stop. Although she tries to, 'No, no, please, don't, stop, oh my God.' Continuing, he says, 'Do you want me to stop?'

'No, but, what about you?'

'I'm fine,' he says, and yet she can feel him, big and taut through her clothing. She doesn't understand why he is doing this, doing this so exquisitely, and not making love to her, but her thoughts are overtaken by ripples and then waves, and soon she is convulsing in his arms while he laughs with a dark brown laugh, and says, 'Do you really want me to stop?' She hangs around his neck saying she'll die if he carries on, and pulls his hand away.

She remains still for a few moments, and then she touches him, 'What about you?'

'What about me? I'm okay.'

'No you're not,' unzipping his trousers, and stroking him. Moving her head down to meet him, she kisses him gently, wanting to incorporate him, to give him all the pleasure her imagination can muster.

He ruffles her hair roughly. Soon he too is beyond the point of no return, then pulls her head to kiss her lips, tasting his bitter taste in her mouth, and kisses her all the more.

She has found a way of being with him that feels right, where the delicate dance between them is as natural as sunshine on a flower, the petals opening because that is the way it is.

They lie together in an untidy embrace on the old sofa. Peter soon falls asleep – a light sleep she thinks, from his breathing. Her whole body trembles from the miracle of the combination of the two of them. She thinks about his forcefulness, and the paradox of it not frightening her away: his assuredness giving her confidence and rightfulness. And yet, and yet, she puzzles, about 'him' – as she calls Harry nowadays – he was so bloody sure too, so insistent, so why, now . . . . ?

Peter half awakens, perhaps sensing her anxious thoughts, strokes her shoulder dreamily, moves onto his side to face her, and holds her tightly before slipping back into sleep.

She tries to sleep too, but knows she can't. She thinks that if Peter had been more tentative, cautious, it may have fed into her own insecurities, but somehow he – or was it she? – met like with like: a strong medicine as an antidote to a strong poison.

Thank you, Elizabeth, Liz, thank you, Emily finds herself thinking.

The late afternoon light is waning rapidly with the approach of winter. Over Peter's shoulder she sees the Virginia creeper framing the window, the leaves as if eroded by rust.

'What're we going to do tomorrow then? I want to see the sea. How near is it?'

'Sure. About half an hour by bus. Or much longer if the bus doesn't come. Won't be like the Aegean, though! Nor the Pacific for that matter. Have you seen much of the North Sea?'

'Only Brighton, and the sea near Edinburgh. Is that the North Sea?'

They stand side by side, arms over each other's shoulder, swathed in pullovers and scarves, facing a brown rolling sea. Peter has to shout to be heard above the crashing waves. He says he's never seen a sea this colour; he thought the sea usually reflected the sky – so why is it the colour of milky tea? She says that she thinks it's because it's whipping up lots of sand, but is not convinced by her answer. His long hair dances over his face from the wind; she wears a crocheted cloche hat pulled over her ears. They clutch each other more tightly.

'It's not always so grim you know!' she bellows. 'Can be calm, and even hot.'

'Suppose so. But I guess it made the English what they are: good sailors, and hard-working, and industrious, having to survive in his climate. No, I'm joking, Emily. I've spent months in Norway. I don't think this is that bleak.'

'Would you swim for a thousand pounds?' she shouts.

'*What*?'

She roars the question again.

'A *thousand*? Yes, you bet! For less!'

'How much less?'

'For . . . oh, five hundred pounds. How long would I have to stay in for?'

'Three minutes. Submerged. I mean, you're allowed to breathe!'

'Okay. Is that a wager then? If I swam now, would you . . . ?'

'No! I didn't mean to take you on, was only imagining!'

'What a pity.' He pulls a disappointed small-boy face.

'Peter, if I wasn't so hard up, I'd take you on. But, sorry – struggling artist and all that . . . .'

He lifts her off the ground and swirls her round as if he cannot contain his energy, looking at her laughing face, making her feel light and lithe and beautiful. And for once not awkward and too tall.

'Peter! *Peter!* Put me down!'

'Race you!' he calls, already yards down the beach.

She charges after him as fast as she can, determined to overtake. He tears ahead, until she drops on the beach, and lies there. He looks round, gallops back, and lies by her side like a panting dog.

'Wasn't fair, was it? I had a head start. You were pretty good.'

'For a girl.'

'Didn't say that.'

'But you thought it.'

'Don't know. Maybe.' He turns onto his back and looks up at the clouds. They too are racing.

They both lie silently. She can feel her heart beating strongly, the cold sand beneath her body, and a sensation like being on a boat of the world tipping and tilting. The reeling seagulls screech and a dog yaps at the water's edge as if trying to command the waves. A man strolls by in wellingtons, his posture implying a search for something along the shoreline. In the distance, clouds are evaporating, shrinking, defeated by the power of the encroaching blue.

Again, Peter seems to be in his own world. Like on Hyrdra. She is so unused to being with anyone for long that she cannot comfortably find her own thoughts as she would if she were truly alone. Instead she wonders what he's thinking, what he really thinks of her. She doesn't know how people ever combine a relationship, an intimate relationship, with intense work; how she could ever be in a partnership and still paint the way she does.

As if sensing her anxiety, he gropes for her hand and holds it firmly, still looking at the sky.

Maybe that's how people manage, she thinks, by scrabbling blindly for each other, and sometimes connecting, but still remaining separate.

Her womb somersaults when she remembers the night before, how they eventually found each other fully in her bed.

She had made up the bed with clean sheets, and was prepared to sleep on the sofa so that he could have the bed.

He laughed the next morning, 'Did you really think I'd have let you sleep on that lumpy couch? I would've sat in a chair all night, and then neither of us would have used the bed. You didn't really think we'd not sleep together, did you?'

'I don't know, Peter. Not that I didn't want to . . . but I was trying to leave it open, open to whatever you felt . . . . You know, on Hydra we didn't . . . .'

'Ah yes, true. But that was because you were going off the next morning, early. I didn't want to leave you sort of exposed, you know – after all you'd told me. You see, if you'd felt uncomfortable about anything, and then we go our separate ways. Oh boy, did I want to . . . .'

She nods, touched that he took what she had confessed so seriously. 'I thought you didn't really like me. Like me enough. Or that you were still involved with someone else, somehow.'

'Wrong on both counts. You silly thing! So little self-confidence. It implies that somewhere, hidden away, you think you're wonderful!'

'Rubbish! What makes you say that?'

'Read my Freud. No, seriously, I've found that people who think very lowly of themselves often idealise others, or secretly entertain fantasies of their own superb qualities.'

'*Huh*,' she says dismissively, but knows that he has said something that she needs to think about.

'How about fish and chips for lunch? If we're cold we can eat in a café, otherwise, find a sheltered spot on the beach,' she suggests.

They join a short queue in *Fish 'N' Chips* – its sign both bold and modest, for the letters are large and attempt three-dimensionality, and yet the soft blues, greys and white of the paint are flaking. Emily enjoys being a couple in a place where no one knows her, where they discover each other with every moment – even in the decisions of how much vinegar and salt, and her insistence on hot tea in plastic cups. Peter gestures towards the huge jar of pickled eggs in murky liquid high on the counter, and whispers in her ear, 'Grue-some. Like specimens in a medical museum.'

'Thought you were going to say, "They *grew* some eggs,"' she replies. 'You should see pickled walnuts – like kittens' brains.'

'What would those be, then?' indicating gherkins. She raises an eyebrow and purses her lips.

Meanwhile the woman behind the counter never smiles; her curls, like springs, are kept under a net to prevent escape.

They are both glad to be outside again with their bulging carrier bag, where they can laugh freely.

'If it was fragile porcelain they couldn't have wrapped it much better,' says Peter, passing a parcel to Emily. They sit on a bench in a bus shelter, to escape the wind.

'You should see this place in mid-summer! Ice-cream vendors, seaside knick-knacks, crowds, cars, windbreaks on the beach. You know, lots of red-skinned families – awful really. I much prefer it now.' She snuggles closer to him.

She thinks of all the things she and Peter don't talk about, about the two of them, about last night, about the alive feeling in her womb now.

The sun has finally burnt the clouds away. 'Rule, blue sk-ai-ey, blue sk-ai-ey rules the waves!' Peter sings tunelessly. Together they bundle the debris of the meal into a bin and run down to the water's edge to rinse their hands. She is not as swift as he, and her boots get wet. She dries her hands on her jeans, he shakes his in the wind. She notices that the sea has changed now, from brown to gunmetal, with brighter blue along the horizon.

They find a sheltered spot against rocks, and lie back with the October sun on their faces.

She notices Peter looking as if he could go to sleep. She envies his capacity to sleep anywhere. The night before she hardly slept. He seems to pull himself out of somnolence, perhaps not to leave her alone and wakeful again, and says, 'Emily, you know what you told me in Greece, about your need – compulsion – to hang onto visual details all the time. Well, for example, just now when we had lunch, were you doing it then?'

''fraid so! Now that you ask me, yes. I can recall everything my eyes took in while we ate and talked. Do you want to know what? The graffiti on the inside of the shelter, the exact details and colours of it – I could easily draw it for you; the cigarette stubs on the ground, the torn packet of *Benson and Hedges* lying in a corner, a damaged green *Smartie*, part of a match box, a *Wagon-wheel* wrapper, a piece of cellophane, oh yes, and pigeon feathers . . . .' She senses that if she expunges all this rubbish maybe she will be able to relax with him. 'Oh, and a crumpled tissue that looked like a dead dove. That's enough to be going on with, isn't it. So now you know. Bit of a nut-case, aren't I?'

'Okay, Emily, but what puzzles me is what happens to all that detail. How you store it all away. I mean, don't you get sort of clogged-up by it all? Or does it fall away after time, and disappear?'

'Well, I guess lots must fall away, and disappear. But I can still recall that sort of detail about loads of things from ages ago.'

'Well, let's try something now?' He has turned on his side, propped on an elbow to look at her. She notices grains of sand adhering to his wrist. 'Let's see what happens if you are here with me now, and of course you take in details, but the main thing is you and me . . . . The sky, the rocks maybe, the sound of the waves crashing, that sound of the waves withdrawing, rattling, over pebbles . . . our conversation, what that makes you feel . . . . You know, isn't that enough to . . . to fill you up? To satisfy you? So perhaps you don't need all the minutiae of whatever.'

'If it were so easy to give up the habits of a lifetime! You know there are reasons why I do all that.' She sits up; lying on her back felt too exposed. 'But yes, I wish I could give it up; I know sometimes I don't hear what people say, because I'm so distracted. That's awful, for me, but really for whoever I'm with.'

He puts an arm around her shoulder, gently pulls her back onto the sand, blankets her with his jacket, and breathes in the smell of her hair.

'I'll always remember this moment, the . . . completeness of it,' he says, as if talking to himself. She sees him half opening his eyes to take in a glimpse of sea and sky above her hair, sating all his senses.

She feels cared for. A bubble of happiness in her chest seems to float upwards, and then, as if suspended by it, she relaxes, and, in minutes, drifts into sleep.

'I'm glad I slept. Can't usually manage that . . . . Lovely, sounds of waves, on and on forever, like a gigantic heartbeat. I dreamed for a moment it was your heart.'

'Maybe it was.' He strokes the hair back from her high forehead, traces her profile with his index finger, softly, as if he was going to sculpt it. When he reaches her lips his finger stops, moves sideways along the top lip and then follows the lower one. 'Can barely feel your lips, they're soft beyond my sensory perception.' But she feels a tingle that connects with a shiver of pleasure between her thighs.

'Makes me feel something . . . deep inside . . . when you do that,' she confesses, pleased to be so alive after years of dormancy.

She can think aloud with Peter, possibly for the first time with anyone. She senses he has been able to do that with her almost from the beginning.

'Another cup of builders' tea, then, Em'ly! I think I'm becoming addicted.'

The same woman serves them from behind the counter, her freshly rouged cheeks, large nose and permed hair reminding Emily of Mrs Punch.

'Okay then, now let's complete the English seaside experience by having a cream tea,' she suggests.

They wander along the out-of-season shuttered seafront, past the forlorn grandeur of The Majestic Hotel, which looks as if it is beyond repair. Some windows are boarded up, a balcony hangs perilously from below a bay window.

'Enough to make anyone feel dismal – luckily I don't,' says Peter. 'Even the sun, after shining so strongly, has decided it's not the season. Surely we won't find a cream tea.'

Emily runs into *Bonbon,* a small sweet shop, to buy fudge. She comes out shrugging, offering Peter a cellophane bag.

'Nothing more disappointing than disappointing fudge,' she says. A memory of her Aunty Sarah's crumbly vanilla fudge seems doomed to remain a memory. Peter agrees, 'Too smooth, factory-made.'

They come to the Hotel Royale in the centre of the esplanade, its Victorian face triumphantly brilliant white. It looks as if it could never go out of season. A blackboard outside proclaims in capital letters: CREAM TEA'S, followed by a list of what is on offer.

'I wish they'd get their punctuation right,' Peter mutters. 'Do you think it means scones *or* bread, or both? And "*homemade* cakes" – do they really mean that?' Her spine tingles when he whispers to her conspiratorially, making her feel special and singled out.

They enter through swing doors and over brass polished stair rods. The place is vast and dark. Wondering if her eyes have not adjusted after the bright light outside, she discerns mahogany surfaces and ruby carpets. Something like lavender room spray does not mask the smells of stale cigarettes and beer. She and Peter separate to find the toilets, indicated by a gothic sign. Here there is the smell of disinfectant overlaid by fake pine.

She returns to a corner seat on an upholstered velveteen bench, next to a Babycham model of a deer. Her hair is brushed, her outdoor clothes bundled by her side. A young woman in a white apron jumps out of the shadows, startling Emily.

'Can I, can we, have a full cream – clotted cream – tea, for two?' She has become unpractised at using the word 'we'.

While she waits for Peter, she overhears a young couple sitting nearby. The woman is saying, 'Ooh I don't like snails – eating them with those little prongy things. *Ugh,* no.'

'I like oysters', the man says.

'Oh no, slithering down your throat, alive. You don't even taste them do you? I don't see the point.'

'Yes you do taste them. I like them. Like mussels.'

'Oh no, don't like mussels.'

'Mussels cooked in white wine, with herbs.'

'With crusty bread, a sort of soup. Yes, that's nice.'

Emily smiles to herself, recognising a former self in the woman. She thinks the man is rather like Peter.

'Y' know, you glow, it all goes to show,' Peter says when he returns, touching Emily's cheek gently with the backs of his fingers. 'Must be all that fresh air. Glad I found you in the murk. Like Orpheus descending to find Eurydice . . . .'

Even in this dull light, his dusty blue soft pullover brings out the crystal blue of his eyes so sharply that she feels pierced by them.

They talk quietly about the way these establishments never change, how there are 'English' places like this in Sydney and Johannesburg, providing an illusion of solidity and tradition, and affluence. She confesses unpleasant associations to stuffy tea-rooms just like this in department stores in Jo'burg, with their silver plated tiered dishes displaying *petits-fours* in lemon, mauve, pink, or blue icing, or coated with jam and desiccated coconut, each one decorated with a fraction of crystallised violet, or angelica, or a sliver of glacé cherry, nestling in paper doilies. 'And dainty white-bread sandwiches with the crust cut off, looking naked, a smear of fish paste inside, sprinkled with salad cress – brought by waitresses in frilly aprons,' she continues.

'Oh God Peter, how I hated those shopping trips with my step-mother: you know, to be bought a few babyish clothes not of my own choosing.' She looks dreamily into the middle distance. But then her eyes becoming radiant, 'But when we went to a haberdashery department – to buy ricrac, or bias binding, press-studs, hooks and eyes – I would stare at the rows of Gutermann's thread: shiny spools of every colour in all their gradations. It was thrilling, like buying oil paint nowadays.'

Peter looks at a woman walking through to the bar. Emily is shaken out of her reverie. 'On top of that Phyllis was always preoccupied with Georgia, or Alex, or Paul, and if the boys weren't there she'd be worrying about them. I told you about my half-brothers yesterday, didn't I?

'But Peter, listen. Coming to England on the *Edinburgh Castle* was just like this, this impersonal place,' taking his hand to claim his attention, tucking a leg under her and turning to face him. 'Only it smelt different. A sort of limbo, where I didn't belong, going from one insecure place to another. Like a piece of flotsam.' Her face closes in, her brow becomes ruffled.

Peter listens, and nods. She waits for him to contradict, to reassure, but he doesn't. Despite his attempt on the beach to shift her perspective, now he seems patient to stay with her way of telescoping time so that past and present merge. Or, is he just not bothered by my neuroses, she worries. Perhaps he doesn't care enough?

A waitress who looks about fifteen trundles a trolley up to their table, glances at both of them, and seems to perceive something about their intimacy. Her high colour becomes more florid.

On the trolley everything, including the jam and lemon curd, is on pretty pink and white floral china. The scones' irregular shapes suggest that they are indeed hotel-made, if not homemade; the Victoria sponge cake is moist and crumbly.

'I can see why the English keep up this culinary feast,' says Peter, sinking his teeth through layers of thick clotted cream, gooseberry jam, butter, and finally scone. He dissects his next scone horizontally into four thin slices instead of two, and concocts layers with double the amount of cream. He gives it to Emily, before making one for himself.

'Typical architect!' she says. 'My goodness, what a treat. After weeks of living off cream crackers – that's an oxymoron if ever there was one – and Marmite, or sometimes digestive biscuits as a treat. And apples.'

Her sense of oppression lifts – though more sparing than Peter in what she eats, she enjoys his appreciation, and begins to taste afresh, while over loudspeakers a guitar strums a familiar tune. The sound wraps round the counters and the chandeliers' fake candles, spreads over the button-upholstered banquettes, reaches up to the treacle-black beams with their artificially chipped edges, settles on the rough plaster, mingles with the cigarette smoke, creeps around the empty whisky bottles on display on a high shelf. Then come the words,

> *Blackbird singing in the dead of night,*
> *Take these broken wings and learn to fly,*
> *All your life*
> *You were only waiting for this moment to arise.*

This familiar song stuns Emily. And then the music fades, to become a background beat as general as the hum of a motor, while a row of coloured lights comes on above the bar in determined jollity.

The waitress offers to refill their teapot. When she has gone Emily pulls herself out of her dream, 'That girl makes me feel old, in a way – yet I can remember feeling just like that, so shy and awkward. Still do sometimes. But, just think, I'm probably old enough to be her mother. Biologically, I mean.'

'How old are you then? I know you said, in Greece – thirty-two?'

'Thirty-three now.'

'So young.' He becomes wistful and remote. He stirs his tea, though it does not need stirring.

She wants to check out his age, but is unsure whether to try to follow his sudden shift of mood. She knows how he can let her be. So she sits quietly. This waiting to see what emerges is not that different from the painting process.

The music becomes louder again,

> *Blackbird fly*
> *Blackbird fly*
> *Into the light of the dark black night.*

The notes of the last line are shocking in their unexpectedness, though she has heard it countless times.

Peter folds her trembling hand in both of his.

The next verse is almost unbearable:

Blackbird singing in the dead of night,
Take these sunken eyes and learn to see.

Her mother's eyes. That day in the kitchen. And she freezes, staring at a cricket bat propped next to a print of cricketers on a green, lit by a brass picture light.

'Hey, they've changed the order of the verses, as far as I remember,' Peter mutters.

But the music rolls on,

All your life
You were only waiting for this moment to be free.

Emily doesn't know if this is true for her. If she can trust Peter. How can anyone know, ever? Can she risk, dare, hope? No, safer to be free of anyone and everyone, with her own magical vision as her lifelong companion, and her painting. Like suppurating wounds, tears seep through her tightly closed eyes.

He wraps a long arm around her shoulders, and stays still.

She sees herself through his eyes, the beautiful cream tea laid out before them, the pot of tea going cold.

She can almost see the funny side, as she says, 'You didn't expect me to spoil it, did you. Sorry.'

'You nincompoop,' he says calmly, his Australian accent compounding the absurdity of the word, and of her. She remembers Liz Fell using the same word about her. Perhaps she really is a silly hopeless person.

'Well, I guess I'd rather be here with you than with anyone else I know, or have known . . . except, except, my mommy.' She buries her head in his shoulder and tries to suppress big sobs in such a public place.

'I guess that's a big compliment then,' he says gravely. 'I suppose if you've not had enough Mom, Mommy, you'll always want her, in a way.'

They both sit like this for a few minutes, silently. She is relieved that the music has stopped, replaced now by the insane clatter and razzmatazz of a pinball machine, which helps to keep her emotional juices in check.

'What does "enough" mean, anyway?' she thinks aloud. 'I don't think I know. Like, like when you leave, will I feel a great chasm where you were, or will I be able to get back to my painting and just miss you in an ordinary way?'

'I don't expect you want me to answer. When I go, I'll miss you.' He lowers his face to smell her hair, that fresh baby-shampoo smell. She senses that he is trying to shut out the loud clatter of coins of a jackpot from a fruit machine, accompanied by a triumphant fanfare, for he says 'Won't miss this seedy place though. Let's go, back to Dingly Dell or whatever it's called. Pick up something to cook tonight?' He seems gentler than she has known him, less aloof, more concerned, although he says nothing more about her distress. He gobbles a scone in one large mouthful and gulps down lukewarm tea.

He continues to astound her: how he simply is, without undue attention to her, and yet she doesn't feel neglected by him. Yet again she doesn't know what to make of the paradox, that somehow his way of being so firmly himself gives her more possibility of feeling rooted herself.

Smiling wanly, 'Are she sure you want to? Want to . . . be with me? Tonight anyway? When I'm such a mess?'

He wraps the knitted scarf that Liz had given her around her neck and pretends to strangle her, forcing laughter to break through her depression, 'Aaarh! Yes, Emily Samuels,' his eyes mock-scary wide. 'I, Peter Johansson, do solemnly swear that I want to be with you. Tonight anyway.'

She has been to find a bakery up a side street while Peter went to a grocery shop.

He rounds the corner with a huge bunch of white chrysanthemums which he holds downwards – as if they are no big gesture, just as ordinary as a bottle of milk – and a carrier bag of provisions. His eyes are the only bright colour. She notices the flowers. She never liked chrysanthemums, so uniform, dull, almost artificial. But she imagines placing them in a cream enamel bucket in the cottage, together with spruce and trailing ivy – too bad if Phyllis said it was unlucky to take ivy indoors – and making them look special, even vestal.

Later, as they sit on the rug in front of a wood fire, leaning back against the sofa, finishing their dessert of the apple pie which she had bought at the bakery, she says, 'Sorry about my gloom earlier today.'

Peter begins to interrupt, to protest at her apologising. She talks over him, something she has only recently been able to do. She is unsure if she is being unthoughtful by continuing, 'Been thinking, I'm now four years older than my mother was when she died. Imagine that. She was twenty-nine! So, so young. Each year that passes I'm outliving her, more and more, having what she never had. Especially now, when I'm happy . . . . Don't know if I can bear that.'

'In another way, you could say,' his tone becoming tentative, 'you are carrying on a life for her? Don't you ever think like that?'

'No.'

'Why not?'

She looks at Peter. It is the first time he has challenged her so directly. 'Don't think I have a choice. Can't just decide to look at things differently, you know!'

'How do you think people ever change then?'

'Oh shut up Peter. If it was so fucking easy . . . . You don't know half of it. You know, for example, I told you how my eyes take in everything indiscriminately? Well, as well as the usual detritus on the pavement, for example, I see the dog shit, the vomit, the different kinds and shapes of bird poo, the phlegm people have coughed up. Yes, sorry to be disgusting, but I've never told anyone the extent of my mad visual collections of everything. You know, I sometimes see blood too, blood from I don't know what, blood that can be beetroot-coloured, or orangey, if it's fresh.

'You see, you don't know how full of death I am, how I see it everywhere. Well, I used to. I think it's changed, though – gradually – since I left Marcus, since I've been painting more, since I've tried to confront my bloody step-mother, and to some extent my father. I know I can't be a victim all my life, can't live in dread. I know now that the bad "characters" that tormented me lived – yes, resided – inside me. I really don't want that. But still, death pops out at times, it's always somewhere there, like a gaping pit that I could fall into.'

She's determined not to cry, not to feel hopeless again. But nor does she want to be that tough soldier she can be.

Turning her head to look at him, she says in a soft little voice, 'Who are you anyway? What are you?'

He begins to smile.

'And don't laugh at me! Don't make a joke of things as you usually do!'

'Okay Em'ly, I'll be serious.' She doesn't know if he is trying not to smile. She looks away, thinking again that it is easier not to be in a relationship with anyone.

The wood in the fire crashes down as logs burn through and sparks fly like the filings of wax crayon from her pictures as a child. They both sip wine and watch the flames.

Peter puts his hand firmly on her thigh. She looks at his big hand with its long tapering fingers, how his skin contrasts with her amethyst silk skirt, and yet how the delicacy of his fingers suits the richness of the fabric, both blessed images somehow connected. She wonders if she is being fanciful, or, once again, caught up in visual distraction.

Like that time in the *taverna* when they had only just met, she senses his doggedness, his way of just being solidly there. She wishes he was more like her now, more mercurial, more reactive. And yet she knows that if he was, it really would be hopeless.

'I don't really know why I got so worked up just now. I just felt . . . felt you were trying to change me, to make me "normal", like you. Normal and . . . ,' biting her lip to censor herself.

'Boring?' And now he does laugh, heartily. 'Can't help laughing. Sorry. Not at you, but at me being boring. Maybe I'm heading that way. No one has ever said that before.'

She regains her view of him as a free spirit, swimming out to sea that day, pining for his son in Australia, his inspired aspirations for new towns, his passion for so much, including her, so what is she doing, making him 'boring'? Now she has an image of him not tugging at her to come out of her traumas, but saying simply that there is another world, where people want to be alive; and even if they have suffered terrible things, life can go on meaningfully for them.

'. . . all the more,' she says.

'What?'

'Not surprised you couldn't follow that,' she smiles. 'Just finishing a trail of thoughts – and it's difficult for me to say this, to own up – that thank goodness you haven't been traumatised in the ways I have. I now see you describing a world that doesn't have to be so hard – that if I can really come out of my fearful world, I might want to live all the more, to sort of make up for all the years of crap.' She sighs.

His hand on her thigh is not so wooden after all, not so impassive. He slides it up towards her groin, gently gripping her flesh beneath the thin fabric, and slowly moves his hand up and down her thigh. He closes his eyes and stretches out his legs. A glance at his jeans tells her something of his thoughts.

He turns towards her and kisses her. This time it is not like that first time, an end in itself. But he wants to be sure she is with him, as he feels her beneath her skirt, feels her in a giving way, with an intuition that astonishes her.

As he lies upon her before the fire, he throws off his warm plaid shirt and pulls up her jumper. Chest on breasts, he seems to devour her neck, her shoulders, her tongue. By the time they fully join, they are both intensely ready, ready to give up their separateness and to squirm and dance in an inside place that is also the vast universe.

Afterwards she cries with gratitude, and with sadness at so many years of paucity. When he kisses away her tears she protests,

'Peter, stop, stop being so kind, or I'll cry all the more. Can't explain . . . .'

'That's alright. You don't need to.'

'Explain? Or stop crying?'

'Both.'

She stops crying, for her mind has taken over again.

With Peter, she feels that she can really breathe, not suffocate beneath the surface of life.

That night she barely sleeps.

1978

From time to time Peter writes poetry, mainly about the countryside, but also about the relationship between a woman and a man. He has shown her some of his poems, stuck into a hardback notebook.

She finds one of them on the desk in his flat in Chalk Farm. It is typed, signed and dated. February 1978. It is called 'Venice', and is about a love affair with a dark long-haired woman called Colombine. Emily reads, 'Full lips stained with wine', cheeks with the flush of lovemaking that never fades completely, a woman with the look of being truly loved. Her long shining hair trailing down her back is the Grand Canal reflecting the lights at night. She sounds just like Stella, his ex-wife, Emily thinks.

The poem lies brazenly on top of his 'In' tray. She does not know if it is an inspiring poem, or if her jealousy emblazons it, but it is as if she has discovered him *in flagrante*. She wants to tear it up, or to photocopy it. She casts her eye over it again, noticing that it is at the time of the *Carnivale,* and that the poet's heart is 'harlequined' as he 'masquerades outside/inside unmasked'. At the same time as being shocked that he has had or is having an affair, she feels she has no right to mind. Why is she surprised? Of course she can't be good enough for him. She flirts with feeling relieved, because then she wouldn't have to bother that much. Of course, Peter was away in Italy in February, visiting a friend in Verona and then having a brief break in Venice, from where he sent her a postcard.

Perhaps he left this out on purpose for me to see, or, in his laissez faire way, he doesn't think it significant, she wonders.

He calls her to have supper. The table is laid with a bottle-green linen cloth offsetting the white damask laundered napkins. Shining Swedish cutlery reflects the light from fat cream candles squatting on a wooden board. There is a loaf of fresh walnut bread, and a salad of rocket and young spinach with fine shreds of raw beetroot in a large wooden bowl. He has opened a bottle of Chianti, and filled two glasses whose stems are as fine as drinking straws. She examines the candle flame through the glass, finding safety in being sucked into visual perception rather than struggling with the difficulties of relationships.

'Cheers, Em'ly!' holding up his glass to her. She quietly responds to the salutation, not wanting to spoil the effort he is making.

He does not seem to notice that she is subdued as he eats the pumpkin risotto and roast vegetables, and discusses if they should go and see *Wild Strawberries* at the Everyman.

Her retreat into colour and shape and abstraction does not prevent her from feeling beset with memories of Marcus's – albeit very different – infidelity: that all too familiar feeling of being a second-class citizen. And yet how she needs this to be different. So she summons her courage to say, as light-heartedly as possible, 'Peter, that poem on your desk, about Venice. Couldn't help but see it. She seems to have made quite an impression on you!'

Peter too now holds his glass up to a candle, one eye closed, to squint at the flame. 'Interesting, a city as feminine, as it is in French, and Italian. Yes, Venice did make an impression on me. You know it did. You know I think it's the most beautiful city in the world.'

She nods, trying to swallow her food.

'You're not jealous, are you, of a *city*?' He seems incredulous, and amused.

She looks at him, confused. She does not know if this is a brilliant ploy, a way of wriggling out of an affair, or if he was really writing metaphorically. She will have to re-read the poem and see if she could understand it that way.

'Sorry, Peter. Yes, I was jealous. She – or Venice, if that's what it is – sounds so different from me, so voluptuous, so rich, so warm, so deep. But, but, I know I mustn't be possessive – especially if you find something you need in, say, Venice, and yet, and yet you want to be with me now. I know that we can't get everything we need from one person. And yet sometimes, mostly, if I'm honest, I want to be everything to you, I want to be special, and I want you to be the main person in my life. But I also know that there's a danger of pinning you down and . . . and killing you in the process.'

'Hey, my lovely risotto is getting cold. Eat up!'

She puts her plateful in the microwave for a few seconds and pours herself more wine, while gathering her thoughts. She knows she's finding a way of being with this man that she has not known with anyone else, of being loved for what she is, but how hard she is finding it to love him for who he is.

'By the way, if it is a metaphor, it makes it a much better poem.'

'Of course. Don't you like the vegetables?'

'Now you're being insecure like me. Just because I'm not praising them, or you . . . ! Yes, I think it's all delicious. Really. Especially the small bits of crispy – what is it – butternut squash?'

She pours the walnut oil dressing on her salad. How enjoyable it is to be with a man who really can cook. And have such an attractive flat. And make love with such intuition and sincerity.

Not for the first time, she wonders what it would be like to have a baby. Would she have to fall into greater dependence on him – just what she senses he resists – or could she feel confident enough to follow her instincts, and sustain hope that he would be at her side.

She thinks of his dark-haired son in Australia, and the pangs that he feels for Adam. What if she and Peter went to live in Australia, for Peter and Adam's sake? She has a sense of the climate and the landscape, some of it similar to South Africa. She has pondered if she would want to leave the London art world altogether – even though she avoids it – and the big galleries and shows. And if she would still be able to sell her work out there. These thoughts are like a familiar journey, one landmark leading to another. What about her father, would she miss him? How often would she still manage to see him? Does he need to have her nearby, even if their relationship is not particularly close? She has had moments of thinking that could alter, since he and Phyllis separated.

Peter meanwhile has put on a tape of Mahler's First Symphony in the background, unaware that it is one of the significant works that helped Emily to find meaning in Suffolk: its insistent rhythm, at times too loud; the pulse of life almost forced, but ultimately, through the noise of all that, how she found a quieter beat – like the funeral march in the work – that epitomised her lifelong struggle with life and death.

Peter stacks the dishwasher before preparing fresh pineapple in delicate half-moons. Overlapping segments curl from the centre, round and round to reach the edge of a large blue and white Moroccan plate. He casually places this offering of love on the table, like an exotic flower, with a small jug of syrupy Cointreau. She smiles inwardly.

His way of looking after her so well takes her back to thoughts of having a baby.

Babies. Years of barely acknowledged sadness when her periods came; her many dreams of breastfeeding a baby, often of neglecting one – realising with a shock that she had not fed him or her; her awe, and increasing fascination, with other people's babies and small children, although usually at a distance. And sometimes sadness, sadness if she was not to have a baby of her own.

Her niece Alice, Alex's daughter, was the first baby, and then child, she has been close to. Fearful of holding her as a very new baby, she was sure she would cry, that she needed her mother all the time. Through Alice's mother – Chloë's – gentle encouragement and permission, Emily found her own capacity to relate to this miracle with pale lilac eyelids and touch-delighting skin. She sensed that untampered quality, which she could barely bear to dwell on, and marvelled at the tiny packaging, the knowledge that within that miniscule body were not only miniature tubes and gullies, ligaments and culverts as thin as tissue paper yet far stronger, soft bones, kidneys, a heart, and so on, but ovaries miraculously already containing minute eggs, and a womb. The future generation unbelievably laid down, and within that, further generations, like the design on the Royal Baking Powder tin, intimating infinity. That is, if baby Alice chose to put all that to use. And if she, Emily, chose to take such a momentous step, of giving life to someone: life with its pitfalls, uncertainties, blind corners, the complete absence of any guarantee.

Could she meet her own baby's needs, or would she be having a baby for what she senses are the wrong reasons: to meet her own needs, to be loved and needed by a small snuffly creature. But perhaps she and Peter could work that out, and round-faced plump Chloë would be around. And Liz Fell, like an eccentric aunt, always seeing the potential in Emily, maybe she too would be somewhere there.

Fears that Liz would be envious if she had a baby, never having had one herself, have been lessened by elliptical conversations and encounters with her. Once Liz said she had 'missed the boat'. Living with another woman for a time had not helped her to make a family of her own. Emily senses that just as Liz supports her creativity in her painting – like an engine at times pushing her along the tracks – she would continue in that vein in other areas. Yes, Emily thinks, Liz is one of life's facilitators, not exactly living vicariously, but finding real satisfaction in watching, caring, and helping others grow.

That evening, Emily wants Peter to take her in his arms. After dinner he clears up, while she stretches out on the sofa and reads his Ruskin on Venice. He comes and sits quietly in an armchair, and begins to read the newspaper.

'I'm tired tonight, Peter. Think I should get back to my place; early start tomorrow.' She yawns languorously. 'Oh dear, yes, look at the time.'

He stands up and briefly ruffles her hair, muttering 'Sorry we didn't make love.'

She senses that when she is needy she becomes unattractive, as if she has a stale smell about her. And yet she knows how easily Peter can alter all that.

He finds his coat and scarf, to accompany her to her car, saying something almost to himself that she cannot fully catch, but it sounds like, 'There's nothing worse than feeling one has to make love. It's wonderful when it just happens.'

She is perplexed. She still doesn't understand how this magic can just happen, and yet of course sometimes it does, she knows. But why can't she ignite his spark? Why does she wait, like an open flower, to be visited by a bee? What is she – or is it he – afraid of, she wonders.

Now he looks particularly striking in his brown felt fedora and long red cashmere scarf that she had given him – like a Toulouse Lautrec poster. Jovial and gentlemanly, he swoops her long skirt into her orange *Deux Chevaux* before gently closing the tinny door for her. Through the closed window he taps his lips querulously. She opens the flap of the side window and they kiss briefly on closed lips. Determined to show her independence, she accelerates harder than usual as she drives away, although the little car sounds like a lawnmower.

She can still feel the imprint of his soft but firm lips as she observes in her rear mirror that he has turned, and is not watching her drive off.

1979

Her belly is tight, swollen with heavy life, as firm as an unripe mango. It is so stretched that the navel has popped out, truly a belly button. From time to time a hard almost pointed bulge moves out sideways, subsides; another fatter shape pushes up centrally before slowly sinking down. Then stillness. But if motionlessness continues too long, she worries, 'What if . . . ?'

At times she fears that there is not enough to protect the baby from shocks and bumps. Only a thin covering of tight skin covers it. She doesn't want this baby to be as thin-skinned as she is.

She marvels at how primitive pregnancy is: so natural that it feels almost unnatural to return to a primordial process, with all its dangers and uncertainties. She senses that she has lost her connection with her deepest biology, and her connection with her mother. If Mommy were here, surely it would be different. But then she smiles at the memory of her time in Suffolk, her way of finding a deep connection with nature.

At seven months of pregnancy, Emily dreams of ripe figs the colour of dark amethyst, squeezed open, their visceral purple-carmine interiors looking bruised, and yet with a sense of rightfulness. Of course, a purple fig's interior would be so dark, she imagines, like the colours of a woman's genitals beneath the skin.

She feels glad to have had such a dream.

PART FOUR:

MOTHERHOOD

1980

Fresh and slightly wrinkled like a windfall apple, a gift from she knows not where. His forehead bears a soft frown; his minute chin, the size of Peter's thumbnail, an exact replica of his father's. His lips curl up in the corners. He is in his own dark womb-world, safely furled in papery flaking reddish skin – except for brief moments when his arms fly out as if taking sudden flight. He muzzles her breast, blindly finding the nipple, and latches on as if he has been doing so for months.

Emily does not want to wash off his womb stain, like burnt sienna, in his creases and hollows. She can relate to the long stick-thin limbs, her own thin legs and arms mocked all her growing-up years. And now she and Peter have made their own stick-insect that can be loved and nourished, and that may eventually fill out.

Expressions visit his tiny face like gusts of wind ruffling water, before it settles back to peaceful being. A moment of utter anguish, or grief, a little later a smile, then a yawn that almost turns him inside out, or a grimace as if his whole body is wracked with poison. She holds him and watches, incredulous at this repertoire, offering soft murmurings. *How does he know? Where does it all come from?* 'Baba, little baba! It'll be alright!' Her expressions change too, more frequently than his, from amusement, to rapture, to wonder, to concern, to curiosity, to fear, to disbelief, to delight.

Phyllis visits Emily in hospital, hardly looking at the perfect little creature slumbering by his mother.

'*"Jack,"* what kind of a name is that?' Phyllis asks, proffering a box of liqueur chocolates.

Emily phones Peter in tears, 'Phyllis just visited. Perhaps she minds that "Jack" is like "Jake". She barely looked at him. Goodness knows . . . . But then . . . I feel so, so, liquid! Don't know what's the matter with me. Can't wait for you to take me home.'

Her father comes to visit, separately. He beams at her and at the baby, hugs Peter warmly. She tries to ignore the sour smell of whisky on his breath. He brings a small carving he has made for the baby, out of the trunk of a gorse bush. It looks like a dragon, the swirling wood almost white except for some dark gnarled knots. She remembers his hands when he used to garden, and how he would crumble the soil to break it up. He seems too rough now, his chin so bristly, hands like sandpaper, so different from the smooth baby and her own soft self. She does not know what she feels about the carving.

In a haze of adoration, of sleepy pink and mauve and cream, watery cerise and lilac dreaminess that she will paint one day, she cocoons herself and her baby, not allowing the nurses to care for him. Within twenty-four hours, Peter takes them home to their flat in Chalk Farm.

There, she and Peter spend hours in their king-size bed under the goose-down duvet, in the dead of winter, with baby Jack brightening the darkness. Winter sunshine glows gold on the white curtains, casting shadows of the candelabra with which Peter lights the nights. Time is measured by the tides of sleeping and feeding. Emily feels they are like a family of mice, snuggling under the covers, involved in serious nest-building.

She and Peter dine on softly boiled quails' eggs dipped in salt, nibble the finest macadamia nuts, eat the most delicate Beluga caviar, the finest Alaskan smoked salmon, sip the best champagne – although she has little of that because she does not want what is already a heady experience for her and baby Jack to become distorted – and eat *blintzes* stuffed with cream-cheese from a Jewish delicatessen, for this is the time to indulge delicacy and fancy. Sometimes all she eats is freshly baked olive bread – which Peter forays to Islington to find – smothered in French butter. One night he ventures to Golders Green to find real Jewish chicken soup with *kneidlach* for her (and for Jack, for he is feeding from her lustily). 'Your hunter has returned, fair maiden,' he announces from the hallway. And figs, fresh figs in the middle of winter, which Peter jokes come from the Smyrna merchant, but which he had asked a friend to get at Fortnum's.

All this emphasis on feeding, because Jack and Emily (and Peter) are working out a pattern of supply and demand, or, more usually, demand and variable supply. But Jack is quite tolerant, and even patient.

She leaves the phone off its hook, despite Peter's occasional pangs of anxiety that someone could be trying to contact him. But he knows that what they are both doing has to be given its life-blood; he wants to be here to provide the roof over their heads and the ground under the baby's swaddled feet, to be here for this baby boy with his blurry beginning-to-focus eyes, eyes that are dusky blue, hanging onto his mother's nipple.

And she, she sleeps and dreams and smiles and oozes tears and milk and blood, and knows that the feel of Peter's taut skin and silken hair and his male smell enables her to be in this strange new world with Jack, a world she knew once in what feels like a previous life. Her breasts fill up, almost concrete-hard, when the baby sleeps a long time; sometimes she gently places him next to a leaking nipple, 'Come on, Jack, Jack Spratt, you're out in the world now, y'know, you have to work hard sometimes, help Mommy to feel comfortable . . . .' When she hears him crying in the night her breasts respond before she has decided what to do, like a tap turned on.

'Peter, darling, should I have a bath?'

'Don't know. Up to you. I can help you . . . . '

'What about Jackie?'

'What about Jack?'

'What will happen to him . . . if I have a bath?'

Peter can enter her world, and yet be in the other world of rationality. 'Well, my love, I can pass him to you in the bath. Or look after him . . . .'

After a few minutes that could be a few hours – for who is looking at a clock? – Peter puts down the journal he is reading, and says, 'If you'd like a bath, a gentle warm bath, it may feel good – y'know, sort of a time for you to find, to refind, who or what you are.'

How does Peter know? How could any man know that this bath would be the first time that she fully realises, since the birth of Jack – no, since four or five months into the pregnancy – that she is separate from this wondrous creature, that Jack is not part of her, but out there, separate, overarched by Peter and herself.

Lying in the warm water, she touches her soft belly, like a deflated balloon, and realises that there is no baby in there, no movement of another, although, like someone after a long sea voyage who feels that the ground is moving, there are moments when she thinks she feels some stirring. She touches her ever replenishing breasts and marvels, marvels at their beneficence and bounty, and thanks God. Incoherent thoughts about her mother, about missing her, wishing she could see Jack and her and Peter, bob around in her mind. But maybe she can see me, in a way, through my thoughts, she thinks.

Warm tears course down Emily's cheeks, over her full breasts, to merge with the tepid bath water, water with traces of breast milk, semen, and blood. All about life, she knows. Not death.

The afternoon sunlight is fading through the frosted glass, giving the bathroom a gloomy tint.

She pulls herself out of the bath, her frame heavy, and enfolds herself in the soft white towel Peter has placed on the hot towel rail. Urgently, she needs to return to Jack. Is he crying? Or, if, what if . . . . She almost stops breathing, and rushes out to find him.

There he is in his wicker crib at her bedside; his soft aqua blanket – almost the colour of Peter's eyes – snugly as high as his chin. Pink and resplendent and perfectly content, he stirs slightly. She breathes out heavily and returns to find her dressing gown and sanitary pads.

In the steamed-up bathroom she realises she had not noticed if Peter was in the big bed – where he spends so much time these days with her and the baby. But that is the way it is, she tells herself; he can look after himself. She gives a small laugh, more an exhalation of air, at how relaxed she is in believing his being somewhere in her new universe, a universe that feels like a discovery of a place from which she was expelled and to which she has returned.

Peter finds himself comparing this soft fair baby with dark Adam, thousands of miles away, and knows this is his second chance to work at being a father. But being here for this baby does not make him feel better about Adam. With a pang of concern for his firstborn, he feels, as he often does, that he is letting him down. He makes a silent promise that he will go and visit Adam, preferably with this new family, as soon as it is feasible.

Peter has to return to work in the town-planning office in Camden Town when Jack is three weeks old.

Maybe it's just as well Jack isn't a girl, Emily thinks weeks later, for she would have been too strongly reminded of her own babyhood and what she had. And what she lost.

Emerged from the cocoon of early infancy – although sometimes he compacts himself and recreates it – Jack is long-limbed and quite thin, but she knows he is healthy. He has a good appetite, his eyes latch onto hers with consummate curiosity, and sometimes he smiles. The most beautiful smile in the world. And then the smile disappears with the suddenness of an apparition.

The beams become more frequent: first with his eyes, a raising of one eyebrow, and then a chuckle breaks out in waves over his whole face and through his body, reaching his fingers and toes, and he becomes one big fat laugh. He is all there, in body and soul.

She and Jack are alone for hours every day – although on some days Peter pops home for lunch, bringing fresh rolls and sometimes thick soup from an organic café.

She carries Jack in a sling, and walks on Primrose Hill in all weathers, quite enjoying defying the elements: the two of them, almost conjoined, beneath thick coats and macs. What would it be like to have a baby in summer, she wonders. She notices the way figures and trees and dogs always make satisfying pictures, sometimes silhouettes, in this particular park: how the steep hill emphasises everything on the edge, against the bright sky, a tableau that she might paint one day. The phrase 'on the edge' makes her heart beat faster. It reminds her of that ridge of land in Suffolk, as she approached the sea, always dotted with silhouettes of people.

Yet the idea of drawing or painting feels like another world. She sketches Jack one day though, to capture his repose: his round cheeks and big brow, the soft wisps of hair, her crayon as delicate as a breeze brushing the textured paper.

On one walk in the slant winter sun she catches herself seeing crimson carcasses of bloodied meat hanging from a climbing frame in the park – dead pigs, or skinned sheep. Almost immediately she knows they are little girls in pink and red coats and trousers. It unsettles her to have had such a fantasy.

Emily meets up from time to time with two mothers who she knows from the ante-natal classes. Susanna has had her third baby, and exudes an American exuberance and optimism matched by perfect teeth and glossy hair. Emily may have stayed with this friendship, for she finds Susanna's baby girl lively and attractive, but this young woman seems to assume that Emily is another satellite to her central position in the universe, exemplified by her always setting the venue, and basing the rendezvous around her baby's sleep schedule. Louise, in perfect contrast, is mousey and a ditherer, never looks directly at anyone, and Emily feels is probably quite depressed. Permanently overweight, Louise tugs repeatedly at her jumper to hide the rolls of fat around her midriff. Her baby boy has a wan pasty look despite gaining weight rapidly on bottles of formula. Emily feels sorry for this mother, but realises she doesn't need to take on her troubles as well as her own; she vows to make some excuse the next time Susanna suggests a meeting.

Watching mothers in small groups talking to each other, in cafés or in the park, pushing their buggies, laughing, toddlers running between them as if of one extended family, Emily cannot always work out which little one belongs to which mother. Despite the mothers seeming younger than she, they have a confidence about them. She sidles into *Tumbling Tots,* a Noddy's Toy Town place, all bright colours and soft shapes and slides, for small children to climb like mountain goats. She feels a usurper, with her papoose, which has hardly separated from her.

In her unreal world, she increasingly wonders if she is a real mother. Is she allowed to be one? Who gave her permission? Certainly not Phyllis, and not Georgia, and maybe not even her own mother, for she disappeared long before completing her own tenancy as Mother. And her father? She does not know about him either.

Despite Jack being delightful, and Peter providing a strong frame within which she can regain her strength and mother Jack, she feels increasingly unsure about this little baby. There is something indefinable that impinges on her, like a shadow of a ghost: something threatening, maybe phantasmagorical, but menacing nonetheless. She fears that it is her incapacity to be really there for Jack, to be good enough, and that her old familiar void, the *no-Mommy-nothing*, is, at times, beckoning her or enveloping her.

She dares not mention this to anyone, not even to Peter. Nor to Liz Fell, who she does not want to disillusion, when Liz has such faith in Emily. And certainly not to the perfect Susanna. Her doubts spawn further doubts. Did she trap Peter into all this, with a false promise that she could fulfil her part of the bargain? But what if, now, she really cannot go forwards with this baby – what if it's all too much? What if she wanted a baby for the wrong reasons – to be adored, or to cuddle? What if it's too late: what if Old Man Harry's clutches go even deeper than she realised? What if her mother's absence is a void that can never be filled?

One day she phones Liz in a rather desultory way, not wanting to impose.

Liz sounds pleased to hear from her, and asks warmly about Jack.

'Yes, Liz, fine. He's doing well. You know, they weigh him at the clinic every week – well, every second week – and he's gaining nicely.' Already she feels she's venturing into that mothers' only territory of nappies and feeds and weight-gain – her words sounding hollow – which must either be boring or excluding for non-mothers. As she talks, she feels she's on a crumbling spit of land with sea on both sides. She doesn't belong in the mother-world but she can't go back to the no-mother place. Grappling for something more real,

'But, but, the whole thing, you know, of a baby, of . . . such isolation – admittedly, such joy too – to be honest, at times I'm not sure about it all, you know. Especially with my background, history, you know. Sometimes I even think . . . I've made a big . . . mistake.'

Liz is silent for a few seconds. Emily holds her breath. Then the older woman asks, 'Painting? Are you painting these days?'

She feels that Liz is being ridiculous. How could she possibly be painting, when her brain feels like porridge, when she hardly has time to change her underwear, let alone paint.

When she never knows if Jack will wake in five minutes or five hours. These women who haven't had babies. All she says is, 'Oh no, no way! Out of the question. Couldn't imagine finding time to file my nails, let alone . . . .'

They both recognise the chasm between them.

Liz asks if she would like her to visit. She could stay with her cousin in Finchley, and see her whenever suited her. 'I was going to get in touch with you anyway – you beat me to it.'

Emily feels a well of emotion rising in her chest, unsure if it's the flood of hormones and breast-milk her body is producing all the time, or if she is genuinely touched and hopeful at this friend's offer. The next moment, she thinks that Liz is so out of touch with the demands of motherhood that her visit would be disastrous. She doubts if she or anyone can be any good, for the despair runs so deep.

But she replies resolutely, 'Great. That would be good. Yes, please. If it's really alright with you? You haven't seen the baby since he was one week old.'

They agree that Liz will arrive in a week's time.

Peter asks that evening what sort of day she has had, and if she had a nap. She feels furious that he should think she had time for a sleep – even if in fact she had – when she had to deal with the man who came to fix the boiler, had to go to the shops, and collect the dry-cleaning, let alone all the baby's demands, and . . . . He hasn't a clue.

Biting back her frustration, she replies in a measured tone, 'Jack and I had quite a nice day. I did the washing, and then, oh yes, then we went shopping in Primrose Hill, and took back that Babygro that's too small, you know, that Alex and Chloë gave him, and then we came home, and Jack had a feed. And then he was very bright and played on his mat, and then . . . oh yes, then we both had a nap. And then Liz phoned, and she's coming to visit in a week's time.' Emily has an image of a neatly clipped but dusty box hedge as she talks, her lacklustre account in keeping with her pale face and drab loose clothing. She doesn't want to tell him that it was she who phoned Liz. Peter, usually so sure of himself, is now uncertain.

'Em'ly, yes, but, how're *you*, really? I know this can be a strange time . . . . Don't want to say too much. Maybe you can tell me how you really are?' He looks into her eyes searchingly, leaning forward on his elbows on the table.

She gazes at him across the candles he has lit, and the checked table cloth, across the spinach, orange and walnut salad he has prepared so beautifully, through tears that blur all his efforts and betray her attempt to appear alright. She wonders if she could, or should tell him. But how terrible to let him down.

Oh yes, Peter has had outbursts from her, middle-of-the-night despair, tears, late evening exhaustion when Jack would not settle and she thought she had run out of milk, but not the full extent of how she feels nowadays. All that cosy blissful time before Jack was born, and afterwards, crashing down because she is derailed. *But, but, maybe it's worse to dissemble.*

'Don't want to let you down, Peter. Jack is the most wonderful baby in the world, I know that. I've no doubt about how much I love him, how breastfeeding is the most perfect thing I can do, how rightful, even sensual, how it makes my whole body tingle, but . . . sometimes I don't think I have it in me to go on, to go on meeting his – and your – needs, because I feel sort of dry, dried-up at times, empty. Nothing more to give. Even bad . . . at times . . . inside. At times, I doubt if my milk is any good.' Sobs interrupt her speech. She struggles to continue, 'Now that I'm being honest, it's when he cries and cries, and what I do doesn't sort him out, when I know he doesn't just need the breast shoved at him, but something else, that I feel desperate, and so inadequate, and even, even . . . angry . . . and rageful . . . and murderous towards him. Don't worry, don't think I'd actually do anything, but the thoughts shock me, frighten me.' Now she begins to cry, holding her face in her hands.

She knows she cannot tell Peter about the occasional terrifying chasms in the whole structure of her love for the baby, when she sees Jack's solid head with its raised blue veins traversing his forehead and skull, and she thinks how easy it would be to kill him. How she quickly stops in her tracks, and makes herself do something practical. Or, sometimes, manages to find something beautiful in the baby that she loves.

Peter stands up and puts his arm around her shoulders. Through her sobs she forces herself to state, in bursts, 'Jack *has* all this, mostly . . . . You know, breast feeds, and all that . . . and still he complains . . . . It's not only when he's crying, but sometimes, even when . . . . he's calm, playing, kicking, whatever, that I . . . . I don't know if I can go on giving to him . . . past the age of four especially . . . . I should have thought of that . . . before having him, but there's a . . . nest of vipers ahead for him . . . and for me. And for you too.'

Peter stays bowed over, still and close, his cheek on the top of her head. 'Em'ly, Em'ly', is all he says.

They both hear Jack waking, at first a creak of a cry, then silence, then a whimper which opens out into a loud demanding bellow. She wants to block her ears. Her crying increases.

'I'll go to him if you like, keep him from getting completely demented, for a while, 'til you feel like taking over? You know I can't keep him happy for long. Wish I could, sometimes!'

She thinks but does not say, I bet you wish you could! I bet you think you'd be so bloody good at it all. And you would be too.

The baby's cries become more desperate. Peter gives her shoulders another squeeze before leaving the room. Holding her breath, she hears him from the next room, saying softly, 'There there little chap. Not as bad as all that. Come on then. You'll just have to make do with me until the milk van comes along. Sorry ol' chap, I know it's tough. There there . . . .'

She begins to feel relief when Jack stops crying, but then all her feelings of inadequacy return as Peter's competence undermines her vestiges of confidence. *Jack's better off with his father. We should put him on bottles, then I wouldn't have to feed him all the time. Peter could do the nights.* Her whole frame quakes with big sobs.

Despite herself, her breasts begin to leak. *Peter's so bloody perfect, doesn't he realise he underlines my inadequacy.*

Anyway, mothers don't last, do they; fathers hang around, for better or worse, but mothers just dry up. A flicker of awareness comes to her, that by suddenly stopping breastfeeding she would do to Jack what was done to her. A mother who disappears so suddenly. She briefly sees how unfair that would be, not only for Jack but also for her, and for Peter, and how she has a chance now to break the mould. But then a deep weariness and hopelessness eclipses her insight, and all she sees is the unscalable tin she repeatedly found herself in as a child in her mind, with no way out, and Phyllis slapping her, '*Now* I'll give you something to cry about!'

She pauses in her sobs to hear the baby's cries starting up again. *Bloody hell, is there no way out? What if I was dead, what would happen then? Then they'd have to feed him some other way.*

Peter puts his head round the door, Jack's little head tossing from side to side on his shoulder.

'Em'ly? How's it? Darling, if I hold you in my arms – I know you're unhappy, desperately unhappy – and you feed Baba? Then we'll get some peace, and later, later, I promise I'll try and help you with whatever it is that's upsetting you so much. Look, the little man just won't have me for his tea.'

Jack turns his head towards his mother, crying lustily.

She stands up and allows Peter to lead her to the sofa, where she sits stiffly in his arms and opens her dressing gown and takes the baby from him. At first Jack chokes and cries and fretfully tosses his head from side to side, but then feeds as if he has been starved for a day.

She does not know if all this – the powerful surge of milk from her breasts, the baby's strong sucking, his tiny hand delicately tickling her bare skin, Peter gently massaging the back of her neck – this primitive world she inhabits, is what she really needs, a chance to get back to a primal place and to have a second chance to work it out. Or if she feels trapped and hopeless.

She leans her head on Peter's shoulder, knowing that she does not need to be angry with him.

1982

The baby boy rushes out like a porpoise in a red and purple streak, caught by the midwife and handed to Emily. She holds him on her breast and cries with relief and elation. So different from the birth of Jack, quiet Jack with his soft blonde head, his Pethidine-induced calm.

She thought she could never love another baby as much as Jack, but here is this one, already so different, passionate, impatient, dark-haired, crying so desperately. She gently adjusts his position so that his face is by her breast. He opens his tiny mouth, his tongue half protruding, half licking the nipple. And then, wondrously, he takes it in his mouth and sucks, only seven minutes old, sucks as if he has done so all his intrauterine life. He moves his little wrinkled head up and down, like those silkworms a lifetime ago raising and bowing their heads as they ate into the edge of a leaf.

Peter is at her side, his arm around her shoulders, silently crying with the miracle of it all, his face wracked with a fierce flame of protectiveness and gratitude.

'Emmy, oh the smell. Smell him, like a warm puppy.' Peter's face hovers over the baby's head. 'And marked by blood like a warrior. Nothing on earth can be more beautiful than the two of you.'

She looks at her husband as if through a mist. He kisses her gently on the forehead and licks away her tears.

'Would you like to cut the cord, Peter?' Kirsten the midwife asks, proffering what look like secateurs.

'You're not going to have another chance, Peter!' Emily says.

'Oh that's what they all say,' says Kirsten. 'But you never know!'

Shakily Peter scrunches through it, 'My God, it's tough!' as blood spurts. 'A bonny *bairn*!' Kirsten exclaims. 'Just look at that! He knows what it's all about! Dr Brown'll be along in a few minutes to stitch you up, Emily. I'll leave the three of you alone for a wee while.'

'The three of us, Peter. Can't help but feel it should be "four," that Jack should be here.'

Peter nods, 'Me too. We'll all be together soon enough, soon as possible.'

'Look at his little hands! And feet! Bit red and flaky. I've got so used to Jack, that this one – Max, oh it is *Max*, isn't it? – seems unbelievably tiny.'

'Yes, he really is a Max, isn't he.'

She goes on, 'Can't remember Jack ever being this small. Oh Max, sweet Max, you've fallen asleep. They haven't weighed him yet. Or really checked him over.' She winces, 'I can feel strange pains in my tummy, guess that's normal.'

A small knock on the door heralds the return of Kirsten, carrying a tray of tea and toast, followed by the doctor. 'Dr Brown here to do the embroidery now, Emily. You know him – he popped in when you were in labour – though I don't think you were feeling very sociable then. And I'll just check over the wee fellow, and all that.'

The dimmed Leboyer lights are turned up, her legs put in stirrups, a bright lamp switched on over her lower half, and the baby gently lifted and wrapped in a flannel sheet and laid on a sloping bed. His eyes remain closed.

Saying something about a local anaesthetic, Dr Brown seems far away, for Emily's focus is on the baby.

Peter whispers, 'Can't wait to hold him. Can I hold him, Emmy, when he's been checked over?'

''course! And then, they'll trundle me and Max – strange, saying "me and Max", not just me-and-baby-in-one.' She hardly notices Peter passing her a cup of tea. 'I remember all this with Jack, but each time it's new, as if I haven't experienced the rift, that separation . . . . I know I'm babbling on.' Peter has sipped his tea and now sits and holds her arm. She continues, 'Oh my God, I feel so excited. We thought it was a boy, didn't we? I think that's wonderful – two boys. I know I wanted Jack to be a boy; didn't mind this time either way . . . .'

She wishes they were home already. Ignoring the stitching that the doctor is quietly performing, she hears Max, out of her line of vision, make a thin moan, and then stop.

'Eight pounds, three ounces!' announces Kirsten, her Scottish accent making it sound even more of an achievement. 'All fine. Excellent form.' She continues, 'The paediatrician will do a few little tests on him in the morning – routine things.'

Max is given to his father to hold, wrapped now in a pale blue sheet and a cellular white blanket. His little bony fingers wave near his chin.

'How're you doing, Dr Brown?' Emily asks. 'Can hardly feel a thing, with the local.'

'Fine, only a few to go. It'll feel a bit like sitting on a pincushion for the next few days, but I expect you know that from last time. You only had a small cut this time.'

Kirsten helps Emily to have another sip of tea. She is amazed at how life goes on after a cataclysmic event, as it always does. The optimism of this thought registers, knowing how she used to think that earth-shattering events irrevocably altered life in a negative direction.

Loud sucking noises come from the direction of father and baby. 'He's sucking his fingers! Two fingers in his mouth!' Peter exclaims.

'I was sure it was you, Peter, making that sound!' The loud smack of the baby's lips and tongue continue. Emily watches Peter's tall frame, his face bent over the tiny bundle. It feels so right.

With Peter walking at her side, she and Max are wheeled along a corridor, the trolley pushing apart the thick transparent plastic flaps that replace doors, taking her to a world that is growing larger.

'It's okay, Maxie, just snuggle up, you and me,' she whispers.

She has a small side room where Peter can stay as long as he wants. It is almost four in the morning.

He looks more exhausted than she, for she is still suffused in the rosy afterglow of the effort and triumph of childbirth. Neither she nor Peter have slept for over thirty hours.

Feeling as if she is being pulled to consider life on another planet, she says, 'Darling, you go home, get some sleep, you'll need to be there for Jack in the morning. Even though Chloë is there.'

She had planned for Peter to bring Jack to the hospital in the morning.

'I s'pose I should try and get some rest. I so, so don't want to go,' reaching for his jacket. 'Jack, oh yes . . . especially after he told me the other day that he was going to bash the baby.'

'Poor Jack. And poor Max,' she says.

'Not really, lucky Max. Bye-bye little chap. No doubt about how strong he is.' Yet, the next moment, Peter is reminded of the baby's extreme vulnerability, for his kiss is as soft as goose down on the baby's fontanel. 'Such a thin covering, look, over such an insistent beat.' He seems to fill his lungs with the caramel womb-smell in an effort to take it home with him.

'What a wrench, Em'ly. Darling, I love you.' And then he kisses her on the cheek with almost religious adoration.

She disentangles one arm from the baby-bundle to loop it around his neck, and returns the kiss.

She watches him step towards the door. He turns round, blows her another kiss, as she knew he would.

'Bye-bye brave hunter,' she says, summoning her own courage.

She can see he is shattered almost beyond endurance, and that the leaving depletes him further. 'Drive safely!' she calls.

Weeks later she came to understand what Peter was thinking, when he tells her that he saw Adam in this tiny baby. He'd thought Adam's dark colouring came from Stella. But here it was again; some throwback in his genetic makeup, or in Emily's. He says to Emily that he knows in his bones how the miracle of birth forged indelible impressions on himself and Stella, and yet even that imprint became damaged when things went so wrong between them.

1983

Walking with her father on Hampstead Heath, almost two years after he and Phyllis have separated, Emily plucks up courage to say as nonchalantly as possible, 'Dad, I've been thinking, been wondering, what you made of Phyllis, you know, thought about . . . her depression? Well, it must have been depression, despair at times, her fire and her frost as I saw it. You know, something that I think she and I both had – a turning away from life, a withdrawal.'

Birds tumble out of a tree randomly, like leaves, only to pick themselves up in graceful flight. Father and daughter look ahead, or all around, but not at each other as they walk.

He replies, as if summoning strength from a very diminished supply, making her feel that she is depleting him further. 'Don't know if you know, Emily, know much about the baby boy that died? Maybe that's got something to do with it. Phyllis's mom, Milly, was distraught when her baby died – that must have been when Phyllis was about eighteen months old.' He continues dispassionately, 'I think Milly never recovered.' Out of her peripheral vision she senses him glancing at her with some concern, as if aware of the impact of these events. She nods.

She had heard mention of this dead baby once or twice, but never focused on it, as Phyllis did not seem to think it was important. 'That was then, this is now. People have to move on,' Phyllis used to say. Emily knew the baby was a few months old, and was 'taken away' as Harry recorded in his copperplate writing in his diary on the day his baby son died.

'Phyllis always felt that her mother shut her out of her mind,' her father continues, 'because she was not the baby who died, and not a boy. Actually, she said she felt blamed for the death, was haunted by a memory of the pram tipping over and not knowing if she had tipped it over, though that was before the baby died. Phyllis once told me that either her mother looked right through her, or clasped her so tightly that she could hardly breathe.'

Emily begins to make sense of Phyllis's attempts to make her into someone else. She glimpses some greater explanation of Harry abusing her, if his wife was depressed. But, still depressed, about thirty years later? she ponders. She stops herself from that line of reasoning, for no explanation can fully smooth out the rough dark place she knows remains within her.

As they both walk on, she remembers how she felt invisible at times, whilst Phyllis focused so much on Georgia.

Looking obliquely at her troubled father, she doesn't want to upset him further.

They come to a clearing in the trees. Kicking the carpet of beech husks and mouldering leaves releases the rich humus smell, a smell of such promise, while the sunlight turns mossy tree-stumps into a vital viridescence that she longs to rest her cheek on. Jake sits on a low jutting branch that looks like a dislocated elbow.

She cannot resist one last attempt, knowing that she would regret it in years to come if she didn't try, now. 'But Dad, I still wonder if you believe me about Grandpa Harry?' She can almost hear her heart beating.

'Em, we've been over that so many times. I don't know.' There is a pause that feels very long. 'It upsets me that you still go on about it.'

Oh no, she thinks. That, again.

He sighs heavily. 'Upsets me for your sake . . . .'

'Yes, Dad, I know. I guess, I hoped, hope, that you could see, you know, what you just touched on, that I wouldn't have got the idea out of thin air. It's no longer crucial to me to be believed by you – I've given up long ago hoping for that from Phyllis – but, but I would feel greatly relieved, at peace inside, if you . . . .'

'Well, you . . . you know, I can't say, either way. I know my Mom – Gella – never liked Harry. She distrusted him, and his wife, Milly. I can't say I really got on with him either. But you know, you were really alright in those days, after Mom passed . . . died. You were well cared for by Phyllis – well, I know you and she clashed sometimes, but that's not surprising. But I was there, and Lizzie.' This reminder of his lack of emotional succour during all those years is almost as upsetting as the other denial. She wishes she'd never raised any of it. He continues, 'Now I sometimes wonder if Harry became a scapegoat for you, not consciously of course, because you needed to put your hurt and anger somewhere.'

She tries to put her renewed hurt and anger aside at this dance he is performing, and recognises that, for him, he is being remarkably psychological. She is still puzzled by what stops him from really believing her. She has a flash of realisation that this truth is unbearable and he is too cowardly to believe it.

'Did Phyllis suggest all that to you?' she says. Her voice sounds flat.

'Oh I don't know. Maybe she did. Can't really remember.' She hates the way he hides behind confusion, or amnesia. 'All so long ago. I think we should be turning back now.'

Hah! He wants to go back in time, to a time of peace, but we can't really do that, she thinks. He puts a hand on her arm. She senses that he's trying to mask his rejection of her.

'Lots to do today,' he adds, compounding her feeling of frustration. So all his petty stuff is more important than my bad old stuff, she thinks.

They walk back in silence, except for the rustle of leaves and the hoarse agitated cry of crows.

She is sure that he has an urgent need for his pre-lunch whisky. She feels helpless.

A flock of starlings propel themselves across the sky like thrown stones.

That night she dreams of a very large roast chicken – as big as her – half eaten, the carcass exposed, with Phyllis's dead head where the chicken's head would have been. She is shocked at the extent of the damage to this mother in her dream-life, how beyond repair she seems.

1984

After a concert in a local church in Gospel Oak, wine and canapés are served in the crypt. Emily shyly hopes to meet the solo soprano, Jane Copeland. She had been captivated by the way the singer glowed as the purveyor of those timeless notes, her voice soaring to the top-most arches of the church.

Emily has hardly been out since Max was born. Her sister-in-law Chloë had offered to babysit, so she and Peter went to a *tapas* bar in Belsize Park and then to hear Bach's Coronation Mass.

'I know that work, the Mass,' Emily says tentatively to Jane. 'But there was something about the quality of your voice that . . . sent shivers down my spine. Oh gosh, this sounds sycophantic,' she adds with a little laugh, 'but I only feel that, that sort of . . . frisson, when something rings true. Maybe it's Bach, maybe it's you!'

'That's very kind of you. Really. Thank you. I'm sure it's the Bach though. I don't sing much these days – I used to be professional. Now I just sing with the Highgate Chorus, and accept other occasional invitations.'

Not knowing if it is the wine, or something about this new acquaintance, leads Emily to say, 'I paint, you know . . . .' Jane begins to say something in response, but Emily continues, 'I was thinking, during the concert, that singing is, in a way, quite close to painting: something that comes from deep within, that has to be authentic, you know, felt, from one's guts. Somehow more revealing – perhaps – than playing an instrument? There's nothing to mediate between you and what emerges: the voice, or the paint on the canvas. Maybe singing is even more "from within" – as if, directly from . . . from the soul – except that you're singing someone else's composition and words. I don't know. . . . Oh I'm saying far too much. Sorry.'

While Emily talks, she likes this new acquaintance's quiet, accepting way of listening, the spark in her eyes behind the glasses she wears now. Jane replies with utter seriousness,

'Yes, I find that all very interesting. I suppose there is a sort of nakedness about singing in public, and I guess that's true too if you show your paintings. But whether the activity is altered by having an audience isn't the main point you were making. Yes, I think for singing to be any good, there has to be an integrity, of course, a sincerity, and, and *passion*. And, probably, you'd say that was true of painting. I know some singers who are very good technically, but somehow lack this "something", I suppose a kind of spark. After all, the voice is so full of meaning, as you know – "finding one's voice", and so on, beyond any development into singing.'

A young man brushes past Jane and she spills some of her wine. He seems unaware in the jostling group. She chooses to make slight of it, checking her skirt.

'Oh dear, shall I get something to mop you up with?' Emily says.

'No, it's fine. Mainly on the ground,' wiping her skirt. She continues as if there has not been an interruption,

'But more than that, you know,' Jane continues, 'what I was saying, I learnt from one of my singing teachers years ago: to listen, to really listen, to the singers next to me when singing in a choir, or even in a duet, or indeed in any group, that enabled me to encompass a much wider mental space than my own self, even when I'm singing solo. And I think that gave my voice more body. The lovely thing about a Mass is that even when I'm singing a solo, there's a sort of collective power of the chorus: all their energies coming together, out of which a solo rises – so I never think of it as separate.'

'Oh yes. I can see what you mean. And as you talk, I find myself thinking about small children, babies, and how singing – the mother's voice, lullabies, rhythm, the sort of pattern of interaction between mother and baby – across cultures, is so fundamental to their feeling sort of "held" or rocked in the mother's mind. I guess it's a necessary precursor of speech. Well, it seems to be, from my own two small children. The babbling stage is very musical, and then out of that comes speech, as well as song.'

'You have children? How old are they?'

'Jack is four, and Max two. Pretty tiring stage, for me, but . . . ,' shrugging, 'working out alright now. Was hard at times.' She frowns slightly, and looks away briefly before she is drawn back to Jane. 'What about you? Do you have children?'

'Yes, one daughter, who's nineteen. Lily. I had her when I was first married – to my first husband, I mean. I often wish I'd had more, but by the time Tom and I got together, and felt settled enough, I was too old. Well, we tried, and even went through all that infertility palaver, but it didn't work. I suppose we could have persevered. But sometimes, you know . . . . Well, we decided to stop those attempts, with its hopes and, well, steep disappointments, and to accept that I had Lily, and, although Tom would have loved a child of his own, it was not to be.' She sips her wine and adds with a slight laugh, 'Goodness, we are getting to know each other!'

'I'm sorry to be hogging you, lots of others must be wanting to talk to you.' Emily glances at other guests.

'Oh I don't think so,' the singer replies with a modest laugh. 'But maybe we could meet up some time, for a coffee, or whatever? I'd really like to see your paintings – if that's alright with you. You've hardly talked about them.'

They exchange telephone numbers just as Peter comes up and puts a hand on Emily's shoulder, suggesting they get back soon. 'You know, babysitter and all that,' he adds to Jane.

Emily introduces him to Jane. She feels quite proud of her husband, as she often does. 'Peter and Jane. Wasn't there a reading book called that, when we were young?'

On the way home, she thinks that in Jane she has met someone as shy as herself, who clearly has a bright personality, but who, like her, tends to be the foil for others to shine. She is not sure if they really did connect, or if they kept missing each other. Emily worries that she was too pushy. Now that she is finding her confidence, she cannot gauge if she really stayed with Jane's ideas. But she is intrigued to see how they both relate another time.

Later that night, as she undresses for bed, she says to Peter, 'She's a bit special.'

'Who?'

'Sorry. Jane. Jane Copeland. You know, the solo soprano. Wasn't her dark green velvet dress marvellous? I mean, I know there's a tradition of solo singers dressing up for these occasions, but hers was particularly lovely. And it suited her grey hair.'

'Didn't notice. The dress I mean. I would recognise her again though.' He stops brushing his teeth to say, 'But you probably noticed everything about her.'

' 'fraid so. Still a habit of mine. A visual inventory. Yup. Can tell you exactly what rings she wore on which fingers, can describe her ear-rings, the silk scarf or wrap she draped loosely around her neck: its texture, the colours, etcetera. Ridiculous, isn't it. It's not as if I wasn't really transported by the music, and watching the conductor, and all the other musicians too. I just have to accept that it's a habit – there are worse habits, I guess.'

'Yes, Em'ly, and I have a habit, a bad, bad habit, of wanting you most nights . . . .' He stands behind her as she brushes her hair in front of the mirror, and she can feel him so powerfully through her nightdress that she replies,

'Luckily, my habit fits in with yours, so that's okay isn't it?' as she turns round to face him, amazed at her weak-kneed feeling of desire after all these years, even when she is so tired. The renewableness of it, freshness even.

1985

Emily paints every day while Jack is at school and Max at nursery for a few hours. She feels that her painting life had temporarily dried up while she had babies. But now, if she does not keep her work moving, on-going, she feels the old flatness to life returning.

Her gallery wants her to have a show in the Autumn, and her paintings are commanding higher and higher prices.

She smiles as she reads a review by Roger Fisher, curious what he has to say. She remembers how angry critics used to make her, how she felt that were scavengers. Now she understands how self-protective she had to be, when she had been violated as a child.

April 1985

Samuels' first show for five years (Delaney Gallery, Cork Street, London W1) does not disappoint. She has continued to struggle nakedly with an untamed inner world, her palette familiar in its Prussian blues and burnt ochres, but with moments of peace and even ecstasy. She continues to disturb the viewer. But now there is a development, which is that, although there is horror, she conveys that she herself can – indeed must – live with it. The moments of peace are like sunshine inexorably creeping through leaves after a tempest: fulgent cream and lime green splatters, almost unbelievably, through the wreckage.

So, it is a relief to see that she courageously struggles with her – or are they our? – demons, but somehow she is not overwhelmed by them.

And then, there is something about the accidental, and the incidental. And thus something is revealed, something revelatory.

I find myself thinking about subject and object in these canvasses: that the two come together. I think about duality: a synthesis, or the forces in her inner world, made now into an outer world for us all to see, and feel.

Her canvases have grown bigger. Indeed, their size reflect her ongoing development.

She and Peter sit at the bottom of the garden under the apple tree, laden with pearly white blossoms and pink buds. They share a fresh baguette with French butter and succulent apricot preserve, and Italian coffee. The bees provide a background buzz to their conversation.

It was Emily's idea to take a morning break like this, while the children are out: to celebrate the warmest day of the year so far. Kicking off her shoes, she takes off her purple linen shirt, and sits in a plum cotton vest and long turquoise skirt.

Preparing a chunk of bread for Peter, she spreads it with care, taking the butter and the jam right up to the edges. She has learned this way of preparing food from Peter over the years. His attention to detail was such a sign of love that she absorbed it, now dispensing it to him and the children. She is beginning to do the same for herself.

Biting into her bread, she devours most of an apricot in one gulp. She senses him looking at her.

'Peter, I'm worried about you.'

'*Hah*! No need for that. You've enough on your plate. Not being rude about your hearty snack!'

'Yes, but my plate is quite big these days.'

'What're you worried about, then?'

'Well, you know . . . you seem less enthusiastic about life these days. Sort of tired.' Her tone turns statements into questions. 'I worry that you're missing Adam, or, if you feel neglected by me. Or if your work isn't so satisfying.'

This is the beginning of several conversations about Peter's frustration with his work.

A few days later, as Emily undresses for bed, Peter says, 'I don't know if I should just put up with it, you know. My job. After all, there's enough satisfaction in other areas of my life. But now that you're earning well, selling so much, and at decent prices, you know, it makes me wonder if I should . . . take a risk, do more what I've always wanted . . . .'

'Of course you should!' she interrupts. Yet, after so many years of living with Peter she has absorbed his way of generally being free of 'should' and 'ought' and is mainly guided by inner conviction. So she stops in her tracks, and sits on the bed with a leg tucked under her, and turns towards him. 'Well, what do you really think? If you were on your death bed, would you have any major regrets?'

'Yes, I think I would.' He looks down at the bedcover. 'I sometimes think along those lines. It's up to me. The longer I leave it, the harder . . . to make something, something different, of my, my vision. You're much better at all this than I, you know. You've struggled, and battled all your life in some ways it seems. Maybe my earlier life was too cushy and I've just sailed along in an expected way, instead of challenging myself.'

She goes around to his side of the bed and hugs him. At first it is because she wants to show him how much she loves him, and is sure that the conversation will continue. But it transforms into one between their two bodies.

Later, as they lie together and she sees her usual post-lovemaking rich tapestry of colours – deep ultramarine, turquoise, and emerald – she says, 'Darling, didn't mean to stop you in what you were saying.'

'Oh, oh that. No, I know. I know it's up to me, always, in the end, what I do. I know. I'm beginning to be prepared to take risks.'

She mutters a *mmnnn,* and briefly tightens her arms around him. Nowadays she falls asleep long before he does.

Emily doesn't know if a particular painting is finished. What does 'finished' mean? She could go on with it for ever. This one is an abstraction of doors and windows, where the gaps or holes can be read as an absence or a solid presence. But it is too angular, too geometric. A shape in the centre in flesh tones, filled with a Prussian blue ground sprigged with tiny red and white and blue and green dots, evokes a floral dress her mother wore.

Max walks into the room. His round cheeks and the shape of his thick head of hair are perfect. His legs are now long and slim, like hers, his eyes dark hazel – a mysterious colour from she doesn't know where.

He begins to whine about not being able to find one of his Scalextric cars.

'Where's Daddy?' Emily asks.

'Don't know.'

'Come on Max. Go and look for Daddy. He's looking after you. He's probably in the garden. Call him.'

'You call him,' looking at his mother petulantly.

She begins to doubt if the deal she made with Peter to give herself time to paint today, is worth it. She has indigestion in her stomach, and feels anger gathering like a storm cloud. Why isn't Peter more in charge of the boys? Max has attention and love from both his parents and still he's fussing.

Somewhere, in a corner of her mind, always, is the fact that she was more or less that age when her world collapsed.

She pulls herself round from facing her canvas, to look at Max lying on the floor, his head on his arms, drumming the floor with the toes of his heavy Kickers. She fears that lifting him up, appealing to him, showing him that she is here for him, will make him fight and shout and run to his room, as he sometimes does these days. She doesn't know if she can bear that today.

Her frailty is exacerbated by her recent disappointment in her friend Jane.

The last time she felt like this, a week ago, she phoned Jane. Her outpouring was met with long silences. She hates that enigmatic uncommitted side of her friend.

'Jane, are you sure it's okay to talk now?' she checked, even though Emily had ascertained at the beginning that it was alright.

'Oh yes, fine, but I'm just not that good with small children. Maybe it's just as well I only had Lily – and then we had a nanny most of the time. But I don't want to get into "me" now, Emily.' Precisely, thought Emily.

Emily tried to continue to talk about her bleakness, her anger with her boys, her feeling of being a bad mother, how hard it was to invent the mothering that she rarely had beyond the age of four and a half. Again she met a silence, and then, 'I don't know, Em. It's really hard, I know. But . . . oh dear, no, I don't know what to say, other than I'm always impressed how you manage to paint and look after . . . .' Her friend's voice trailed off.

'Yes, but . . . .' Emily found it hard to accept that Jane could not really enter her world of small children. Jane was fine when she talked about painting, or music. She knew that Jane's mother was a musician who had led a bohemian life with many lovers and she too had not been there for Jane. Yes, Emily realised, again, that paucity in Jane.

'Okay, sorry, Jane. I've gone on a bit. I'm premenstrual – perhaps that's part of it. Anyway, haven't asked how you are today?'

She knew that this residual pattern of the soldier in her was not helpful to her or to this relationship. She resolved to talk to Peter, and to go back to her painting as soon as possible.

She thought then of Liz Fell, in Derbyshire, whom she rarely saw. No. Liz could not easily fit into her London life, even for a few days, and Liz and Peter found it hard to relate to each other.

'What, what did you say, Phyllis?'

There is a silence and then she hears Phyllis at the other end of the phone more clearly.

'Georgia. She died two days ago, in South Africa. It . . . was an accident.'

'Oh my God. I'm so sorry. How terrible. What kind of accident?'

'Thought I should let you know. She fell, fell from a window. She was cleaning the outside, leaning out it seems, on the second floor of the cottage where she was staying.'

'How are *you*?' Emily asks with feeling.

'Terrible, terrible. But that's not the point . . . . Going . . . flying out there tonight, funeral's on Thursday, in Pretoria. Alex and Paul are trying to arrange flights too.'

I can't possibly go, won't go, don't want to go, Emily thinks. *No.* She reminds herself that Alex and Paul are Georgia's half-brothers, different from a step-sister. Or is it?

'I'm so sorry, Phyllis. It must be such a shock, unbelievable. And how awful to have to ring everyone. At least her brothers will be there, at the funeral, hopefully. And my dad, is he going?'

'I must go. So much to arrange. But I thought I should let you know.'

Now it really is too late to do anything about Georgia, Emily thinks.

She stammers, 'I hope it all goes . . . as well as possible, you know, under the circumstances,' deciding not to explain, nor make excuses, but to phone Phyllis when she returns.

'Dad . . . .'

'Oh Emily. So glad you rang. You know about Georgia? Was just going to ring you.'

'Yes, Phyllis rang a minute ago. Terrible, shocking. Are you going to the funeral?'

'No, can't manage it. Hurt my back recently, may be a slipped disc, have to lie flat on my back most of the time.'

How convenient, she catches herself thinking, before mustering some sympathy, not knowing how genuine his injury is. His speech sounds slurred. Perhaps it's painkillers. Or drink.

'Oh dear, Dad. I'll pop over soon – will ring you. We must talk, about all this . . . . And about you.'

Her sinking feeling as she puts the phone down is relieved when she realises that he did not ask if she were flying to South Africa. Perhaps no one expects her to.

Emily hesitates about ringing Jane. Perhaps she was simply being honest, not pretending that she had the resources, when she talked to her about her sons.

'Jane, have you got a moment? Is this an okay time to talk? Are you sure? Just need to share something with you, something shocking. Can't get hold of Peter. It's about my step-sister, Georgia – you know, who's two years older than me. Just heard that she died, suddenly. An accident.'

'Oh dear, how awful. What . . . how – the accident?'

'Fell out of a window which she was cleaning.'

'Oh goodness, dreadful. Maybe this is the wrong time to say this, but people generally don't fall out of windows – well, not usually. Doesn't it make you wonder if she . . . jumped?'

'Oh my God, yes. Only I was loath to come to that conclusion, well, hypothesis, entirely on my own. Her mother said she fell. But of course it's much easier to bear the death if that was the case – whereas suicide . . . .'

'Exactly, Emily.'

'Now that I think about it, I think Phyllis said it was the second floor of a cottage. Cottages in South Africa don't usually have two or three floors – in fact, most homes are built on one level.'

'But how are you feeling?'

'Don't know – yet. I only heard a few hours ago. You know I had such a negative, hateful at times, relationship with Georgia. Don't know if that makes the . . . the finality of her death more difficult. But I am sad, shocked, for her mother, and for her – to have had her life cut so short. I must pick the boys up soon – but . . . thanks, Jane, yes, thank you, for being there. Speak to you soon. Thanks.'

The next day, Emily goes for a walk on her own across the Heath. The detail of a large maple tree, its yellow leaves a mass of dots, makes her stop to marvel. Long grasses silvered by the sun, leaves flame against a forget-me-not blue sky smudged with clouds. Planes' vapour trails criss-cross into the distance.

The news about Georgia pulls her back to remembering her own attempt at suicide when with Marcus, and her frequent thoughts about it – the magnetic appeal of that beam in the cottage in Suffolk, fantasies of rat poison, knives, and of jumping from a great height.

Now, life is too short, precious, at times miraculous. She thinks of Jack and Max. She wonders if she would feel this degree of appreciation of life if she had never shunned it. She thinks of Peter, his lows and highs too, but a much calmer view of life. He has never been suicidal.

1986

The sun creeps below the curtains at six in the morning and wakes Jack.

'Max?' A few seconds later, 'Max! Are you awake?'

'Ye-es . . . ,' still drowsing, unable to resist his big brother's attention.

They look at books in bed, have their 'bed-night snack' as Jack calls it, of apple and sultanas and juice, which Emily had put out at night to buy more time for her and Peter in bed.

At seven o'clock the boys burst into their parents' bedroom – the time when they are allowed to come in. They begin a game of Jack's design: Max is the Mummy "Maxine," Jack the Daddy, somehow named Anthony. Emily and Peter are content to be the children, cuddling and giggling under the duvet, pleased to have extra time in bed, but not like siblings.

Jack finds two shoes which he says are the baby in Max's tummy. Max accepts this, stuffing them up his pyjama top and pats his pregnant chest. Emily asks how the baby got into Maxine's tummy.

Jack says, 'The Daddy put it there.' Then Jack announces that the baby is born, and the shoes are pulled out. 'But wait a minute,' he says, 'there are six, no seven, no eight, no twelve babies. Plus Mummy and Daddy, I mean, Emily and Peter, that makes fourteen.'

Emily wonders to herself why Jack imagines such a nest of babies – at some level, inside her.

Peter says, 'What about the changing of all those nappies?' Emily is pleased he is not taking the chance to doze, but is actively engaged in the game.

'I can't know,' says Max.

Jack pretends to buy hundreds of nappies.

She asks, 'But how will all the babies be fed, when Maxine has only two breasts?'

Jack looks worried. Peter says they could have bottles, as well as turns on the breast.

Max briefly breast-feeds an imaginary baby, but then becomes wild, crawling around speaking nonsense.

'Stop it Max, it's not part of the game. Max!' says Jack.

Max becomes more demented, truly acting crazy.

Emily says, 'Oh dear, the Mummy has gone mad! Now who will look after all the babies?' She thinks it understandable that Max turns to craziness when landed with so many offspring.

Jack looks worried. Peter says he could phone for some help, there are people from the hospital who will help with all the babies. Jack is relieved and mimes phoning up, but just in time Max recovers.

Now Jack finds Emily's silky bra thrown over a chair, and says with a smile, 'Can Max, I mean, what's his name? Can Maxine wear this?'

Max takes off his pyjama top, and the bra is put on and tied by Jack to fit at the back. Max looks down and pats his breasts approvingly. He repeatedly strokes them.

Joyfully finding their mother's bold red beads on the dressing table, and her bracelet, evening bag, and shoes, Jack amiably asks each time if Maxine can wear them. Jack finds a vest-top, which Max happily puts on. Meanwhile Max slightly wiggles his shoulders, and holds his head in a particular way, his blonde hair so like a pretty girl's style at that moment. Emily thinks of the girl she never had, even though she probably does not want another baby, and wonders if Peter is thinking similarly. She briefly thinks about herself at more or less that age, playing similar games with her mother, but without a brother or sister to fill out the story. She pulls herself back from that fateful day as she watches Max patting his breasts again.

Then Jack finds a black half-petticoat, which makes a marvellous long silky skirt, belted at the waist. Max calmly accepts his status, stroking his breasts again as he looks down at them. Jack (always one for more), finds a makeup bag for Max; now Max calmly carries a bag over each shoulder. Jack finds the alarm clock and gives it to Max to put in one of his bags.

And so the game goes on, with Jack very helpful as the facilitator and driving force of the transformation. He decides that the family go to a fairground to ride on a Helter Skelter and then a roundabout, and win lots of fluffy toys. The twelve babies are forgotten by now; only the Emily and Peter children come to the fair.

She is beginning to think about the washing she must unload, the Sunday lunch to prepare, the book she wants to read over coffee.

'Who's coming with me to Homebase?' Peter asks. 'Sorry boys, in a few minutes we'll have to end the game. What happens now in the story, at the end?'

Jack frowns. 'It's not fair.'

'Well, Jacko, it is a fair, a lovely fun-fair you and Max, I mean Maxine, have taken us to . . . .'

'Not funny,' Jack interjects.

'Mummy and I have to do other things soon.'

'Can we watch *Loony Tunes*?' asks Max.

Emily looks at Peter and gives a little shrug.

'Alright boys, just for half an hour. Can you put the video on, Jack?'

Phyllis's face is sallow, for she rarely goes out, rarely feels the sun or the wind. Her cheeks are hollow; her eyes look inward, further shielded by the grey-tinted lenses of her glasses. Her dyed hair, a dark unchanging mahogany, adds to the pallor of her skin. She always dresses neatly, immaculately in fact – except for her now small sagging breasts which she no longer supports in a bra – favouring cream silk blouses with ecru embroidery and neatly pressed slacks in dark grey or tan. On the rare occasions that she goes out, her handbag is of discreet brown leather, matching her shoes. Nowadays, she walks as if her shoes are too tight.

In her always-clean apartment, the surfaces are polished, the cooker gleaming immediately after she has cooked, the Amtico floor tiles polished, the corners and under-bed places vacuumed weekly by her cleaning lady.

The windows of this small ground-floor flat in Highgate – which she bought when she and Jake separated – peer out through the rectangles cut in the Virginia creeper. Yet the glass is never cleaned, except by rain. If windows are the eyes of a house, these have cataracts. When new little stems of creeper foray across the panes, Phyllis tugs at them, pulling the suckers from the glass, and cuts them back with sharp scissors. But she will not allow anyone to clean these murky shrines.

On one of Emily's rare visits, she is struck by the connection between her step-mother's determination not to clean windows, and the way Georgia died.

Occasionally people comment on the strangeness of her dirty windows, especially as the privet hedge looks artificial in its neatness, the front path always swept. The smooth soil in the flowerbeds defies weeds; the rose bushes never display an overblown rose for long, so fallen petals are not a problem. When a rose bush begins to show signs of black-spot, Phyllis has it dug out. She does not replace it.

'I should never have let poor Georgie go back to South Africa like that, should have kept an eye on her, close by,' she says to herself, over and over. 'That Bernie in Cape Town! Doesn't deserve the name of "father", not paying her attention, too busy with his other family.' Phyllis often thinks sorrowfully that Georgia must have gone back to South Africa to try to salvage something with him. 'I should have warned her, protected her . . . . Jacob wasn't a bad father to her, but still . . . her real father . . . .'

'Never, never, will I get over it,' she intones. This becomes more of an instruction to herself than a lament.

'Georgia was the sunshine of the family,' she says to every visitor and acquaintance. She often passes them a framed photograph of Georgia smiling at the camera. 'The death of a child . . . it's not normal, not natural,' looking away.

She knows that it was the wrong child who had taken her life. *It was never meant to be Georgia.*

1987

Waking to find himself at the bottom of the stairs in his house in Hampstead, with his left leg at a strange twisted angle upon the bottom steps, the pain in his back and hip is eclipsed by piercing pressure in his temples. Jacob Samuels lies still, hoping to slide back into the oblivion from which the fall wrenched him.

He does not know how much time passes before he opens his eyes again, and remembers drinking whatever spirits he had in the house. He notices a bitter taste in his mouth and smells vomit. Wiping his mouth with his sleeve, 'Oh-God-oh-shit. My leg.'

Hours later – the bright dawn now streaming through the high landing windows, casting blue and red jewel colours through the stained glass – he drags himself to the phone to call an ambulance. The pain in his left leg is unbearable.

And now he cries, weeps at the state he is in, the total mess. Should have finished myself off properly. Maybe still can. Either that, or . . . no, this can't go on.

He knows how hard it will be to open the front door when the ambulance arrives. He thinks of phoning Alex, who has a key. Vestiges of pride prevent him from letting his son see the state he is in.

Shivering, Jake realises his trousers are wet. *No, ambulance men see it all – but not Alex.* Imagining Alex telling Phyllis about what has become of his father, he resolves to pull himself to the front door, to see if he can open it.

'Bloody stupid,' through tears of rage. 'Disgusting old fool!'

The two paramedics find him lying inside the open door. He had managed to push the low hall table towards the front door and levered himself up.

'Sorry, gentlemen. Not as bad as it looks. Or . . . maybe . . . it is . . . .'

They carry him out on a chair, covered by a red blanket and strapped in. A semblance of care and order. Convulsively shivering while trying to control the tears that rain down his cheeks, he whimpers, 'Sorry, what a mess . . . . Drink. You see, either I stop now, not a drop again . . . or . . . .' The effort to appear rational is considerable. 'Or . . . I top myself.'

The paramedic with him in the back of the ambulance lays a hand on Jake's arm while taking his pulse with his other hand,

'Don't you be worrying about all that now. They'll sort you out at the hospital. Fix that leg, clean you up.'

Jake shakes his head, and begins to cough. 'My God, my head!'

A few minutes later he mutters through tears, 'What we do with life, with the life we've been given . . . ,' before sliding into a half sleep in the dim light. The words 'Rae, Raychie . . . ,' tumble out when the ambulance stops abruptly.

'Daft place for someone with a broken leg!' Jake calls out as he descends from the taxi awkwardly, hopping to balance himself on his crutches. He wants to state the obvious before anyone else does. The path up to the cottage in the Black Mountains is so steep that he has to rest several times. He stops to adjust his cap, and to look around. And pauses again ostensibly to check something in his pockets. The taxi driver walks ahead with the two suitcases.

The young couple are glad to have a tenant, one who keeps himself to himself, and who seems pleasant enough. They put his bloodshot eyes and florid complexion down to his being weather-beaten. In a way they are right: he is beaten by life, by its relentless lashings, as well as his own self-inflicted attacks. He had told them on the telephone that he had fallen down stairs, was having a hard time generally, and wanted to get away from city life.

Jake's leg has healed well enough by the time Emily visits for two days in May, soon after the plaster has been removed.

The last stretch of her drive from London tugs her back to previous stays here in the Black Mountains: the steep decline of the little road from Crucorny, then the six miles to Llanthony along winding lanes with lay-bys for cars to pass each other, and machine-cut hedges. The steep grassy fields are populated with sheep, and a few horses, statue-still.

Arriving when her father is out, Emily sits on a low wall in the late spring sunshine, waiting, tired from the journey and from the pace of her life. The sounds of sheep and cockerels and birds and bees weave a cloak of heavy peacefulness.

The tranquillity reminds Emily of her Suffolk retreat, one that she could anticipate and ache for when she was not there, with the knowledge that it would never disappoint. She does not know if it is the prospect of seeing her father again after two months – since he was in hospital – or this blessed place, that moves her.

She sees the silhouette of an approaching old man loping sideways, as if leaning into the slope of the hill, surrounded by a halo of the lowering refracted sun. As the ground levels he continues to walk at an angle, with the same lopsided gait. Life itself seems to have bowed him.

When he catches sight of her he speeds up his hobble. Shading her eyes, she discerns his smile.

'Emily! You've arrived! Should have warned you, about my . . . posture. Not to worry. Yes, I know, like a tree that's grown crooked,' while hugging his only daughter. 'Seems the only way I can walk now; less painful that way. Not too bad, you know, since the leg . . . the injured one is somehow shorter than the other. I think it's my back, too.' Pulling away to peruse her face, 'You look good!' He returns to explaining, 'But, except for a bit of pain, I'm fine, really. Come on in. Door's unlocked. Can't offer you a drink – you know all about that – apart from some really good apple juice, or tea.'

He seems to have shrunk. So fragile, she thinks.

The terracotta tiles and roughly plastered walls with exposed areas of grey stones, windows in deep recesses in the thick walls, an old pine table and rickety chairs, the buff stone sink, again evoke memories of her Suffolk hideaway: a sparse place like this, but where, like a chrysalis, she was slowly transformed to emerge into life.

'Tea you said? Now where's that special tea?'

'Actually, Dad, I said apple juice, please.'

While he finds glasses and a bottle from the larder, she notices the book on top of a pile by the fireplace, *The Life of the Bee*. She peers to read the author, Maurice Maeterlinck. She takes in the pile of cassettes of Beethoven and Schubert, *The New Statesman*, that old Meerschaum pipe in an ashtray, the familiar *Balkan Sobranie* black and white tobacco tin, the brown leather tobacco pouch, the *Swan Vesta* matches he always bought, ash from a fire in the grate. And here he is in his usual taupe cavalry twill trousers and old suede shoes, probably made in Poland and bought at a bargain price. She feels reassured that he will be alright.

Huddled in her coat she sits on one of the bentwood chairs and sips a glass of apple juice, although she would have preferred wine. She senses that this cottage never warms up even in hot weather.

Her father collapses into the armchair. 'Well, Emily, how long is it since I saw you? Well, must be several months, since before my accident.' He becomes more serious and a little remote, smoothing back his still-dark hair. He has forgotten that she visited him in hospital several times.

She does not know if she can bridge the gap, find a sincere way of relating, after in fact years and years of . . . . No, she tells herself, since Mom died. She feels like shouting, Since I was four, I lost you . . . . Phyllis . . . Harry . . . . The obstacles mount up and her face clouds over. But she so wants to refind hope, the hope she felt on the drive here, to reach over the abyss like a cantilever bridge, and find him, before it is too late.

'Well, Dad, we have the rest of today, and all day tomorrow, and I don't have to go back to London 'til Wednesday afternoon. Plenty of time, really, to catch up with each other, if we can.'

As she talks, she feels doubtful about words. There seem to be holes in her sentences through which anything could fall. She doesn't know if he notices the strain in her voice. Perhaps it really is too late. How easily she could slip into despair, despair with its gravitational pull.

She lowers her head to see out of one of the small windows, to look at the hills, searching for their old magic. There they are, exultant, an overarching presence now bathed in sun, beckoning her. Remembering her father's expression – 'as old as the hills' – renews her hope that something instinctive from deep inside both of them will find a real connection.

Jake had bought fresh trout from the trout farm near Crucorney. He had hired a taxi specially, asking it to stop at a small shop to buy fresh vegetables and raspberry home-made ice-cream, honey, and sunflower-seed bread. He prepared the trout with flaked almonds and fresh dill, dotted with butter. He wanted this meal to be an act of love, a libation. He considered buying good wine for Emily, but knew he could not risk it.

Dinner is a quiet affair, her father seriously and slowly dissecting his fish, mindful of bones, his hands trembling, as they do generally these days, talking about little things since he arrived here three weeks ago. He talks about the two boys – Gareth and William – of the couple who own the cottage, and how they come and chat to him, or kick a ball around outside his cottage. Gareth collects beer bottle tops, and was grateful for those from ginger beer that Jake kept for him. Jake smiles as he tells her that William did not want to be outdone, so he said he collected rubber bands. But then, Jake's face darkening,

'You know, Emmy, what makes me sad? Lots of things, but at this moment, the fact that I don't really know your two boys that well. I really feel sorry about that. And I don't know Peter's Adam at all. I know it's my own fault. Not sure that "fault" is a helpful way of thinking, but, anyway, I take responsibility for that.' His shoulders become more hunched.

Emily feels so full of emotion that she says nothing, allowing him to flow on.

'I hope it's not too late now,' he says, glancing up at Emily with a frown. 'Let's see, Jack would be how old now? Seven? Eight? And Max, he'd be six then. A bit older than the two lads here. Ridiculous really, that I could have strayed so far from what was, is, important. And now, when I'm so, so, disabled, well, not completely, but my body . . . . '

He seems to pull himself together. 'No, the main thing is, my mind is far clearer, and my . . . emotions. The body, well, that's just an encumbrance at times.' With his paper napkin, he mops his mouth, although it does not need wiping.

Her mind and heart feel overfull with impressions, her father now this old disabled man with a fine spirit despite everything. She tries to brush aside her concerns about his mind – he seems forgetful and unclear at times, and she does not know if that is his way of defending himself from reality, or if he is beginning to show signs of dementia. How will she convey this to Peter? She holds onto her husband in her mind now, as someone who has never judged people. He has his likes and dislikes, but it will not be too difficult to gain his understanding of her father's transformation. A lesser man would not trust or believe it.

'Well, Dad, of course, it's never too late. Of course you must see more of the boys. They would love it. Maybe I could bring them here, with Peter, and we could stay at that little place, you know, Penny Maes, at Capel-y-ffin, and spend time with you.' She doesn't know why a feeling of apprehension fills her chest. 'Would you like that? Or have you come here to get away from all that? I'll understand if you have.' But she knows that in fact she would not really understand.

He stops eating, lays down his knife and fork, sips his water, and looks at her through brimming eyes. She can hardly bear moments when she perceives him as pathetic. She is poised between that impression and the opposite: admiration. Holding her breath, she waits.

'Yes, Emmy. Oh goodness, calling you by your little girl name. Feels right, somehow, now . . . . I'm sorry, Emmy, sorry for . . . well, for Mom dying . . . .'

Burying his face in his hands, he sobs, mucous running down his jowls and perilously hanging over his trout.

She stands up and walks round to his chair, putting her arms around him. His shoulders are as delicate and bony as a bird's skeleton.

'Dad, Daddy, yes, I know, yes, I don't know who should be comforting who now, but, yes, I know . . . terrible, for you . . . and for me . . . of course.'

She breaks through the silence, 'You know, Dad, in a way it was worse for you, because you hardly gave yourself time to really feel what you'd lost, and what I'd lost. You sort of got on with life, you know, earning a living, and finding another wife, and . . . . So, in a way, you couldn't really find, re-find, Mom – Rae – later, if you never really felt her loss.'

'Don't be silly, Emmy,' stopping his tears to look at her. 'How could it have been worse for me? You lost your only *mother*! I . . . .' She worries that perhaps she is avoiding her own pain. But as he talks he stops, realising the weight of her words. 'Oh God.' He breathes deeply, and continues, 'Maybe. I've begun lately to think along those lines too. But you . . . you sort of lost me too . . . .'

'Yes, I know, Dad, and it was hell. I'm not underestimating the . . . the madness that my life became, as suddenly as an earthquake. But somehow, and maybe it's a miracle, I have come through the fire, more or less. No, more rather than less, and found painting, and Peter, and Jack and Max, and a life, a good life.' She pauses, staring at the candle flame. 'A blessed life. And you, you're what now, about seventy, no seventy-two, and you're still struggling. Well, maybe finding something authentic, at last . . . .'

'Maybe it's footling to compare lives.'

'"Footling!" Haven't heard that word for ages. I think you're the only person who uses it. But I love it, because it's your word. Like *Balkan Sobranie* and *Swan Vesta*, and that gadget lying there that you use to press the tobacco down in your pipe, that I remember from when I was little. You see, at least I have a father.'

'Yes, but an unworthy one, my dear.'

She smiles at him. 'Better than nothing! No, seriously, you don't realise how much you have been there for me, despite everything. Partly as an antidote to Phyllis at times, partly as the only other person in the world who loved Mom. Even if you didn't let on much about that.'

'When's your next show, Emmy?'

'What's that got to do with the price of eggs?'

'Well, I was thinking, it's not only your boys, but your painting, that I've missed out on. If Mom were alive she would have appreciated your painting. But when she died, as a painter herself, I turned away from that world.

'But you know, now, here,' he continues, 'I have so much time, for once time is expansive, it's on my side, not my enemy, and I can follow what my heart and mind want. No, it's not as simple as that. I'm much more aware of the passing of time, the . . . finiteness . . . and, strangely, well, not strangely at all, that makes me value the moment far more. You know, I feel a hunger. Like, I went to an exhibition in Abergavenny of David Jones's work, and a photography show by that Australian – what's his name? My memory! All black and white images, landscapes, rocks. And I read a lot. Been buying art books in Hay – such a treasure trove – and I found that Maeterlinck book I loved when I was young, and one about van Leeuwenhoek, who discovered the microscope. And Jack London – *Call of the Wild* – some of my old favourites. Oh Emmy, the ice-cream.' She wonders if he perceived something in her face that was not really in accord with his stories. 'In the freezer part of the fridge,' he continues. 'Will you get it? Anyway, with all this looking, and thinking, and discovering, rediscovering, I really want to know more about your work.'

'You don't have to go to one of my shows, Dad. You can come to my studio any time. And choose something you like, if you want . . . .' Years ago she would have added, 'Don't suppose you'd like it,' or 'Don't worry if you don't want anything . . . .' But now she knows that her offer is of value.

She insists on washing up. She can see that he is tired, and is pleased when he stretches out in the one armchair, and nods off while she potters. The overture of *La Traviata* playing on a tape sounds more profound than she ever realised.

She too is weary after the long drive and the intense emotions of the evening, and would like to retire to bed – which is a mattress on the floor in the small sitting room. Aware how her own needs can jostle with what she supposes the other wants, over the years she has absorbed from Peter the capacity to be more solid and able to state what she desires, and knows it can be a relief to others not to have to second-guess. Deciding to quietly prepare for bed, she puts the kettle on for camomile tea, and finds night clothes in her small case.

When Jake opens his eyes, he sees her in her nightdress, a coat for a dressing gown, smiling at him.

Through bleary eyes he apologises for dropping off, 'The ways of an old man.'

'Oh, don't be silly, Dad,' she says gently. 'I'm quite tired. I'd like to go to bed. Tomorrow's another day. Can I make you herbal tea?'

'Good to have you here, my girly,' as he gets up slowly and seems to topple sideways before more or less righting himself to go to the bathroom, holding onto furniture and the wall on the way.

After a few minutes, he reappears to ask if she is warm enough, and whether she needs anything else. She is reading by the light of a small lamp, enjoying this new experience of camping with her father.

'No, Dad. I'm fine ta. Very comfy. Sleep well.'

He goes quietly into the small bedroom and closes the door.

She hears the sound of the wind, the leather-creak of branches outside, a strange scratching – probably of branches on the roof – and the occasional cry of a bird. Now the prickly sound of rain on the roof. She dreamily thinks how layer upon layer is laid down in her memory, Suffolk overlaying that first spring in England, which resonated right back to her first years, years full of wonder. Before the ice age set in.

Jake, meanwhile, lies awake too.

He knows there is much to work out with his only daughter. He wonders whether to share with her the full horror of the depths to which he had sunk, how he nearly died before he could shock himself into claiming life. The terrible trembling and sweating he endured when he first came here, the images of drink that appeared before his eyes like mirages, the seductive words, *One, only one, won't do any harm.* And how the lines of the whole embroilment in *Hamlet* came to him, stopping him, 'It is the poison'd cup ; it is too late.'

His mother's voice, 'You can only do what you can do,' came to mind many times – how he could hear it as defeatist, or the opposite. He had teetered on the brink between those two poles, but it was this country place that pulled him towards life, and even, a lifelong atheist, towards something he began to call God – the mystery and wonder of nature all around him.

He re-found this valley near Abergavenny, where he had been one summer two years after he and Phyllis brought the children to London from South Africa. He did not know why he felt so at peace, that summer of 1958, so connected with the place. Perhaps there were associations with the Orange Free State where he had lived as a boy – the freedom of his childhood, the uncomplicated barefoot happiness. But maybe it arose out of his love of Dylan Thomas' poetry, excited at experiencing first-hand the place he often invoked without pause, like a brook, *Now as I was young and easy under the*

*apple boughs about the lilting house and happy as the grass
was green the night above the dingle starry time let me hail
and climb golden in the heydays of his eyes* – words he offered
up breathlessly to the 'new made clouds' and the 'moon that
is always rising', like a prayer.

The simple air of the Brecon Beacons, the sounds of
cocks crowing, and sheep, and birdsong, the physicality of
a landscape that he could feel in his own body, the timeless
farming life measured out by the seasons, reconnected him
with the rhythm and pulse of a life that he had lost.

He falls into a deep sleep, cushioned by dreams that he
does not remember.

In the next room, Emily lies awake. She needs to tidy
her thoughts, to travel with them and see where they take
her. Gratefully connected with the world – its beauty and
its terror – her father's bent frame somehow personifies her
own life, except that she hopes she has more time to slowly
straighten up than he. Or, perhaps, like a bent tree, she has
grown strong branches in unexpected places, that balance
the precarious structure. Yet she knows that if the gale is too
strong, in that tearing ripping cracking way that wind has,
the tree could topple. Then, what is that word? It would all be
footling. Yes, life is so bloody precarious. She tells herself not
to take it too seriously.

Not until she hears the sonorous snores from the next
room, does she begin to doze.

The next day they clamber slowly, pausing every few
steps, to a vantage point behind and above the cottage, soon
rewarded by views of the valley: sheep in flurries like snow,
the graceful twisting road through the valley, the fuzzy blur
of regimented conifers on the opposite hillside. So as not
to draw attention to her father's incapacities, Emily pauses
frequently to survey the view, and climbs slowly, as if that
is her chosen pace. She senses that he is being stoical about
his pain; she would be happy for him to lean on her, but his
pride does not allow it. She begins to perceive his bent gait
as an expression of determination, a dogged way of thrusting
himself into whatever he does.

They sit on the low bent trunks of hawthorn trees, some parallel to the ground, that provide seats and backrests, and lean back to take the sun on their faces.

Tattered shreds of sheep's wool cling onto thorns and sharp branches, as if from threadbare bridal gowns of some druidic people that inhabited these sparse hillsides. A young sheep, half-way between lamb and sheep, the sun back-lighting its ears so that they look red, comes closer to these humans, and stares at them with curiosity. Its mother calls anxiously from a little way away. Father and daughter, ewe and young sheep, remain still, and wait. Eventually Jake says, '*Baa-aaa!*' The ewe's entreaties increase. The youngster starts, and gambols back to its mother.

'As if it suddenly realised which species it belongs to,' Emily laughs.

'Emmy, there's a big thing in the air, in the way, isn't there?'

'What d'you mean, Dad?' She holds her breath, the peaceful place suddenly suspenseful.

'You know, my dear. What you approached me, me and Phyllis, about. Years ago, now.'

Her heart misses a beat and she clenches her teeth, unsure if she wants all that dredged up now, again. It's bound to spoil the peace. But then, the peace has already been spoilt, not only now, but throughout much of her life.

'Well, Emmy, just like that youngster, that lamb, knew where it belonged, knew where safety lay, so you need to know . . . feel . . . that I . . . do, I really do, believe you, about old man Harry.'

This does not seem to point to a resolution of all the years of struggle, but to open them up again, emphasising the years of not being believed, and the loneliness, even madness, of that. She does not know if she feels angry, angry with her father's cowardice all those years, his blindness, his . . . . Perhaps it really is too late. The bright world around seems subdued now. She waits.

She knows he is looking at her, although she is still leaning back, her eyes half closed.

'Emmy?' She senses he does not know what to do. But that's alright, she thinks. I don't want to punish him, but it's not that easy.

'Emmy my dear, what're you thinking? Emily, please say something.'

She sighs, pulling herself together. 'Dad, I don't know. Thank you . . . ,' beginning to cry, unexpected sobs rising in her chest. She feels let down by her emotions now. How many more times will I be overwhelmed, she thinks. Trying to fight against it, *pull yourself together, don't go there, all that is behind you.* But then she remembers Liz, Liz Fell, who believed her, believed the unmistakable evidence before her eyes in her paintings, and her gratitude and relief. Now she knows she feels something similar. It doesn't matter when belief comes, in time there can be forgiveness.

She can begin to forgive and to feel relief, but like a river whose flow has been altered by the accumulation of alluvium or silt, only gradually can it flow more freely when some of its sediment has been washed away.

1988

Early forced red tulips with gaudy yellow centres in a vase on a windowsill in the Royal Free Hospital. They splay in the only way tulips know: with grace; petals drop, until the black pollen-laden stamens, as furry as bumble bees, are all that's left. No one notices, except Emily. Nurses in their buttoned-up blue dresses, the darker the blue the higher the rank, perform their duties kindly and efficiently.

Jacob Samuels, his hair uncharacteristically ruffled, his false teeth in a glass next to the dead flowers, lies back on his pillows. His distended belly is a cruel parody of forthcoming progeny. Sunken cheeks mock his once handsome bone structure. Now and again he requests music: symphonies not sonatas, grand orchestral works a befitting coda for his final days.

Emily, and Phyllis, Alex, and Paul, take turns to sit up at night. Phyllis has insisted on being involved, and no one has the strength to question her; Emily wonders if it can be for the good in the long run, or the short run of her father's last days.

It is Emily's shift. She leans on pillows in an armchair by his side, dozing in the half-light of the little side room with familiar views across Hampstead and beyond which no longer have a meaning, a backdrop disconnected from the drama. Her father rears up, crying out in pain, clutching the trapeze support above him. She calls a nurse. The breezy one.

'More morphine?'

'No, he's not written up for more for another hour.'

My God. What can he do? What can I do? The old man slumps back into sleep. Emily is caught in a terrible dilemma.

She wants him to have as much morphine as he needs, and so do the nurses and his doctor, but Alex, who is a doctor, argues that too much morphine will hasten his death. What's the difference if he dies today or next week, as long as he's not suffering too much? The power of Alex being male and a doctor – and having a mother – all rolled into one, rules the day.

Later, years later: Dad, I'm sorry. I'm sorry I only found my voice much later, and then only sporadically. I'm sorry.

She feels as useless as a child kicking a stone in the dust: her questioning over-ridden with barely an acknowledgement. But then Alex too has his own desperate fears and need to prolong his father's life – more, at any cost.

A primordial cry escapes her father's lips, as if from a fledgling trapped deep down. She tries to comfort him as once he comforted her. She combs his hair to make him more the father she knows. Or knew. And drinks tea, unusually with sugar, wishing it could go through to him via an invisible umbilicus.

The next evening, he rallies, sits up, puts in his false teeth and makes jokes to an appreciative audience. She feels guilty that she had wanted him to die in the night, to get it over with: that rock-hard belly, like breasts engorged with milk; his excruciating pain, and hers, at this symbol of death, not life.

Now the life and soul of the party, he wants a sip of iced water. It is not immediately forthcoming. He quips 'What does a man have to do to get a drink?' He doesn't refer directly to the inevitable. Of course he knows, knows that they all know, maybe knows some of them are still hoping for a miracle.

Her own need to talk openly would have been more pressing if she hadn't talked with him months earlier about his dying, told him how much she loved him. That trouble with his leg and his back were metastases, she later realised.

He had said then that he was sorry to be causing so much disruption to her life. She replied that of course she wouldn't want to be anywhere but nearby, involved. Her words felt inadequate, but she thinks they got through to him.

They both had a chance to go to their last opera together – *Rigoletto*. Phyllis could never stand sopranos, so Jake rarely had been to the opera all the years they were married. The love between father and daughter in this opera, against a background of a dead mother, was almost too painful for Emily.

The next day his breathing becomes more laboured. He is given oxygen. His eyes are closed all morning. She doesn't know if he can hear her. A nurse tells her that he can. She holds his capable hands with their rough corrugated nails, a few black hairs on the backs of his fingers, and bruised raised veins. Other than Peter's, she has never loved any hands more than these, hands that soothed her cheeks or brow, that patted her back. Hands that were often covered with the 'clean dirt' of pottery clay or gardening, that made the soil 'friable' and got it down to a 'fine tilth' – those beautiful words of his that she has never heard since. Now she cannot connect them with the hand that slapped her twice, or useless hands that could not or would not stop Phyllis. Or, much worse, did not stop Grandpa Harry.

Paul and Alex arrive.

Slowly, the great machine grinds to a halt, and then, when she thinks he has died, he breathes some more. A slow, irregular, further breath, in, and . . . out.

Such silence.

They cry. She cries. She doesn't know what she feels.

Half-light of the room. Has a big cloud eclipsed the sun? It is mid-day.

Phyllis returns from lunch. She sticks her hard breasts into Emily's chest as they dutifully hug.

She had got Jake to sign an open cheque to her the previous day. This emerges later when the details of his finances are discussed by a lawyer. The nastiness that had been beneath the surface for months and years like a festering abscess has begun to erupt.

Her father's forehead, with its wide sweep, looks less lined. She kisses it. Cold so soon. The hardness astonishes her. No one ever told her that death was so hard. A memory of precisely that hard coldness has been buried. And yet she feels strangely calm in that irrevocable silence.

Peter arrives. Emily hugs him and he hugs her. There's nothing else to do. A desolate, unreal hug, enveloped in his large navy-blue-woollen-jumper-arms, she is unable to cry as she stares at the reeded glass of a window. The corridor beyond is obscure, distorted. Another image to latch onto, file-away, delineate a significant event, and thereby – for the time being – avoid the feelings.

She doesn't want to leave the hospital, to go home, leave her father all alone. Alex's son Joe arrives on his way home from school in his royal blue blazer with its optimistic badge of a yellow oak tree, to visit Grandpa Jake. He hadn't known Grandpa had just died. He still wants to see him. He opens his mouth wide and bites the white knuckles of his clenched fist as he looks at the dead body through runnels of tears. This makes Emily cry. But she has to comfort Joe.

Emily wears her best black coat. It is the one her father admired when it was new, gave it his ritual blessing, 'Wish you well to wear it.' In the little synagogue smelling faintly of oranges in the Jewish cemetery – for though her father was an atheist he was also a conformist, and observed some of the Jewish rituals – she reads to the gathering:

> What though the radiance which was once so bright
> Be now forever taken from my sight,
> Though nothing can bring back the hour
> Of splendour in the grass, of glory in the flower,
> We will grieve not, rather find
> Strength in what remains behind –
> In the primal sympathy
> Which having been must ever be,

In the faith that looks through death,
In years that bring the philosophic mind.[2]*

- more to comfort herself than because she fully believes the meaning. She knows she will grieve and grieve, and yet perhaps find strength in what remains behind. Later, she thinks she should have read something he really liked, like *The Ballad of Reading Gaol*, or *The Highwayman*.

The room is familiar: the cart, the rabbi, the people, all like Grandma Gella's funeral – who lived to the age of ninety-six – except her father isn't here grieving too, centre stage, holding everyone together, like the centre pole of a tent. She laughs inwardly at the pun her father would have made – after all, he was a Pole, because his mother was.

To one side is the familiar shaped box covered in a navy velvet cloth. It looks too small. He can't be in there. She can still see him in 'The Property of the Royal Free Hospital' pyjamas.

The thin winter light streaks in, illuminating a plaque on the wall, *This tablet is dedicated to the memory of the six million.* It evokes infinity, like the stars at night as she leant against her Daddy's side for anchorage, to allay a weak-kneed feeling. Now her legs tremble. There is no room in her heart for more deaths, let alone six million.

The pitiable cart with long curved handles trundles towards the open grave, followed by its reluctant flock. The uncushioned wheels bump harshly over the ground. She wants his last conveyance to be as comfortable as a well-sprung high quality baby's pram. She imagines sun beaming through green grass, and wild flowers growing on her mother's grave in South Africa, all alone, so far away. Now, passing Gella's grave, and then her niece Natasha's outrageously small grave – for she died at the age of two – is all too much. She wails at the lowering of the coffin, so deep, so far down, clayey clods of earth clomping on it. How can they?

She thinks she will never feel comforted again.

---

2   *Wordsworth, *Ode on the Intimations of Immortality*

1992

Wandering in a desultory fashion around the shops of Heathrow airport, before being snatched from the safety of her life, her husband and children, to fall, Alice-in-Wonderland-like, down tunnels towards the plane. A feeling of 'there's no going back now' reminds Emily of being trundled on a trolley to an operating theatre, knowing that when she wakes up 'it will all be over', with the underlying fear of dying. She cannot believe that this return to South Africa after thirty-eight years is really happening.

As the vast plane soars up, London's November lights evoke Johannesburg's, blurred by tears and raindrops, at the beginning of that last Trans-Karoo train journey. An edge of sadness pokes through her 'high' as the plane climbs but she falls into the unknown once again.

'We don't want the children to grow up in a country like South Africa. If it was only us, we might have tried to stay. You can't live here unless you wear blinkers' – these familiar statements by her father were justified by his name being published on the régime's list, which he called the 'Roll of Honour,' of banned 'undesirables' after they all arrived in London in 1956.

The taste of plums with their bitter-sour stones and skin but their so-sweet flesh remains a deep memory, along with all the other brilliantly clear memories and pictures of sight, smell, sound, texture, beyond an increasing distance of experience.

She has not returned all these years, not even for a holiday, for she felt it would be like picnicking at the gates of Auschwitz. But once there was the beginning of an end of apartheid, with Mandela's release, the unbanning of the African National Congress two years previously, and freeing of significant political prisoners, she felt she could accept the invitation.

And she would be able to visit her mother's grave.

A curator had seen Emily's 1991 one-woman show in London, in a gallery in Cork Street. He offered her a show in Cape Town in a new gallery on the Waterfront, plane tickets and hospitality.

Her old discomfort with the country begins on the flight: the strident South African accent of a woman behind her – 'Yaw spelling moy drrrink!' – feels as irritating as a rough broken finger nail. She does not know if, after years of boycotting, she can drink South African wines on the plane, or watch tourist 'filims' with pleasurable expectation. Yet she feels a sense of great privilege and gratitude as she reads the sumptuous menu.

In Cape Town, she is in a depersonalised state, too stunned by the brightness, abundant agapanthus as blue as the sky, women with babies tied to their backs – like her memories – only this is real and she can't believe it. Her cousin, who is driving, stops at a robot – she gratefully slips back into this, and other, 'proper' names and ways of feeling, like a long-dislocated joint at last being aligned, with some strangeness and stiffness. Her euphoric dazed smile gets caught up with that of an Indian woman chatting to her friends. As their eyes meet the other woman's smile fades behind puzzlement.

She is deposited by her cousin in lodgings near the harbour. The symmetry of leaving from this very spot and now being invited to return to it is the first of several attempts at integrating past and present, lost and found, white and black, hate and love, good and bad, mother and father, work and play, child and adult, coming together. If the original dislocation – from mother and mother-country – left her with a serious limp, this re-alignment leaves her with an ache that is not always visible.

She is struck by the number of whites who build fortresses around themselves – walls within garden walls, electric fences, razor wire, armed response alarms, panic buttons, guns – creating a sterile prison, ironically echoing the barren townships and settlements to which they committed the blacks, enslaving them with curfews and passbooks. She hears a joke: 'Rottweilers now go for walks in pairs.' She senses that this extreme on-going legacy of apartheid deprives both sides of experiencing the richness of the other, just as her erstwhile denial of much of the good in her mother-country impoverished her.

Not knowing whether to distrust the black man who walks out of a bathroom naked in the little guesthouse where she stays, she loses her usual common sense in this massive upheaval. She grapples with her immediate response of fear, and later, anger: how much is she resisting being caught up in the pervasive paranoia and how realistic is it to be frightened? The speech in Xhosa of the men in the room next door, shouted to each other as if across the *veld*, explodes attractively like bubbles bursting, whilst Afrikaans sounds like the rasping of metal files or a lawnmower on full throttle. Noticing a fat pink Afrikaner in the street she is reminded of a polished pig. She fears that she is as prejudiced as those who upheld apartheid.

Through her adrenalin-charged vision she sees the private view of her show like a speeded-up film of a giant hibiscus opening, marred by occasional dismissive remarks by some of the white people towards the black visitors.

Gladys, a black artist, who produces vibrant woodcuts on handmade paper of dancers, and who works at the Waterfront Gallery, becomes a friend. She is the same age as Emily. She responds to Emily's, 'It's not good enough until everyone has the vote, even though we know it's heading that way', with 'It has to take its time. I'm happy. A few years ago I couldn't be here with you. I used to avoid going near "Whites only" places – I felt humiliated. Now I can hold my head up high. You have to be patient.' (Emily wonders what Gladys's childhood was like, compared with her own. What was Gladys doing when they were both little girls aged six?)

She is puzzled by the patience in Africans she observe many times. Nannies giving good quality maternal care to white children, people waiting by roadsides in the middle of nowhere, crowds waiting for trains and buses that seem never to come, mothers and infants thronging hospital corridors all day waiting to be seen. Perhaps it's resignation, the hopelessness of the dispossessed. She senses that years ago she may have so identified with the 'uninherited' that she was unable to ponder their state of mind. How different they are from the young Afrikaner men on a station platform wheeling their trolley into a confused old black man, hurling '*Gaan loop, vokken kaffir!*' – 'Go and run, fucking kaffir!'

She continues to struggle with what she has been missing for thirty-eight years. The pulsing forests where she can feel the heart of Africa; the insistent loud throb of the invisible bullfrogs at night in the game reserve against a background of a seething mass of life and stealth under the cloak of night. The sinister jagged laugh of hyenas, strange shrieks of birds, crashings in the undergrowth, and sometimes the roar of lions. Warthogs appear to teeter on high heels. Snails as big as her foot; animals with a timeless rightness-of-being where she is the interloper; sugar birds perfectly designed to poke into flowers for nectar with their sharp beaks, their iridescent turquoise plumage vying for attention with flame orange flowers; sunsets of such splendour that she is over-awed; the wild and violent oceans; flour-white powder-soft beaches; pawpaws oozing fecund sweetness; the clear, clear light across the vastest vistas culminating in lavender mountains surmounting taut flanks of unripe green.

The sweet flesh of the dark plum would not taste so sweet were it not for the sour skin.

Is there not enough abundance and bounty for everyone?

She thinks how the soil of Africa is so stained with the blood of beast and man, so wracked by violence, and yet nature herself is forgiving with her splendid capacity for renewal.

She recognises how much her life echoes this.

Visiting the little cemetery on the outskirts of Pretoria, her heart feels like a thin-skinned sack of sadness that could easily burst – not dramatically as her mother's did, but that it could begin to leak. How small her mother's grave looks, how worn and old, the inscription almost merging with the darkened headstone.

Rachel Samuels, née Solomons
1919 – 1948
✡
deeply missed by
Jacob, Emily, & Maurice

She looks at the words with detachment, reminding herself that Maurice, Rae's father, died a few years after his daughter. She reworks the mathematics of her mother's age at death. Emily, at forty-eight, has already outlived her by nineteen years. With a shiver, she remembers that she was more or less the same age when she died as Emily was when she began to turn her life round, began to find her own life source within her.

Pulling the petals off a few of the blood red roses she has brought – for somehow it would feel wrong to leave them intact – she scatters them over the slab and surrounding grass, *Mommeee, Mommeeeeeeeeeee*, wailing into a desolate desert. Her voice and a few petals are carried away on the wind. She imagines lying face-down, splayed on the cold stone, staying like that for ever, trying to get close to her. How different from the pleasant longings she had in England, when she imagined soaking up the warmth from sun-baked stone.

Returning to her hired car, she finds she had not put the handbrake on. She is grateful to the ground for being flat.

Emily visits the house in Emmarentia where she used to live. The front garden is now populated by palm trees, and odd clusters of rock which look as if they have been abandoned by a glacier that passed this way and melted.

The front doorbell chimes a loud and alien tune. A woman with peroxided hair opens the door.

'When I saw you from the window I *knew*, with your camera. Someone else came, a few years ago, who used to live here.' She readily invites Emily in for a quick tour.

Emily hardly listens to her chatter, just as she cannot take in the chintz furnishings, brocaded pelmets, curtains looped back with shiny ropes and tassels, thick pile carpeting, and the modern bathroom in the latest shade of avocado. But she connects with those familiar arched windows of the bedrooms – *Spanish mission style architecture*, wasn't it? – trying to make time stop still, to wipe out the intervening thirty-seven years. By the time she is bombarded with the new kitchen and more improvements, she has an overwhelming headache. She marvels at the woman's persistence, her unawareness that these are precisely the things that the visitor is not interested in.

On the way to being shown the new servants' quarters, Emily stops in the back yard and gasps, 'Oh the old sink!' It is like a reunion with a very dear old friend.

'Oh that old thing. That's the next thing to go. The maid still uses it sometimes . . . must get rid of it.'

If only this woman would shut up.

This beige stone sink is where Emmy was washed down if she was too muddy for the bathroom, and where she would see Ellen washing, in this corner of the yard that was always cool.

As if her survival of this ordeal depended on these flashes of connection, she finds another. In the back yard, least expected of all: a place between the bottom of the dusty privet hedge and the earth below, a foot or so of in-between nothingness, that has not changed at all. The soil is dry and stony, the colours almost monochromatic. No one has desecrated this, this memory of which she had no conscious recall, a place more substantial and miraculous than any other in and around the old house.

She must have lain on the grass here, looking at the space beneath the hedge. She must have stared, in the close-up way that children have, at the stones, and the parched soil, and the branches of the hedge. Maybe it was here that she pulled the wings off a dead grasshopper, lying on her stomach. Maybe it wasn't dead. Perhaps this empty in-between space, when she was six or seven or eight, connected with her own emptiness. And now she feels a loneliness and a deep quiet.

On the return journey, the plane soars like a metal monster, snatching her away from her country. She dozes and dreams of rolling down grassy hills dotted with cosmos daisies in the sunshine.

1994

Peter steps off the plane in Sydney, into air that is so hot that his eyeballs hurt. He glances back gratefully at the Qantas aircraft with its lively red tail sporting a white kangaroo.

As he pushes his trolley past customs and out of the exit, to the sea of faces, helium balloons, small children held aloft, *welcome home* banners, signs displaying names, a loud hubbub of voices and cries and calls, he sees to one side a tall dark young man, his straight hair flopping over his forehead, scanning the arrivals. Their eyes meet. Peter pushes his trolley as fast as possible, then hugs his son, aware of Adam's broad muscular shoulders, the way he has become a man without him.

'Let me take a look at you, my boy!' stepping back slightly, arms still enlaced. 'My goodness . . . .' How beautiful, earnest, searching, those dark eyes are. Peter tries to control his tears; the lump in his throat aches. The depth and translucency of those eyes had escaped his memory. And yet how complicating that they are the epitome of Adam's mother's.

'How many years is it? Three and a half, since you came to London? Feels too long, far too long. Yes, you were twenty two then.'

'Parked in the International Arrivals place. Let me take your trolley, Dad.'

'I'm not too old to manage! But it's good when your son can look after you.' Peter takes his lead from Adam's matter-of-fact stance, aware that his son may be trying to keep under control similar feelings to his own.

'How's the flight? And the stopover in Singapore?'

350

They enter an ordinary conversation as the young man wheels the trolley between revolving doors and over ramps to the carpark, stopping on the way to feed the ticket into a pay station. Peter notices how unflustered his son is, how competent. He recognises his own more youthful self, a self that felt intrepid. But then, can he claim any of that, when he wasn't there?

All Adam's clothes seem lopped off: he wears long khaki shorts – or are they short trousers – and a sleeveless tee-shirt. Perhaps December was not such a good idea, Peter thinks, sweat pouring down his back as they trundle across the car park.

'That's my limo,' the son announces with muted pride, stopping at an orange Saab, certainly not air conditioned. Peter thinks he must find a way of talking to him about his finances, to see if the allowance he sends is enough.

As Adam drives away from the airport following signs to the city, Peter worries if two weeks will be enough to re-establish contact, to feel how this boy really is, to begin to know him. Long-distance phone calls and emails have been so inadequate.

'Y'know, mate, I'm really looking forward to the time we have – just the two of us – in that lodge you booked on the East Coast – *Rainforest* something or other?' Peter notices his slide into a strong Australian accent.

'Yeah, *Rainforest Retreat*. Yeah, me too.'

'So how's Stella? How's your mother?'

'She's fine, yes, she's good. Had that operation about six months ago, as y'know – one of those "women's" ops – but she's well now.' He nods, keeping his eye on the road.

'Her work? How's that going?'

'Fine. I think she enjoys her teaching at the uni. Yeah, well, you can ask her, I'm sure you chat to her?'

'Of course, yes.'

They drive in silence past large expanses of indigenous trees interspersed with flashes of red bottle-brush bushes. Peter thinks that Adam wants to make sure that his parents talk to each other – something that took years to establish after the divorce.

'Didn't want you to think I was using you to find out . . . about Stella. I guess, my boy, that's an ordinary thing people do in families, ask about each other, and hear different points of view.' *Oh God now he'll think I'm lecturing. Or that I'm too defensive.* He continues, 'But I s'pose when there's been a divorce, even though it was ages ago, all that is potentially fraught. Sorry.'

Adam does not make it easier for his father. A repetitive twitch in his cheek conveys the young man's tension. As they are driving fast on the Expressway, Peter senses they should stick to lighter subjects for now. But he has never been good at small talk.

'D'you want to put on a tape, Dad? You still like modern jazz? Got a Miles Davis compilation somewhere,' gesturing towards a plastic box at Peter's feet, amidst the debris of empty drink cans and wrappers.

Peter does not feel like listening to music now – his head throbs, and he feels the gap between him and Adam widening. He thinks that Adam wants to shut out any conversation.

'Y'know, Dad, I always think it figures, you liking the MJQ – you, as an architect.'

'Oh really?' raising his eyebrows, 'Say more?' He doesn't tell Adam that he does not listen to jazz these days, that he finds the tighter geometry of Bach more satisfying.

'The clean lines of modern jazz, the precision, the structure, and yet, and yet, the playfulness.'

Peter briefly wonders if his son is mocking him – but no, the young man seems serious, his knuckles white as he grips the steering wheel. Who are you? Peter feels like asking. But 'the sins of the fathers' then comes to mind: sure that this boy's strangeness, the way Adam switches in and out of contact, is his own doing. Peter swigs water from a bottle, winds down the window, and stretches out. 'Okay, well then. Let's give it a go!'

With his eyes closed, he allows the music to fill his head.

The beat and exhaustion take him back to the days when he was a student, when he smoked cigarettes and dope, drank a surfeit of cheap wine, went to parties, and laughed more than at any other time of his life. When he discovered Bach, and Mozart, and the Beatles, and modern jazz. When he lived in Japan for seven months, and discovered a passion for architecture, form, and the way it can affect everyday life. The days when he took political issues so seriously; when he fell in love with T. S. Eliot, and three or four women, holding himself back a little with each girl, not fully believing that she was quite right. In his memory, he sees the pellucid dawn rising over Sydney as he walked home across town, to sleep until afternoon. That invincible feeling of possibilities, of the world open to him, of choices he would make.

He comes out of his reverie as they enter More Park Road and then South Dowling Street, past the surviving clusters of simple terraced cottages that still line the road, pleased that they have not been demolished.

Adam deposits him at the little guesthouse where father and son will spend the first night of Peter's visit, before they begin their journey north the next day. Adam says that he has to do some things, but will return late afternoon. Peter thinks he is minimising the contact.

That night Peter finds it difficult to sleep. He is saddened that Adam is not the free spirit he was at that age, does not seem to feel blessed. Of course he cannot repair years of absence in these two weeks. He struggles with thoughts of whether he is overestimating – or underestimating – his contribution to Adam's life. Adam has had a sort of Dad in Phil, Stella's partner, he tells himself. Adam knows it wouldn't have worked between him and Stella . . . . People have worse lives. I haven't been so bad . . . . And yet, Peter feels as if something in his heart will never be quite right while he is out of alignment with Adam. He wonders if all parents who have separated and 'lost' a child feel this.

He phones Emily early in the morning, which is late at night for her.

'Emmy, I feel so bad about Adam. He's okay, ostensibly. But he and I are so out of . . . out of touch. I feel wrong-footed much of the time. I blame myself . . .' Peter pulls himself together, knowing that self-pity would not be helpful. 'No,

Em'ly, maybe you could help me, help me think about it, help me get my bearings, so I can make the most of the time here.'

'Why? What happened when you arrived?'

'Nothing much. I mean, Adam was polite, sweet really, but so remote. Not so much in what he says, but in his manner, his mood. So different from our boys. Maybe that's inevitable. You see, I don't know how much is him – his disposition, his . . . inheritance from Stella, and me – and how much is as a result of my lack, my absence. The damage I've caused.'

In the ensuing silence, Peter's sense of disconnection is increased by the actual distance between him and his wife.

'Peter, I'm sorry it's so hard. Maybe you can only do your best – which I know you will do. Maybe you can't perform miracles.' There is an awkward silence. Then Emily continues, 'I'm thinking of the struggles I've had with my father and with Phyllis – let alone my lack of a mother. You know, the thing you could do, that may make all the difference, is acknowledge to Adam that you're sorry, sorry that you weren't there in his growing-up years – after the age of five or six, wasn't it? You know, if you tell him that you think of him, you really do, that you've always had a place in your heart for him . . . . You know, in your own words. I know that's true, that you worry about him, that you've never abandoned him emotionally. I remember even when Jack was born, you became quite sombre, thinking of Adam's birth. He mayn't be comforted by that, mayn't believe you, but it's the truth. What do you think?'

'Maybe. I'll see. It's hard. I don't think I've ever given enough credence to my Dad dying when I was fifteen – and how that may've led to my having to . . . sort of . . . invent a father after that age, you know, made me sort of weak in that respect . . . .' As Peter talks, he knows that has not been the case with Jack and Max, that he had it deep in his blood and bones to be there, because he was wedded to Emily in all senses. He has often had an image of him and Stella being like two pieces of a jigsaw puzzle that really could not fit together. He thinks how it led to her trying to force him to fit in with her – only he wouldn't, couldn't comply, if he was to survive. 'Emmy, okay. I wonder if I can offer Adam something, something more: if he wants to spend time in London, to study, maybe he could live with us? Maybe Jack and Max would get on with him, despite the age gap, maybe belatedly I could be there more for him?'

He senses a longer than usual silence, before Emily says, 'It's a big thing you're saying, you and I would have to think, think through the implications, the practical side.' He quickly feels that he was wrong to expect her to make up for his and Stella's deficits.

'Yes, of course, I'm sorry – this isn't the time . . . for us to decide. I won't make any rash offers – without you and I thinking it . . . .'

Emily interrupts, 'Peter, you must do what you feel is best, and if it's best for you and Adam, it's best for me, and the boys, I'm sure. Really. Sorry if I was so, so cautious just now. I often feel that this is the one area of your life – besides the problems in your professional life, but that's in another sphere – which sort of eats away at you. And I know – as you know I know – what it's like to be the rejected one. So the least we can do is offer Adam a second home in London – if he wants it.'

'Love you, Em'ly. Y'know, this sort of conversation we're having, about Adam, Stella and I could never have. Makes me think that it's not only his lack of a present father, but of a couple – parents – who could think together. I felt quite low – maybe it's jet lag. But much better now. Better go – thanks, darling. Love you . . . .'

She has put him in mind of his own parents, their seaside holidays in Terrigal, how he and his sister were free to play and invent games and find friends, because all the time their parents were so happily there, relaxed and not shy about their love for each other.

Poor Stella – her need to control . . . . It's not surprising that Adam is fraught, he thinks.

1995

Emily is taken by two friends to visit Sally Mthethwa, in her shop in Soweto, a township outside Johannesburg. It is during her next trip to South Africa, three years since the last one – where she has been commissioned to paint four pictures.

Sally's hair is scraped neatly back, baring a fine-featured face which matches her dignified, forceful delivery. 'My first vote? I couldn't believe it! I thought the piece of paper would drop into the box and go right through the floor. Can you believe it, an ol' tramp in Joubert Park had the vote, but all our people didn't, jus' because we had the wrong colour skin.'

There are no customers for the few cuts of fatty beef in a glass case. Sally offers *Coca Cola* from paper cups that she expects her visitors to wash even though they are from a new package.

The two friends with Emily – both 'liberal' white South Africans – notice a starving dog in the yard outside, which they gather isn't Sally's dog. This emaciated chained-up animal becomes their main focus. Appalled, they want to know whose dog it is. The dog's plight feels irrelevant to Emily. She wonders if extreme suffering leads to a hierarchy of suffering, and if these two people turn to a dog because the black people's problems are so overwhelming. Or because their guilt is unbearable? Emily stops speculating and focuses on the bright spark in Sally's eyes.

She says that the Soweto protests of 1976 were planned in her back yard. 'If the government doesn't do something soon about education and health and housing, there'll be another '76,' she explained. The second time she was in jail for protesting a policeman with more badges on him than she could count said to her, 'If you don't stop causing unrest you'll be in jail 'til you're an ol' woman!'. She told him she didn't care, 'If our children weren't prepared to die, if we weren't prepared to go to jail, there'd still be apartheid.'

Her fervour is optimistic and not bitter. Emily is reminded of that impressive patience. Sally adds, 'It takes time. Rome wasn't built in a day.'

One of Emily's friends returns later with a packet of dog biscuits, and then worries that having a proper meal would make the dog more ill, or make it miss real food all the more.

Another day Emily is taken to see the hospital in Soweto by a friend who is a social worker there. She notices 'no guns' signs next to 'no smoking', each equally prominent.

One afternoon, she sits in her aunt Selma's kitchen. The fluorescent lights compete with the bright sunshine coming through the window. Selma asks Grace, her black maid, 'Gracie, what do you think we should have for supper tonight? What's in the fridge?'

'Ma'am, I leave fish, curry fry fish I make yesterday, in Pyrex. Before I go off I put it in oven. You take it out seven o'clock. I put on boil potatoes same time, you find potatoes on stove when you eat. And baked custard in fridge, Ma'am.'

'Thank you Gracie.' Selma doesn't look up as she snips her emerald green thread with sharp silver scissors shaped like a stork, and continues to embroider over a blue iron-on cross-stitch pattern of a cottage. She has a cupboard-full of similar tablecloths, tray-cloths, napkins, mats, runners, and aprons.

'Oh yes Gracie, have you seen my secateurs, cutters, you know, garden scissors? I left them in the garden I think.'

'I go look.' Grace wipes the sheen of sweat from her forehead with her apron, and lifts a wicker basket of damp washing to hang on the line. 'Yes Ma'am, you pick flowers this morning,' she adds over her shoulder. 'I think I find them. You want me buy milk after? *Baas* drink lotsa milk today. And onions, I pick up onions from Sammy, nearly finished all the onions.'

Selma, in her flower-sprigged dresses and white cardigans, her girlish voice, dyed hair, a face unlined despite her fifty-nine years, is now as dependent on her nanny as when she was a small child – though that nanny died years ago, and nowadays the servants are called 'maids'. Emily notices how Selma leaves her dirty cups lying around for Grace to clear, as well as her cuttings from flower arranging by the sink.

It occurs to her that the black servants have considerable power after all. She wonders what they really think of these whites who cannot manage the simplest things.

She sees that it is still a country of a privileged few, of an economic apartheid, of enormous inequity, of whites in vast houses with swimming pools, tennis courts and servants. Fortressed whites' houses have security-guard booths and barriers in residential areas, whilst many of the blacks' schools, hospitals, and tiny houses are similarly protected with razor wire and high railings. Her friends say as they drive past small brick houses in townships that house four families each, 'These are really nice houses.' Well, only compared with the corrugated tin or packing-case squatter huts that still proliferate, she thinks.

She worries how all these impressions will shape the work she has been commisioned to make here.

That old vagueness, at times a drugged sleepiness, creeps over her: the escape route when she is in touch with feelings of abuse. As if sucked down into oceanic depths, almost beyond control, it carries the promise of a sort of peace.

It is a relief to get down to the work.

Her patrons have supplied some of the tools and materials she requested, in a garage converted into a studio attached to accommodation. She shuts herself away for days in this large concrete-floored space in the aptly named green suburb of Orchards in Johannesburg, venturing to a shopping mall for basic food supplies, and, with the help of a young man from the gallery, a builders' yard for sand and concrete and gravel and plaster.

Laying her canvasses flat on their backs she makes a raised frame for each one, boxing them in. They remind her of wide graves, now flooded with topaz sunlight. She returns to her old emollient: wine – now fine Stellenbosch white – to ease the flow of her vision, a way of bypassing her intellect.

The red earth she squelched between her toes after the rains as a child, the pebbles she wanted to suck, the poplar branches, the afternoon sun slanting across the lawn, Lizzie's ripe skin, the breeze, the no-nothingness, the torment, the fire and the ice, the soft and the rock hard – she wants to recreate and transform all of this.

Poured wet sand mixed with paint and concrete, gravel, rusty barbed wire, dried leaves and twigs, and red rose petals, all formless and chaotic. Yet they convey fixity, not transience. She almost gives up in tears. Surface textures, the same old literal stuff. She cries for her father, and her mother, but she can't find them. This country baffles her: she doesn't know if it's deep in her blood, or if she will always yearn for it and not be requited. For now, all she can do is try to stay with her frustration.

With a deep breath, she closes her eyes, and feels how her body is made from these amethyst mountains, these rivers where she taught herself to swim, the veld and the animals that hide in it, the violent oceans, yellow rocks, and the sun.

She remembers her canvases in Suffolk, when Liz Fell appeared and understood her struggle. That wasn't enough, she realises. Suffolk, although intensely beautiful, was not the earth of her birth.

The next day, through a headache like a constricting iron band, she knows that all she can do is continue to wrestle with calamity. She looks at her work as though it has been carried out by someone else, and feels desolate, sad for all that she has been through. Perhaps the next painting will satisfy her more.

She struggles with impasto of paint that is like petrified lava, like Pompeii, which captures life in death.

She inscribes words in the wet paint, in her own handwriting – forgetting that years ago she scratched *Hope is a lie* into a self-portrait. On one, lines from Emily Dickinson:

A Lava step at any time
Am I inclined to climb

On another, etched into thick paint, two lines from the same poet that intrigue her:

Perception of an object costs
Precise the Object's loss

But the words feel like embroidery. Or stealing.

Her old love of patterns in nature becomes her guide now. The way that veins in leaves follow the same principles as the circulation of blood, or the delta of a big river; the way waves leave prints on the sand that perfectly depict mountain ranges; the structure of some sea shells: so like rams' horns; the patterns from cracked dried earth, reminding her of dried paint, or a crackle glaze. The way some sea coral is so like the brain, which in turn is like the insides of a red cabbage: how brilliant is nature's design, to maximise the surface area.

She wants her canvases to breathe, to be alive, to capture her love of weeds growing in the most inhospitable places, and the way ferns can shoot out of vertical walls. Possibly to grow mould or fungus or lichen or rust on the canvas, to dry and flake, and to die. A curator's nightmare, she laughs. Above all, she wants every inch of her canvas to speak, to carry weight. If some areas recede and take on a background quality, she wants them to zoom forward if focussed on, in the way that peripheral vision can cease to be peripheral. It is not enough to create the equivalent of nature's miracles, she has to transform nature into her story of her life and her story of this exquisitely painful country.

On another painting, full of natural trickles and whorls, she scratches – in tiny writing that only close perusal would discern – a part of her old quotation by Flaubert,

Even the smallest thing has something in it which is
unknown. We must find it.

She is not only challenging herself to make work that breathes, but that has a life cycle, where everything is related to every other thing. And where the only certainties are space. And time. And transience. And death. But yet, where she can challenge all those things, by making space that is constricted, time that is unbounded, transience alongside fixity, and work that defies death because it lives on.

An Afrikaans woman, Lisette van Rensberg, of the Waterfront Gallery, is a calm presence who takes Emily to different bays to swim in the always-icy Atlantic, and to restaurants with views of Table Mountain. Lisette wears simple linen tunics in aquamarine or burnt sienna over baggy white cotton trousers, silver earrings like miniature mobiles, her face haloed by fair hair as soft as thistledown. One evening, in a quiet corner of a café, she reads Emily some of her poetry in Afrikaans, and translates it for her. From Lisette, she learns two words that she writes in her notebook, to remember: *motrëen* (moth rain), and *douvoordag* (dew before daybreak), wonderful words that contain an essence of the language of her paintings, the delicate thing itself, which cannot really be explained or adequately translated.

Lisette inspires her to make a fifth small painting, more feminine than the others, with dull graphite and grape blue, dusty pink (like flowers), and smoky green (like eggs), all overlaying a bedraggled square of earth. The more she looks at this work, the more she discovers and the more hopeful she feels. It calls to mind something she had as a child – the Golden Book that her mother used to look at with her. Forgotten until now, she remembers the pictures of woodland, with ducks' eggs hidden on each page amid the fallen leaves.

She goes back to the four new big pieces, and – with help from Lisette, for they are heavy – stands them up, then asks to be left alone. She steps back, right back. Her knees feel weak when she sees how the years when her eyes promiscuously gathered everything they saw – from that silver milk bottle top on the kitchen floor to dust on her father's shoes, from phlegm on the pavement to cobwebs on a branch – have been alchemised into more than an encrusted patina of her South Africa. She looks at the paintings, as if for the first time. She knows they are about love, the love that emerges out of the pain of labour, when a mother holds her baby, her blood on the baby's head, her womb still contracting. Life that could so easily have been death. She hardly dare say it, but the paintings feel monumental, inspiring reverence.

That is the moment when she can be fully herself, when she knows she has embraced life and death in a delicate balance.

Of course there had been moments like that before, in Suffolk, when she found a way of painting from inside, when she tramped across shiveringly beautiful countryside where the reeds rippled under her skin. Maybe moments before at the Slade. Certainly Peter allowed her to risk being more herself because he was so solidly himself: when she could be herself in his presence. And years and years before, when held in Lizzie's arms, Emmy could refind a soft place inside herself.

But there came a tipping point in the making of these paintings, when she knew she no longer needed to retreat to another house in which she had laboriously lodged since she was four and a half. After the death, sometimes the distance from the 'observatory' house to her real house was vast, sometimes very close.

She often conjectured what she was like before her mother died. She thinks that she had a sense of 'I', who could talk to 'me', who could play games where she was safely herself, and could risk imagining things happening to herself in the game. In a dusky memory, she thinks she used language and stories and play to think about herself, calling herself 'Emmy', because her mother and father were there to hold her. But she suspects she may have been a child who, even before the tragedy, used her eyes in a particularly clingy way, as a way of latching onto things that anchored her.

In the Orchards studio, in this moment of homecoming, she can feel a fluidity, an exhilarating freedom, to being both outside and at the same time inside her paintings, outside and inside herself. Her paintings speak to her and yet are her. She feels loss – a heavy lump-in-the-throat loss – of the old known pattern of distance, and a glimpse of retrospective massive loss of so much wealth when she was in a world of surfaces. And yet, at one and the same time, she feels the warm-blooded aliveness of possession: encompassing a heady experience of ecstasy, close to a wild madness, desire and loss all in one.

The closest description of her epiphany is to say it is like an orgasm.

Of course she can still go into the other house to see her house, if she wants to. But it feels just that: like a brief visit to a neighbour, where she sees her house from an unfamiliar angle.

1996

Since Peter's crisis in his professional life, when he gave up his job in a drawing office and started his own practice, he began to enter plans for competitions and to tender for projects. But his output was slow, and sometimes he missed deadlines. In returning to a reformulation of his work, he spent far more hours sketching and studying than addressing actual projects.

He tried to put into practice his fascination with form and structure in nature – the hexagonal cells of honeycomb, the symmetry of crystals, the spiral of a ram's horn in D'Arcy Thompson's *On Growth and Form,* the double helix of DNA. He pored over Haeckel's late nineteenth century drawings of domes and hexagons and pentagons, and found a book that showed the microscopic ribbed structure of shark skin, and another on the structure of bones, and how they withstood stress. He compared the physics of waves with that of sand dunes, revisited the drawings of Frei Otto for buildings inspired by the shapes of soap bubbles, and studied Joseph Paxton's design for the Crystal Palace – based on the ribs of a water lily's leaves – which Le Corbusier once described as the victory of light over gravity. In going right back to the Golden Section, the underlying principle of the Parthenon, he returned to ancient Greek geometry, and struggled to arrive at his own synthesis of the classical and the romantic, to integrate the fundamental laws of the universe with imagination and expression that was not superimposed, but grew out of it. He knew he was following in the footsteps of a long line of architects.

Peter felt that nature could not be improved upon; what mattered was how people used it, breathed their own individual soul into it. So, taking nature as his mentor, he elongated, or rotated, or made mirror images or opposites of the fundamental structures, never losing their basic configuration, and adapted them for the requirements of his vision for his building. He used colour sparingly, sympathetic to the ancient Greeks for whom the fundamental colours were black and white.

Incorporating his earlier love of contrast, of smoothness with roughness, he used materials that conveyed high technology juxtaposed with corroded metals or rough stone. But he was dissatisfied with his work, for he felt that some of it was too dryly mathematical, while some was the very opposite, lacking coherence. When he tried to combine the regular with the irregular, he became unsure of why and how, and how to achieve the right balance.

One Saturday afternoon, Emily senses Peter watching her in her floral cotton dress, the navy 1940s one dotted with small colourful flowers that she found in Portobello Road. She knows he always likes her in this dress – he said it accentuated her slim waist and full hips – although generally she cannot believe the good things he says about her. She pulls the skirt up to expose her legs to the late summer sun, as she sits on the old bench she'd painted so often that it is hard to tell which of the many flaking patches of colour it is meant to be.

She is shelling peas, one of the time-consuming jobs that she enjoys – like mincing food with an old-fashioned mincer, or grinding coffee beans, or making a paste of spices with a pestle and mortar, or kneading dough for bread – because it stops her feeling hurried or anxious.

The small fresh peas with their grassy smell slowly accumulate in a large Prussian blue colander. She likes the look of this green against this blue. Now and again she munches some of the pods until only the fibre is left, which she spits out into a bucket.

'You know, I think in some ways your work and mine aren't that different, Em'ly.' He puts his newspaper down.

'What d'you mean? Shelling peas and reading the paper? Both ways of keeping in touch with the world, I guess!'

'You're joking, of course. No, seriously, I mean, I know how you get excited about organic form, and how it informs your work, and, and your attention to the visual world, where you're not trying to impose some idea on your painting, but are thinking through what you observe and what you feel – you tell me how you simply feel what is out there: the truth of the object, or the integrity of the object, I think you call it. And how something is revealed, something you didn't already know – different from a fact – and it comes out on canvas. I don't mean to give a seminar on you – but I sometimes think that we're . . . complementary.'

She remains silent, continuing with her simple task. She wishes he had not broken the spell of her meditation, her way of just being there. She wants to jokily tell him to shut up, but is unsure if he needs her attention, and if she should try and respond.

'Not sure about that. Not sure I can see much of a connection.' She pauses to take a deep breath. 'Well, I think your approach is intellectual. I think you have an idea, and then yes, of course you do feel your way through it, through and beyond to a structure that you create. But somehow, I am still painting from I don't know where, from my life's blood, somehow. I know that sounds dramatic, but it's true. I don't know if I really want to analyse what I do – I'm almost superstitious that the magic, the mystery, might disappear. In fact, you know how I've told you that the better my life becomes, with you, and the children, the more I fear that my painting will dry up. Perhaps it's no coincidence – for me – that painting has the word "pain" in it. I'm not thinking of the real etymology. You know, if the source, for me – which has always been awful things – recedes, where will my impetus come from? I could end up painting pretty pictures.' She pauses, and then, with a slow shake of her head,

'But I guess that's not so; there's always more to dredge up; or to try to paint, even if it's beauty, and joy . . . and all kinds of ways of finding meaning, without being clichéd about it.' She becomes dreamy, looking at the middle distance in an unfocussed way. A handful of pea pods fall to the grass.

'Well, for someone who didn't want to engage, you're doing okay,' Peter says quietly.

A rather tense silence follows while he stretches out his long legs, arches his back, and stretches his arms skywards, before refolding himself into the canvas chair. And during this silence she goes back to her task, running the small peas through her hand like sand, letting them form a little hill, and watching the hill remain more or less the same size, no matter how fast or slow the rain of peas. She knows Peter would have some law of physics to explain what she is observing; she remembers his use of the word 'determinism'. But at this moment she does not want predictability. Predictability feels lifeless, mechanical, ruling out surprise, or even chaos.

'What're you thinking, Em'ly?'

She stares at the peas, 'Years ago you'd never ask me, or, hardly ever, ask what I was thinking. I used to stop myself from asking you that sort of thing. You were so, so, sort of self-sufficient. I was in awe of that. And now . . . .'

'Now it's the other way round!'

'Not sure. Well, I was thinking something like that. At that point anyway.' She realises she has avoided some of the truth of what she's been thinking.

He gives a little laugh. 'Yes, I think there's something in that. Well, you know, you've really got somewhere in the past ten or so years: gradually, since Max was in the reception class. You know, I think you are more *in* the world, without that much anxiety, and I . . . well, you know I'm struggling . . . .'

She looks up at him, at Peter's strong chin that reminds her of her father, at his long thin fingers, his delicate collar bone glimpsed through the opening of his faded shirt, his flat firm belly, and she knows she loves this fine man, who is now risking uncertainty, who is honestly engaged in questioning his place in the world.

'Peter, I'll tell you what I was thinking just now. You know I go into *dwaals*, as we used to say in South Africa – dreamy states. Sorry. I was thinking about the peas here, about the way they pile up like an anthill and some roll down, and how I didn't want to hear some physical law that explained it, or made it predictable – you know, how or why it never goes beyond a certain conical shape, and so on, because I didn't want to lose the magic.'

She doesn't have to wait long to gauge his reaction.

'But Em, yes, you're right, that connects with something I've been struggling with: the more I study the natural laws of the universe, the more I have to acknowledge that alongside the appeal of symmetry and order, is chaos. I don't yet know if it's a system that I don't understand, and that "chaos" simply may be a system of incredibly complex rules that just appear to be chaotic. But, yes, I don't want to lose sight of the essential counterpoint between regularity and irregularity. You know, the extraordinary movements in, say, flood water meeting opposite currents, which may appear chaotic but are governed by rules of physics.'

He interrupts himself with a rush of self-consciousness, 'Oh God, if our neighbours could hear us . . . *Pseud's Corner!*' he whispers, glancing at the fence.

She replies as straightforwardly as she can, 'I think your job is incredibly hard, to have to wrestle with mathematical and physical laws – otherwise your buildings would fall down – and yet to find that alchemy that, say, a painter hopes to find: that . . . transformation of the prosaic, or even of chaos, into something that may be an emotion, or a vision, but a rendering nonetheless.' He seems to be listening calmly, giving her a sense of spaciousness, so she continues,

'I was thinking the other day that the notion of hubris may embody what I mean: that it wasn't just an intentional mistake that the ancient Greeks wove into their weaving, say, so as not to threaten, or anger, the gods, but, paradoxically, the very human element of inspiration, the thing that does not conform to rules. Only a god could make something that's perfect. And yet, and this is the paradox, I think that it's these deviations that can be "god-like", you know – we don't know where they come from. Oh goodness, now I'm going on . . . . You know, what I said just now, that I could lose the mystery, the inspiration, if I talk too much.

'But Peter, I wonder sometimes if you try too hard, if you want to create the most breath-taking building in the world – not that there's anything wrong with that, of course, and . . . maybe . . . . ' She stops, and puts the colander on the ground, and folds her arms. She doesn't know how to talk about a vision that could be ideal but has to suffer inevitable disappointments and failures; and that would be, in the end, only a step towards the next building, or the next painting. She stutters, 'Oh dear. I can't explain. Sorry.'

She stands, stretching her back, longing to return to her studio, knowing that he has to work this out for himself. Yet she also longs to help him, if she could.

'Darling, must get on with my painting.' She stands behind his chair, gently kneading his shoulders, and brushes her cheek against his forehead. It feels warm and silky. 'I think you will find a form, forms, you know, some way of working that will feel inspired, but I can't really help you . . . .'

He looks up at her with a frown, and nods. They are looking at each other upside down. His mouth tries to smile.

PART FIVE:
ACCEPTANCE

1999

Emily is no longer so negative towards critics, and sometimes enjoys conversations with them. But she approaches interviews fairly quizzically, with wary curiosity. She knows that her paintings are the real diary of her life, that she does not need these word-makers and markers. But occasionally a sensitive interviewer throws new light on something she is pondering – like Angela Bellamy, the art critic, who interviews her on BBC 3's *Nightwaves*:

> *A.B. I know this is an enormous question, Emily, but could you try and expand on the ways in which your work has developed over the past thirty years?*
>
> *E.S. My goodness! Yes, it is a huge question. Well, let's see . . . I don't know if my "signature" nowadays is that different from forty years ago – like one's fingerprints, perhaps it hasn't changed fundamentally. Or like the key in which a piece of music is written, the overall atmosphere is consistent. Although if I use a musical analogy I think my work has changed from D minor to something more like E flat. You know, that's the key of my favourite of Mozart's piano concerto, number 22.*
>
> *Now, especially, I try to convey what I actually encounter in life: my painting is an interpretive interface between the outer world and my inner world. And between my inner world and the outer. I was less clear about that thirty years ago. Then, I was either rigorously recording the outer world – you know, struggling to find the essence of it – or awash in my*

inner world. Now, I think, I'm caught in the tension between the two.

But this quest always makes me anxious: how to make something that is perceptible to the viewer as well as to me. Yes, I think that thirty or so years ago I didn't worry much about others' perception. Well, I guess I did, but I had given up on that. Strange, I know it's often the other way round for artists. In those days I was driven by a compulsion to render my vision, almost as catharsis. But now I do want others to be offered a glimpse of my object, my relationship with it – haunted by memory and by dreams, attempting meaning where there may not be any – my object, as I was saying, even though it is for ever enigmatic and elusive, searching for but not fully finding. Goodness, back to that. Perhaps I haven't moved on that much after all: presence that is about absence, having but not having. As Plato said, ". . . a thing is not seen because it is visible, but conversely, visible because it is seen . . . ." That, for me, is the endless fascination. And, I have to add the obvious, that my object can never be the same as your object, so if I paint my object you are seeing it at "two removed": through my distorting lens as well as your own. And, incidentally, my object tomorrow will be different from, but not disconnected to, my object today. But that way, perhaps, what you see is enriched. Or, impoverished? It would depend on your vision and on mine.

I realise I could go on and on. At times I am aware that my vision, my experience, can never fully be shared by anyone else: indeed it is my very inalienable separateness from you that may make me more mysterious, more challenging, more enigmatic. Perhaps what you end up with is your very own experience. Oh dear, I hope I am making sense?

A.B. Yes, Emily, I think I do see what you're saying, and how that elusiveness has fascinated you for decades, and intrigued the viewers of your work.

Can we go back to your earlier work, in the early 70s: it was often extremely detailed – like rich tapestries – semi-abstract, but preoccupied, I think, with what you once described as a need to see the foreground and the background equally – to value the whole patina before your eyes as well as, I guess, in your imagination. That gave it a particular richness. In what ways does that particular vision still feature?

E.S. Well . . . yes . . . . My South African paintings of a few years ago were still preoccupied with the tension between peripheral vision and the thing we are trying to look at; surface versus depth; trying to integrate the micro with the macro. It's hard, if not impossible, to do all that justice with words. I guess that what I began to really feel then, in the South African series, was the delicate balance between life and death. I don't want to get too autobiographical here, but there is a pivotal tension between the two that I have always been preoccupied with, but it was only a few years ago that I got close to some way of conceptualising it. And, you know, in a way, the realisation that the sadness those paintings evoke in me is more about beauty, and goodness – something about the precariousness of those qualities – than about death.

But to return to your question: nowadays I still automatically take a mental snapshot of most things I encounter, partly to draw on later if I choose to, partly to absorb it and, in a way, to love it, whereas when I was much younger, long before I committed myself to painting, my mind took "snapshots" indiscriminately of everything: there was hardly any selection or censoring in my brain. It was as if there was celluloid behind my eyes. Whereas now I can choose, and can bear to focus on one thing to the exclusion of another; you know, to home-in, and to leave aside. Well, more or less. You see, when I was younger, to make choices would have involved a capacity to bear loss: the loss of all the things I was choosing not to 'capture'. So I

clung to everything that my eyes lit upon because I had
lost so much of what I had inside when I was a young
child. I was forever hungry, taking in, possibly stealing,
the appearances of everything, and only latterly,
gradually, in my 40s and 50s, have I not needed to live
like that, because only relatively recently have I found
the life source within me, and I don't have to cling to
appearances out there. I know I'm saying huge things,
but it's what I mean.

But Angela, I want to go back to what you were
saying just now, about my erstwhile approach of
trying to capture the whole: I think rather than
painting landscape, or trees, or people, my paintings
are landscape. The way the paint runs or falls or
pushes or winds or coagulates or forms furrows – the
tensions between all that movement and colour: that
is landscape, or is a person, and at one and the same
time, is my feeling inner self.

A.B. My goodness. I think I need to take all that in.
Luckily this is recorded – so I can come back to it later.
But what did you mean by 'stealing' just now – that
you used to 'steal' because of a sort of hunger? Can you
elaborate on that?

E.S. Well, yes, I think so. I mean that, like a magpie, I
would steal from all over the place in my images, in my
techniques, partly from other artists – we all do that
to some extent, we can't not; it's a part of working in a
context. But I mean more than that. I was constantly
'hungry' and so I was a sort of visual kleptomaniac. I
had a compulsion to take and to appropriate, without
feeling that I could find the source of richness within
myself.

But hold on, I don't mean that we, I, am the source
entirely: I mean I can find a flow, une source, within,
but of course it is because over the years I have taken
in so much from outside. It is like kneeling in gratitude

and wonder at an altar, and finding a prayer or a poem or inspiration in one's mind.

I know we have to end soon – so I want to add that I do worry about integration, emotional maturity, lessening my drive to paint – you know, that age-old question. In essence, I don't think that becoming more fulfilled has or does lessen my drive to paint. If it did I'd be a better gardener or cook. No, seriously, I think we are always striving to repair internal damage, and it's never-ending. Even if the internal damage lessens, there is so much that is disastrous out there in the world – no shortage of subject matter. Not that as a painter I see that as my mission – far from it. I mean that we cannot avoid destructiveness, as part of human nature, and so there is little danger – I hope – of ending up painting pretty sentimental pictures.

2000

She looks deep into Peter's eyes. Those Aegean blue eyes on some days, deep Nordic fjords on other days. They have faded slightly with age, softened. She feels that he is inviting her in, to know more, to find him deep inside. And to find her own depths, unfathomable depths where she might sink for ever. She travels into their nadir, and when she feels his strong arms around her, and reminds herself that he will always be mysterious, she travels back and back, a vortex in reverse, to seeing him for who he is: kind, vulnerable, yet with a particular strength that comes from his acknowledgement of his vulnerability. Now his eyes are more beautiful than ever, but only because they are part of that smile of his, with feminine lips that turn up at the corners, and his strong arms, and his stiffening between her thighs until it is not only his but hers too. Or neither of theirs. And his mind, holding it all together, and her mind and his mind sometimes sparking each other off, and sometimes enigmatically separate, sometimes two bodies with one soul, sometimes two souls with one body.

But that's alright, she says to herself.

She knows that her knowledge of Peter, in and out of focus, so close one minute that neither of them exist in their own right, and then her sense of his place in the world, and the beauty of that, beauty that is almost unbearable, alongside her, two souls who travel but never arrive, is so like her process as a painter.

And that's alright, too.

She feels immensely sad about all her years of deprivation. The least she can do is gather herself up into her heart and let it sing its achingly blessed song, a song that dimly remembers the infinite tenderness of her early life.

2001

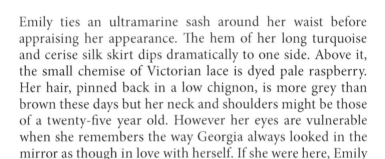

Emily ties an ultramarine sash around her waist before appraising her appearance. The hem of her long turquoise and cerise silk skirt dips dramatically to one side. Above it, the small chemise of Victorian lace is dyed pale raspberry. Her hair, pinned back in a low chignon, is more grey than brown these days but her neck and shoulders might be those of a twenty-five year old. However her eyes are vulnerable when she remembers the way Georgia always looked in the mirror as though in love with herself. If she were here, Emily thinks, I would feel less attractive; and is immediately cross with herself for allowing that ghost to appear.

'It's not *de trop,* Peter?' she asks, seeing him in the mirror stretched out on the bed. He raises his head slightly,

'No, really. I don't mind if you upstage me. I'm only the architect.'

'No seriously, don't I look like an over-decorated Christmas tree – at my age?' She turns to face him. 'I know I'm going on, it's not that important, but . . . . What're you wearing anyway? Not your Oxfam suit?'

'You know that's too tight for me nowadays. No, the linen number I bought in Florence – mafia-style, white suit, black shirt.'

She goes over to sit on the edge of the bed, and leans over to kiss Peter lightly on the forehead. 'You silly, it's not white, your suit. *Cream.* And the linen shirt you mean, it's dark green, isn't it? Mr Subtle!'

She knows he always looks good in his slightly crumpled clothes. Something about his build, his fine greying hair now well cut in a long crew-cut, and his nonchalant handsome face giving him an unexpectedly debonair look. His neck and chin have slackened into what might be called jowls in a plumper man, but in Peter have a softer, feminine quality.

'You know Max and Jack are meeting us there,' she adds. 'Jack said he'd be late – after his shift in the deli. Poor chap, I suppose it's good he works, but such a boring job – such poor wages – to keep solvent.'

Peter gets up to change, preoccupied. She notices him making a few notes on a card before slipping it into his breast pocket.

She drives them to the reception, fifteen minutes away.

Standing within the brand new space as if it were a venerated cathedral, Emily breathes deeply. She cannot quite believe that it is completed, and in use, after years of struggle. She feels excited as she watches Peter raking back his hair, sipping champagne, and smiling at one of his architect friends, Charles Newman.

She takes a step towards them to hear what Charles is saying.

'Congratulations, old chap. Wonderful. I knew you'd make it.'

Peter puts his arm on Emily's shoulder, 'You know my wife, Emily, of course.'

Charles shakes her hand, 'I was just saying to Peter, I knew he'd win the comp. You know, Peter, when I saw your drawings for that pavilion in Venice, three or four years ago was it, I thought this—'

He is interrupted by a journalist, 'So sorry, Mr Johannsen – I'm Andrew Jennings, *Guardian*.' With a nod towards Emily he continues to Peter, 'I emailed you . . . . Have to leave straight after the formalities today – catching a plane. Just wanted to set up an appointment for an interview, if I may.'

Emily can tell Peter is genuinely overawed by the impressive gathering – the line-up of friends, the vice-chancellor, lecturers, architects, artists, photographers, students, journalists, and a few politicians. She recognises his old boss, Robert de Haas, from Peter's early days in his practice in London, and Alfred Sylvester, the art critic. She hopes that Sylvester will not seek her out, to talk about her recent show. She identifies several other architects, and the celebrated designer, Juliette Norris.

It is a relief to see Max, with his latest, Tammy, in tow, holding one of his fingers. Emily observes how he always seems to pull her along, which the girl, in turn, accepts willingly. Squeezed into tight jeans and a black sequinned top, Tammy looks exotically Mediterranean. The toss of her long auburn mane turns the heads of many of the men. Max has made an effort for this occasion, found a white shirt and a grey tie that looks like faintly stained antique silk, and proper trousers. His freshly washed hair is left – by design – tousled and curly. 'Cherubic' comes to Emily's mind when she sees him.

Light-headed from half a glass of champagne and excited for Peter and for their sons, she steps away from a group of friends, and takes a deep breath. She has visited this site several times during the construction, discussed with Peter some of the problems in its realisation, but only today does the building breathe with a life of its own. The autumn evening sunlight slants through the glass: gleaming panes broken up into man (or woman) sized rectangles, so that the mass of the whole, the weight and volume of this huge building is reduced here, for Emily, to human proportions. Her very own sense of her body – with its insides and outsides, its cavities and projections, its solidity and spirituality – seems to be here, externalised.

Turning her back on the animated crowd, she walks towards an area beneath the wide twisting staircase that leads to an open mezzanine. She needs to gather herself, to discover if her rapture is something anyone could feel here, or if it is because Peter has arrived at a work of art that is a fusion of so much that has grown within him and between them as a couple.

She notices the ancient flagstones, smoothed with age and use to a high gloss, and remembers how Peter had rescued them from an old workhouse in the East End that was being demolished.

Through some of the windows, she can see the High Street, a busy Saturday evening in Highbury, now like a colourful silent film of grime and detail and movement, in startling contrast to this glass and steel and stone. She had not anticipated how the location would complement this construction. Of course, she thinks, Peter would not only have factored that in, and shut out the noise – how could she have thought otherwise – but used it positively to juxtapose the rough with the smooth, the buzzing messy outside world with this now hallowed inner space.

She notices those glass panes he had told her about, where the glass is not transparent and yet not fully reflective either, on windows where he chose to shut out the moving outside world. They seem, with a controlled rhythm, to semi-reflect the life within the building, and take on the hues and tones of the throng and of the opposite walls. At this moment her dress appears as a smudge of pink and green, like watercolour on wet paper. Not wanting to draw attention by distancing herself, she wipes her tears before rejoining her husband.

Standing by his side Emily squeezes his hand, trying not to interrupt his conversation. He quietly asks, 'Okay darling?'

'Yup, very okay. Moved. Moved to tears,' she whispers.

'Oh no. Really?' He looks at her anxiously.

'No, really. It's good. I'll tell you, explain, later.'

Both of them notice Jack arriving in the lobby. Carrying a Muji black canvas bag across his shoulder, he looks around rather shyly, his head towering above others. Emily notices the way he bows his head, compounding his gentleness. She feels a pang of understanding, as for most of her younger life she too felt too tall. She observes his black tee-shirt, jeans and a denim jacket: an art student not just in appearance but in reality.

'Sorry I'm late, Mum. Trains not running.' Then, looking into his mother's eyes, 'How're you?' He always seems to really want to know, more than anyone else she knows.

She embraces him briefly, 'I hope you can join us later for a meal – just the family . . . ? Catch up then? That Bistro on the corner – nothing fancy.' He agrees, just as Jane Copeland comes up. Jane and Emily hug.

'So glad you could make it – all the way from Chelmsford.'

By now Jack has begun to make his way over to Max and Tammy.

Emily takes her place at Peter's side during Robert de Haas's introductory short speech. Not really listening to the phrases, she feels anxious for Peter, sensing his tension at what he will soon have to put across.

'You have been one of the most facilitating clients of my career,' Peter states with sincerity in the speech everyone has been waiting for, his blue eyes compounding his earnestness, acknowledging his gratitude to the vice-chancellor of the university, whose vision first led to this building being commissioned in this way.

The vice-chancellor stands nearby, his flushed face becoming more florid, as if trying to suppress a smile out of modesty. Emily detects a nervous tremor in Peter's voice, when he carefully thanks the whole team of workers and sponsors without which all this would not have been realised. He names the main players, nodding to the ones he can see. She knows this is the boring duty stuff, and is keen to hear the main body of his speech.

She glances sideways at him as he smiles softly, changing his tone from energetically professional to personal, as he adds, '. . . and my wife Emily, without whom, over the years, I could never have persevered with my ideas for long enough for them to be realised.'

She frowns, shaking her head slightly. She doesn't feel directly instrumental in Peter's professional development. But he sweeps on with his speech, switching back to business, leaving her with some discomfort.

She hears him elaborating on what is already in a pamphlet in the lobby – an article he had written – that gives the background to this project. Yes, I know all that, and so do many of others here, Emily thinks. She hears Peter's words, 'cloister, campus, forum, arena, amphitheatre,' thinking, Yes, that is interesting, and becomes more alert, to hear how he wanted to blur the boundaries between the public and private, so that interesting things could happen. She catches something about his not only being stimulated 'by the tension between the two . . . and the empty spaces between various more prominent functions.' Then, he says something about not wanting to make a distinction between 'function' and 'use.' She begins to feel as she did as a child, hearing adult conversation and not engaging with it – those interminable mealtimes, flies circling above the dining room table, while Emmy's eyes clung to the pool of melted butter in the butter dish, or the bread crumbs, slivers of light on the bell to summon the servant, while her hand stroked the damask cloth's starched edge under the table to gain some satisfaction. She daydreams Phyllis waving a fly away from her plate, and Emmy hoping the fly would return, and poo on Phyllis' food. She suspects that she cannot really hear Peter now because of her own fear, fear of standing up there like that, accountable, open to scrutiny in such a naked way.

She studies the faces of others, particularly other architects, to discern if they too are anxious or irritated. Their attentive optimism calms her, and she relaxes as at last he begins to focus on his main preoccupations.

He now talks about something that she knows excites him: the idea of things that are unfinished, half-stated, open to development, to possibility, and to imagination. 'How powerful are Michelangelo's slaves half emerging from the rock that both imprisons them and sets them free. Or the silence after a peal of bells, when the sound hangs in the air, and we are left with the resonance as well as the possibility of a further toll. I am talking about the impossibility of cessation; the human condition carries this fluidity, this movement, from past to present to future, and therefore I hope that my buildings can embody this.'

He pauses. She senses that she feels what he feels, that he is saying something huge, and he needs to allow time for everyone to digest it. Then she half hears him saying something about the way that all buildings carry their ageing on their faces and in their joints, 'just as people's faces show

how they have lived – even if, in a building, it is as a result of, say, rain damage.' He glances at his notes, before continuing,

'So what is it about this building that is unfinished, that carries its evolution, you may wonder?' He jokes that if anyone had come on site a few months ago they'd have joined him not only in wearing a yellow Bob the Builder hard hat but in his panic. Emily is relieved at the warm wave of laughter rising from the gathering.

Now she really listens, as Peter states, with a more serious face, 'If you look around and move through the spaces, you will see how I have tried to give a feeling of great height, of a surge of something opening out into space, not only the sky beyond but a sense of infinity. You can't see the ceiling from some positions, because of the curve of that wall – in contrast to miniscule details within the same line of vision. Maybe you'll have noticed the small oxidised tiles at the base of that window.' He gestures to his left. 'How the . . . roughness of those tiles, the chemical reaction of their glazes . . . .' Again Emily stops taking in his words, but is struck by the way the audience is under his spell, something she would find hard to achieve if she was on stage.

Although relieved that he is finding his voice, conveying his excitement, she is not fully able to follow his argument. Perhaps it is because of her nervousness.

He continues, 'Someone, possibly Mies, Mies van der Rohe, once said "God lies in the details" – and I return to that aphorism time and again, because of the way that *detail* expresses inherent meaning.' His speech slows down, 'A meeting of construction . . . with an idea . . . through the senses.' Now Emily listens attentively, for this is something she struggles with in her painting. 'This last phrase,' he continues, '"through the senses" includes an awareness of cultural and archetypal conditions. I am certainly not privileging detail above spatial concepts – that could lead to being seduced by artefacts.' Yes, thinks Emily, that was me, decades ago, seduced by detail, surfaces, patterns . . . .

He glances at his watch, 'Must stop soon. It must be the champagne – I'm not normally so garrulous. Though Emily tells me that my Nordic blood sometimes unleashes epic sagas!' Again the audience laughs appreciatively. Trying to cool her cheeks with the back of her hand, Emily hopes the flush is not too visible.

'But to return to my wish to leave something "unfinished" here – and I apologise for a walk "all round the houses" – I want there to be a feeling that there are conditions that can allow for things I can't control, that can allow for chaos.' He becomes more passionate. 'The empty space, in this hall more than in the lecture theatre, is a space that is waiting to be filled by people, by sound, by light, by whatever use is made of it, and above all by imagination. I see emptiness not as a void but as the potential for presence.'

Emily feels a shiver running through her body. For most of her life she has struggled with a terrifying void, when 'presence' carried dread of absence. But here is Peter fearlessly embracing the paradox as the cornerstone of his vision. She senses that his capacity to feel this way has been within him all along. That was what attracted her to him. How I forget, forget those things, she thinks. The way he was solidly there, with his big arms, or eyes that focussed on far away, she thinks. He wasn't afraid of being alone.

She catches the next part of his speech, aware that she missed some of it. 'Lastly, I hope that in the way that plane soars,' gesturing with a wide balletic sweep of his arm towards the highest wall, 'and the way it tends towards something aerial, and yet is embedded in those oxidised earthy tiles, I hope that people using this building will feel some transformation within themselves – for whether we stand before a Cézanne, or listen to Beethoven, or watch a sunset, we are engaging with our senses.'

Emily feels herself shrinking when he talks like this. It is not for him to make these links, if they are here, surely, she thinks.

He goes on, 'Forgive me if I am linking this building with some of the giants of creativity – but I hope you understand that we all have to have our gods. So, when we are moved by something, we (hopefully) lose sight of the way it is constructed, or the historical or cultural factors, and feel our humanity.'

She tries to put aside what could sound grandiose, too self-regarding. She has glimpsed his arrogance over the years she has known him, and has tried to ignore it, not knowing if it was normal self-confidence in contrast to her own insecurities.

His words register, again, 'And, even more than that, we may feel inspired, awed, yes, and somewhere our own spirit may grow.'

No, I have to give him the benefit of the doubt. Of course he can shine, now, here, especially, she decides, with some relief. She looks over at Max, and remembers when he was a chubby toddler, how proud she felt of his beauty and intelligence, and the sense of some magic beyond her and Peter.

'That, I think, is what I am aiming at,' Peter concludes, '– our attempt to find what is sublime in all of us. And that is what – mercifully – makes us human: that we are always unfinished, and always have potential.'

Emily joins in the loud applause accompanying the smiles and nods, the flashing cameras, the glasses of champagne held high. But her claps are slow, for she has to compose herself, to manage her uncertainty, to hear what seems to have been some acknowledgement of humility after all. Her knees feel weak.

She knows that the free spirit that she was first attracted to, and Peter's resolute side, has truly come to fruition. Perhaps he had to have that, that confidence, to make this building. She has a flash-back to how he came through that time of serious self-doubt.

As the applause subsides, she notices Adam and Jack in the top gallery, greeting each other with a hug. Both young men seem to be smiling. Adam claps Jack on the upper arm as they stand together, before they look down over the balustrade, and then up at the elevation. Both look flushed. They seemed to be sharing a joke. No one would think they were half-brothers – the one so dark, the other fair; the one wary in demeanour, the other open.

Peter and Emily had not been sure that Adam would leave his architecture studies to come down from Glasgow for this opening. She had not seen him arrive. Perhaps he missed the speeches. She wonders if he was avoiding her. Putting aside her own anxieties, she goes to find Peter, to tell him that Adam is here. She knows that this will be the finishing touch for Peter.

Peter had returned from Australia in 1994 feeling that his trip had been a disaster. All his efforts had been met by Adam's bitter resentment. The unspoken tension in their conversations escalated until either of them withdrew, or Peter wept bitterly while Adam fought to suppress his tears of anger.

Peter phoned Emily frequently to try to think through what was going on, but was unable to put to use Emily's encouragement to continue to be there for Adam, and to understand Adam's apparent selfishness as a means of survival.

On the way to Cairns, Peter became ill – perhaps not surprisingly, although it may have been from some dubious pâté he had eaten. He spent days lying on a bed in the sparse guesthouse, trying to shut out the bright sun beyond thin unlined curtains, overcome by abject discomfort from nausea and diarrhoea and the irreconcilable situation between him and his firstborn.

One evening, in tears, weakened by his illness, his head swimming from a double tot of Black Rat, Peter said jerkily, 'You know, Adam, you can never know what you meant to me, when you shot out – or so it seemed – shot out of your mother . . . . That moment, covered in blood, so lusty and strong . . . . I never realised it would be so . . . so defining. And that never goes away, can never fade.' He felt feeble, crying, dribbling from his nose. 'Oh God, Adam, I just want you to know that *you matter to me,*' with barely disguised anger. 'How could you not? If I've let you down, I'm sorry – as I've said so often. Can't say it any other way – I'm sorry. I want to make things better.'

Besieged by his own distress, Peter walked away from the small café where they were the only customers, with its rusty *Coca Cola* and *Passiona* signs, past the owner's prideful displays of dusty geraniums in large petrol cans, past drifts of fine sand piled up by the wind against a low wall, towards a horizon that could not have seemed more distant. He walked and walked, his boots gathering brown dust, his shirt soaked in sweat, oblivious to the slashes of red in the sky reflecting the already set sun, walking out the last vestiges of energy he had.

And then he turned back, slowly. He knew he had done all he could.

Something had altered inside him. He realised that he could not make any more appeals. He would simply be there now, because that was all he could do.

When he returned in the semi-dark, Adam was immutable. With relief, Peter registered that he only had two days until he left for London.

Peter could not see that the more he offered, and gave, the more Adam was reminded that this generosity had not been for him; it spoke of the bounty his half-brothers and step-mother had received for so many years. He was too proud to accept the scraps his father now offered him.

Peter did not know that Adam would have to discover his father for himself, perhaps even have the illusion that he created him himself.

2004

Emily returns to Suffolk for a week alone in April, to Holly Cottage, near Wrentham. She and Peter had bought the property a year before.

The little house perches on top of the only little hill in the area, in a green field, catching the sun and wind without protection. At the bottom of the long garden are three ancient cedars, and along one side of the plot a straggly line of poplars rattle softly in the breeze, like rain on water. She is pleased that this place is so different from damp Dingly Dell.

Peter had told her that architects talk about people either preferring to live in caves, or in nests in trees. She used to be a cave dweller and he a nest dweller. Now she thinks she prefers nests.

One night, she is disturbed by a dream of being late – she doesn't know for what – and of donning her mother's crumpled skirt. She is being accused of man-handling a child in her dream.

Early the next morning she tries to enjoy the new shining day as she walks around the wet garden in wellingtons with a mug of tea in one hand and toast in the other, still in her nightdress, a red shawl around her shoulders. What was that Afrikaans word for dew before daybreak? *Douvoordag*, she remembers. But the dream leaves her dismayed, for there is a child, abused in her unconscious, after all these years. And she is arriving late, with her mother in poor shape with a dishevelled skirt. She has to admit that she has not resolved her mother's place in her mind. She remembers Jane Copeland telling her that, from time to time, she wrote to her dead mother in her diary. Perhaps Emily needed to write herself a letter from her mother, to try to discover her mother's voice?

Dressed in jeans and a jumper, an hour later she covers part of a log with a rug, and sits with a cartridge pad on her lap, a 2B pencil and a rubber. She closes her eyes. A robin sings insistently. She can feel the gentle sun on her head and shoulders.

She has to begin somewhere.

My darling Emmy,
I want you to know that although I died a long time
ago, I am still here, alive in your mind.

She pauses, hesitating. She can hear a mocking 'Ha!' deep within; already this feels a false exercise, the words hollow. And yet she feels tearful. She struggles to continue, trying to discover an authentic voice for her mother.

I want you to know that I love you, care about you,
watch over you, want you to be happy. You and Peter
and Jack and Max. And Adam.
But maybe you don't know how frantic I was for
you, after I abandoned you, when your father was lost
in his grief, when only dear Lizzie – God bless Lizzie –
was really there for you in her solid way, when I could
not protect you from – I hesitate to honour him with
the title 'Grandpa' – Harry, and Phyllis, and Georgia.
As you know, you developed a carapace to protect
yourself; your soul nearly died hundreds of times; in
the end you could have died. But then you sensed that
I wanted you to carry on living, for what good would
it have done for you to give up on your life. And, little
by little, you too wanted that, for yourself.

Emily frowns, losing her mother's voice, just when she thinks she is finding something; stopped by knowing that it is her version, and not her mother's, knowing that this is wishful thinking, the essence of denial. Denial of the fact that

Mommy could not think about me. But then, Emily thinks, alright, so this is my imagination, but that's alright isn't it? Although her shoulder aches she writes on.

Emmy, I feel a deep sadness at being robbed of years of watching you grow up, sharing your trials, maybe giving you a brother or sister. Years of not being able to hug your beautiful body, of admiring your long neck, your fine hair, your miraculous perfect child-shoulders, smelling your little girl smell.

An image of the bones inside a bird come to Emily's mind: their delicate form, the achievement of evolution, the almost transparent and yet strong scapulae. She thinks of Jack's strong body when he was little, a miracle of Peter's and hers, and yet assuredly his own. But she forces herself to continue with what her mother would say.

When I say that I missed out on so much, I mean that because you felt you lost me, I was not granted life by you, and so I was dead to you. Do you follow me, gentle Emmy? It is difficult to explain more clearly, that I could only exist after I died by being kept alive in your mind. And, unfortunately, you were unable to do that all by yourself.

But I also know that regret is fruitless. We cannot alter the unpredictability of life and inevitability of death, so we may as well rise to its challenges. It is its very uncontrollableness, the potential for chaos, that gives life its fascination, as well as its terror.

Fearful that she is slipping into superficiality and sentimentality, and into her own theories, she pauses again. The sun has disappeared behind a bank of clouds. She goes indoors to sit at the old oak table with a view of the three huge cedars – of which she and Peter are the guardians – to take in their presiding strength. She rereads what she has written, and then continues with greater conviction that she is grasping her mother's voice inside her.

> *I want to share something with you here. I feel a yearning for life, for more life. Is this only because I have died, that I am so desirous of this? Isn't all art an attempt to prolong life, to perpetuate the moment? Hearing, registering, or feeling the moment defies death. Or does it? Is the moment alive only because of death?*

Emily rereads all she has written, sighs, and continues in a different gear.

> *Emmy, you've often been angry with me and your father for not looking after my health adequately. Believe me, I have pondered this too, many times: could I have prevented the massive thrombosis that killed me? I know I smoked heavily, but most of us did in those days, and I was quite depressed, unfulfilled in my life – though not in my marriage. I didn't really apply myself to painting. Unsure that I had the talent, I gave up on that, trading it for a life of tea parties and tennis. And a life of being hard on myself: never really allowing myself to develop into the person I could have become.*
>
> *I need to add that I don't mean that one ever arrives, or 'becomes' someone, because of course, as you know, one is always 'becoming'.*
>
> *Your father and I loved each other deeply, irrefutably, as I think you sensed – which partly explains why he went to pieces after I died, and perhaps even why he then married someone very different from me, who did not threaten his memory of me.*
>
> *But I've digressed. Back to my health: so, perhaps I should have had more check-ups, should have gone to the doctor about the strange sensations in my chest. But who knows if that would have made a difference.*

*I don't want to dwell on the last half-hour of my life,
when you and I were alone at home, when I was in
excruciating pain – it was all so rapid, and I worried
desperately for you, what would you think if I was ill,
and I tried to get to the phone, everything began to
slip away, and then . . . . I can't remember. I draw a
blank for the hours of my actual death – yes, it was
hours, not minutes – when I can only assume that you
froze. While for me, it was as if under an anaesthetic,
timeless, when my soul was stuck in my useless body
– until later, when I could see you, see you wandering
around the house like a lost soul, searching for me, for
days and weeks. And oh, my helplessness, at not being
able to reach you.*

Emily stops writing then.

Staring at the cedars, she tries to go back to that day, 22nd
March 1948. Putting her mind right back, a shivery fear and
panic make her hold her breath.

There are segments of her mother's body – not the whole
big body, but the chest and the head, then the arm, the
hands, later the feet – prone on the hard tiled kitchen floor.
Terrifying bits. And she is full of a sense of wrongness, the
inside-out, upside-down-ness of it all, her mother becoming
someone, yes, something else. But then there is the bright
light of the silver milk bottle top, the shiningness of it, the
one sparkling thing she holds onto in that grey blurriness.

After that, she cannot be sure what is memory and what
she's been told. Her father coming home. His panic. The flurry.
Action. Telephone. Strangers marching in. Details fuzzy.

Her mother carried out on a thin tray.

Emmy is carried out too but in the opposite direction,
away, away from the open front door, away from Mommy, her
own voice becoming a thin trail of nothingness, as people –
which people? – hold her back. Her father all tight and hard,
Lizzie coming back, soft Lizzie, holding her in her arms,
enveloping her, shielding her eyes with her hand, muttering
something as soft and warm as kneaded dough.

The bed feels cold that night at Aunty Sarah's. *Tickly-nankin* isn't there. Even the crumpets and syrup Aunty gives Emmy taste strange. There's a frightened look in Aunty's eyes the whole time, though she won't look properly at Emmy, as if she's waiting for something even worse to happen.

'Mommy, where's Mommy?' Emily thinks she asks a second time, sounding assertive, demanding to know.

'Darling, I don't know for sure . . . your Mom . . . Mommy's sick, Mommy in hospital . . . .'

That is all.

A grey-mauve haze, the world through gauze.

'Want Lizzie. Where's Lizzie?'

Then, in her reverie, still staring at the huge cedars with an animated bird-life of their own, Emily sees her father alone with her, his forehead as furrowed as corrugated cardboard. It must have been the next day. He must have said something like 'Emmy, Mommy, Mommy . . . has died. Her heart . . . .' And then he cries, that she does remember, big sobs that shake his whole body like the fish she'd seen at Hermanus, its mouth gasping open and closed, open and closed, pounding against the rocks.

No, Daddy, stop it, no! she wants to say, but she can't. Her voice just isn't there.

Perhaps he tries to pull himself together, 'Emmy darling, Mommy has died. She won't be coming home . . . . My sweet girl . . . . I'm sorry,' – or something like that.

She remembers, he becomes tender as a young flower, passionate in his tenderness, his voice, his body, his hands, his lips, caressing her. Perhaps he feels that his heart, like his wife's, would break. She doesn't know what to do with this, this love, this grief, this surfeit of feeling, the confusion of marvellous yet overwhelming adoration from him.

No space for her to feel anything. Her father fills all the space.

But Grandpa Harry had no such excuse.

So on this day of sitting down to write the letter from her mother Emily begins to configure why Harry's attentions were familiar, why they were not all bad: that tenderness and passion can be good and bad. Daddy's expressions of love and regret and anguish, and imponderable confusion, had all happened before Harry. And the person who would have mediated big things for her, her mother, wasn't there.

She held her breath, making herself go back to when she was four and a half, and began a long, long hibernation.

From which she occasionally awoke to suffer pain, or to find millions of things like that first shiny thing, the silver milk bottle top: the world encrusted with things, patterns in everything; curtains like skirts; a leaf on the ground was a rock; a stone a bald man; folded linen became the creases of a woman's stomach; the bars on a bed-head were arrows; the silk lining of a dress was soft skin; the crossed legs of two aunties a big 'M' as they sat – their toes almost touching – and sipped tea; the knot on a plank a fish's eye; the hunger in her tummy was an emptiness that stretched as big as a desert; the poplar leaves glinted and danced in the breeze: branches bowed to each other, one was king, the other a servant, bobbing respectfully.

She takes a deep faltering breath and forces herself to continue with her letter,

I think you still have a sense of me, your Mommy, for those first four and a half years of your life: the usual challenges of separating, and growing up, but deeply loved by me and by your father.

Emily knows she is mourning her loss. 'Deeply mourned', as they say on gravestones.

Perhaps you remember the day before I died, how we – you and I, for Daddy was at the office – walked down to the dam to feed the ducks. You wore your little tweed coat – pale green it was, with a dark green velvet collar – as there was a chill wind. And your black shiny patent leather shoes decorated with a stitched pattern. You wanted to eat the bread, the ducks padding on the bank near us expectantly, while you held the crusts with both hands and gobbled. I let you, even though it was stale. (What emptiness were you feeling, even then?) You made me laugh. Perhaps you were perplexed by my amusement.

At this moment the sun emerges and shines through dusty windows, casting bright light on the vase of dark pink and purple and mauve tulips. She pauses before really seeing, anticipating the pain of the beauty of these open pink petals, membranous and lambent, and leaves so green they might have been harbouring an inner light. She thinks of the difference between looking and seeing; like that between hearing and listening. The tulips' dusky shadows on the buttermilk wall, the whine of the wind around the cottage, the stiff creak of branches outside, all comfort her, while the jar on the window sill of tight catkins, like small caterpillars waiting to stretch and grow, suffuse her with an aching fullness at this bounteous world.

Buoyed up by so much blessedness she continues with her task.

Well, Emmy – of course you'll always be "Emmy" to me – I haven't mentioned painting yet. I will in a moment, but first: a word about that low time, your marriage to Marcus.

Emily sighs at how difficult it is to broach this.

How I struggled when I watched your already fragile spirit dying, when you succumbed to something so annihilating in that relationship. I could see why, and how, that happened: how you repeated Phyllis's and the dreadful Harry's negation of you, and even your father's difficulty in really seeing you. Of course you hoped, at the beginning, for a different outcome. And you lost me, really lost the sense of me, during those Marcus-years: like a recapitulation of the early years after I died, but without resolution until, as you know, you began to find me through your painting.

Painstakingly you first created – perhaps "imitated" would be a better word for that period – your world of fragmentation and surfaces and appearances, and slowly, perhaps after you broke down, in Suffolk, you found something that sprang from your life-blood and from me, and somehow it flowed along your arm and hand and onto the canvas. Yes, of course the paintings were mediated by your mind, but not in a very intellectual way: you allowed an eruption of feeling onto canvas. (You know, this is something I could rarely do when I painted. I was far too tied to classical principles I learnt at art college, and somehow having you at a young age became my creative output, rather than a more symbolic struggle.)

And you are still engaged in that struggle and always will be. I hesitate to say that you are doing it for both of us, because that could be burdensome. But I am glad for you, my love, even though your life has been tough. The struggle now is not the same. Nowadays it is your way of thinking things through, whereas before you could not really think: painting was a way of holding yourself together.

If you ever have a retrospective you will see what I mean. People may talk about the 'mature Samuels', which, I think, is when you began to come through the fire, burnt and scarred, but stronger. Perhaps 'burnt' is not a bad metaphor: the skin is more sensitive after it has been burnt, even when it has . . . .

A loud thud on the window pane startles her. It sounds like someone flinging a clod of earth.

She rushes to the glass. Beyond she sees the black tracery of silver birch reaching, dancing to the wind, and clouds shredding the blue sky.

She runs outside, looks at the window from the other side, then finds a chaffinch lying on the ground. Its chalky-terracotta head lies back at a strange angle, its eyes tiny slits. She strokes its tiny chest. Still warm. *Poor, poor bird, poor silly bird.* She shakes her head. *Didn't you see the glass?* – lifting the small creature tenderly, wondering if it is only stunned. Somehow the heaviness of her sadness feels out of proportion to this feather-light creature. Placing it back on the soil, 'I'll come and see you later. Maybe you'll wake up.'

Inside the cottage her heart thumps insistently. She prays that the bird has a heart that is beating.

She wants to end the letter, wants to ring Peter.

She rereads the last sentence:

Perhaps 'burnt' is not a bad metaphor: the skin is more sensitive after it has been burnt, even when it has . . . .

and adds the word *healed*. After a long pause she writes a final sentence, which emerges clumsily. She leaves it as it is:

And perhaps it is because you lost me that you too paint, and yearn for perpetuity, paradoxically with an awareness of the impossibility of that desire.

You know, Emmy, that I will continue to keep in touch with you. Lots and lots of love,

Mommy

She thinks that she will try to write a letter from her to her mother another time.

2006

Darling Mom, or Mommy,

It's two years since you 'wrote' to me.
I want to reach you in this letter, work out what and
who you are for me, so that I can talk to you.
Maybe I'll find something about you and therefore
about myself that I don't already know.
I really let you go, let you die, on my second trip to
South Africa. Through my paintings at that time, and
since, you have become more present for me:

- *visible in the pale chartreuse sky gradually*
  fading into transparent turquoise.
- *in the first bright evening star.*
- *in a wind-buffeted blossom that keeps pace with*
  me along the pavement as I walk.
- *in the sudden warmth of blood rushing to my*
  cheeks.
- *Janet Baker's voice, the colour of caramel, singing*
  Kindertotenlieder.
- *in the back of little Max's neck, with an*
  overhanging tuft of hair, when he was three or
  four; I know now, from my love of him when I
  stroked it, that I was expressing your love inside
  me.

I want to tell you about a dream last night of a dragonfly
dancing with the wind and the sun. At first the wings

looked black and white, and then I zoomed in and saw that they were a delicate iridescence of all the colours in the world, strengthened with fine wires of steel.

I knew I was going to try and write to you today. So this astonishing dream must be about me, my evolution, and about you, and Phyllis. She delighted in the story of whether the sun or the wind was stronger: the might of the wind only made the man button his coat tighter; the sun shone brilliantly and the man took off his coat. (What stories would you have told me over the years?)

I doubt if Phyllis recognised her connection with the forceful wind in that story, nor her defences against it.

I have battled with a dragon wind outside and inside. Maybe the struggle gave me that steel in my wings.

But I have also basked in sun-warm soft black arms, arms which carried me through the desolate years, keeping alive the residual warmth of your skin and your blue-grey eyes.

She stops writing. Wanting to create her own atmosphere, without recourse to the waning evening light or the view of the cedars, she draws the old plum velvet curtains, and puts on a CD of Rossini's *Petite Messe Solennelle*, the volume high. Emily lights a range of candles, including Jane's gift of a fat burgundy candle smelling of spices, with three wicks, each nestling in its own visceral wax grotto. Now her shrine is rich and heady. She pours herself a glass of South African Sauvignon Blanc. If the phone rings, she won't answer it. She needs times like this, away from everyone.

Blackthorn blossoms, white and virginal, stand in a cobalt vase near the candles, each stamen crowned with its pinhead of pollen, opening to the candles as if they were sunshine.

The Rossini rolls out into the room, measured, immensely serious and mellow, until the bass gathers a masculine intensity and passion.

She closes her eyes. And then lifts her pen.

Do you remember that time when you and Dad took me to the seaside? Was it Hermanus? There was a shallow lagoon of turquoise water in the sand, left by the receding tide, connected to little streams of water which flowed out to sea. I was running behind you and Daddy, in my pink coat with the hood up, to keep out the wind. I saw you both holding hands, ahead of me. Your bodies cast long shadows behind you, which I tried to catch by jumping on them, but they kept slipping away. Daddy turned round and smiled, waiting for me. I ran and held his hand, the hand you had been holding. You had stopped too. You took my other hand. And then you both swung me over a rivulet, my legs high. I thought I was flying.

Do you remember the coppice of poplar trees in our garden in Pretoria? Poplars seem to have followed me throughout my life. After you died, when we moved to Jo'burg, a row of poplars lined the drive. When I was about six, I looped a horseshoe over a branch, low down. Over the years, the tree slowly enveloped the horseshoe as it grew. One day, I tried to dislodge it but it would not budge.

Now I imagine a faint depression discernible in the bark above the branch. The iron object is within the much bigger and stronger tree, but tiny particles have broken away and been carried along by the sap into the limbs. Some of those branches have broken off with age. Other fragments have worked their way to the surface like splinters in flesh. The core of the horseshoe is still there, a cold metal place, dark and heavy. But I know that the tree is painfully alive, a rich rust colour.

A horseshoe is supposed to bring good luck.

Dad told me the story that the midwife who delivered me said, as I emerged, 'She's going to be a lucky baby: she has a double crown,' commenting on the way my hair grew.

I didn't feel particularly lucky as a child, or as a young adult.

I think I have had three lives: before, after, and now. Of course the 'now' incorporates the 'before' and 'after'. In my latest painting, I have been struggling with a wide area painted around the centre: I want to make neither the interior nor what is framing it more eye-catching, and yet each needs to be distinct. This wish not to privilege certain areas, not to promote subject over object or background, has been one of my preoccupations in painting for decades. I think I am still trying to work out how my background informs my present, and vice versa. And how what is visible is only a fraction of my rich life. (I can hardly believe that I have written that last sentence.)

When I was six or seven I cut open a silkworm's cocoon in order to examine the creature. How I waited for the ugly brown chrysalis to transform into a moth. But it never did. Perhaps painting the pain, giving it a name and a shape, runs the same risk.

I cannot resolve that painting with its frame yet. Or, that painted frame with its portal which could be a hole or the whole. Perhaps I shall leave it that way.

If you were still alive you would be eighty-seven. I'm not sure why I needed to work that out now. Perhaps to bring you into the present, to make you less obscure.

I don't think I need to write to you again. Why put on paper what I sense you already know about me, know through me.

So I will end by saying, not goodbye, but welcome back, Mom, welcome home.

Lots of love,

Emily

By now the mezzo-soprano is singing with the baritone, their voices weaving in and out, together then separate, and then, with the chorus, forming a golden skein, the piano punctuating everything like Emily's breaths as she listens, knowing that if she were to die now she would have truly lived.

Perhaps the real work of living is not through painting but in allowing the universe to show itself. When Emily has a mind to, in those still moments of realisation, she feels how most everyday things are beyond the ordinary: they seem to contain the whole world. When such a moment passes – which it must, like the shadow of a cloud on a green hill – she is left with the sense of it, and its loss.

But each such instance changes her.

For they endure, they glow in her inner life. So different from the sparkle of that milk bottle top.

And she trusts there will be more.

Bibliography

Dorothy Judd was born in 1944 in apartheid South Africa, and as a child of 11 faced the profound experience of loss and exile when her family emigrated to London. It is not surprising that those early experiences informed and enriched her professional life, first as an art therapist and then as a child, adolescent, adult and marital psychotherapist.

Her first degree in Fine Art partly inspires the story here, in *The Other Side of Night*.

In her clinical and research work, disability, loss, transience and bereavement were her key contributions that culminated in her seminal book, *Give Sorrow Words – working with a dying child* (Karnac, 2014 – 3rd Edition.)

She has published a previous novel, *Patch Work – Love and Loss* (I Am Self-Publishing, 2018.)

Dorothy is married to historian and writer, Denis Judd, and they have four children and six grandchildren.

In 2016, she was longlisted by Cinnamon Press for *Patch Work* in their debut novelists' competition.

Acknowledgements

Thank you to:

Leila Green for detailed editorial attention and encouragement, and for rescuing this novel from the slush pile many years ago. It has taken me many years to decide to self-publish it, with Leila's help.

Denis Judd for steadfast encouragement.

Sonja Linden, Sara Collins, Valerie Sinason, Tessa Dresser, Jill Yglesias, Margot Waddell, Rebecca Mascull, Anne Lanceley, Felicity Weir, Prophecy Coles, Mary Adams, Sylvia Paskin, Olive Somers, Emile Woolf, Anita Woolf, Judith Edwards and John Woods – all of whom have offered different types of encouragement. And thanks to many colleagues and friends, who can't be mentioned individually.

Iona Doniach, an artist and warm friend.

Ron Britton, Dina Rosenbluth, Alex Tarnopolsky, and especially Margaret Rustin – the analysts and therapists – for their implicit encouragement, and for helping me to think over many years.

Lindsay Clarke for his inspiring workshops.

The Arvon Foundation, for creative writing residential courses.

Inevitably my children and grandchildren have given me immense and rich inspiration.

And to 'Lizzie', my nanny in South Africa, for her abiding love.

Printed in Great Britain
by Amazon